Kristin Harmel is an internationally bestselling novelist. She spent many years as a journalist, including more than a decade writing and reporting for *People* magazine. Kristin now focuses on book tours, book club visits and, of course, writing her next books.

Kristin has lived in Paris, Los Angeles, New York, Boston and Miami, and she now resides in Florida, USA, with her husband, Jason.

Also by Kristin Harmel

The Sweetness of Forgetting

Kristin Harmel

The
Life
Intended

Quercus

First published in 2014 in the United States by Gallery Books.

First published in Great Britain in 2015 by Quercus Editions Ltd.

Quercus Editions Ltd
55 Baker Street
7th Floor, South Block
London W1U 8EW

A CIP catalogue record for this book is available
from the British Library

PB ISBN 978 1 84866 488 3
EBOOK ISBN 978 1 78429 087 0

10 9 8 7 6 5 4 3 2 1

Printed and bound in Great Britain by Clays Ltd, St Ives plc

To anyone who has ever loved and lost.

And to the love of my life, Jason.
I can't imagine a world without you.

"Music is the space between the notes."

—FRENCH COMPOSER CLAUDE DEBUSSY (1862–1918)

One

It was 11:04 when Patrick walked through the door that final night almost a dozen years ago.

I remember the numbers glowing red and angry on the digital clock by our bed, the sound of his key turning in the lock. I remember his sheepish expression, the way his five o'clock shadow had bloomed into an almost-beard, the way his shirt looked rumpled as he stood in the doorway. I remember the way he said my name, *Kate,* like it was an apology and a greeting all in one.

I'd been listening to Sister Hazel's *Fortress,* my favorite album at the time, as I waited for him to come home. "Champagne High," the fourth track on the CD, was playing, and just before he walked in, I was mouthing the lyrics, thinking to myself how "the million hours that we were" was such a poetic way to describe a life together.

Patrick and I were just four months into our marriage, and I couldn't imagine a day when we'd no longer be with each other. I was twenty-eight then, Patrick twenty-nine, and the years seemed to stretch before us into an endless horizon. I remember reflecting that a million hours—just over a hundred years— didn't sound like enough time.

But as it turned out, our hours together were almost up. The number that defined us in the end was only fifteen thousand and nine.

That was the number of hours that had passed since we'd met at a New Year's Eve party on the last night of 2000, the number of hours we'd spent knowing we'd found our soul mates, the number of hours we'd spent thinking we had it all. But fifteen thousand and nine isn't even close to a million.

"Honey, I am so, so sorry." Patrick was all apologies as he fumbled his way into the bedroom, where I sat on top of our comforter, knees pulled up to my chest, checking my watch pointedly. The relief that he was home safely was being quickly supplanted by annoyance for making me worry.

"You didn't call." I knew I sounded petulant, but I didn't care. We had made each other a promise the year before, after my uncle had been killed in a hunting accident, that we'd always make an effort to let each other know when we were going to be late. My aunt had been blissfully unaware of her husband's death for nearly twenty hours, which had horrified Patrick and me.

"I just got caught up in something," Patrick said, averting his gaze. His thick black hair was mussed and his green eyes were full of concern when he finally looked back at me.

I glanced at the phone on our bedside table, the phone that had been silent all night. "You were stuck at the office?" I asked. It wouldn't have been the first time. Patrick was a risk management consultant for a firm in Midtown. He was young, hungry, one of those people who would always pitch in if there was extra work to be done. I loved that about him.

"No, Katielee," he said, using the affectionate nickname he'd been calling me since the night we met, when he'd mistaken my maiden name, Kate Beale, as I shouted it above the din of the crowd. "My beautiful Katielee," he murmured as he crossed the room and sat down beside me on the bed. The back of his right hand grazed my left thigh, and I slowly unfolded my legs, melting into him. He inched toward me and wrapped his arm around my shoulders. He smelled like cologne and smoke. "I was with Candice," he said into my hair. "She had something important she needed to tell me."

I pulled away from him and scrambled out of bed. "*Candice?* You were with Candice? Until eleven?"

Candice Belazar was the girl he'd dated just before me, a bartender at a smoky dive in Midtown. It had been a short-term fling and they'd broken up two months before we met, but she'd been a thorn in my side as long as I'd known him. "It was just a physical thing," he'd tried to explain the first time he told me about her. "I was in a rut, and she was there. I got out of it as soon as I realized how wrong we were for each other." But that hadn't been much comfort.

We'd run into Candice once at a restaurant in Little Italy, and having a face to put with the name only made things worse. She was several inches taller than me, with huge, obviously fake breasts, stringy bleached blond hair, and hollow eyes. She had smirked as she looked me up and down, and I'd heard her stage-whisper to her friend that Patrick apparently couldn't handle a real woman anymore.

"Kate, honey, nothing happened," Patrick said quickly, reaching for me. "I would never do anything to hurt you."

"Then why didn't you call?"

"I'm so sorry." He raked his fingers through his hair. "There's no excuse. But I would never, ever cheat on you. Ever. You know that." His voice caught at the end of his sentence, but his eyes were as guileless as ever. I felt my shoulders relax a little as some of my indignation rolled away.

"Whatever," I huffed, because I couldn't think of a better response. I knew he was telling the truth, but the thought of waiting at home while he sat in a bar with his ex-girlfriend still stung. I wasn't going to tell him it was okay, because it wasn't.

"I'm totally wrong here," he said, spreading his palms in a mea culpa. "But it was a heavy conversation, and I didn't feel like I could walk away to make a phone call."

"Yes, heaven forbid you offend Candice," I muttered.

"Kate . . ." Patrick's voice trailed off.

"I'm going to bed." I knew I was supposed to soften, to tell him it was all right. But I couldn't bring myself to.

"Don't you want to talk about this?" he asked.

"No."

Patrick sighed. "Kate, I'll explain everything tomorrow."

I rolled my eyes, stormed into the bathroom, and slammed the door behind me. I blinked at my reflection in the mirror, wondering how, nearly two years after they'd broken up, Candice still managed to hold some kind of power over my husband.

But as I climbed into bed ten minutes later, I could feel myself thawing a little. After all, Patrick had told me right away where he'd been. I knew he was being honest. And besides, he'd chosen me, and deep down, I knew that he would choose me every day for the rest of our lives. As I pulled the sheets over me, my anger receded in slow, steady waves.

I was already half asleep when Patrick came to bed. I turned away from him, facing the wall, and after a moment, I felt his arms encircle me. He moved closer, pressing into my back, entwining his legs with mine.

I thought for a moment about pulling away, but it was Patrick, my Patrick. He would tell me in the morning what had happened, and I would understand. So after a pause, I relaxed into his warmth.

"You know I'd never hurt you, Katielee," he whispered. "Ever. In a million years. Nothing happened."

I closed my eyes and breathed in. "I know."

Patrick kissed the hollow beneath my left ear, sending a shiver up my spine. "I knew before I met you—" he murmured, just as I began to drift off to sleep.

I smiled. "—that I was meant to be yours," I replied. It was the way we always said *I love you,* our own special language.

I knew I'd feel that way for the rest of our lives.

Sunlight streamed into the bedroom along with the scents of coffee and bacon when I awoke the next morning. I blinked and rolled over to look at the clock. It was 6:47, and Patrick was already up, making me breakfast. I knew it was his version of an apology, but in truth, he was already forgiven.

"Morning," I said, covering a yawn as I walked into the kitchen a few minutes later. Patrick turned around holding a spatula, and I began to laugh. He was wearing a yellow KISS THE CHEF apron over his I LOVE NY boxers and white T-shirt. His feet were bare, his hair sleep tousled.

"*Le chef* eez at your service," he said in an exaggerated French accent, which made me laugh again. "Sit, sit," he said, gesturing toward our tiny kitchen table with his spatula. "Breakfast is served, madame."

He set two plates of scrambled eggs, crispy bacon, and toast with strawberry jam on the table with a flourish. A moment later, he returned with two steaming cups of coffee, already lightened with cream and sugar, and sat down beside me.

"You didn't have to cook, honey," I said with a smile.

"*Mais oui.*" He kissed me on the cheek. "Nothing but the best for my girl."

I took a bite of my eggs and looked up to see him watching me, his gaze intense. "What?" I asked, my mouth still full.

"There's no excuse for me not calling last night," he said, his words tumbling out. "I feel terrible. I didn't mean to make you worry."

I take a sip of my coffee, then I draw a deep breath. "It's okay," I said.

Relief spread across his features like a sunrise. "You forgive me?"

"I know I overreacted."

"No, you didn't," he said quickly. He took a bite of his bacon, and I watch his strong jaw work as he chewed. "Look, there's something I'd really like to talk to you about," he said. He blinked a few times, and his expression made me suddenly uneasy. He seemed almost nervous. "Can I take you to dinner tonight? The restaurant at the Sherry-Netherland, maybe? I know you love that place."

I smiled. "Sounds great."

"Aren't you forgetting something?" Patrick asked a moment later, as I crunched on a piece of bacon.

I looked up. "What?"

He pulled his apron taut and turned to face me. "It says Kiss the Chef." He smiled at me, and when I met his eye, he winked. "And it's only polite to follow apron instructions."

I laughed. "Is that right?"

"It's one of the laws of kitchenocracies around the world."

"Kitchenocracies?"

"Of course. Sovereign kitchen nations. Like this one."

"I see," I said quite solemnly. "Well, I don't want to violate any laws, sir."

"It's probably in your best interest to just follow along, then." He smiled at me, stood, and held out his arms.

I laughed and got up. He bent his head, I stood on tiptoe, and our lips met.

"Good enough?" I whispered after a moment as he wrapped his arms around me, folding me in.

"Not even close," he murmured back. Then he was kissing me again, parting my lips gently with his tongue.

We made love that morning, quickly, urgently, drinking each other in. Then I cleaned up our breakfast dishes while he showered and dressed for work.

"Looking good!" I marveled with a whistle as he reemerged into the kitchen with freshly washed hair, charcoal pants, a crisp blue shirt, and a striped gray tie.

"I didn't think the apron and boxers would cut it at the big meeting I have this morning," he said, "although—and I don't want to brag here—I *do* have some seriously sexy legs."

I laughed and stood on tiptoe to kiss him good-bye. "Good luck with the clients."

"Who needs luck?" he asked with a crooked, dimpled smile. "I have the greatest wife in the world. Life is good."

"Life is good," I agreed. I kissed him again, and this time, it was Patrick who pulled away too soon.

When I opened my eyes, he was holding up a silver dollar from his grandfather's old collection. "Listen, would you hang on to this for me until tonight?" he asked.

I took it with a nod. "What's this one for?" Patrick had a tradition of tossing a silver dollar somewhere nearby whenever something good happened to him. *You have to pass the good luck on,* he always used to say. *That way, someone else gets to make a wish.* We'd thrown a silver dollar into Central Park the day I'd gotten into graduate school, another into the fountain outside

City Hall when Patrick got a big promotion last year, and a third into the ocean near his parents' house on Long Island after we got married in the spring. "Must be something big," I added.

"It is," he promised. "You'll see. I'll tell you at dinner. We can throw it into the Pulitzer Fountain after we eat. And Katielee?"

"Yeah?"

He stood in the doorway and stared at me for a long moment. "I knew before I met you—" he finally said, his voice soft.

My heart fluttered. "—that I was meant to be yours."

The door closed behind him at 7:48 a.m.

I never saw him again.

I was out for my morning run when it happened. While I was jogging north along the Hudson River greenway, marveling at how bright and clear the sky looked after a few days of rain, a thirty-seven-year-old woman named Gennifer Barwin, a tourist from Alabama, was finishing off the bottle of vodka she'd started drinking at three in the morning after a fight with her boyfriend. While I was mentally replaying a lecture I'd heard the day before in the music therapy graduate program I'm just started at NYU, she was strapping her seventeen-month-old daughter Lianna into a car seat in her 1997 Toyota Corolla. While I was thinking how lucky I was that Patrick had encouraged me to quit my banking job to pursue the career I'd always wanted, she was pulling out of the parking lot of Hoboken's Starlite Motel.

You have to do what your heart tells you to do. Patrick's words of encouragement rang in my ears as my feet pounded the pavement. *Life's too short not to follow your dreams, Kate.* As I looked up at the sky that morning, reflecting on how wonderfully supportive my husband was, Gennifer Barwin was swerving through the Lincoln Tunnel, headed for Manhattan. As I turned south to head home, she was taking the exit for West Fortieth Street, side-swiping a sign after she got off the highway.

And as I smiled to myself, wondering what piece of good luck had made Patrick hand me a silver dollar that morning, Gennifer Barwin was driving at 47 mph directly into the back passenger-side door of the taxi my husband was riding in.

Thirty minutes later, I rounded the corner to our fifth-floor apartment, still breathing hard from my run, and found two uniformed police officers standing outside my front door.

"Mrs. Waithman?" asked the younger one. I'm not sure whether it was his eyes full of sympathy, his somber expression, or the way he said my name, but in an instant, I knew something was terribly wrong.

"What happened?" I asked, my knees buckling beneath me. The young officer caught me before I could hit the ground.

"Ma'am, we're very sorry, but your husband was involved in a serious car accident this morning," he said, his voice flat. "He was in a cab, ma'am. Near Times Square."

"No, that can't be right," I protested, looking back and forth between the officers. Their faces were suddenly blurry. "He's at work. He takes the subway to work." But he had that meeting, I realized immediately, the one with some of his most important clients. He would have taken a taxi from his office to theirs. "*Oh God.*"

"Ma'am—?"

"You're sure it's him?" I choked out.

"Yes, ma'am, I'm afraid so."

"But he's okay, right?" I asked into the strangely heavy silence. "Of course he's okay?"

"Mrs. Waithman—" the younger one began uncertainly.

"Where is he?" I cut him off, glancing at the older officer, who reminded me of my dad, someone who would surely make everything okay. "Which hospital? Can you take me? I have to help him."

From the thin slice of stillness that lingered between them, the way neither of them made a move, I knew before they said the words.

"Ma'am." The older one finally spoke, his eyes watery. "I'm afraid your husband was pronounced dead at the scene."

"No. Absolutely not." My reply was instant, for the very concept was impossible. No more than two hours earlier, Patrick and I had made love. He'd held me in his arms. He'd kissed me good-bye, just like any other day. He'd been warm and alive and mine. "That can't be right," I mumbled. "Of course it can't. There's been some kind of mistake."

"Ma'am, I'm afraid it's true," the younger officer said, reaching out again and catching my other elbow so that I was suspended between the two men. I hadn't even noticed that I was falling. "Is there someone we can call for you?" he asked gently.

"Patrick," I answered irrationally. "Patrick's my emergency contact." It had never occurred to me that he could be the emergency. I let them help me inside the apartment, where they placed me gently on the couch. I handed them my cell phone, and somehow, they must have managed to find my sister Susan's number, because my daze was interrupted some thirty minutes later by her flying through my front door, her hair a mess.

"I got here as soon as I could," she said, but all I could do was nod. It wasn't until I noticed the tears streaked across her face that I realized I hadn't cried yet. "Mom and Dad are out of town, but Gina's on her way."

"Oh," I managed.

"Kate," she said softly, sitting down beside me on the couch. "Are you okay? What can I do?"

I just stared at her blankly. It was like she was speaking a different language. I knew that I'd have to call Patrick's parents, reach his friends, arrange a funeral, and do all those things you're supposed to do when someone dies. But the thing is, I wasn't ready to admit he was gone yet. As long as I sat there on the couch, the couch where we'd spent hundreds of hours together, believing in our future, I could convince myself that the world hadn't ended.

My best friend, Gina, who'd lost her husband a year earlier in the September eleventh attacks, arrived some time later, and the two of them stayed with me, rubbing my back in silence, until long after the time Patrick should have come home from work. I watched the door for hours, hoping beyond hope that he'd walk through it, that it would all be a crazy mistake.

But it wasn't. And as the clock turned to midnight and September nineteenth became the first day of my life that Patrick wasn't on this earth with me, I finally began to cry.

Two

Twelve Years Later

"Raise your hands up high!" I sing brightly, strumming my guitar as I smile at Max, my favorite client.

"Kick your feet up too," I continue. "Now twirl 'round and 'round! Bend down and touch your—"

"—shoe!" Max cries.

"Good job, Max!" I'm making it up as I go, and Max, who has autism, is giggling madly, but he's playing along. In the corner of my office, his mother, Joya, laughs as Max straightens up from his toe touch and begins to jump up and down.

"More, Miss Kate!" Max begs. "More, more!"

"Okay," I tell him solemnly. "But this time, you have to sing along. Can you do that?"

"Yeah!" he exclaims, throwing his hands in the air with joyful abandon.

"Promise?" I ask.

"Yeah!" His enthusiasm is contagious, and I find myself laughing again.

"Okay, Max," I say slowly. "Sing with me, okay?"

I've been in private practice as a music therapist for five years now, specializing in kids with special needs, and Max was one of my very first clients. Joya first brought him to me on the recommendation of his speech therapist when he was five, because he wasn't making progress with her and was refusing to speak. Slowly, in our weekly sessions, I managed to coax one-word answers, then sentences, then entire conversations out of him. Now, our sessions are a time to sing, to dance, to be silly together. On the surface, I'm helping him with his verbal and motor skills, but this is about more than that. It's about helping him to socialize, to trust people, to open up.

"Okay, Max, fill in the blank," I begin. I strum the guitar and sing, "My name is Max, and I have—"

"—brown hair!" Max cries, giggling. "My name is Max and I have brown hair!"

I laugh. "Good one." I play another chord and sing, "I'm so handsome that all the girls stare," I sing, raising an eyebrow at him.

Max collapses in giggles. I wait until he straightens back up again and says, "Miss Kate, that's so silly!"

"Silly?" I exclaim in mock horror. "Silly is as silly does, mister. Now are you going to sing with me or not?"

"Sing it again, sing it again!" Max says.

I wink at him. "I'm so handsome that all the girls stare," I repeat, strumming my guitar.

This time, Max sings it back to me, so I move on to the next line.

"I'm just turned ten; I'm getting so—" I sing.

"—old!" he cries, puffing his chest out and holding up ten fingers. "I'm getting old!"

"You got it, old dude!" I strum again and conclude my on-the-spot verse. "But the best part of me," I sing, "is my heart of gold."

I stop strumming and put my hand over my heart as Max sings back, "The best part of me is my heart of gold!" He giggles again and claps his hands over his mouth "But my heart's not made of gold!" he exclaims through his fingers. "That's silly again!"

"You're right!" I tell him. "But what that means is that I think you're a very, very nice person, Max."

He breaks into a grin and throws his hands in the air. "You're nice too, Miss Kate."

I put my guitar down so that I can hug him. Today, I needed him and his cheerful innocence more than he needed me. But I don't want him to know that. These sessions aren't supposed to be about me.

"Thanks, Miss Kate!" Max cries as he squeezes me hard around the waist, pressing his head into my shoulder. "I love you!"

"Max, you are very special," I reply, surprised to feel tears prickling my eyes. "You be a good guy for your mom this week, okay?"

"Okay, Miss Kate!" he says cheerfully. Then he bounds over to give Joya a hug.

"Thanks, Kate," she says with a smile, getting up from her chair as she returns her son's squeeze. "Max, why don't you go out and see Dina in the waiting room? I just need to talk to Miss Kate for a minute."

"Okay!" Max agrees. "Bye, Miss Kate!" he cries as he dashes out of the room, slamming the door behind him.

I turn to Joya. "Everything okay?"

She smiles. "I was going to ask you the same thing. You don't seem like yourself today."

I shake my head, chiding myself for letting my personal life bleed into my professional one. "No, I'm fine, Joya," I say. "Thanks."

She takes a step closer, and I can see doubt in her eyes. "Things with Dan are still going well?" she asks.

"Things are great," I answer quickly. Joya and I have gotten to know each other well in the last five years. I know, for example, that she's a single mom struggling to make ends meet and that she'd do anything to make her son's life as normal and as easy as possible. She knows that I'm still struggling with the grief left over from Patrick's death nearly a dozen years ago, but that I'm finally dating a guy I'm serious about, someone everyone in my life agrees is perfect for me.

"Is it something else, then?" she asks gently.

"Really, it's nothing," I respond too quickly, too brightly. I see something in her eyes flicker. "Don't worry about me," I add with as much confidence as I can muster. "I'll be fine."

But after Joya takes Max's hand and leaves, her face full of doubt, I sink into the chair behind my desk and put my head in my hands. It takes me another five minutes before I can force myself to open the file folder my doctor gave me today, the one filled with terms like *chronic anovulation* and *primary infertility*.

Two hours later, I've finished up my notes on today's clients and I'm headed south on Third Avenue toward Zidle's, the intimate bistro on the corner of Lexington and Forty-Eighth that's become a favorite of Dan's and mine over the last year. We have a reservation at seven, and the closer I get, the more ferociously my heart thuds.

I'll have to tell Dan about the news from my doctor, the fact that my ovaries have basically shut down, but what if this changes his mind about being with me? He's the first person I've been serious about since I lost Patrick. I've made the choice—

finally—to blend my life with someone else's. I can't lose that. I can't be alone again.

You don't know what *Dan will say,* I remind myself as I turn the corner onto Forty-Eighth. We've never really talked about children, save for a few surface-level conversations when we first started dating. I had just turned thirty-eight when we met, so I suppose my biological clock should have been ticking, but it was strangely silent. I thought—even though I knew intellectually that it would be harder to get pregnant the older I got—that I had all the time in the world to make my mind up about kids. I certainly didn't expect to be told at barely forty that my chances had all vanished. I'm not even sure I *want* to be a mom, but I've realized I'm not ready for that door to close.

What if Dan isn't either?

I check my watch as I arrive outside the entrance to Zidle's. I'm already ten minutes late, but there's a piece of me that wants to turn around and go home. I could text Dan with an apology, tell him I got caught up with a client, and suggest we order takeout. It would buy me an extra hour to keep things just as they are.

"Kate?"

My intentions evaporate as Dan emerges from the restaurant, his brow creased in concern.

"Oh." I force a smile. "Hey."

"What are you doing just standing out here?" He takes a step closer and puts a hand on my shoulder. Right away, I feel better. This is Dan. Perfect, blond-haired, hazel-eyed, friends-with-everyone Dan, who's reasonable and rational and loves me. Everything's going to be okay. He's not going to give up on me just because my ovaries have.

I take a deep breath. "Dan, there's something I need to tell you."

Something flickers across his face, but then he smiles and shakes his head. "Think we could go in first?"

"Well—" I begin.

"You can tell me once we've gotten our table, okay?" He grabs my hand and turns around without waiting for an answer. I sigh and let him pull me through the door.

"Surprise!" A chorus of voices greets us the moment we step inside. I gasp and take a step back as my eyes adjust to the dim lighting of the restaurant. It takes me a moment to register that the entryway is filled with some of the people I love most: my sister, Susan, and her husband, Robert; their kids, Sammie and Calvin; my best friend, Gina, and her husband, Wayne; a dozen other friends and acquaintances from over the years. Dan's brother, Will, is there too, as is his best friend, Stephen, and a handful of the couples we sometimes go out with.

"What's happening?" I ask, directing my confusion toward my sister, the one who always seems to be able to untangle me, even if she's usually judging me at the same time. But she merely smiles and points over my shoulder.

In slow motion, I turn back toward the doorway, where I'm startled to see Dan down on one knee. I blink at him, my heart thudding. "You're proposing?"

He laughs. "Looks like it." From his pocket, he pulls a robin's-egg-blue ring box, cracks it open, and holds it up. "Kate, will you marry me?"

Our friends break into applause, and it feels like time freezes as I stare at the perfect Tiffany solitaire inside. For a split second, all I can think is that it's different—too different—from the antique engagement ring Patrick proposed with. Then, my mind shifts into high-gear guilt. I shouldn't be thinking about Patrick. What's wrong with me? I should be thinking about whether I can say yes to Dan without telling him the news from my doctor. Then again, I can't say no in front of all these people either.

Of course I don't *want* to say no, I remind myself. Dan's perfect. Always holds doors. Never forgets to say please and thank you. He's the kind of man every mother wants for her daughter. In fact, my own mother never misses the chance to remind me how lucky I am to have found him. I hadn't been thinking marriage, but it's the next logical step, isn't it? It's what people do when they love each other.

"Kate?" Dan's voice jars me back to reality.

I feel my mouth shift into a smile as my pulse races. "Yes," I hear myself say. And then, because I know it's the right thing—obviously it is—I say it again. "Yes, of course, yes." This is what's meant to be, and when I tell myself that, my heart fills. "Yes, I'll marry you, Dan," I say, smiling at him.

He whoops and jumps up, pulling me into his arms and dancing us around as our friends whistle and cheer. "Kate Waithman," he says, "I'm going to make you the happiest woman in the world."

I laugh with him as he slips the ring onto my finger, where it catches the light, diffusing it into a million tiny stars.

"I love you, Kate," he murmurs, pulling me close. But I can barely hear him over the rushing sound in my ears.

For the next hour, I smile and laugh on cue, but it feels like I'm in a daze as our friends mill around, telling stories about both of us, calling us "the golden couple," slapping Dan on the back, and kissing me on the cheek. At least a half-dozen people tell me they're glad to see me moving on; a dozen more tell me what a catch Dan is. I notice the waitress behind the bar staring lustily at him a few times, and I'm grateful that he seems oblivious.

Susan is busy corralling her two rambunctious kids, so it's Gina who sticks close to me as Dan mingles with his friends. I know she understands the weird roller coaster of emotions going on inside me right now. She remarried six years after her husband Bill died, and I remember her telling me how it felt like there was a storm going on inside of her after she said yes. Guilt for moving on. Joy at finding love again. A cautious optimism about a new life beginning. A regret at putting the old life definitively to rest.

"You okay?" she asks as she brings me a glass of champagne.

"Yeah." I smile. "Thanks."

She gives me a quick hug. "I can't believe he rented this whole restaurant just so he could propose in front of all your friends." She grins and shakes her head. "What a guy, right?"

"Gina?" I ask, grabbing her arm as she starts to walk away. "Do you think Dan would still want to marry me if I couldn't have a baby?"

"What?" She stops and stares at me. "Kate, what happened?"

My eyes fill. "I had a doctor's appointment today." I shakily recap what the doctor told me. "It's okay; I'm going to deal with it," I add quickly when I see how concerned she looks. "I'm just worried about Dan."

"Oh, Kate." She folds me into a silent hug. "But does he want kids?" she asks after a moment.

I shrug and pull away. "I don't know. We've never really talked about it."

"You've never talked about it?" Her tone isn't accusatory, but I still feel like I've done something wrong.

"It just never seemed like the right time." It sounds stupid when I say it aloud. "Besides, I was supposed to have kids with Patrick," I add in a whisper.

Gina's eyes fill with understanding. She chews her bottom lip, and I know her well enough to know that she's literally biting back something she wants to say. What finally comes out is, "Do *you* want kids?"

"I don't know. But I'm not ready to be told I can't have them." I wipe my eyes before they can overflow.

"No one's telling you that," she says firmly. "Maybe you could do IVF. Or you could hire a surrogate if you still have healthy eggs left. You could even adopt. There are plenty of options. Don't you dare let yourself believe that your chances are all gone."

"Thanks." I smile weakly.

"As for Dan, you have to tell him," she adds. "But it's not going to change his mind about you. He loves you. Don't worry about it tonight, okay? Just enjoy this. But talk to him, Kate. You're supposed to be able to talk to the man you're going to marry."

"I know. I will. I shouldn't have said anything. Don't worry, okay?" I walk away, a smile pasted on my face, before she can get another word out.

It's seeing Patrick's mother come through the door twenty minutes later that finally undoes me.

"Kate!" she exclaims, rushing over. She pulls me into a tight hug. She smells, as she always does, of cinnamon and flour. "Gina invited me; I hope it's okay that I'm here."

"Of course it is!" The two of us have remained tight since Patrick's death, and we grew even closer after her husband, Joe, died nine years ago. Patrick was their only child, and with Joe gone too, I feel responsible for her. But it's a responsibility I relish, because I love her like a second mother. "I'm so glad you're here, Joan."

"I just wish I'd been on time!" She rolls her eyes. "Wouldn't you know I missed my train? It threw my whole schedule off."

Joan lives in Glen Cove, a small town out on Long Island, in the same house Patrick grew up in. Sometimes I worry about the fact that she's living all by herself, surrounded by the past. I'd had to move out of my downtown apartment three weeks after burying Patrick because I couldn't stand the emptiness in the space we'd shared. Every time I walked through the door, I had half expected to see him standing there. Besides, the neighbors had started to complain about the fact that sometimes in the middle of the afternoon, I'd stand in the living room and start to scream. I couldn't stop. The landlord had been only too happy to let me out of my lease.

"Don't worry," I say. "You're here now. That's what matters." I'm startled to realize that tears are rolling down my cheeks. "Listen, Joan, I'm sorry."

"For what?" She looks at me blankly.

"I . . . I don't want you to think I'm forgetting Patrick," I sniffle as I wipe my eyes. I avoid her gaze for a moment, then I look up.

"Sweetheart," she says gently, "you're allowed to move on. You're *supposed* to move on." She puts her arm around me. "Let's go get a breath of fresh air, shall we?" She leads me out of the restaurant, and once we're around the corner, she takes a tissue out of her purse and hands it to me. "Kate, sweetie, it's been almost twelve years. Patrick would want you to be happy. I know he's up there in heaven, smiling down at you."

We both glance skyward at the same time, and I wonder if she's thinking, as I am, that the city is covered tonight in a canopy of clouds, obscuring all the stars. It makes heaven feel very far away.

"Do you still wear the coin?" she asks softly when I don't say anything.

I nod and pull the silver dollar out from beneath my shirt. It was the last thing Patrick gave me, and a few months after he died, I found a jeweler who agreed to drill a hole through it and string it on a long chain.

She smiles slightly. "Patrick believed in all kinds of good things in the universe, Kate," she says, reaching out and touching the coin. "He believed in love and luck and happiness, and he would have wanted you to find all that. That's what these coins are about. You have to remember that. He would want the brightest possible future for you, dear."

"I'll never stop loving him, you know."

"I know," Joan says, folding me into her arms for another warm hug. "But that doesn't mean you can't love someone else too. Life has to go on. You're happy, sweetheart, aren't you?"

I nod.

"Well, then, you're doing the right thing," she concludes. "So shall we go back inside to your party? I'd love to meet your fiancé."

After I introduce Dan to Joan and down another glass of champagne, someone puts Eric Clapton's "Wonderful Tonight" on the jukebox. Dan holds his hand out to me with a smile. "Let's dance, my beautiful bride-to-be."

He spins me dramatically onto the makeshift dance floor, and we fall into an easy rhythm, just like we always do.

"Pat's mother seems nice," he murmurs as our friends begin to appear alongside us, swaying to the music in pairs.

"Patrick," I correct. Dan has the annoying habit of calling my husband by a nickname that was never his. "And yeah, she's great. I'm lucky to have her in my life."

"Sure," he says. He pauses and adds, "So do you think you plan to stay in touch with her?"

I pull away and look at him. "Of course." When he doesn't say anything, I add, "Why wouldn't I?" I sound more defensive than I mean to, so I try to soften the words with a small smile.

Dan pulls me back toward him. "I just thought that once you and I got married, you might let that piece of your past go. But I don't mind. She seems like a nice woman."

"She's family, Dan. She always will be."

"That's fine," Dan says quickly.

But it doesn't feel fine. It feels like Dan thinks I'm doing something wrong, which makes me wonder if I am.

As soon as the song's over, Gina sweeps in with another glass of champagne for me, and as we walk off the dance floor, I down it in two gulps. She gazes at me with concern. "Anything you want to talk about?" she asks as she takes my empty glass from me and motions for a waiter to bring us another.

"Nope," I say. The bubbles are starting to go to my head.

"Was that about Joan?" she asks. "Whatever Dan said?"

I nod and glance at Dan, who's dancing to "YMCA" now with some of his buddies from work. Somehow, he manages to make the dance look cool. "Yeah," I say. I don't bother explaining, because I know Gina understands.

"You're not doing anything wrong, in case you're wondering," she says. The waiter arrives with another glass of champagne, which I sip more slowly than the last. My head is starting to spin.

"You're sure?"

"Positive," she says firmly. "Joan is a part of your life. She always will be. There's absolutely nothing wrong with that."

"Okay."

For the next few hours, I down glass after glass of champagne as the party winds into the night. I dance a silly version of "Call Me Maybe" with Sammie and Calvin before Susan takes them home to put them to bed. I hug Joan good night around ten and put her in a cab with instructions to call me once she gets home safely. And I dance with Dan, who pulls me close and tells me that he's the luckiest man in the world.

Around midnight, Dan's friend Stephen puts Guns N' Roses' "Sweet Child O' Mine" on the jukebox and pulls him away to rock out on the dance floor with a bunch of his friends. I drift back to a seat at the bar, and as I listen to the song, even though I know that it's not actually about a child, the chorus gets me thinking about kids.

Maybe it's the champagne or the fact that the world feels a bit like a whirling merry-go-round, but as I put my head down, I'm all of a sudden wondering what would have happened if Patrick and I had tried for a child when we'd first married. What if I'd gotten pregnant before he'd died, long before my ovaries had given up? I'd have an eleven-year-old by now. I'd have a piece of Patrick with me forever. Regret surges through me, tightening my throat.

When the song ends and a Rolling Stones song comes on in its place, Dan drifts over and puts an arm around me. "I'm happy too," he whispers, and it takes me a moment to realize that I'm crying and that he's mistaken my tears of loss for tears of joy.

I let him make the mistake, because I *am* happy. So happy. So many people never get a second chance. And so I kiss him deeply until Stephen and a few of his other friends whistle and catcall from across the bar. I pull back and look into his eyes.

"Thank you," I say solemnly.

"For what?" He smiles and kisses me on the forehead.

"For loving me," I tell him. "For making me feel special and for marrying me and for trying to understand me and for . . ." My voice trails off, because I've forgotten what I was going to say.

Dan laughs. "Looks like someone's had a little too much champagne," he says. He helps me to my feet and I realize he's right when I sway a little. "What do you say I take my beautiful bride home and put her to bed?"

"But I'm not a bride yet," I protest, surprised to hear my

words slurring together like they're made of syrup. "But yeah, okay. Bed."

He laughs again, sweeps me into his arms, and after waving good night to our friends, he carries me home as I fall asleep against his solid chest.

Three

The next morning, as I blink into the sunlight, I have the dim sense that something's off. There's far too much light for our western-exposure bedroom. Dan put up blackout shades when he moved in six months ago, so mornings usually dawn in near pitch-blackness.

Where am I? I squint, my head pounding from what is undoubtedly a massive champagne hangover. I sit up and look around, confused, as my eyes adjust and the room comes into focus. Indeed, this isn't our apartment. The curtains on the windows are white and gauzy; the bed is a teak sleigh queen instead of a burnished black king, and the sheets and comforter are pale blue and soft instead of gray and sleek. The room is oddly familiar, but I can't put a finger on why.

Had Dan put me to bed at a friend's apartment last night for some reason? I struggle to remember, but the last thing I recall is falling asleep in his arms just after leaving the restaurant.

"Dan?" I call out tentatively.

I hear footsteps in the hallway, then the sound of someone whistling softly. Again, I have a strange feeling of familiarity, but it only unsettles me. Dan never whistles. In fact, he'd told me on our first date that he considers his inability to whistle one of his greatest failures in life. It was the first time he'd made me laugh.

"Babe?" I venture a bit more uncertainly.

And then the person whistling rounds the corner into the bedroom, and my heart nearly stops, because it's not Dan standing there at all.

It's Patrick.

My husband, Patrick.

Who died a dozen years ago.

"Morning," he says with a smile, and the sound of his sweetly familiar deep voice hits me like a punch to the gut. I was so sure I'd never hear it again. *This is impossible.*

As I gape at him, I realize that he doesn't quite look the way he used to. His dark hair is a little thinner around the temples, his laugh lines have deepened, and he's more solid than he once was. It's how I always imagined he might have looked if he'd lived to grow older with me. His eyes are just as brilliant and green and warm as I remember, though, and for a long moment, I forget to breathe.

"What's happening?" I finally whisper, but my voice barely makes a sound. I notice with a start that there's a sort of haze filling the room, the kind of softening of the light that happens when the sun's rays hit particles of dust in the air just the right way. Those gossamer moments have always made me think of fairy dust and wishes come true. I wonder if that's what's happening now, something magical and unreal.

But as I stare at Patrick, something strange happens: my disorientation begins to fade. I look around and realize with a start that I *knew* somehow that there would be a slender Dyson vacuum cleaner propped haphazardly in the corner; I knew there would be a Word-of-the-Day calendar on the bedside table; I knew there would be a small cluster of yellow roses in a blue vase on the bureau.

This is our old apartment, I'm startled to realize, the one on Chambers Street, the one we were living in when Patrick died. The furniture is mostly new, but I recognize the layout, the hardwood floors I'd once loved, the walls I'd once pounded on while screaming and demanding to know how God could have taken my husband away. I can't understand what's happening.

"Katielee? You okay?" Patrick asks with concern, cutting into my confused train of thoughts and bringing me back down to earth.

I can feel tears rolling down my cheeks as I struggle to say something in return, but the only thing that comes out of my mouth is a meaningless string of vowels. A part of me is wondering if this is a dream, but the longer I'm here, the more convinced I am it's not. After all, I've never dreamed this vividly and in this much detail before. Then again, if I'm not dreaming, what explanation is there?

Patrick sits down beside me on the bed. "You must have had a rougher night than I thought, honey," he says with a chuckle.

Then he reaches out to stroke my arm, and my whole body feels suddenly like it's on fire. He feels so real, and it startles me so much that I pull away and then instantly regret it, because I'd do anything in the world to have his hands on my skin.

"What is it, Kate?" he asks, reaching up to wipe my tears away. "What's wrong?"

"You're alive!" I finally manage to choke out between sobs. His hand on my face is the only thing grounding me. I have the sudden feeling that if he moves away again, I'll simply drift straight out the open window and back to the reality in which I belong.

"Of course I'm alive," he says, looking puzzled.

I sniffle and try to explain. "But you . . . you died twelve years ago." As soon as the words are out of my mouth, the whole room goes fuzzy. I reach out in a panic, groping for him.

"Honey, what are you talking about?" His voice sounds very far away. "Why would you say something like that?"

"Because—" I pause as the world around me continues to fade. Abruptly, I wonder whether my doubt is making this reality disappear. Isn't that what happens when one shakes the foundation of a dream? All of a sudden, regardless of what this is, I'm desperate to stay here for as long as I can, so I take a deep breath, force a feeble smile, and say in a rush, "I don't know. I don't know what I'm saying. I'm sorry. You're obviously right here."

The room comes instantly back into focus—*Patrick* comes back into focus—and my heart skips a beat. For a few seconds, I look around in wonder, taking it all in. The impossibly blue sky outside the window. The technicolor yellow of the roses on the bureau. The searingly red glow of the numbers on our digital bedside clock. It's like someone has turned up the color dial by fifty percent, making everything more beautiful. I look back at Patrick, and although he seems to almost glow in the overly saturated room, he still looks like himself. Except that he's frowning.

"Katielee, you're scaring me," he says. The room flickers again, and I grab his hand in a panic.

"No, I'm sorry," I hurry to say. "I think I was having a bad dream."

The minute the words are out of my mouth, I find myself wishing fervently that they're somehow true. What if *this* isn't the dream? What if everything that has happened in the last twelve years is instead the strange fiction?

"You dreamed that I was dead?" He looks concerned, and I can feel my eyes filling with tears.

"Patrick, it was the worst thing I could have imagined. You have no idea how glad I am that you're here."

He gives me another strange look before pulling away. "You're being really weird this morning. Why don't I go get you some ibuprofen and a cup of coffee, okay?" He stands up and takes a step toward the door, and before I know what I'm doing, I lurch out of bed and grab his arm in a panic.

"Please don't go!" I cry. I'm terrified that if I let him stride out of the room, I'll never see him again.

"Okay," he says slowly. "Would you like to come with me?"

I nod, feeling foolish, and after giving me another concerned look, he helps me out of bed. I feel dizzy and disoriented the moment I'm on my feet.

As Patrick takes my hand and leads me out of the bedroom, I glance out the window in the hall and notice that the dilapidated funeral home that always stood there has been replaced by a little green space with a jungle gym, a yellow slide, and a poplar tree. "Everything's different," I murmur.

"Kate," Patrick says, his voice hoarse, "what's wrong with you?"

I turn to face him, and he's so close that I can hardly breathe. I move into the space between us, and as I feel his body against mine, I remember with a jolt the way I used to fit so perfectly into the nook between his arm and his chest. I touch his face, and the stubble on his jaw feels so real. "I . . . I'm not supposed to be here," I say, because I don't know how else to explain what's happening to me. The hall flickers and sparks at the edges, and I realize that I've again threatened the fabric of this world.

"Where else would you be?" Patrick looks at me for a moment and then gently turns me around and begins moving us back toward the bedroom. "You know what, honey?" he asks. "Maybe it's better if I just bring you that ibuprofen. You seem really off this morning. Let's get you back to bed for a bit, okay?"

I let him lead me back to the bedroom, because he's right; I feel dazed and unsteady on my feet. "Don't leave me," I murmur.

"I'll be right back," he says as he tucks me under the covers. "I promise."

"But you promised me you'd be with me forever too," I whisper after he's gone. For a moment, I just lie there, staring at the ceiling, trying to figure out what's happening. Why does everything here feel so familiar? How do I know, for example, that the ibuprofen bottle Patrick is going to get is the generic brand from Duane Reade, that it's on the second shelf beside the sink in the bathroom, and that there are only a dozen pills left? How do I know that the shopping list attached to the fridge has *ibuprofen* written on it, directly below *milk, marshmallows, peanut butter, frozen onions,* and *toilet paper*—all in my handwriting? How do I know that when I reach for the lamp on Patrick's bedside table, it won't turn on, because the bulb burned out last night? I take a deep breath and just to be sure, I reach across and flick the switch at the lamp's base. Nothing happens, and I exhale heavily, more confused than ever.

I can't shake the feeling that I'm really here, that this isn't actually a dream at all. But that doesn't make any sense.

My heart thudding, I reach for the phone on my bedside table. We still have a landline, I know in a flash, because Patrick thinks it's safer, just in case we ever need to call 911. *How do I know that?* I shake my head and dial my sister's home number. Surely she'll explain everything.

But a second later, a recording comes on telling me the line has been disconnected. I hang up and redial, assuming I've hit the buttons wrong in my confusion, but the same recording comes on again. I try her cell, but there's a man's voice on the outgoing message instead of hers. I'm getting a bad feeling in the pit of my stomach. What if something happened to her?

"Is Susan okay?" I demand as Patrick walks back into the room. Could this dream world have traded my sister for my husband, one horror for another? "Please tell me she's okay. Please tell me she's alive."

Patrick's brow furrows. "Of course she is, honey," he says, and relief floods through me like a river. "What are you talking about?"

"I just tried calling her," I say as I feel myself begin to shake again. I rattle off the digits of her home phone, as if saying them will bring her back.

He shakes his head. "Katielee, that's her old number."

I stare at him, and suddenly, as if someone is uploading my memory files as we go, I know exactly what he means. "She moved," I murmur. "For Rob's job. Eleven years ago."

Patrick looks concerned. "Of course. To San Diego."

"Right," I say slowly. I also know suddenly that Sammie is taking surf lessons, that Calvin broke his arm falling off his skateboard three weeks ago, and that they live in a little yellow house with blue shutters seven blocks from the beach. "How do I know everything?" I whisper.

Patrick climbs into bed beside me and slips his arm around me, pulling me close. "Honey, what are you talking about?"

"I don't know," I murmur. I close my eyes and breathe in his woodsy cinnamon scent, the one that's so specifically and intimately his. I lean into his warm, solid chest, something I'd never imagined doing again. I reach up and kiss him, and it feels just like it always did. His lips are soft and gentle, and after a moment, he reaches up and strokes my right cheek with his left thumb, like he always used to do. He tastes like toothpaste and love and life, and I consume him eagerly, hungrily, as tears sting my eyes. As long as I'm kissing him, I'm not scared.

But then I'm hit with a sharp pang of guilt, and I pull away.

Am I cheating on Dan? I shake the thought off. Of course I'm not. This isn't real. It can't be.

"Tell me you love me, Patrick," I whisper urgently, because I need to hear him say it before reality comes crashing back in.

Patrick pulls back a little to look me in the eye. "More than you could ever imagine," he says. "I love you, Kate. I knew before I met you—"

"—that I was meant to be yours," I murmur, feeling the salty path of tears down my cheek.

He leans in to kiss me softly, gently, and it feels like magic. Our kiss is beginning to grow more intense when we're interrupted by a voice from the doorway.

"Dad?"

I turn in slow motion to see a girl standing there in a pink nightgown. Her wavy chestnut hair falls just past her shoulders, and she has big green eyes the exact color of Patrick's. I feel my heart flutter.

She's immediately familiar to me, and although I can't quite grasp the thread of memory that ties everything together, I know instantly that she'll be thirteen in four weeks, on July eighth. I know she loves One Direction and that her favorite member is Louis, because he's the mature one. I know she loves to draw and play the piano. And I know she got a B+ on her vocabulary test last week because she misspelled the words *sagacious* and *countenance*.

"Hi," I whisper.

The girl is staring at me with concern. "Mom?" she ventures, and something inside me bursts wide open.

I turn to Patrick with wide eyes. "I'm her mother?" I whisper, but of course I am. I know it instantly, and just as quickly, there's a sudden buzzing in my ears. I see Patrick open his mouth to reply, and I feel him wrap his hand around mine, but already, the light is growing brighter, and he's beginning to fade into it.

"Come back!" I cry, but I know he can't hear me.

I lose sight of him as the room disappears. The last thing I can feel is his strong fingers slipping from mine.

Four

My alarm jars me awake, and it takes me only a split second to remember the feel of Patrick's touch, warm and solid and alive. I sit bolt upright, blinking into the darkness.

"Patrick!" I call out, but there's only the bleating of the alarm clock in return. I hit the snooze button, and in the sudden silence, I already know that I'm back in my real life, the one I share with Dan, the one in which I'll always be a widow. "Patrick?" I repeat feebly, although I already know he's not here.

As the room comes into focus, the last shred of hope disappears. The blackout shades obscure most of the light, and I'm wrapped in the cool silk sheets I've grown accustomed to.

"It was just a dream," I say aloud. "A dream. That's all. Patrick is gone." But I can't get over how real it all felt. His touch. His taste. The weird way everything seemed to glow.

And although the details are fading fast, I can't shake the image of the little girl with the beautiful eyes that were unmistakably Patrick's. I can't erase the way she felt so real and so *mine,* the way I actually loved her. My breath catches in my throat as her single word to me—*Mom*—comes floating back.

But I'd known, somehow, that she'd be thirteen on July

eighth, which means she'd been born just four months after I slept with Patrick for the first time. There's no weird alternative universe in which she could actually be mine.

"I'm not her mom," I whisper, surprised at how crushed this makes me feel. "It wasn't real." I know I'm being irrational. But my heart is still thudding, and I can still see her face in the darkness.

I turn on the lamp on the bedside table. Just in front of my alarm clock is a glass of water, a bottle of Advil, and a note from Dan telling me he had to head into work early but he hopes I'm not too hungover. *I've never seen you drink so much champagne!* he has concluded helpfully.

My hand shaking, I take out two pills for my throbbing headache. I wash them down then lie back on my pillow and stare at the ceiling. "What's happening to me?" I whisper into the silence.

After a few minutes, I reach for my iPhone and pull up YoungWidowTalk.com, a website I visit every once in a while, though never around Dan. I enter *vivid dream of husband* into the search field, and several threads pop up. I begin clicking on messages, looking for an instance of a widow having a bizarrely vivid dream about her husband being alive in the present day, but all I find are mentions of dreams about people's husbands in the past. I search next for *imaginary child,* and *child who doesn't exist,* but I come up empty. Apparently, I'm the only one losing her mind in that particular way.

I sigh, set my phone down, and get out of bed. The marble floor is cold beneath my feet, and it jars me back to the here and now.

I float through my morning appointments, and by lunchtime, I know I'm too distracted to be much use to my clients. I ask Dina, the receptionist I share with three other therapists in my office suite, to cancel my afternoon sessions.

"Everything okay, Kate?" she asks, eyeing me with concern. "You've never canceled on your clients before."

"I'm just not feeling well," I tell her. It's not entirely a lie.

While I wait for her to let me know she was able to reach everyone, I head back into my office and dig in my middle drawer for the framed photo of Patrick I took off my desk after my fifth date with Dan. I'd told myself then that it was time to put Patrick away. And I had. Mostly.

From time to time over the last two years, I've pulled out his picture and stared at it when I needed answers. There's always something about seeing his calm, sea-green eyes that seems to untangle everything in my head.

But today, looking at him just makes everything more confusing. He's so young in the photo, a sharp contrast to how he looked last night. *It wasn't real,* I remind myself. *It couldn't have been.* Still, I run my finger lightly over the outer corners of his eyes and think how endearing it was to see the laugh lines that would have formed there. I touch the deep black of his hair and think about how beautiful it looked laced with gray.

The intercom on my desk buzzes, startling me.

"I reached everyone, Kate." Dina's tinny voice fills the office. "You're all canceled for the afternoon." She hesitates. "You sure you're okay? Can I get you anything?"

"No, I'm good!" I force a chirp. "Thanks!"

There's staticky silence for a minute. "I'm going to take lunch now."

"Okay!" I reply brightly. "See you tomorrow, then!"

I shove Patrick's photo back into my desk drawer, beneath a stack of files, and then I reach for my phone. Susan picks up on the first ring.

"I'm off for the afternoon," I tell her. "Can I come over?"

"What's the matter?"

"Nothing. Can't I come see my sister without something being wrong?"

"We'll talk about it when you get here," she says firmly, letting me know she sees right through me.

Twenty-five minutes later, I'm pulling up outside her brownstone in a cab. She greets me at the door with a glass of white wine, which she hands to me wordlessly.

"It's only one in the afternoon," I say, taking the glass anyhow.

"I know by your voice when you need a drink. And now is one of those times."

She walks away before I can respond, so I shut the door behind me and follow her in, taking a sip as I go. She's right.

"Hi, guys!" I say as I pass the living room, where Sammie and Calvin are glued to the television. On the screen, a cartoon mouse I've never seen before is giving a cartoon bear a lecture, and Calvin is giggling. Sammie turns around, grins, and waves. I feel a sudden pang of longing for the green-eyed girl in my dream.

I find Susan in the kitchen, leaning against the counter with her own glass of white wine. There's an open bottle of chardonnay on the counter beside a bowl of kettle chips. "Well?" she says as soon as I round the corner. "Spill. Is this about you getting engaged?"

"No," I say immediately. But when she just raises an eyebrow at me, I look down and mutter. "It's stupid. I just had this crazy dream last night. I mean, I think it was a dream . . ."

I let my voice trail off, and when she doesn't say anything, I force my gaze up to meet her eyes. She looks calm and pulled together. Exactly how I should be feeling right now. Instead, I feel jittery, like a drug addict going through withdrawal.

"Go on," she says calmly.

And so I tell her about waking up beside Patrick, hearing his voice, feeling his touch. I tell her how his hair was speckled with gray; his frame was sturdier; his touch was just as achingly familiar. Her expression grows sadder as I speak, and by the time I'm done, I can feel tears rolling down my cheeks.

She sighs, puts her glass down on the counter, and pulls me into a hug. "It's just nerves, sweetie," she says into my shoulder. "Saying yes to Dan is a big deal. It's totally normal to have a dream like this."

"But it didn't feel like any dream I've ever had before," I say in a small voice. "It felt like it was actually happening."

"Of course it did." She releases me and steps back. "I think there's a part of you that feels like you're doing something wrong by moving on. But it's time, Kate. It's okay. Patrick would want this for you."

I take another tentative sip of my wine. I contemplate telling her about the girl with the green eyes, but I already have the feeling she thinks I've lost my mind. "It just felt like I was getting a glimpse of the life I was supposed to have," I say instead.

Susan grasps both of my arms firmly and waits until I look at her. "*This* is the life you're supposed to have. Right here. Right now. Losing Patrick was terrible, but it was a long time ago. You can't keep retreating to thoughts of him every time you have a chance to move forward, or you're going to let life pass you by. Is that what you want?"

"No." I sniffle. I look down for a long time, then I look up to meet her gaze. "It's just that it felt like I was meant to be there. I knew things I couldn't have possibly known. I felt like I was totally at home."

"Kate, listen to yourself. It was just a dream," she says firmly. "Let me hear you say it."

"But—"

"Kate, seriously!"

"It was just a dream," I repeat obediently after a pause.

Sammie appears in the doorway to the kitchen then, and I quickly try to hide my tears by taking another sip of wine. She's not fooled. "What's wrong with Auntie Kate?" she asks Susan, glancing at me with concern. "She's crying."

"We were just talking about your uncle Patrick, and Auntie Kate got a little sad," Susan says.

Sammie looks puzzled. "But I don't *have* an uncle Patrick."

I choke on her words as Susan hustles Sammie out of the room. I can hear her reminding Sammie that I used to have a husband, and that I'm very sad sometimes that he's gone.

Susan returns a moment later, her cheeks a little flushed. "Sorry about that," she says. "We don't talk about Patrick much in front of the kids, because it's confusing for them to think about people dying. I didn't mean for her to hurt your feelings."

"I'm just an emotional wreck today. Not her fault." I force a smile and try to lighten the mood. "By the way, you may be interested to know that in my dream, you lived in San Diego. I bet you had a great tan. So there's that."

Susan goes very still. "San Diego?"

I nod. "Yeah, apparently you'd moved there eleven years ago, because Robert had gotten a job offer. Lucky you, right?"

Susan presses her lips together. "I told Mom and Dad not to tell you that," she mutters. "How long have you known?"

"Known what?"

"About Robert's job offer."

When I look at her blankly, she sighs. "The year after you lost Patrick, Robert got a pretty great job offer in San Diego."

"He did?" Goose bumps prickle on my arms.

She nods. "But we decided to stay here."

"For me?" I venture in a small voice.

Susan hesitates. "You would have done the same. But how did you know about California? Mom?"

"No." I look down at my hands, more perplexed than ever.

"Well, who told you then?" Susan asks.

I shrug helplessly, my heart thudding. "Patrick did."

It's impossible, isn't it? Seeing Patrick and the life I could have had in such finite detail can't be anything but a dream, but then how could I have known about San Diego?

That's what's swimming through my mind as I head out of Susan's apartment and make my way toward the subway station on Eighty-Sixth. It's not the dream itself that's haunting me, although seeing Patrick has unearthed feelings I thought I had closed away for good. What's bothering me is what it means. And if I'm divining information that actually matches up to reality, is there a chance it's something more?

"Don't be a lunatic," I mutter to myself, earning a pitying glance from a passerby, who cuts a wide path around me on the sidewalk. I smile an embarrassed apology and put my head down until I duck into the subway station.

I catch the 6 train, but instead of getting off at Grand Central, my usual stop, I find myself riding the train to the Brooklyn Bridge–City Hall station and walking west on Chambers, toward my old apartment. I have to see it, if only to remind myself once and for all that Patrick is gone, as is the life we shared long ago.

I've deliberately avoided this area of Manhattan since I moved farther uptown. I've declined invitations to birthday dinners in the neighborhood, taken cab drivers on roundabout, nonsensical routes, and mostly convinced myself that it could be stored away in a lockbox with all my other memories of the years before Patrick's death. But the lock was broken last night.

I reach the doorway to my building, walk up the steps, and take a deep breath before looking right, to the listing of tenants.

My gaze stops at Apartment 5F, where *P + K Waithman* used to be written in block letters that seemed so permanent. The line beside the buzzer now reads *Schubert*.

Despite myself, I'm disappointed, but what did I expect? That Patrick was still here, living a secret life with a fictional preteen daughter, their names listed in plain sight? I shake my head. "You're being ridiculous," I say out loud.

Still, I can't resist pushing the buzzer. When there's no answer, I back away from the door, and that's when I notice that the funeral home on the corner is gone, just like it was in my dream. I hold my breath and duck into the narrow alley along the right side of the building. Through the slats in the new wooden fence, I can just make out a new jungle gym with a yellow slide, shaded by a sinewy poplar tree.

"Impossible," I murmur, backing away, out of the alley and into the fading sunshine on Chambers Street. I haven't been here in more than a decade, so how could I have known about the swing set and the tree? How could I have seen them in such exact and correct detail? How did I know they'd be here?

I walk back up the steps and buzz apartment 5F again, but there's still no reply. I'm half expecting to hear Patrick's voice through the intercom, vibrating with static, but that's crazy.

I buried him on a bright September morning long ago.

Five

I arrive home by four thirty, and after a half hour of sitting on the couch and staring straight ahead in confusion, I stand up and head for the liquor cabinet in the corner, the one I rarely touch.

I like a glass of wine with dinner, and I have a pint of Guinness from time to time at happy hour with Susan, but I've never been a big drinker. So maybe if I have a few shots of something strong, I can force myself back to sleep, back to the dream, back to Patrick. I'm desperate to see him again, to prove to myself that I'm not going crazy. Then again, that's probably what a crazy person would say.

I reach for Dan's bottle of Basil Hayden's and pour several ounces into a rocks glass. The bourbon burns going down, but I can feel it almost immediately. I'm woozy after a few minutes, but I'm still wide awake, so I fill my glass almost to the top, take a deep breath, and drink it down.

Ten minutes later, the room growing foggy, I make my way to the bedroom and climb between the sheets, yawning gratefully as my head begins to spin. "Please let me wake up with Patrick," I murmur into the silence, but I'm not sure who I'm asking. God? The bottle of bourbon?

I drift off soon after and although I sleep soundly, I don't dream. When I wake the next morning in my real bedroom, with Dan lying beside me, I'm crushed.

"Morning, baby." Dan's voice is cobbled with sleep as he rolls over and pulls me toward him. He nuzzles my neck then pulls back, a look of his confusion on his face. "Geez, Kate, you smell like a distillery."

"Sorry," I mumble, my head throbbing like I've been run over by a truck. "I had a few drinks last night."

"Again? You okay?"

"Mmm hmm." I force a sunny smile, which just makes my head pound even more insistently. I get up to brush my teeth and swallow three Advil, then I crawl back into bed, hoping I'll have time to close my eyes for a few minutes before I have to be up, just in case.

But Dan wraps his arms around me and presses his body into mine. "What time do you have to be at work?" he asks, his voice low and suggestive.

I glance at the clock, my hopes of falling back asleep fading. My first appointment isn't for ninety minutes, so I tell him, "I've got time," because I feel guilty that I spent the night hoping desperately to wake up with another man.

We make love slowly, lazily, and I manage somehow not to think about Patrick at all until Dan gets up to go take a shower. As I lie in bed alone, my head still aching, I feel my eyes filling with tears. I quickly wipe them away and get out of bed to begin getting dressed.

Fifteen minutes later, Dan and I kiss good-bye at the front door, but he grabs my arm as I begin to walk out. "Kate?" he says tentatively. "Is something up? It feels like you're somewhere else today."

I haven't told him about my infertility yet, but now isn't the right time, not when I'm on my way out the door, not when my head is still swirling with thoughts of Patrick. I'll tell him tonight, after dinner, and it will all be okay.

I take a deep breath. "No, I'm fine."

He looks into my eyes. "You sure? You're not yourself."

I'm still mulling over Dan's words—and the fact that he's right—as I arrive at my office. Dina asks if I'm feeling better, and I mumble an excuse about nausea, because I *am* feeling ill. Liquor and confusion will do that to you. Her eyes light up.

"Maybe you're pregnant!" she says in a stage whisper.

"Doubt it," I say, avoiding her gaze and reaching for my flat belly. I hurry into my office to prepare for a long day in which I don't have to think about my own life at all.

I'm just packing up my bag a few minutes after five when my sister strides into my office, a binder in her arms and a determined expression on her face.

"What are you doing here?" I ask, because she's only been to my office once in the five years I've worked here. "Are the kids okay?"

"They're with Robert," she says. She holds out the binder. "You and I are going to Hammersmith's to plan your wedding."

I feel my headache returning as I take the binder from her. It says *Mrs.* on the front in glittery script. "I told Dan I'd make dinner tonight."

"It's just for an hour," she says. "You can bring him takeout."

"Susan—"

"Look." Her tone is instantly businesslike. "You're freaked out about this engagement. I know. It totally explains the dream. But I think that if we start planning the wedding, you'll start feeling better. The more real it feels, the more you'll be able to detach from the past. Okay?"

I eye her. "You talked to your therapist about this, didn't you?" Susan sees a therapist every Thursday afternoon, although I've never understood why. Her life is perfect. What could she have to talk about?

She shrugs. "She agreed with me that getting you to focus on the present will help. So are you in? Or do I have to drink alone?"

I sigh. I might as well seize the opportunity to try out the speech I'm planning to give Dan tonight about my infertility. And I need to tell Susan anyhow. "Are you buying?"

Ten minutes later, we're settling into our usual booth at Hammersmith's, the British pub down the street from my office where we've been meeting for happy hour every few weeks for years. Our regular bartender, Oliver, comes over with a chardonnay for Susan and a Guinness for me, but I make a gagging gesture and order a Sprite instead.

"I need to tell you something," I say once she's taken a long sip of her drink. "I haven't told Dan yet."

"Told him what?" She laughs. "You sound so serious."

I give her a look. She's always been terrible at reading me, but I'm blown away that she can't see pain written across my face right now. "Susan, it *is* serious. I can't have a baby. I found out from the doctor a few days ago. My ovaries have stopped producing eggs."

"Oh." She stares at me for a minute. "Well, I'm sorry to hear that."

It's not exactly the reaction I was expecting. I'd anticipated tears or immediate consolation. Instead, she just looks puzzled. "That's it?" I ask.

"It's just that I didn't know you wanted kids," she says, avoiding my gaze. "I mean, if you were trying to get pregnant, I could see how this would be devastating. But you're forty, so I just kind of figured . . ."

"What, that I don't have the right to want a child?" I snap, interrupting her. "Because I didn't do it on the same schedule you did?"

She shrugs, unperturbed. "No. I'm just saying that forty's a little late in the game to be making up your mind about it, isn't it? I just assumed that you and Dan had already made the decision. You're saying you didn't?"

I glare at her. "*No*. And forty isn't old."

"I'm not saying it's old, obviously. I'm two years older than you are."

"Two years and ten months," I mutter.

She gives me a dark look. "Right. But I had Calvin and Sammie in my thirties, because it's safer that way, Kate. Surely you've seen the statistics. It's much healthier for both mother and baby if you have your children before forty."

"Well, gee," I say faux sweetly, "I'm so sorry I didn't start dating Dan in time to suit your baby-making schedule."

"I'm just saying that you basically spent your thirties with your head buried in the sand, obsessing over Patrick. Look at Gina; she moved on, didn't she? If you'd wanted a child, you should have seized the opportunity while you still had the chance."

I stare at her as my chest grows tight with anger. "It doesn't work like that, Susan. I couldn't just snap my fingers and be okay. You have no idea what it feels like to lose a husband."

"No, I don't. But I know that Dan's a good guy. And you could really screw things up if you start obsessing about babies and fertility now when it's not even something you really want."

"How do you know whether it's something I want?" I demand, my voice rising an octave. Out of the corner of my eye, I see Oliver glance at us with concern.

"Well, is it?" she asks. "Do you want to have a baby?"

"Yes! Maybe. I don't know." I avoid looking at her, because I'm sure she's wearing her infuriating I-knew-I-was-right expression. "It's just that I'm not ready for that decision to be made for me."

"Kate," Susan says, and her tone is gentler than it was a moment ago. "Can you really imagine Dan as a father?"

"Of course!"

"But he hates my kids," she says softly.

"What? He doesn't hate them!"

"Okay, maybe he doesn't *hate* them. But he doesn't like them either. Have you ever seen him interact with them when he doesn't absolutely have to?"

I open my mouth to defend him, but I realize I can't think of a single time I've ever seen him exchange more than awkward, obligatory hellos with my niece and nephew. "He's just not comfortable around them," I finally say. "He's not used to kids."

"Sweetie, he doesn't *like* kids," she says. "So if you're worried about how he's going to react to your news, don't be."

"Really?" I ask. I can feel some of the tension drain from my shoulders. But at the same time, there's a knot forming in the pit of my stomach.

"I'm absolutely positive he's going to be fine with it," she says firmly. She waits until I look up to add the rest. "But the question is, are you?"

She waits a beat before clapping her hands together once and smiling. "Now. Let's get down to wedding talk, shall we?"

I stare at her. "Are you kidding?"

She looks blank. "Why would I be?"

I clench my jaw. "Look, thanks for doing this, Susan. The wedding binder—it's a good idea. But I really need to talk to Dan before we dive into all this planning, okay? Say hi to the kids for me."

I drop a ten-dollar bill on the table and walk away before she can respond.

Outside, I head downtown. The longer I walk, though, the worse I feel. Sure, Susan doesn't quite get me, but her heart's in the right place most of the time. After a minute, I pull out my phone and call her, intending to apologize, but she doesn't pick up. I start to put the phone away, but then I retrieve it from my bag and dial Gina instead.

"So how did you do it?" I ask when she answers.

"Hello to you too." I can hear the smile in her voice. "Okay. I'll bite. How did I do what?"

"Put Bill behind you," I say in a small voice. "Move on. Get married to someone else. Have a child with someone else."

"Oh," she says sadly. She and her husband Wayne have a three-year-old daughter named Madison now. "You just have to think of it as a different life," she says after a minute. "Maybe not the life you were intended to have, or even the life you *thought* you were intended to have. But it's still *your* life, just like the old one was."

I absorb this for a second. "Do you still miss Bill?"

"Every day. But not as much as I used to."

I contemplate telling her about how vividly I saw Patrick, but I know it'll sound crazy. It probably *is* crazy. "Was I wrong to say yes to Dan?" I ask her instead. "When there's still a part of me that's in love with Patrick?"

"No," she says firmly. "You'll always love Patrick. And that's okay. You just have to keep reminding yourself that he's not here anymore."

"But what if he is?" I whisper.

"What?"

I hesitate. "I just don't think I know how to let him go."

* * *

I use the remainder of the walk home to think. New York is swarming with people, but there's something about walking down a crowded street that can feel almost peaceful and solitary. I don't make eye contact or talk to anyone, and by the time I get to our apartment, I feel like I've spent the last twenty minutes in a silent bubble.

Dan's in the kitchen, drinking a glass of red wine, when I walk in the door. "You okay, babe?" he asks. "Susan called and said you seemed upset. She's worried about you."

"I'm fine," I say. I force a smile. "Really. Thanks, sweetheart."

He sets his glass down on the counter and crosses the room to pull me into a hug. "So? How's my beautiful bride-to-be? I heard you and Susan got together today and talked wedding planning?"

"A little," I say, and he smiles at me.

"Hey, I don't want you to stress out about any of this," he continues. "There's no rush. I know some brides go kind of overboard with the details, but I don't want to add anything to your plate. How can I help?"

"You really are perfect, aren't you?" I say with a sigh. "But really, don't worry. I'm not that kind of bride."

"Well, I took care of dinner tonight, anyhow, so that's one less thing on your plate," he says, and I feel terrible. I was supposed to cook. The doorbell rings, as if on cue. "That must be the delivery guy."

Ten minutes later, Dan has set the dining room table, lit two taper candles, and plated our Chinese takeout to make the whole meal look like a fine dining experience.

"Only you would serve take-out lo mein on fine china," I say, shaking my head with a smile.

"Healthy vegetarian lo mein," he clarifies. He pours me a glass of Bordeaux and kisses me on the top of my head. "Nothing but the best for my girl."

"I have to tell you something," I say after we've taken the first few bites of our food. "I went to the doctor a few days ago." I watch his face closely. "My ovaries aren't producing eggs anymore. I—we—won't be able to have a baby."

"Kate—" He reaches for me, but I'm not done yet.

"Do you still want to marry me? I mean, I know we haven't talked about this before, but if this changes things . . ."

He stares at me for a moment as my heart thuds. Then he leans across the table and kisses me. "Of *course* I want to marry you, Kate." He pauses and adds, "It's fine. It'll just be us. We don't need to have children to be happy." He smiles broadly, comfortingly.

But my stomach rolls uncomfortably, and I blink a few times. "We could adopt," I venture.

He shrugs. "Babe, maybe being parents just isn't in the cards for us. Stop worrying about it. This isn't your fault." Then, before I have a chance to say anything else, he switches tracks entirely. "So did you and Susan make any decisions about wedding venues today?" he asks. "Your sister said she had a whole binder of ideas, and I thought some of the outside locations might be nice for the fall . . ."

I shrug, and as he continues to talk, I tune him out and focus on the wall behind him, trying not to cry.

That night, Dan sleeps peacefully beside me while I stare at the ceiling, thinking of the way Patrick and I used to lie in bed, talking about what we'd name our kids, all the fun things we'd do as a family, and the life we were so sure we'd create together.

For the first time, I find myself wondering if I've traded all those things away without realizing it. Maybe it's too late to find my way back to the kind of life I thought I would have. Finally, I drift off into an uneasy sleep.

Six

When I wake up the next morning, I know instantly that I'm back in my old apartment again, back in the strange, overly bright world I can't explain. I gasp, close my eyes, and murmur a small prayer of thanks, even though this might just mean I'm losing my mind. When I crack my eyes open again, the sunlight is catching a few particles of dust in the air. I turn my head slightly to find Patrick lying next to me.

For a moment, I don't move. I just study him as his chest rises and falls. I don't know I'm crying until my vision gets blurry. As I sit up to wipe away my tears, Patrick stirs and rolls toward me.

"Good morning, Katielee," he says, and it's still his voice, his green eyes with the crinkles at the corners, his wide smile with the slightly crooked bottom row of teeth.

I'm too overwhelmed by a rush of gratitude to say anything.

I lie back down and nestle against Patrick as he puts his arm around me. I stroke his hair, noting a solid sprinkling of gray strands that weren't there before. I marvel at the passage of time, the way the years can change a person.

"I would have loved to see you grow old," I murmur, running my hand down his still-solid chest. The color-saturated room flickers a bit, and my heart skips a beat. I remind myself to play along, to do my best to believe I belong here. After all, maybe I do. Why else would it all feel so familiar to me?

Patrick laughs, and I can feel the sound reverberating through his body. "Don't I look old now?" he asks.

I can't even joke back, because my breath is caught in my throat. He pulls me closer and kisses me gently, threading his fingers through my hair. His stubble is scratchy and his lips are warm, but it's not until I feel his tongue against mine that I begin to sob again.

"Kate?" he asks with concern, letting go. "What's wrong?"

I shake my head, not wanting to pull us out of the moment. So instead, I say, "So, our . . . daughter?" I don't know how to ask about her without destroying the fabric of this world, so I let the words hang there.

Patrick touches my cheek and gives me a strange look. "Hannah? What about her?"

Something bursts open inside of me. "Hannah," I murmur. "What a beautiful name."

Patrick looks at me with concern. "You're being weird again."

The room fades a little, and I rush to add, "I was just thinking how lucky we are, that's all."

He smiles. "Oh, I'm pretty positive I'm the luckiest man in the world. Now come on, weirdo, let's get moving."

He gets out of bed, but for a second, I can't move. His statement—the idea that he's lucky—stabs me right through the heart. In fact, he never got to experience any of this: fatherhood, the approach of middle age, the comfort of waking up beside someone you love after years and years together. It all makes me feel profoundly sad.

Patrick is filling the coffeepot at the sink when I finally get out of bed and head into this kitchen. I come up behind him and press my cheek against his bare back. I breathe in deeply, wishing I could just hit the pause button and stay here forever.

"I'm sorry I'm acting so off," I say as he turns off the faucet. "I don't know how to explain what's going on with me. I just feel like . . . It feels like you've been gone a long time."

He sets the coffeepot on the counter and turns, pulling me into his arms. "I'm always here, honey," he says. "I've always been right here. But you've got to stop acting like you don't belong here or something. You're scaring me a bit."

"I'm sorry. I *do* belong here." As I say the words, I find myself fervently clinging to them, hoping there's a way they're true. The room gets a little brighter, comes into focus a little more. I'm struck again by how overly saturated things are here, how everything seems to glow.

"Of course you do." He looks puzzled again. "Let's get some breakfast in you, okay? Maybe you're just hungry. What do you say to crispy bacon and scrambled eggs?"

The knife twists a little deeper in my heart; it's the same breakfast he cooked for me the morning he died. "Sounds great," I manage to say, forcing a smile.

"Good." He turns to grab bacon and a carton of eggs from the fridge and a couple of frying pans from the cabinet while I watch him with tears in my eyes. As he cracks eggs into a bowl and begins to whisk, small pieces of this life begin to drift in from nowhere, and I realize there are things I know with absolute certainty. For example, I know that Patrick left his old financial management job nine years ago, because he wasn't feeling fulfilled, and I know that I supported him in going back to school the way he once supported me. I know that he works in the strategic policy initiatives department of the mayor's office now and that in his spare time, he spearheaded the creation of a new community garden a few blocks from our apartment, calling it Little

Butterfly Garden, because Hannah, who was eight at the time, loved butterflies. I know he took a huge pay cut when he left his old job, but I also know he's a thousand times happier than he used to be and that he feels he's in a position to make a difference in our city. I feel a sudden surge of pride for my husband.

I close my eyes and try to figure out what I know about Hannah too, but for some reason, my knowledge of her is spottier. I know bits and pieces—that she broke her right leg when she was a toddler when she slipped on the playground; that she spent all of kindergarten firmly believing that she was a fairy who just hadn't sprouted her wings yet; that she didn't lose her first tooth until second grade, which was a source of great distress because all her friends had lost teeth earlier—but I can't bring to mind more than snippets. While Patrick is an open book, Hannah feels like a novel with all the important chapters missing.

When I open my eyes again, it's as if my train of thought has summoned Hannah herself, for she's padding down the hall toward the kitchen, wearing pajama pants and a Mickey Mouse T-shirt, her thick, dark hair piled into two messy pigtail buns. "Morning," she says, smiling at Patrick and me, and I notice for the first time that there's something unusual about the way she speaks, although I can't put a finger on exactly what it is. Even in the single word, her vowels are longer and her consonants rounder than they should be. I wonder vaguely if she has a minor speech disorder like some of my clients. Something tickles at the edges of my memory, something I *should* know, but I can't quite hold on to it.

"Good morning," I say, returning her smile. The girl standing in front of me is everything I've wished for so many times over the last twelve years: a piece of Patrick, a way for him to live on. I blink back tears, and before either of them can see me crying, I get up quickly and pretend to be absorbed in getting ready for breakfast. With shaking hands, I reach up and pull three plates down from the cabinet. They clatter loudly onto the counter, because I can't keep my grip steady.

"Kate—?" Patrick begins, but I cut him off.

"No, I'm fine. I'll just set the table." But when I reach into the silverware drawer, which is exactly where I knew it would be, I'm trembling and paying so little attention to what I'm actually doing that when I reach for a butter knife, I grasp a paring knife instead. It slips through my shaky fingers, slicing the tip of my pinkie. "Ow!" I exclaim as a ribbon of crimson opens up and begins to pour down my palm.

Patrick steps forward and takes my hand. "Well, that looks like it hurts. Hannah, can you go get Mom a Band-Aid, please?"

Hannah nods and hurries away, and Patrick turns back to me. But I'm no longer looking at him. I'm staring at my bloodied hand. "I cut myself," I say in awe.

"I know, sweetheart." Patrick grabs a paper towel and gently presses it to my sliced finger. "Hold that there for a minute, okay? Does it hurt?"

But all I can do is look at the blood in awe. "I cut myself," I repeat. *If this were just a dream, cutting myself would have woken me up, right? The way that pinching yourself is supposed to?*

Hannah returns to the kitchen and hands a Band-Aid to Patrick, who opens it quickly and wraps it around my finger. "There you go," he says. "Good as new."

"Good as new," I echo, still staring at my hand in disbelief.

Patrick squeezes my shoulder then turns to Hannah and smiles. "All right, kiddo," he says, grabbing a spatula from the counter and waving it around dramatically. "French toast, or bacon and eggs? Your old man's taking orders."

Hannah laughs, a beautiful sound, and tilts her head to the side.

Then she does something that catches me off guard. She replies to Patrick in sign language.

And what shocks me even more is that I understand it. *Eggs, please,* she signs. Then she glances at me and signs, *What's wrong? You're looking at me funny.*

My jaw falls. "She's deaf," I murmur, more to myself than to Patrick, but he looks concerned, and a shadow crosses Hannah's face. I raise my hands to sign back, intending to say, *Nothing's wrong, Hannah. I'm sorry.* But I realize suddenly that although I can understand Hannah in the dream, I have no idea how to use sign language.

I look to Patrick for help, a panicky feeling rising inside of me, but he's already fading, as is the whole kitchen around us. "No!" I cry. "I'm not ready yet!"

"Kate?" Patrick takes a step toward me, but the light flooding in through the windows is erasing the room.

"I love you, Patrick! Tell Hannah I love her too!" I manage to say before there's a blinding flash, and everything fades to black.

Seven

I wake up with my head spinning and my finger throbbing. It takes a few seconds before the details—Patrick's kiss, my cut finger, Hannah's sign language—come pouring back in. I sit up and gasp, which awakens Dan.

"What's wrong?" he asks groggily, sitting up too. He blinks at me and his eyes widen. "Kate! What did you do to your finger?"

I look down, and my breath catches in my throat as I realize that the tip of my right pinkie, the one I cut in the dream, is sliced open and bleeding. "Oh my God," is all I can manage.

"Let me get you a Band-Aid!" Dan is already out of bed, heading for the bathroom. "How deep is the cut? Do I need to take you to get that stitched up? How on earth did you cut yourself sleeping?"

"I'm fine," I murmur, holding my hand up and watching the blood flow down my palm. "Aren't I?" I add to myself.

Dan eventually stops panicking after he has applied Neosporin and a Band-Aid and has assured himself that the wound isn't actually all that bad. I mumble an excuse about going to get a glass of water in the middle of the night and slicing it on the edge of a knife when I reached into the dishwasher, and he seems to buy it.

After he heads out to go with his friend Stephen to a ball game, I text Gina and ask if she can meet me at the emergency room at Bellevue.

Oh my God, what's wrong? she texts back immediately.

I hesitate before answerng. *Something weird is happening to me.*

She texts back a series of question marks, but when I don't reply, she writes back, *On way. U ok?*

I don't know, I reply.

I'm waiting to see a doctor a half hour later when Gina rushes in. "Kate, what the hell?" she demands. "How could you just send me a text like that without explaining? What's the matter? Is Susan here?"

I shake my head. "Susan wouldn't understand."

"Understand *what*? Kate, you've got to tell me what's going on. You're scaring me!"

I hesitate. "I've been having these dreams about Patrick. Or at least I think they're dreams. What else could they be, right? But I know things in them that should be impossible for me to know, things that turn out to be true in real life. And they're so vivid, Gina. I don't know what's happening to me."

"Oh." I see sadness and concern in her eyes as she sinks into the seat beside me. "Why don't you begin at the beginning?"

And so I do. I explain about waking up with Patrick the day after the engagement party. I tell her how strange and beautiful it was to see him in so much detail, right down to his salt-and-pepper hair, his laugh lines, and his broader belly. I explain how real he felt: his touch, the familiar scent of him, the steady beating of his heart.

I go on to tell her about last night too, but I don't tell her about Hannah, because her presence somehow makes everything seem less authentic. Patrick once existed, so it seems like there's some sort of possibility he could be crossing the thin line between heaven and earth, as unlikely as that sounds. But how do I explain Hannah, a girl who can't possibly be our child but who calls me "Mom"?

Gina listens intently, and I'm relieved not to see judgment on her face. When I'm done, she looks at her hands for a moment, and when she glances up again, there's sadness written across her features. "I used to dream about Bill sometimes too," she says. "Not quite as vividly as you're describing. But seeing him once in a while, even if the dreams were sort of vague, always threw me into a tailspin for a few days." She pauses and adds, "It's never going to go away, is it? The way we feel right now?"

I shake my head, and some of the stress melts out of my shoulders. Having lost a husband is a bit like belonging to a club. It's a club no one would ever want membership in, but it's comforting all the same to know that you're not alone.

"But the dreams, Kate, they sound more or less normal. Don't you think?"

"Then how did my finger wind up sliced open?" I ask, holding up my bandaged pinkie.

"What?" Gina stares at my hand.

"In the dream, I cut my finger," I tell her. "And when I woke up, I was bleeding on the sheets. How is that possible?"

She gapes at me. "Well . . . It's not. Maybe you sleepwalked in the middle of the night and cut it on something."

"Wouldn't that have woken me up?"

"I—I don't know." She pauses. "But you're not saying that you think these dreams are actually real, are you?"

I avoid her gaze. "I know it sounds nuts. But how could I be dreaming things I don't actually know, like the fact that Robert got a job offer in San Diego eleven years ago?"

"Maybe it's a coincidence, or maybe you overheard something Susan or your mom said at some point," Gina says slowly. "As for the rest of it, maybe your brain just has to wrap itself around the reality that you're about to start a new life."

I take a deep breath. "But what if seeing Patrick is reminding me just how much I want my old life back?"

"But you can't have it, Kate," she says softly. "Those chapters are closed. It took me a long time to realize that—to *really* realize it—but when I did, everything felt a little better. Maybe you're just not there yet."

The cranial CT scan, neurological exam, and blood tests all come back clean, and the doctors assure me I don't have a brain tumor or anything else physiological going on. After sending me to get two stitches in my pinkie, they refer to me to psychiatry, and after a brief meeting with a doctor, I'm sent on my way with a prescription for sleeping pills, an antidepressant I know I'll never take, and a reassurance that what I'm describing sounds perfectly normal, save for the sliced finger.

"Sleepwalking isn't that uncommon," the doctor adds with a shrug. "I'm certain that's what happened."

"But how could everything be so vivid?" I ask. "How do I know things that I couldn't possibly know in reality?"

He shrugs again. "The subconscious works in strange ways, Ms. Waithman. Trying to figure it out will only make it feel more confusing. My suggestion would be to get some rest and forget about this. Dreams can be very powerful, but it's important to remember that none of it is real."

Still, over the next few days, I can't stop thinking about Hannah. My inability to sign back to her was what yanked me out of the second dream, and I find myself obsessing about how I'll communicate with her if I wake up in the alternate life again. Would knowing sign language myself help me to stay longer next time, to fit into the dream's landscape a little better? The thing is, the cut on my finger, still throbbing, doesn't feel like my subconscious speaking at all.

On Monday morning, after a weekend of going to bed early and trying in vain to dream, I arrive at the office twenty minutes before my first appointment and spend a few minutes googling American Sign Language. I quickly learn how to say *mom, dad, love, daughter,* and *here.* Then, before I have a chance to question what I'm doing, I click on a pop-up ad for an eighteen-week GothamLearn sign language class being offered within walking distance of my office.

The class began last week, but when I e-mail to ask about enrolling, I get a quick return message from GothamLearn's online director telling me that it's not too late to join if I'd like; I should just arrive a few minutes before seven on Wednesday night with a check for my tuition to hand to the instructor, a man named Andrew Henson.

I'll be there, I reply before I can talk myself out of it, and as I hit Send, I'm buoyant. I also feel idiotic for doing this; I know intellectually that Hannah can't be real. But at least taking a class will be more constructive than day drinking and trying to force myself to sleep.

Dina buzzes to tell me my first client of the day has arrived, and I shut my laptop quickly, as if I'm looking at porn rather than hand signs.

Leo Goldstein strides in a moment later, the circles under his eyes dark and his jaw set belligerently. "Okay, I'm here," he announces, throwing himself onto the couch opposite my desk. "What do you want me to do?"

Leo looks paler today, I think as I move to sit beside him in an armchair, and when I look closely, I see the shadow of a bruise on his right forearm, where he has pushed his sleeve up. The skin around the purpling stain is a soft yellowish green.

"Leo, what happened to your arm?" I ask.

He looks down and frowns, tugging his sleeve over the mark. "Nothing," he says, quickly amending, "Tripped on the basketball court."

Leo's mom started bringing him to me about four months ago, when he began having behavior issues at Tompkins Square Middle School, where he's currently in seventh grade. He made it clear from the beginning that he hated being here—and hated me as a result—but older kids often resist therapy at the beginning. I knew if I waited him out, chances were he'd come around. And he did.

Little by little, even though he always complained that singing was for babies and banging drumsticks against bongos was pointless, he had come out of his shell. Now, we're in a routine that seems to work: he huffs into my office, sulks for a few minutes, tells me nothing is wrong, and then brightens when I pull out my double xylophone.

Most weeks, we play Beatles songs, which Leo calls "retro-cool." The Beatles theme to our sessions was his idea; I like to let my clients lead whenever possible, because the more comfortable they are with the music we're playing, the easier it is for them to open up.

Getting Leo hooked on playing the music rather than just listening to it was an important step, because it has allowed us to develop a common language. Sometimes it's hard, for example, to say you're angry. But pounding an instrument gets the point across without words. Kind of like sign language, I think: meaning without articulation. You just have to know how to communicate.

"Anyway, I learned 'You Can't Do That' this week," Leo tells me, his eyes sliding away from mine. "I've been practicing on my iPad keyboard app."

"From the *Hard Day's Night* album."

"Yeah. From 1964," he says with the authority of someone who was around then. "Want to hear it?"

"Sure." I shuffle a few papers then grab the xylophone mallets, purposely taking a long time. "So about that bruise: You must have fallen pretty hard, I guess."

"No big deal." His voice is gruff, his eyes shifty. "It didn't even hurt anyways."

"Was Tyler there?"

He hesitates, and from the way his eyes flick to mine and then dance quickly away again, I know I've hit upon the truth. "Maybe," he mumbles. "Don't remember."

"Did you hit him back?" I ask softly.

He looks at his hands for a minute. "No," he says finally. "All his friends were there too."

"Bunch of jerks," I mutter under my breath. Leo is tall and slender, with the kind of shape he'll grow into when he's older. But for now, he's a stick figure, and Tyler Mason, who's a year older and forty pounds heavier than Leo, teases him mercilessly about the way he looks. His friends join in too, probably relieved not to be on the receiving end of bullying themselves.

Tyler's also the kind of kid who can talk himself out of situations, so when Leo began fighting back, it was Leo who was labeled the problem kid. Somehow, the teachers never saw Tyler throwing the first punch or hissing under his breath that Leo was a beanpole. As a result, Tyler's halo was intact, and Leo was becoming a frequent visitor to the principal's office.

His mother had brought him to me on his school guidance counselor's recommendation; she couldn't understand why her son had started acting inexplicably violent. It took me three sessions to grasp that Leo wasn't the aggressor. He was being bullied and didn't want to admit it. By the time I sat his parents down and explained the situation, they'd already decided to keep sending him to me on a weekly basis, because they were seeing marked improvements in his schoolwork and behavior at home.

I hand Leo the mallets, and he grins at me—the first real smile since he's gotten here—and begins playing the Beatles' song. He impresses me, as he always does, with his skill. I join in on my guitar after a moment.

"So what does the song mean to you?" I ask after we've finished. It's one of my ground rules with Leo; he has to tell me why he's picked a song. It's another way to open up discussion between us.

"I don't know," he replies, looking down.

I'm silent, waiting patiently for him to go on.

"I guess when the singer says 'leave you flat,' I was thinking about when Tyler said he'd flatten my face," Leo finally mumbles. "And then the singer says people would laugh at him, and sometimes that happens to me too."

I nod, pleased that we're at a point where he can say things like this to me. Of course the Beatles song is about a guy telling his girl that he'll break up with her if he catches her talking to a particular guy again, but Leo has gotten something entirely different out of the lyrics. That's one of my favorite things about music—that the same words, the same notes, can mean completely different things to different people.

"Did you talk to your teacher about Tyler?" I ask.

He shakes his head. "Tattletales get beat up worse."

"How about your mom and dad?"

He doesn't answer. Instead, he bangs his mallet on the xylophone for a minute before asking abruptly, "You got any kids?" I see him looking at the two framed photos on my desk of me with Dan. "Who's that guy anyways?" he asks before waiting for an answer.

"That's my boyfriend." I pause and correct myself. "Well, actually, my fiancé. And no, I don't have any kids."

"Why not?" He's twirling one of his xylophone mallets now. "You seem pretty old. Like older than my mom."

It's common for kids to try to turn the therapy sessions around on me, but the purpose of these visits isn't so that we can bond and become friends; it's so that they can find out more about themselves. I try to walk a fine line between answering their questions honestly—because I think adults should always take children's questions seriously, and I want Leo to feel like I respect his feelings—and deflecting questions that are too personal.

I shrug. "Why do you ask about kids?"

"I just want to know."

Again, I stay quiet, waiting for him to go on. Silence can often be as effective as sound when you use it correctly. After a moment, he returns to playing the melody of the Beatles song, almost absently. "I bet you wouldn't let someone beat up on your kid," he says in a small voice when he stops playing again. "I bet you'd care enough."

So that's what his questions are about. "Leo, what's happening at school isn't because your parents don't care about you."

His jaw tightens. "My dad keeps saying I got to just stick up for myself and hit Tyler back. But Tyler would beat the crud out of me. Or his friends would. You think my dad wants me to get beat up?"

"Absolutely not, Leo. He's just telling you that sometimes, bullies won't push around someone who stands up to them."

"Yeah, well, I bet you wouldn't let your kid go and get creamed, if you had a kid," he grumbles. "I bet you'd fix things and help your kid to be happy."

I'm at the stove making shrimp scampi that night when Dan gets home.

"Dinner smells great," he says, coming up behind me and nuzzling my neck. "I love it when you cook, babe."

"Why don't you open a bottle of wine? And would you mind setting the table?"

"Sure." He opens a bottle of sauvignon blanc, pours us each a glass, then heads into the bedroom to change out of his suit and tie. A minute later, I can hear the shower running, which annoys me a little. He knows the meal is almost ready. *Patrick never would have done that,* I think, but I catch myself and banish the thought. It's not fair to compare my former husband with my future one.

But as I set the table myself, top off my wine, and pour us each a glass of water, I can't help but think how different this feels. Dan's a great guy, just like Patrick was, but in a way, the similarities end there. For the first time, I find myself wondering if what attracted me most to Dan is simply that he was so different from Patrick. He's perfect and glossy, a storybook prince, while Patrick was rough and warm and endearingly imperfect.

As I pile pasta onto two plates and add shrimp and buttery garlic sauce, I feel a pang of sadness. Patrick and I used to cook for each other all the time, and I loved that we had a sort of intimacy in the kitchen. We were a team; if he was cooking, I was chopping vegetables or washing dishes. If I was cooking, he was pouring wine or setting the table. We had an easy sort of we're-in-this-together camaraderie that's just not there with Dan.

Patrick and I used to communicate in our own sort of shorthand too. I could say a single word, and he'd almost always know exactly what I meant. He'd say, *Lynn,* for example, and I'd know he'd had a tough day at the office with his boss and that he needed a few minutes alone to unwind. I'd say, *Five,* and he'd know dinner would be ready in five minutes and he should start pouring our water. He'd breathe *Katielee* in a low voice, and we'd always look at each other for a moment before dropping everything we were doing and heading for the bedroom. There were a thousand words between us that spoke volumes, but I can't think of a single one that Dan and I share.

I don't even know the stories of Dan's childhood, the things that shaped him. I don't know what he wanted to be when he grew up, or what his school social life was like, or what books and movies he liked as a boy. Yet I can still name Patrick's elementary-school best friend, tell the tale of the day he got into a fight in seventh grade defending a girl he had a crush on, and recite a list of his career aspirations in chronological order from garbage man to astronaut to chef to pilot to financial analyst.

Does the fact that I don't know those kinds of things about Dan mean that something's broken between us? Or is it just a logical result of beginning to date when we were older, at a time in our lives when childhood felt further away?

"What were you like in high school?" I ask almost desperately as Dan sits down at the table a few minutes later. He's wearing pajama pants and a T-shirt, and he smells like soap.

He takes a bite of pasta and a sip of wine before answering. "I don't know. The same as I am now, I guess. Why?"

"I just feel like I don't know about your past as much as I maybe should."

"Okay," he says, giving me a strange look.

"So tell me about it," I say. Maybe I can use the shreds of information he gives me to patch the holes I'm beginning to see between us. "Your past, I mean."

"You're acting weird."

"Just humor me."

He shrugs. "All right. School was never really an issue. I always did well. I played soccer in junior high and football in high school, so I was always pretty popular. Never really had any problems with the other kids. I was actually the prom king. Haven't I told you that before?"

I ignore the question, because in fact I've heard it at least a dozen times. "But there had to have been a time when you struggled," I protest. "A time when you were bullied, or when you were sad, or when you just had a bad few months."

"Not that I can recall." He looks at me more closely. "Why? Were you bullied?"

"No," I say, suddenly desperate to share. "But I had rough patches in school. Fifth grade, for example. We'd just moved to a new school district, and all the kids in my class wore designer clothes and arrived in their parents' expensive cars. I took the bus, and my favorite outfit was a Superman T-shirt and polka-dot skirt, which I wore all the time. I got made fun of a lot that year." I smile, intending for the words to be funny, but he just looks confused.

"But why would you keep wearing something that made you the butt of jokes?" Dan asks, taking another bite of his pasta.

I stare at him. "I was just being myself," I say. "And I was ten. What did I know about fashion?"

"Just strikes me that it would have saved you a lot of trouble if you just tried to fit in," he says with a shrug. "But maybe I'm not getting it. Why are you telling this story, anyway?"

"I don't know," I say in a small voice. "I just thought it would be nice to learn a little more about each other."

He shrugs and goes back to eating, but I've lost my appetite. I pick at my food and try not to think about the fact that when I told Patrick about my fifth-grade fashion sense and the trouble it caused, he came home from work the next night with a Superman T-shirt for me. *This is to remind you that you should never stop being yourself, no matter what,* he'd said. *Because I think you're the most incredible person in the world.*

That night, Dan sits in the living room and answers e-mails while I take my laptop to bed and once again google American Sign Language. When Dan comes to bed just past 10:30, he walks in on me signing the sentence *I love you more than you can imagine.*

"What are you doing?" he asks.

"Nothing," I say, snapping my laptop closed.

"Is that sign language?" He nods to my hands. "Were you signing?"

"Well . . . yeah."

"Why?"

"For a client I'm working with." As I hear myself lie, I know it's too late to take it back.

He laughs. "You're a music therapist," he says. "Why would you work with a deaf kid?"

I resist the annoyance that washes over me. After all, there's no reason to expect someone outside my field to know that people who are deaf can still experience sound though vibration and visual cues. "Music therapy with deaf kids actually isn't that uncommon," I tell him. "And hard-of-hearing kids can usually hear some residual sounds anyhow."

He chuckles. "Next you're going to tell me you're setting up stargazing trips for the blind."

"I'm sure there's a way to do that too," I tell him. "Braille constellations or something. People shouldn't miss out on something just because they have a disability."

"But music? For deaf kids? C'mon, Kate."

"Music isn't just about hearing with your ears."

"Now you sound like one of those nutty new-age people."

I exhale slowly through my nose. "No. I just sound like a music therapist trying something new." But I realize as I say it that I don't know much about music therapy for deaf and hard-of-hearing kids at all.

I make a mental note to look into it further when I have time. Then again, maybe that's foolish. What am I going to do, comb through the journals for information on music therapy for deaf children just so that I can pick out a few songs on the guitar if I ever dream about Patrick and Hannah again? It sounds crazy even to me.

Eight

The entrance to St. Paula's, the Catholic church on the corner of Seventieth and Madison, is lit by two torches that illuminate the shadow-cloaked stairs, and as I push open one of the heavy wooden doors, the faint scent of frankincense lingers in the air, triggering a handful of memories. I'd gone to church almost every Sunday with Patrick, but after he'd died, I'd had trouble understanding how God could have taken my husband like that. As a result, I'd simply stopped attending, and now I feel guilty as I look up at the cross. "I'm sorry," I murmur.

"Looking for the sign language class?" asks a deep voice behind me. I whirl around, startled, to see a man with glasses, a square jaw, and sandy hair sprinkled with gray standing a few feet away, near an open door to the left of the front entrance. When I nod, he smiles. "You can continue your conversation with God if you want, but when you're ready, we're down in the basement. Welcome."

He doesn't wait for a reply before disappearing down the stairs. I glance once more at the crucifix, feeling foolish, and hurry after him.

In the small church basement, I find three women and a man sitting on folding chairs in the center of the room, facing a big easel on which the sandy-haired man from upstairs is currently writing. One of the women, who looks about my age, with dark, pin-straight hair, nods at me as I enter, and the man at the easel turns as I sit down in a squeaky chair.

"You must be Katherine Waithman," he says.

"Kate," I tell him.

"Well, welcome to class, Kate," he says. He sets down the marker he was using, and I see he's written several phrases on the easel. "I'm Andrew Henson, the instructor from Gotham-Learn. These folks started with me last week, but if you want to stay a few minutes after class, I'd be happy to catch you up. Sound good?"

"That's nice of you. Sorry I wasn't here for the first class."

"Hey, what matters is you're here now." He turns to the others in the class and says, "We're just waiting for Vivian, then we'll get started, guys."

He turns back around and continues adding phrases to the list on the easel. I see *I love you*, *New York City*, *My name is* ____, and *Have a nice day*. He's just adding, *How's the weather,* when the dark-haired woman scoots her chair toward me.

"I'm Amy," she says.

"Kate." I shake her hand. "So you were here last week?"

She nods. "I work at a bank; I've been meaning to learn the basics of sign language for a while because we have a few regular customers who are deaf."

"Well, that's nice of you."

"Actually, that's a lie." She shrugs. "I mean, I do work at a bank. But a friend of mine took this class last semester and told me how hot the instructor is. I figured it was worth the price of the course to see for myself."

I smile and follow her eyes toward Andrew, who's shuffling through a stack of papers. "I guess he's pretty cute," I say. "In a nerdy professor kind of way."

"Yeah, if Matt Damon was playing the role of nerdy professor," she says with a laugh. "Looks like you already have someone anyhow. Good. Less competition for me."

I follow her gaze to my left hand and am almost startled to see a ring on my finger. "Oh, right. I'm still getting used to this thing."

"Well, you're lucky," she says. "Dating in New York is a nightmare. Hang on to that guy."

I force a smile, feeling uneasy. After all, I'm here because of my old husband, not my future one. "I will," I tell her anyhow. Then, because it's polite, I add, "I'm sure your guy is out there."

She glances at Andrew. "Or in here."

We're interrupted by the arrival of a sixtysomething woman with her hair dyed carrot orange. She's wearing a long purple skirt, a black sweater, and a flowing green scarf that grazes the ground. "Sorry I'm late!" she says, still panting from her rush down the stairs. "Begin, begin, don't wait for me!"

Andrew smiles at her. "Ah, Vivian," he says. Then he signs something to her as she slides into the seat to my right.

She looks perplexed. "I assume that means 'Get your act together, crazy lady,'" she says.

He laughs. "It actually just means welcome to class."

She sighs loudly in mock relief and wipes the back of her hand across her forehead. Andrew waits to begin while she digs in her giant bag for a notebook and a pen.

"Ladies and gentleman, welcome to our second night of American Sign Language for Beginners," he says, pausing to go around the room and lock eyes with each of us. "Vivian, Amy, Diane, Shirley, Greg, you all began this journey last week. Let's all give our newest student, Kate, a big welcome."

I expect a smattering of claps, or a chorus of hellos, but instead, Vivian and Amy both give me what appears to be a salute, and the others move their outstretched, upturned right hands toward their rib cages. I glance at Andrew, who grins at me. "Kate, Vivian and Amy just said *hello,* and the others said *welcome.*" He turns his attention back to the rest of the room. "Great job, guys! I see you retained at least some of what I taught you last week. Kate, how about saying *hello* back?"

I hesitate, feeling foolish, but Vivian smiles encouragingly, and I give her a weak salute.

"Great start, Kate," Andrew encourages. "But make sure you own the action. In American Sign Language, hesitating or flimsy-arming, as I call it, is sort of like mumbling out loud. Want me to show you how to thank your classmates for welcoming you?"

"Uh, sure," I say.

"Watch this," he says. He puts his right hand in front of his chin, just below his lips, and moves it outward, almost like he's blowing me a kiss. "That's *thank you,*" he says. "You try it."

I put my hand in front of my chin uncertainly, but he arches an eyebrow, so I finish the motion with a definitive kiss-blowing motion forward.

"Nice!" he says. "You're a natural. Now, folks, I know we learned a bunch of basic phrases last time, and I'll show those to Kate after class. Today, I thought it would be handy to learn and memorize the alphabet, and then we can conclude the session with each of you choosing a phrase for me to teach you. So as we work today, be thinking about what you want to say."

Andrew passes out printed charts of each of the letters in American Sign Language and spends the next hour showing us each letter and patiently waiting for us to repeat them back to him. It should feel tedious, but it doesn't. Andrew keeps us laughing by demonstrating sign language puns as we go, such as using his right hand to make a D and his left to make a U, then knocking the U over with the D to form an H. "That's an ASL pun for *duh*," he tells us with a grin.

He also peppers the lesson with explanations about why knowing the letters is so important. "Most people who are proficient in sign language know somewhere south of ten thousand signs," he explains, "and many know far fewer than that. But there are a quarter of a million distinct words in the English language, maybe one hundred fifty thousand of which are in regular usage today. Think about what a huge gap that is. So knowing how to fingerspell is important, especially for names or other proper nouns and for words you simply don't know yet. For beginners like you guys, fingerspelling will be your lifeline for a while. When in doubt, spell it out."

He has us practice with each other while he steps out to make a quick phone call, and when I pair up with Vivian, I find myself really appreciating the beauty of signing. There's something graceful about fluidly moving one's hands into shapes that represent words, but by the time Andrew returns to the basement, Vivian and I have abandoned elegant signing and are repeating *duh* to each other and giggling like children.

"Okay," Andrew says, coming back into the room and looking at us with an amused expression on his face. "I see you've all mastered the art of *duh*-ing. How about we conclude class by learning one expression each of you would like to say? Who wants to go first?"

Greg, who looks like he's in his midtwenties, raises his hand, and when Andrew nods at him, he says he'd like to learn, *Do you need help with those groceries?* "There's a deaf girl who lives on the fourth floor of my building," he says, his face turning red. "I want to learn to talk to her."

Andrew smiles and nods. "Try this," he says. He points at

Greg, then, with his palm open toward himself and his fingers splayed, he makes a quick clockwise circle in front of his face, closing and opening his fingers again in the final motion before pointing at Greg again. He has Greg repeat the motion a few times, then he asks us all to try. "Good," he says with a grin when we've all mastered it. "Now you all know how to say, *You're beautiful,* which is, I think, what Greg *really* wants to say." We all chuckle, and Greg turns even redder, but he's smiling. "But now, if you insist, I'll show you how to ask about groceries."

We all repeat the motions he shows us, then Amy asks how to say, *How can I help you today?* Next, Shirley, a heavyset woman with graying hair, asks how to ask where the park is, and Diane, who looks like she's in her midforties, wants to know how to say, *My nephew is hard of hearing.*

"You know, folks, I don't think I mentioned this last week, so I'm glad Diane brought it up," Andrew says. "As it appears Diane already knows, *hard of hearing* is actually the correct term nowadays. Remember when we were younger, and people would say *hearing impaired?* Well, over time, that term fell out of use, because *impaired* has sort of a negative connotation, as if the person is damaged or lacking in some way. Most people with hearing loss these days prefer *hard of hearing.* So thanks, Diane, for bringing that up. Here's how to say it: make the letter *h* and sort of hop it to the right."

He demonstrates by putting his right index and middle fingers together, pointing them toward us and making an arc toward the right, then he adds, "It's also important, while we're speaking about terms and political correctness, to know that there's a difference between deaf with a lowercase *d* and Deaf with an uppercase *D*. The first one is broader and refers to the actual condition of not being able to hear. The second one refers to the Deaf community, a group of people with a shared culture and shared language, which is, of course, the language we're learning here today."

We all nod and jot down notes, then he asks Vivian what she'd like to learn. She tells him she'd like to know how to sign *Live long and prosper,* and he shows us all the ASL way to say it, then suggests we use the Vulcan salute from *Star Trek* instead, which makes us all laugh.

Then it's my turn. "Kate, what phrase would you like to learn to say?" Andrew asks.

I take a deep breath. "Can you teach me to say, *I'm sorry I've been a little bit weird*?" It's what I'd like to say to Hannah if I ever see her again. The fact that I can't communicate with her must seem strange, and I want her to know I feel badly about it.

Andrew looks surprised, but he nods. He has me point to myself, rub my right hand over my heart with a closed fist, then point to myself again, flick my thumb lightly against my index finger twice, and finally position my hand in an almost clawlike position and move it right to left in front of my face while wiggling my middle finger, my ring finger and my index finger.

"Good work," he says after I successfully repeat the motions twice. "You're a fast learner. Hang out after class, okay, Kate? You and I can do a quick review of last week, which I'm sure you'll pick up quickly."

He closes by winking at Vivian and giving us the Vulcan salute, then he tells us he'll see us next week. "Same time, same place. In the meantime, practice those letters and phrases," he says. "Practice makes perfect, just like with any other language."

I say good-bye to Vivian, then Amy murmurs, "Lucky you getting to stay after with Andrew. Maybe I'll skip next week to get some one-on-one time." I laugh and wave as she heads out the basement door.

Andrew is looking at his watch when I turn around, and for

a second, I think he's going to cancel on me because it's getting late. But instead he says, "I'm starving. Mind if we grab a quick bite while we go over last week's lesson?"

I hesitate. I can't remember the last time I ate a meal out with a man who wasn't Dan. Besides, I'm eager to get home, have a few too many drinks, and get into bed early in hopes that I'll wake up again in the impossible world where Patrick still exists.

"I don't bite." Andrew clearly sees me wavering, because he adds, "And there's a few places on this block. We can be in and out in thirty minutes. I'm just afraid I might collapse if I don't eat something. My treat."

I force a smile. I'm being ridiculous and I know it. "Yeah, of course. I'm actually pretty hungry too. But you don't have to buy."

As I follow him up the stairs and into the church vestibule, I cast one more glance over my shoulder at the crucifix over the altar.

"It's never too late to come back, you know," Andrew says.

I turn to see him watching me. "What are you, a mind reader?" I ask.

He shrugs. "No. Just a guy who's a little adrift himself."

He heads out the front door of the church without another word.

Nine

We wind up at a diner a few doors down from the church.

"I'm telling you," Andrew says as he holds the door for me, "this place has the best greasy burger in Manhattan. Maybe in all of New York State."

A waitress shows us to a table, and after we're seated, Andrew waves away the menu she offers him. "Oh, I already know what I want."

"And for your girlfriend?" the waitress asks.

Andrew looks amused. "I think she needs a menu."

"I'm not his girlfriend," I tell the waitress then immediately feel like a jerk. "But I hear the burger here is amazing," I hurry to add. "I'll have what he's having."

"In that case," Andrew says, "two burgers, medium, each with your special sauce and a fried egg on top. And two cherry Cokes."

"Cherry Coke?" I ask as the waitress walks away.

"You can't tell me it's not the best drink in the universe when they put real cherry syrup in."

I find myself smiling. "Okay. Agreed. But a fried egg on the burger?"

Andrew widens his eyes dramatically. "You've never had a burger with a fried egg on it? Well, Kate, prepare for your world to be rocked."

The waitress delivers two giant, red-tinged Cokes, and as we wait for our meals, Andrew hands me a small stack of papers filled with illustrations for ASL signs and begins a rapid-fire explanation of sign language.

"As I told the other guys last week," he says, "the grammar rules in American Sign Language can be a little different from standard grammar rules in English. What I mean by that is that sometimes, the direct object often leads the sentence off, whereas in English, the direct object normally follows the verb."

"I'm a little rusty on my grammar terms," I admit.

"That's okay. So here's an example. In English you'd say, 'I love the burger.' In ASL, you *could* structure your sentence that way, but it would also be common to sign 'Burger, I love' or 'Burger, love I.'"

"Kind of like Yoda," I say.

"Ah, the woman knows her *Star Wars*! Charming." He laughs. "Yes, a bit like Yoda."

He demonstrates by cupping his hands and sort of clapping them together twice horizontally, with his right hand on top the first time, and his left hand on top the second time, almost like forming a patty. "That's *hamburger*," he tells me. "And this is *I love*." He crosses his arms across his chest then points to himself.

He goes on to tell me that making eye contact in ASL is very important, and that it's considered rude not to do so. "A lot of people think that ASL is just about using your hands," he adds. "But it's not. It's all about facial expressions, movements with your mouth, things like that. In fact, facial expressions are just as important as what you do with your hands and where you place your signs. Think about having a conversation out loud with me. You'd convey how you're feeling with the tone of your voice, right? In ASL, you don't have the advantage of tone, so you have to rely on visual cues. But like I said to the others, we'll learn more of that as the class goes on."

He's just in the middle of explaining the five key components to signing—hand shape, location of the sign, palm orientation, movement, and facial expression—when our waitress arrives with our burgers. "What do you say we take a break to scarf these down?" he asks.

I look down at my greasy burger, which is on a pretzel bun, piled high with an egg, lettuce, onions, and pickles, and slathered in sauce that's drizzling out from the sides. "Looks healthy."

He arches an eyebrow. "Everyone knows that Wednesday calories don't count." He doesn't wait for a reply before taking a huge bite of his burger and moaning dramatically.

I laugh and take a bite of my burger too. I see exactly what he means. It's incredible. "My husband would have loved this," I mumble without thinking about it.

I see Andrew glance at my ring finger. "You'll have to bring him here sometime."

My cheeks flush red, because I was talking about Patrick, not Dan, who has sworn off red meat. "Oh, no, I'm not married" is what I finally say, which I know makes no sense considering that it was me who just brought up my husband.

Andrew cocks his head to the side and waits.

"What I mean is, I'm engaged. Not married. So he's not my husband."

"But he likes burgers," Andrew says helpfully, like he's coaxing a story out of a difficult child.

"No," I say, my cheeks still burning. I know I should explain what I meant, that I was referring to the husband I lost a dozen years ago. But I hardly know Andrew and I already feel ridiculous enough, so I force a laugh and say, "Sorry. Long day."

He smiles, although I can still see lingering concern in his eyes. "I know the feeling. But trust me, these burgers make everything better. They're magic."

I smile back and take another big bite, marveling at how juicy and perfect it is and trying not to think about fat grams and calories, which Dan would surely be pointing out. I'm so fixated on not thinking about how unhealthy the burger is that I don't register how quickly it's disappearing until I've almost finished. I look up to see Andrew, his plate empty, looking amused.

"Told you you'd love it," he says.

"I can't believe I ate so much!" I exclaim, looking down at my hands as if they were wholly responsible for my lapse in nutritional judgment. "How embarrassing."

"Embarrassing?" he repeats. "No way. Believe me when I say that only chauvinistic pigs are turned off by a woman who can eat. Personally, I think it's awesome."

My cheeks burning, I start to set the remainder of my burger down, but he leans forward and says quickly, "No more ASL until you finish that, young lady."

"Well, you drive a hard bargain," I say, then it occurs to me that I sound like I'm flirting. I quickly wipe the smile from my face and clear my throat. "So, um, what made you decide to go into teaching sign language? Is this your full-time job?"

"You first," he says. "What brought you to ASL class?"

I take another bite of my burger to buy time, since I can't exactly say *I'm learning sign language so that I can communicate with my fake daughter in my fake dream world with my hamburger-loving dead husband.* So instead, I swallow and tell him, "I'm a music therapist." I hesitate and say, "And, um, I've been hearing about advances in music therapy for deaf kids, so I thought it might be worth looking into."

Andrew's face lights up. "Really? That's awesome!" He pauses. "Okay, I'm going to sound like an idiot. I've heard of music therapy, of course, but I've never known a music therapist before. How does it work, exactly?"

"Lots of different ways." I glance up to see him watching me intently, so I go on. "It's hard to sum up, and actually, even in the music therapy community, there are a lot of definitions of what music therapy is, and a lot of applications to what we do." I pause and remind myself that Andrew likely doesn't care about the academic debate over the meaning of music therapy. I try to boil it down. "In music therapy, we basically use music to promote the physical and emotional health of a client—whatever that means in that particular client's context. So for example, a music therapist might use music to help a child overcome a speech disability. But along the way, once he grows to trust you, there might be something about a song lyric that triggers something in him. Maybe he confides a secret or says something offhand that helps you to understand where he's coming from better."

Andrew nods. "So what you do is kind of like what the doctor does in the movie *The King's Speech*?"

"Not exactly. That was speech therapy. Using music, the way the doctor did in the movie, is actually a very common technique in that field," I say. "Music therapy is more about establishing a relationship with a client using music and then working within that relationship to promote whatever it is the client needs. Music can open a lot of doors, once you've built that bridge."

I stop abruptly, feeling a bit foolish, but Andrew is smiling and nodding vigorously. "Yeah!" he says. "I know exactly what you mean. There are more ways to communicate than just saying words out loud. So do you have any deaf patients now?"

I shake my head and dodge his gaze as I finish the last bite of my burger. "Not yet. So how about you?" I ask. "How'd you get into teaching this class?"

"I'm actually a supervisor for an agency called St. Anne's Services," he says. "Have you heard of it?"

"I don't think so."

"But you know about ACS, right? The Administration for Children's Services?"

"The foster system?"

"Right. But some kids with special needs get referred out to various other agencies, like St. Anne's or New Alternatives for Children. We have programs in place to help meet the needs of both mentally and physically challenged kids. I specialize in working with the deaf and hard-of-hearing kids who come to St. Anne's."

"So you just teach the class on the side?"

He nods. "Seemed like something fun to do. This is only my second time teaching it. How am I doing so far?"

"You're a natural," I tell him honestly. "Did you grow up knowing sign language?"

His smile falters for a split second. "My little brother was born hard of hearing," he says. "When he started learning ASL, my parents taught it to me too. I can't even remember a time when I didn't know it." He pauses, his expression softening. "It was kind of like this secret language we knew that no one else was in on."

"Cool."

He winks. "I told you, I'm incredibly awesome. But enough about me. How did you get into music therapy?"

"Long story." I don't want to talk about Patrick. "Let's just say that someone I love reminded me how important it was to pursue the thing I was most passionate about."

He nods. "I've always said that life's too short not to follow your dreams."

I swallow hard. "That's exactly what he used to say."

"Sounds like a pretty great dude."

I smile sadly. "He was."

"So," Andrew says after an awkward pause. He clears his throat. "Can I ask you something?"

"Sure." I eat a few fries and push my plate away. I'm starting to feel queasy, and I'm not sure whether it's because of the huge burger or because being reminded of Patrick is making me sad.

"Look, I'm going to be blunt here, and feel free to say no. But I have a few hard-of-hearing and deaf kids at St. Anne's I'd love to try something new with. Real sweet kids. I can't offer to pay you right away—I've maxed out the budget this year on cochlear implants for two of our kids—but if you're interested in working with the deaf population, maybe this could be a good place to get your feet wet."

"Um," I reply, trying to figure out how to decline politely.

"Actually, okay, let me backtrack here," Andrew adds. "Am I being crazy? It's just that I'm always trying to come up with new ways to reach them, you know? And here you are. But maybe they're not the right fit for the kind of work you do."

I hesitate. "I think it depends on the kids and what kind of help they need," I finally say. "Although music therapy can be used in a lot of different contexts."

He smiles. "Ah, like a secret superpower." He pauses and shakes his head. "Okay. I've clearly been spending too much time with children if I'm making you out to be a comic book hero with, like, a power pan flute."

I laugh. "Sadly, I have no idea how to play a pan flute."

"You're crushing my dreams, Kate. I suppose you're going to tell me you don't wear a cape, either?"

"Only on special occasions," I deadpan, and he laughs. I take a deep breath and plunge in. "So do you want to tell me about these kids? What were you thinking I could do with them?"

"Well, two of the three have received cochlear implants in the last few years, so they're still developing their comfort levels with speaking and processing speech. Of course cochlear implants impact the way in which people hear music, but from what I understand, it can still be really enjoyable. Do you think maybe music therapy could help a bit with their speech and with coming out of their shells? Or am I totally off base?"

I pause. "You know what? Yeah, I think I could help them, and I'd be happy to try," I hear myself say. "Why not?"

"Really? Kate, seriously, you have no idea what kind of a difference you could make. There's one girl in particular who I just can't get to open up; maybe you can reach her." He smiles and shakes his head. "Geez, sorry, I'm getting ahead of myself. I'll have to have you fill out some paperwork, but I can expedite all that, I think. I'm just really happy to get you involved."

"My pleasure," I tell him, and I'm a little surprised to realize that I mean it.

The waitress sweeps by to deliver the check, which Andrew insists on picking up. "Least I can do, Kate," he says. "I'll buy you greasy burgers every week if you help give my kids a better shot."

As I jot down my contact information for him, it occurs to me that maybe that's what the weird visions of Patrick and Hannah were about: a reminder that I still have something to offer, even though I've slipped into a comfort zone of going through the motions. It's the first explanation that's made me feel better instead of twisting my insides into a tangled mess.

Ten

I'm already in bed when Dan gets home that night, so the first chance I get to tell him about Andrew and my promise to help a few kids from St. Anne's is the next evening after work. I call him from the train on the way out to see Joan, whom I've been visiting once a month since Patrick died.

"But, babe, your schedule is already packed," he says, sounding perplexed after I fill him in on Andrew's request and the paperwork I filled out and faxed back to him this afternoon. "You sure this is something you want to take on?"

"I think I can move some things around and volunteer one evening a week."

"Kate, I hate to say it, but are you sure you didn't fall for a recruiting scam or something?" His tone is gentle and concerned, which makes me feel annoyed. "It sounds almost like this St. Anne's place sends out people like this Andrew guy to sign up volunteers like you."

"No, it wasn't like that at all!" I retort. I hate it when he talks to me like I'm a child, even though I know he means well. "What Andrew was saying made sense. I have a skill that can help these kids."

"Okay." He draws the word out and pauses. "Kate, is there something here I'm not getting?"

Like my new obsession with my imaginary daughter? I think guiltily. "What do you mean?" I ask instead.

"Well, you develop an interest in sign language out of the blue," he says slowly, "and then you make plans to start hanging out with some random social worker guy. I just want to make sure I shouldn't worry."

"Dan, did you seriously just say that?"

"I know it's crazy . . ." He lets his voice trail off, and I know I'm supposed to jump in and tell him I understand where he's coming from, that I would never cheat on him, and that nothing is wrong. But my defenses are already up, and I don't feel much like soothing him now.

"I'm just trying to pursue something I think I could love doing," I say tightly. "I would think you'd be supportive of that, but instead, you're twisting it. I'm hanging up now." I push the End Call button and turn to stare out the window. I feel equal parts angry and guilty: angry because he suspects I'm not being entirely honest with him, and guilty because he's right. My phone rings again two minutes later, but when I see it's Dan calling back, I let it go to voice mail. I'm not doing anything wrong. I listen to the message he's left, and some of my anger melts away when I realize it's a heartfelt apology.

"Baby, I'm really sorry," he says. "Sometimes I just worry about losing you. I know it's stupid; I know you love me. I hope you know much I love you."

I consider texting him back, but after a moment, I switch my phone off. I don't want to think about Dan right now.

Joan is waiting for me, as usual, outside the train station in her silver Volvo. I climb into the passenger seat and we embrace awkwardly over the center console, then she gives me a quick peck on the cheek before starting the car. "It's good to see you, sweetheart," she says. "You're looking well."

"You too," I say, and I can feel stress melting off my shoulders as she pulls onto Footemill Lane toward her house. The night has turned dusky outside the car window, and streetlights illuminate her silvered hair. After 2002, it quickly turned from Irish ebony to salt and pepper, and now, the black strands that used to remind me of her son are almost completely gone.

"How's the wedding planning coming?" she asks, and then, before I can answer, she laughs. "I'm sorry. I used to hate it when I was engaged to Joe a million years ago and people asked me that. You probably haven't had a moment to breathe since your engagement, have you?"

"Not really," I reply, although clearly I've had enough time to sign up for a sign language class and commit to volunteering.

"Well, if you need any help, sweetheart, you just say the word," she says. "I know your mom isn't nearby and—" She stops abruptly and sighs. "I'm sorry. This is probably inappropriate, isn't it? You don't want your former mother-in-law helping plan your wedding."

"Joan, you're still my mother-in-law," I say gently. "You always will be. And I'd love your help."

We pull up to Joan's house, the house Patrick grew up in, and Joan suggests I wait on the front porch while she goes inside to grab us some iced tea. "I've got dinner in the Crock-Pot for us," she tells me, "but I thought we could sit outside and catch up for a bit. It's such a nice evening."

"Can I help you with anything?" I ask.

"Oh no, I'll just be a second." The screen door swings closed behind her, and I settle into an Adirondack chair and close my eyes. The sound of applause wafts over from the Little League field across the street, then I hear the sharp, tinny ping of an aluminum bat connecting with a baseball. The crowd cheers, and I smile to myself. This was the sound track to my summer evenings here with Patrick; we'd sit on the porch and talk, but inevitably, the sounds of the game across the street would trigger an animated conversation between him and his dad about something that had happened in a Yankees game the previous week.

I can smell salt in the air from the coast nearby, and I reach instinctively for the silver dollar hanging from my neck as I think about how Patrick and I threw a coin into the ocean just blocks from here after we got married. *A thank-you to the universe for the best thing that ever happened to me,* Patrick said. I wonder if you're allowed to ask the universe to refund your coins when life doesn't turn out the way you planned.

"Did Patrick ever tell you the whole story of the silver dollars?" Joan asks, reemerging onto the porch with two glasses of iced tea. I open my eyes and see her gaze resting on the coin I'm clutching.

I shake my head. "Just that his grandpa—your father—had a collection of them and started throwing them out for good luck when he was a kid."

She smiles. "That's right. It's a tradition my great-grandfather started almost a hundred years ago, after my father was born. He gave my father fifty newly minted silver dollars and explained that each time something really amazing happened to him, he had to return one of the dollars to the universe so that someone else could wish on it."

I smile, recalling how Patrick had once told me a story of his grandfather standing on the Brooklyn Bridge in 1936 and throwing a silver dollar into the water after his beloved Yankees won the World Series. They won it for the next three years too, and his grandfather always believed that it was his coins—good luck returned to the universe—that kept their streak alive. "I remember Patrick saying that. He really believed in it."

Joan nods. "Me too. My father always used to tell me that if you keep the coins, you throw things out of balance. When I was born, he gave me fifty silver dollars, and when Patrick was born, he did the same. It's all about passing the luck on and thanking the world for whatever good things have happened to you."

"I always loved that story."

"Did you know that Patrick threw a coin the morning after he met you?" Joan asks.

Something inside of me lurches. "No," I whisper. "I didn't."

"He called me that afternoon to tell me," she says, her expression far away. "I knew you had to be something special. He didn't take that sort of thing lightly."

"Wow," I murmur, the most I can manage through the lump in my throat. I reach for the silver dollar around my neck again, and Joan watches me closely.

"You know," she says gently, "you'll have to throw that one back someday."

I look up, startled. "But it was the last thing he ever gave me." I clutch the coin a bit defensively.

"I know. But I also know he gave it to you because something good had happened. And he wanted to throw the coin back once he'd shared his good news with you."

I nod, and for a moment, I can see his face in my mind, his expression as he handed me the coin. *I'll tell you at dinner,* he'd said. But he didn't come home. "I never found out what he was going to tell me."

"And maybe it'll always be a mystery. But the silver dollars aren't meant to be kept. Not in our family, anyhow."

Her words pierce me, partially because I can't imagine parting with the coin that I wear every day, and partially because I know she's right. "I'm not ready yet," I finally admit.

"And that's okay." She reaches over to squeeze my hand. "But you'll need to be. Someday, you'll need to be."

I nod, and for a moment, we sit in comfortable silence. I'm thinking about Patrick and how much stock he put in the magic of the silver dollars. But in the end, all that good luck hadn't been enough to save him.

From the baseball field across the street comes another sharp ping, aluminum meeting leather, and the crowd cheers. "Patrick always talked about coaching Little League someday," Joan says, breaking the quiet between us. "He would have been a great coach. He was always great with kids."

I smile faintly. "He's great with Hannah." I realize what I've said a split second later and resist the urge to clap a hand over my mouth.

"Who?" Joan looks confused.

"No one. Sorry," I say quickly. "What I mean is, I'm really sorry, Joan."

"Sorry?" She looks at me blankly. "For what, sweetheart?"

I stare at my hands for a minute. "For not having a child with him."

"Kate—" Joan begins, but I cut her off.

"I thought we were too young." It's a conversation I've had a thousand times with myself, but never aloud. "Patrick was ready, but I was still in grad school, so I told him I wanted to wait a few years, and he agreed. I thought we had all the time in the world."

"Of course you did, Kate," she soothes. "You were absolutely right at the time. How could you have known what would happen? A grandchild would have been wonderful, but that wasn't in God's plans. You can't blame yourself for that."

We sit quietly for a moment, lost in our own thoughts, then Joan breaks the silence, asking, "Do you think you and Dan will have children?"

It takes me a few seconds to muster an answer. "I can't have a baby," I say softly. "I just found out a couple weeks ago."

"Oh, sweetheart, I'm so sorry to hear that. How are you feeling about it?"

"I don't know," I admit.

"In vitro isn't an option?"

I shake my head.

"Surrogacy?"

"Not with one of my eggs."

"Well, what about adoption?" she asks, brightening. "You'd give a child such a wonderful home."

"Maybe. I'm not sure how Dan feels."

"How do *you* feel?"

I think about it for a minute. For years, I've been forgetting to ask myself that. "I think I want to be a mom, Joan," I say softly. "I just don't know if it's too late."

Eleven

A tidal wave of gratitude washes over me as I open my eyes the next morning and realize I'm back in my old apartment, lying beside Patrick.

"Thank you," I murmur, and my words wake Patrick up.

He rolls over, blinks a few times, sleepily, and reaches for me. "Did you say something, honey?" he asks.

"No. I mean yes, I did, but not to you." I hesitate. "I'm just talking to God, I think."

"Oh, well, that's okay, then," Patrick says, pulling me toward him. "I make an exception for the big guy upstairs."

He kisses me, long and deep, and I can feel a tingle of happiness spreading all over my body, but it's interrupted by a sob that bubbles up from the middle of my chest.

"Kate?" Patrick asks, pulling back and gazing at me with concern. "Are you okay?"

"Yes," I manage. "Fine."

"But you're crying."

"I just—I just miss you so much," I tell him. The world flickers and dims, alarming me.

Oblivious, Patrick strokes my hair. "I'm right here, Katielee."

I force a smile. "Yes. You are. Of course you are." The room springs back into focus, the colors sharpening into their familiar near-blinding hues, and I breathe a sigh of relief.

He dries my tears gently, his thumb coarse against my cheek. I'm about to say something else, to ask more, but Patrick rolls over, looks at the clock and exclaims, "Shoot! We're running late. We've got to get Hannah ready to go."

I blink a few times. "Go where?"

"To day camp." He looks at me with renewed concern. "Pete's mom is picking her up. Remember?"

He gets out of bed without waiting for a reply, and I watch, my breath caught in my throat, as he slides a gray T-shirt over his bare chest.

"You coming?" he asks, smiling at me.

"Sure," I whisper. I should be enjoying every second of this, real or not. I clear my throat. "How about I make us pancakes for breakfast? Do we have time for that?" I hesitate and add, "Wait, does Hannah like pancakes?"

The moment the words are out of my mouth, I know the answer is a resounding yes. I also know immediately that her favorite pancakes are peanut butter blueberry, a combination we stumbled upon when she was in first grade, and that she likes them with honey instead of syrup.

"Is the sky blue?" Patrick asks with a chuckle, saving me from having to explain.

"Just kidding," I reply weakly as he strides out of the room. I hurry to throw on a plush blue robe I don't recognize but that I know I love.

I can hear the sink running in the bathroom, and someone rummaging through the hall closet. "My family," I murmur aloud, and all at once, I know I have to stop wondering whether

I belong here. If I keep acting as if I might lose my place in this world at any moment, I will.

In the kitchen, I grab a skillet from the cabinet just to the left of the stove, turn the burner on, and slice a few pats of butter into the pan. *This is real,* I tell myself. I mix flour, sugar, baking powder, vegetable oil, salt, milk, and an egg together in a bowl, then I stir in a half cup of peanut butter. *I'm really here.* I ladle spoonfuls of batter onto the skillet, and finally, I dot frozen blueberries onto each of the pancakes as they begin to sizzle and bubble.

I belong in this life, I tell myself as the scent of butter and frying pancakes fills the kitchen. *I have to.*

Hannah pads into the kitchen wearing a cute floral dress and purple Converse sneakers just as I'm sliding the first batch of pancakes onto a baking sheet to warm in the oven. "Morning," she says, and as I turn to greet her, my heart fluttering with happiness, I notice for the first time that there's a small, oblong node on the side of her head, just behind her right ear, mostly hidden by her hair. It's where her bun was the last time I saw her, which explains why I didn't see it. She looks away for a moment, and I see an identical headpiece on her left side.

"Cochlear implants," I say softly, and although Hannah gives me a weird look, the room doesn't fade, and suddenly, the details flood in. Teaching her sign language when she was a toddler and encouraging her to read lips and to try to verbalize. Deciding with Patrick just before Hannah was two and a half that cochlear implantation was the best thing for her. The maternal panic I felt when she went in for surgery; the relief I felt in the weeks afterward when I knew my daughter was beginning to hear. The knowledge that because she learned to sign before she learned to speak, and the fact that we encouraged her to keep up ASL so she'd always have a tie to the Deaf community, she often switches back and forth between the two forms of language when she's talking to Patrick and me.

"Mom?" she asks aloud, and I notice she's peering at me with concern, probably because I'm standing there, spatula in hand, staring at her.

I gather myself, smile at her, and sign, *Good morning,* one of the phrases I taught myself online.

She looks relieved, and she signs back, *You are acting weird again,* but she's smiling. I'm struck by how well I can understand her here, which reminds me that this can't possibly be real. But then again, calling it a dream seems crazy too, because it's obviously so much more than that.

I try to remember the signs Andrew taught me for the phrase, *I'm sorry I've been a little bit weird.* I point to myself, rub my right hand over my heart with a closed fist, point to myself again, flick my thumb against my index finger two times, and then position my hand like a claw and move it right to left while wiggling my middle finger, my ring finger and my index finger in front of my face.

Hannah looks at me for a moment, and I'm afraid I've said something wrong. But then she says aloud, "You're always weird, Mom," and laughs. Then she signs, *Are the pancakes ready?*

"Just a few more minutes," I tell her. I melt a bit more butter in the pan, spoon five dollops of batter in, and add blueberries. I turn to find Hannah pulling three plates out of the cabinet and three forks out of the silverware drawer.

She catches me watching her again and rolls her eyes. "What now, Mom?" she asks aloud.

I shake my head quickly and look away. "Nothing," I say, then I add in sign language, *I love you.*

She rolls her eyes again. "I love you too, dork," she says aloud. "You don't have to keep signing, you know. I promise, I'm keeping up with practicing ASL, okay?"

Duh, I sign back with a weak smile, using Andrew's pun, and she makes a face at me, but she's smiling.

As I slide another round of pancakes into the oven and prepare the frying pan for a third batch, Hannah sidles up beside me and begins a rapid conversation about someone named Meggie. I know in a flash that Meggie is Hannah's best friend at school and that I've always liked her. Then she transitions right into a long, signed monologue about a girl named Jessica who she sat with yesterday at day camp. *Jessica met One Direction last year!* she signs excitedly, her eyes wide. *So cool!*

I make sure Hannah's looking at me, then I ask, "So you'll hang out with Jessica at camp today?"

She shakes her head. *Only if Meggie doesn't come,* she signs. *Meggie doesn't like Jessica.*

Patrick strides into the kitchen, freshly shaven and smelling of soap. He's dressed for work in a button-down shirt, chinos, and loafers. "Mmm, pancakes!" he exclaims, patting his belly and then coming around behind me to tickle me, like he always did when we were in the kitchen together. He nuzzles my neck, and I sigh contentedly.

Gross, Mom and Dad, Hannah signs, and we both laugh.

We eat in companionable silence, and I'm surprised to realize that Hannah's blueberry–peanut butter combination is sort of ingenious; the tart berries balance out the salty peanut butter perfectly.

After breakfast, Patrick and I walk Hannah outside, where a woman in a minivan pulls up curbside a few minutes later with a teenage boy in the passenger seat.

I hug Hannah good-bye so tightly and for so long that she has to wriggle away from me, muttering, "Geez, Mom, clingy much?" She waves from the backseat as the van pulls away, and I stare after her long after they've disappeared around the corner.

"You okay?" Patrick asks, putting his hand on my shoulder and squeezing gently.

What I'm thinking is, *No, I'm not; I'm terrified I'll never get to see her again.* "I just miss her already," I murmur.

"She'll be back," Patrick says, looking at me oddly before heading back toward the front door. "You'll hardly even know she was gone."

Inside, I find him putting a tie on in the bedroom, facing the window. I stare for a moment, my breath stolen by the familiarity of it all. Then, before I can second-guess myself, I cross the room and put a hand on his shoulder. He turns slowly and murmurs, "Katielee."

The word sends shivers through me, and slowly, deliberately, I loosen his tie and begin to unbutton his shirt. He stares at me for a minute, as if trying to decide something. "Katielee," he murmurs again, but I can see something powerful flickering in his eyes.

"Please," I murmur, shorthand to a thousand unspoken words as I gaze up at the husband I thought I'd never see again.

He only hesitates another second before pulling me into his arms—the strong arms I love and remember so well—and holding me against his chest. I can hear his heart pounding the way it never will again, and then his hands are on me, and we're on the bed.

His body feels different than it used to, more solid, less lithe, and there's a confidence to the way he moves that wasn't there before. It's like he's known my body for years instead of just the precious twenty months we had together. Then I push away all my thoughts, all my endless analysis, and make love to my husband, slowly, tenderly, with every cell on fire.

Afterward, I collapse on Patrick's bare chest, tears streaming down my cheeks.

"That was amazing," Patrick murmurs.

"I love you so much," I reply. But then I think of Dan, and I'm flooded with shame.

I look up at Patrick, into his perfect green eyes, the ones I miss so much. I can't stop crying, even when he takes my chin in his hand and gently tilts it up. "What's wrong, Katielee?" he asks gently. "I'm right here."

"Yes," I murmur, the pain of my words shooting through my heart like a million little daggers. "You're right here."

Twelve

In the morning, a tremendous tidal wave of guilt crashes over me when I roll over and see Dan fast asleep beside me. The way my stomach lurches uneasily upon seeing him isn't normal, and it makes me feel even worse about everything.

As we get ready for work, Dan's kindness is almost torture; I'd almost rather he be distant and removed so that I don't have to think about how in a way, I cheated on him last night. But is it really a betrayal if I imagined everything?

Imaginary or not, as I brush my teeth, I can still feel Patrick's touch on my skin. As I wash my face, I can still smell his musky cologne on me. As I walk to the kitchen, trying to block out all thoughts of him, I can still hear him whispering in my ear. I just can't understand how the dreams feel so painfully real.

"Baby, I want to apologize again for last night," Dan tells me as he brings me a steaming mug of coffee fixed just the way I like it, with hazelnut creamer and a packet of Splenda.

"Last night?" I ask blankly. All I can think is that last night, I made love to my husband.

"Those things I said. About the kids you want to work with. I was wrong. And I'm sorry."

"Oh," I manage to say.

He sits down across the kitchen table from me and rakes a hand through his hair. "I had no right to question you. Honestly? I was jealous. And I know that's a completely unattractive trait, and I'm trying hard not to feel that way. It's an uphill climb. You know my history, but that's no excuse."

I nod. Dan was married in his early thirties to a woman named Siobhan. They were together for three years, and it had ended when she cheated on him with her boss. He'd told me on our very first date that he was a little commitment-phobic because of that, and that he had some trust issues but that he was working on them. I'd told him that my husband dying had made me a commitment-phobe too, and he'd smiled and said we'd just found the first thing we had in common.

"I'm not Siobhan, you know," I remind him.

"I know. I know without a doubt that you would never be unfaithful."

"Never," I mumble into my coffee, but I can still feel Patrick's lips grazing my collarbone, his hands on my breasts, his body pressed against mine.

"Kate?" Dan's concerned voice brings me back to earth. "You okay? You zoned out there for a minute."

I look up in surprise. "Sorry. I just haven't been sleeping well."

He looks concerned. "Anything I can do? If you need me to take anything off your plate . . ."

"That's really nice of you. But I'm fine."

"Hey, about the foster kids and that Andrew guy." He clears his throat. "If it's really that important to you . . ."

"Dan—" I begin.

"No, I just wanted to say I'm glad," he says quickly. "I think you'll really be able to help them."

* * *

On Tuesday, after an appointment with Max, I head to Queens to meet Andrew at the main offices of St. Anne's Services. As promised, he has expedited my paperwork and I've been approved to work with the kids; he just needs a few signatures before I see my first client.

As the subway rumbles along and I flip through an ASL dictionary I've downloaded to my iPad, I feel a surge of excitement. I've spent the last few days poring over journal articles about advances in music therapy for deaf and hard-of-hearing children, and I'm fascinated by it all. What sounds impossible on the surface makes complete sense once you take the time to understand the power of vibration, rhythm, and pitch. I'm a firm believer that music is a huge gift in life; it has the power to connect people to each other in a way that words just can't. If I can share that gift with a handful of kids, I'll have done a good thing.

I find Andrew waiting for me outside St. Anne's, which is housed in a converted midcentury church on a busy street corner in Astoria. He's sitting on the front steps, and he stands when he sees me approaching.

"You found the place," he says, brushing the dirt off his faded jeans and grinning at me as he comes down the front walkway. We shake hands, which feels too formal, then he gives me an awkward hug.

I smile. "I guess I'm overdressed, huh?" He's in a vintage-looking Batman T-shirt, while I'm still wearing a silk blouse, pencil skirt, and kitten heels from a day at the office.

"Not at all," he says. "This is just comfortable, for when I need to get down and play with the kids—or fix stuff around the foster houses. I'm known far and wide as the man who can work magic with a screwdriver and a drill."

"And here I'm just the woman who thinks she can change lives with a guitar and a pair of maracas," I say with a wink, tipping my big canvas bag so that he can see the small collection of instruments I have inside.

"Well, I guess we make a pretty good pair then," he says. He takes my bag off my shoulder, and when I start to protest, he just gives me a look. "I may be dressed like a five-year-old, but I'm still a gentleman. I'm carrying your bag for you."

"Just don't try to take my guitar, or I'll have to hurt you," I shoot back with a smile.

"Ooh, a fictional violent streak. Edgy."

I make a face at him and look up at the St. Anne's building. "So do the kids I'll be working with live here?"

He shakes his head. "This is just an admin office and a place where the kids can meet with some of our workers. Most of our kids are placed in private homes, and the ones we don't have homes for live in a group home run by the city, but we try to make sure those stays are as brief as possible. Actually, if you don't mind, I've brought your paperwork out here—there are just two things to sign—then we'll walk a few blocks to the foster home where two of the kids I'd like you to meet—Molly and Riajah—live. Okay by you?"

"Sure."

He hands me a couple of pieces of paper on a clipboard—a declaration that all the information I provided previously is true, and an official statement that I've never been convicted of a crime—and after I've signed them and handed then back, we begin walking.

"So you never told me what intrigued you about working with hard-of-hearing kids in the first place," Andrew says as we make our way down Thirty-Fifth Street.

I consider the question before I answer, because obviously

I can't mention Hannah without sounding like a lunatic—and lunacy probably isn't high on the list of qualifications St. Anne's looks for in volunteers. "I think music can help everyone," I finally say. "And there are plenty of ways to hear music that don't involve the ears. Just because a child is deaf or hard of hearing doesn't mean he or she can't benefit from exposure to music, even if that's not what people might expect."

We turn left at the corner onto Thirty-Fourth Avenue, and Andrew glances at me. "I love to see these kids defy expectations," he says. "Deafness and hearing loss present their own unique challenges, but coupled with the fact that these kids are also in the foster system, well, some of them are at real risk of getting lost, you know?"

"Lost in the system, you mean?" I don't know Andrew that well, but somehow, I can't imagine him letting that happen.

"Not really. St. Anne's is great, and the other organizations around the city that do similar work are too. What I mean is, I worry about them just losing their chance to develop into healthy, happy kids, you know? Lots of these kids have low self-esteem, and some of them think their parents got rid of them, so to speak. There's a lot of acting out, a lot of anger. And because they have special needs, they're a lot harder to permanently place than the average kid. The pool of parents with the right skills is smaller."

"So what happens to them?" I ask softly.

"Some of them find homes. Some of the kids are reunited with their biological parents. And some, unfortunately, get bounced around from home to home or wind up in a group facility.

"It's why I think I'll be in this job forever," he adds as he leads me up a walkway to a narrow, brick row house. "I want these kids to know that they always, always have an adult who will care about them, a person they can come to if they need anything."

"Andrew, that's really incredible of you," I manage, and he looks instantly embarrassed.

"I'm sorry," he says. "That sounded dumb."

"No," I say softly. "Not at all. I was just thinking that I hope I can continue to be a part of these kids' lives too."

Andrew looks surprised, but he nods. "Anyhow, enough mushy stuff. Let's have you meet Riajah and Molly." He rings the doorbell, and after a moment, a woman with gray-streaked dark hair answers the door. There are bags under her eyes, but she's smiling. She dusts her hands off on her apron and reaches out to shake Andrew's hand.

"Sorry," she says. "I was just baking some cookies. Come on in."

Andrew steps over the threshold and gestures for me to follow. "Sheila," he says, "this is Kate Waithman, the music therapist I was telling you about. Kate, this is Sheila Migliavada, baker of cookies and changer of lives."

"Nice to meet you, Kate," Sheila says as she laughs and shuts the door behind us. Inside, the house smells like vanilla. "I'll find the girls for you, then I'll go check on those cookies before they burn."

"Actually, Kate's going to visit with the girls separately," Andrew says. "In fact, we're just here for a few minutes today to assess them. Mind if we head on down to Molly's room?"

"Not at all. Last door on your right." She points down a narrow hallway and turns back toward the kitchen.

"Sheila's one of the good ones," Andrew explains quietly as we head down the hall. "She's got Molly, who's seven, and Riajah, who's ten. They've been with her for about a year. They're nice girls. They should be okay for you."

He looks nervous, and I realize that he's trying to start me off easy. "We're talking to Molly first?" I ask.

He nods. "She lost most of her hearing when she was four after a bad ear infection went untreated. She'd been living with her mother, but there was an abuse situation at home with the mother's boyfriend. She was removed until the state could verify that he's no longer in the picture. She doesn't interact with other kids much, and she's very behind academically, because she won't participate at school. She's repeating kindergarten this fall, so she'll be in with kids who are a year or two younger than her. She's one of the ones I'm concerned about."

"And you said she doesn't have cochlear implants?"

"Because of the nature of her hearing loss, she isn't a candidate for them," he explains. "So she communicates largely by signing. But I also try to work with her on lip reading and verbal skills. I think it just helps for social development, in general. I thought maybe you could work with her on speech, if you think she's a fit."

The door's open a crack, so Andrew steps in first and stands in front of Molly, a pale, tiny girl with straight, straw-colored hair. He waves, and I watch her face go from suspicious to happy to guarded all in a single second. I understand right away that she has her defenses up but trusts Andrew.

"Hello, Molly," Andrew says aloud as he signs to her. "This is my friend Kate. She's a music therapist. She's here to visit with you today."

Molly's expression darkens. "No!" she says sharply, but the word doesn't sound right; the *o* sounds more like a long *u*. She signs something to Andrew that I don't understand, and he shakes his head.

"I know you don't like therapists, Molly," he says aloud, still signing to her. "But Kate is a different kind of therapist. She plays music."

Molly looks me up and down suspiciously, then signs something to Andrew.

He turns his head toward me. "She says she doesn't believe me."

I nod and dig into my bag. The music therapy itself will be to assist Molly with her ability to communicate, but first, I have to get her to trust me. "I guess I'll have to play my instruments alone, then," I say casually. "Or get Andrew to play with me."

He quickly translates what I've said into sign language, then I give him a handheld xylophone and mallet. I pull my guitar out of the soft case on my back and pluck the first few notes of "Mary Had a Little Lamb." To my surprise and relief, Andrew enthusiastically hammers the next several notes out on the xylophone.

"Piano lessons when I was a kid," he says with a grin, in response to my questioning look. "Although this is about the extent of my repertoire."

I laugh, then we both look at Molly as we continue playing. She's staring at us with her mouth slightly open. It only takes her a moment to reach out and say aloud, "Me!" When I don't respond, she stomps her foot and signs something to Andrew.

"I'm sure Kate would be happy to let you use an instrument," Andrew says aloud as he signs back. "But you'll have to ask her politely."

She signs something to me, and Andrew says softly, "She's asking for an instrument."

Molly looks back and forth between us and adds, "Please," aloud.

"Good job, Molly," Andrew says with an approving nod. "Kate?"

I smile at the little girl and hand her a pair of maracas, which she accepts almost reverently. She shakes them a couple of times and then turns one upside down and inspects it, like she's trying to figure out where the sound and vibration are coming from. Then, with a solemn expression on her face, she says to Andrew,

"Ready." The word sounds more like "Red-uh," and I'm getting an idea of what kind of work we'll have ahead of us.

I start strumming "Mary Had a Little Lamb" again on the guitar, very slowly, and Andrew joins in on the xylophone. Molly watches us for a minute, then she does something that surprises me; she gently sets down one of the maracas and walks over to me. I continue playing as I watch her closely. First, she gives the maraca she's still holding in her right hand a tentative shake. Then she reaches out with her left hand to touch the strings on the neck of the guitar. Her eyes widen, and I know she's felt the vibration. Her fingers on the strings change the notes I'm playing, but I don't mind; I want her to feel that too.

After a minute, she begins tentatively to shake her maraca. She's playing exactly along with the beat of the song, which fills me with relief; the fact that she has an intrinsic sense of rhythm will make it that much easier to help her get comfortable with communicating verbally.

When we finally stop playing—after repeating the chorus an additional dozen times—Molly looks at me tentatively. I set the guitar down and carefully sign to her, *Good job,* which I taught myself to say during my lunch break today.

Her face lights up for a second, and then her smile falls just as quickly, and I'm surprised to see her glaring at me. She glances at Andrew and signs something to him.

"No, Molly," he says gently as he signs back to her. "We're not going to abandon you now. Kate is going to come back next week. Right, Kate?"

I nod vigorously.

Molly studies me suspiciously for a minute. Then she signs something else to Andrew.

"She wants to know if you'll bring your maracas back," he tells me with a slight smile.

"Yes, absolutely." I nod again, and Andrew signs to Molly that I'll be back with all my instruments. She looks at me for a moment, and then she smiles tentatively.

"Okay," she says aloud. "Bye."

"Good-bye, Molly," Andrew says. He makes a sign that's similar to a wave. I do the same thing. Molly nods solemnly and turns away as we leave her room.

"I'm sorry," I say as soon as we're alone in the hallway.

"What?" Andrew looks startled. "Why are you sorry?"

"It probably doesn't look like we made much progress. But with kids, it's better to start off slow, get them to trust you."

"Kate, that was the most I've seen Molly interact with a stranger—ever. Whatever you're doing . . ." He pauses and concludes, "Let's just say I think you have a real gift. I'm hoping you'll be able to get Riajah to open up too."

"What's her story?"

"She was born with only five percent residual hearing," Andrew explains. "Her mom died of breast cancer when Riajah was just two, and her dad gave her up after that. He just walked into ACS one day and said he didn't want to raise a kid on his own. We tried to find a relative who would take her, because she has a huge extended family, but only one aunt stepped forward, and that only lasted a year. She gave Riajah up entirely when she was just four. Apparently, there was some incident at Riajah's birthday party that year, and the aunt wound up yelling at her that she was stupid and would never be normal. She brought her back the next day, like a store return."

"That's horrible," I murmur.

Andrew nods. "And that's the kind of thing that stays with a kid for a very long time. Riajah's had a few placements in the six years she's been with us. Two years ago, we were able to get her cochlear implants, but it's been slow going. She can hear and speak perfectly well, but she still uses sign language a lot too."

"Because that's what she's more comfortable with?"

"I'm not sure," Andrew says. "I'm pretty positive it's more of a defense mechanism. Like she can keep most people out by refusing to communicate in a language they can understand."

"Poor kid," I say.

"Nah, try to think of it this way: Now she's a *lucky* kid, because she gets to work with you." He turns away before I can reply, and I feel myself blushing.

Andrew goes into Riajah's darkened room first and has a quick signed conversation with her before ushering me in. "I told her about you," he says. "She says she's not going to talk to you, but that you can play your music if you want." He shrugs an apology.

"No problem," I tell him. I follow him into the room and find Riajah, a stout African American girl with long hair in little braids, sitting on the floor. She looks older than ten, or maybe that's just because she's scowling at me with the world-weary expression of someone who's seen it all.

"Hello, Riajah," I say aloud, smiling as I greet her with a wave and a careful fingerspelling of her name. She cocks an eyebrow, looks at Andrew, and signs something rapidly. He sighs and signs back.

"What did she say?" I ask.

"She wants to know if you have mental problems," he says. "Apparently you're not signing fast enough for her."

I look at Riajah, who's smirking at me now. I make the letter *A* with my right hand and move it in a circle around the center of my chest, the ASL way to say, *I'm sorry.* Then I follow with the sign for *learning,* by making a motion from my upturned left palm to my forehead, as if I'm extracting knowledge from a book and transporting it to my brain.

Riajah scowls at me for a moment before looking away.

I take a deep breath, and without waiting for her to turn around, I set a tambourine on the floor beside her, hand Andrew a triangle, and begin strumming my guitar. I don't think about what to play, but what comes out is the Beatles' "Yellow Submarine," one of my favorite songs to play with kids.

"In the town where I was born . . ." I sing, and Andrew hits the triangle right on cue, twice after *town* and twice after *born*. As I get to the chorus, and Andrew enthusiastically dings his triangle, she finally turns around.

It takes three times through the refrain before she finally picks up the tambourine and, watching my fingers on the strings closely, begins beating it against her hand, tentatively at first and then with a bit more confidence. She's not quite in rhythm, but she's participating, and that's more than I'd dared hope for on a first visit. I keep repeating the chorus again and again, and Andrew gamely continues chiming the triangle. I can even see a smile tugging at the corner of Riajah's lips.

On the fourth time through, though, she looks up and locks eyes with me for a moment. Then her expression darkens, and she slams the tambourine down and stalks out of the room without looking back.

Andrew and I stop playing and look at each other.

"I'm sorry," I say helplessly. "I don't know what happened. I thought we were making some headway."

I expect him to look disappointed, but instead, he smiles at me. "You *did* make headway," he says.

I look at him uncertainly. "Really?"

We walk out to see Sheila in the kitchen, and as Andrew gives her a recap of the two brief sessions and discusses what day of the week would work best for future sessions, I gaze around at our surroundings. Sheila's house is filled with family photos, many of which include Molly and Riajah and some of which look older and feature other kids. I'm guessing Sheila has been fostering kids for a while. I don't see a husband in any of the pictures, and I'm struck by the strength it must take to do this kind of parenting alone.

Sheila hugs me good-bye, and on the way out, Andrew tells me he has one more child he'd like me to see, a twelve-year-old, but she got in trouble at school this week and is grounded, so perhaps we could drop by her house next week.

"Sure," I tell him. "I really liked working with Molly and Riajah today."

"You were seriously great." He glances at me. "Do you think you'd consider making this a regular thing? I think the kids could really benefit."

"Definitely," I say. "Let me check my schedule, but I think Thursday evenings should be fine most weeks."

"Kate, that would be amazing. And we can be as flexible on our end as you need us to be. We're just grateful for your time. And I promise, we'll try to find some money for this in next year's budget."

"Don't worry about it," I murmur. I'm typically annoyed when people assume music therapists won't mind working for free—it's like they're saying our work is worthless—but in this case, it's different. I'd rather have Andrew spend money directly on the children, and if he's using funds to provide cochlear implants for kids in the system, I'd like him to keep doing that.

We walk in silence toward the subway station on Broadway and Thirty-First, and after a moment, he nudges me and says, "So do you and your fiancé have any kids?"

He glances at my ring finger before looking up to meet my gaze.

I think of Hannah, but that's foolish. "Not yet," I reply.

"Well, watching you with Molly and Riajah today," he says, smiling warmly, "maybe it's a silly thing to say, but I think you'll make a really good mom someday, if that's something you want."

"Thanks," I whisper. The silence between us as we walk feels awkward, so I hurry to change the subject. "Your brother, the one you mentioned, does he live here in New York too?"

The smile falls from his face. "Kevin? It's a long story."

"I've got time."

I know right away from the expression on his face that time isn't the issue. I've hit a nerve.

"I'm sorry," I say quickly. "If you don't want to tell me—"

"He died," he interrupts. He looks away as he mumbles, "We were kids. We were playing soccer in the front yard, just kicking the ball back and forth, the two of us. The girl I liked rode her bike by, so I stopped to talk to her. I turned my back for a second, and Kevin chased the ball right into the street. He—he didn't hear the car honking at him."

"Oh, Andrew," I say, my eyes filling with tears.

"I was twelve. He was nine," he says with a practiced shrug. "It was a long time ago. But it's the kind of thing you just never get over, you know?"

"I know what it feels like to lose someone," I say, although I don't mention Patrick. It's not the same. "But you can't blame yourself."

He shakes his head. "But that's just the thing. Of course I can. I'm the one who turned my back. I was supposed to be looking out for him. And now he's gone, and I get to keep on living, and that's not very fair, is it?"

I open my mouth to reply, but he cuts me off. "I shouldn't have told you all that and made myself sound like some sort of martyr. I'm fine. I was in therapy for a while. I've worked through it. But it'll always be a part of me."

"I know."

"You're easy to talk to, Kate. Thanks for listening." I realize we've reached the stairs to the subway station. We pause awkwardly for a moment, and then Andrew points up the street and says, "I live that way about ten minutes. You okay getting home?"

"Sure."

"Great. Thanks again, Kate." He reaches out to shake my right hand. "See you in class tomorrow."

He gives me a half smile and walks away before I can reply.

Thirteen

My dreams of Patrick and Hannah don't return that week, which leaves me disappointed and missing them. Going to sign language class on Wednesday makes me feel a little closer to them, though. Or maybe it's just that Andrew's warm smiles and the speed at which I'm picking up new words and phrases make me feel pretty good.

I try to catch him after class to continue our conversation about his brother, but he seems to be in a rush and leaves without a word while Amy talks my ear off about some dating advice a friend gave her. I have the feeling the point of her story is to not so subtly let me know that she's after Andrew, and I should back off. She seems to think there's something going on between us. "You already have a fiancé," she concludes tightly. "So there's really no point in you hanging out with Andrew outside of class."

"Amy, it's just work related," I tell her with a sigh, but she makes a face and launches back into a monologue about dating in New York.

By the time I extricate myself from Amy and make it upstairs, Andrew is long gone, and the church is silent.

Before I leave, I glance back at Jesus above the altar and murmur, "Thank you for letting me see Patrick again. But maybe, I don't know, maybe it's not that good for me. Maybe I just need to focus on my real life. Thank you anyhow." I cross myself and hurry out into the warm evening, feeling unsettled.

On Saturday morning, I'm getting dressed to go wedding dress shopping with Gina and Susan when Dan comes up and kisses me.

"You look beautiful," he says, turning me around and pushing my hair behind my ear. "My gorgeous bride-to-be. Looking forward to shopping for a dress? I hear that's supposed to be a big deal for you ladies."

I smile. "Gina and Susan seem even more excited than I am." I hear how the words sound, and I quickly shake my head. "Not that I'm not excited. I just mean that the two of them act like they've been waiting forever to see me in a white dress."

Dan's smile falters. "Since Patrick died."

"I didn't mean it that way."

"I know." Dan studies me for a moment and nods. "Is everything okay?"

"Of course," I say instantly. "Why wouldn't it be?" But when he still looks skeptical, I add, "Work stuff. That's all."

He rubs my back comfortingly, his hand moving in small circles. "So you'll never believe what happened to Stephen."

"He fell off another keg?" I guess, only half kidding. Dan's best friend is a recently divorced forty-five-year-old who seems to think he's two decades younger than he actually is. "Or he dropped two hundred grand on a sports car he can't afford? Or did he talk another college coed with daddy issues into going home with him?"

Dan chuckles. "Good to know you hold him in such high esteem. But you're not too far off base."

I laugh. "Oh, this should be good."

"He got a girl pregnant," Dan continues. "Some girl he only went out with twice. Can you believe it?"

I can feel the smile fall from my face. "What's he going to do?"

"He offered to pay for the abortion."

Something twists inside of me. "She's having an abortion?"

"No, that's the thing," Dan goes on. "She's refusing to get one. She's only twenty-five, but she says she's been dying to have a baby. So she's going ahead with the pregnancy. Stephen is panicking."

"Well, that's her right," I say. "To have the baby."

"Of course," Dan says. "But Stephen's pretty upset. He doesn't want to be a father. Not with some girl he barely even knows."

"Then maybe he shouldn't have slept with her. That's how babies are generally made, you know." I can't keep the edge out of my voice. Suddenly, I'm irrationally furious. I'm technically pro-choice, because I feel like abortion should be an issue between a woman, her conscience, and her doctor, but the older I've gotten, the more I've realized just how valuable life is. Stephen's eagerness to throw it so carelessly away makes me bristle, as does the blank expression Dan is giving me now.

"You're saying you think they should keep it?" Dan asks.

"I'm saying I think it's not my business," I reply. "And I think that Stephen accidentally procreating isn't really something I need to hear about right now."

Realization crosses Dan's face. "Oh. So that's what this is about."

I glare at him. "You say it like I'm being ridiculous."

"You can't compare it to what you're going through, Kate. It's not the same thing."

I flinch at his choice of words. "What *I'm* going through?" I can feel my face getting hot.

Dan looks confused for a second. "I meant what *we're* going through," he amends unconvincingly.

"No, that's not what you meant," I mutter. I know this is a perfect opportunity for a talk—a *real* talk—about what we both want. But I can feel the heat of annoyance radiating through me, and I don't want to fight. The truth is, I *never* want to fight. Unfortunately, Dan seems to subscribe to the same philosophy, so we never really discuss anything. Instead, we simply let potential disagreements go, but I'm beginning to suspect that the things we've swept under the carpet are the things wrapping themselves around me lately, making me feel like I can't breathe.

"Okay, what can I do to fix this?" Dan asks, his tone softening. He waits for me to look up. "I love you."

"Why?" I hear myself ask.

"What?"

"Why? Why do you love me?"

He rakes a hand through his hair. "I just do, Kate. Jesus. Are you deliberately pushing my buttons this morning?"

"No." In fact, I'm not sure *what* I'm doing, but I know it's not fair. I know that my unsettled feeling is about Patrick, and I'm aware that my long-dead husband has no place in the middle of a conversation with Dan. But I can't stop. "I think what I'm doing is saying we don't communicate, Dan. And maybe we should be communicating better."

"Fine. So let's communicate." He looks at the clock on the wall. "But aren't you going to be late for meeting the girls?"

I check my watch and grimace. "Oh."

"Hey, I love you. We'll talk later. Okay?"

I nod. "Love you too." I can feel his eyes on me as I walk out the front door. In the bright morning sunshine, the miniconfrontation feels ridiculous, but I can't seem to untie the knots that have formed in my stomach.

Elisabetta's Bridal Studio looks like something out of a fairy tale, with Tiffany blue carpets, ornate oval mirrors, and rows and rows of lace, tulle, and satin in a spectrum of shades from white to cream.

"Wow" is all I can muster when Susan, Gina, and I walk in and a guy in a tuxedo who looks barely older than eighteen materializes with a tray of champagne flutes. We each take one, and Susan grins at me.

"I *knew* you would love this place," she says. "The appointment was almost impossible to get, but I called in a few favors."

"Thanks," I say, exchanging glances with Gina. I'm sure she's thinking, as I am, that everything in this store is well out of my price range.

But Susan, reading my expression, squeezes my arm gently and says, "Relax; it's just to get an idea of what you like. I'm sure your style has changed in the last twelve years."

She whisks away to sign in for our appointment, and Gina smiles at me and shrugs. "Hey, we might as well enjoy it," she says. "Besides, who knew today would come with free champagne?"

Susan returns with a glamorous-looking woman dressed all in black, her dark hair pulled into a tight bun. "I am Veronica," she says, her voice thick with an accent I think is Italian. "And you are the bride, Katherine?"

"Kate," I say. I begin to stick out my hand, but instead, she leans forward and air-kisses me on both cheeks, European style. I feel clumsy and uncouth as I pull back.

"Very well," she says, giving me an appraising once-over. "We will begin. Do you know what type of dress you are interested in?"

I shake my head. "I wore a ball gown for my first wedding, so . . ."

She shakes her head briskly. "Not right for your frame. You need something that's cut slimmer around the hips. A mermaid gown, perhaps? Or a trumpet style. I'll go pull an assortment in your size." She puts a finger to her chin and studies me for a moment more. "Not white, no, no. That would be inappropriate after a divorce."

"I'm not divorced," I say defensively. "He died. My first husband died."

I feel Gina's hand on my back as Veronica frowns. "Pardon me. I just assumed. Well, still, white isn't right for a second wedding. But we'll find you something special."

She pulls out a tape measure and makes rapid measurements around my bust, waist, and hips, then she disappears into the back of the store.

"Don't let her bother you," Gina says in a low voice.

"She didn't know," Susan says defensively. "How would she know?"

"It's okay," I say quickly. "Let's just focus on finding a dress." After all, a dress will make all of this real. And maybe that's what I need in order to get out of my own head: a reality check.

Veronica returns a few moments later with a rolling rack of cream and ivory gowns, some of which are simple and sleek, some of which are elaborate, with long trains and delicate beading. "Sometimes, the ones that look the most unlikely on the rack are the ones that are the most exquisite on," she tells me with the grave expression of someone imparting a major piece of wisdom.

I nod and accept the first one she hands me, a flowing ivory sheath that laces up the back.

"There's a slip hanging in the dressing room, and strapless bras in several different sizes," Veronica says. "Why don't you get into the appropriate undergarments, and I'll be in to help you lace up the dress in a moment? Just call when you're ready."

She holds the dressing room door open for me, and I quickly pull on the slip and bra before wriggling the dress over my head. It cascades beautifully over my curves, and I stare at myself in the mirror for a moment, struck momentarily mute by seeing myself in a bridal gown again after all these years.

This dress, made of silk, is completely different from the embroidered lace one I chose for my wedding to Patrick, and I'm surprised at how good this makes me feel. I *shouldn't* look the same. *This* isn't the same. And maybe, just maybe, that means it's okay that what I feel for Dan isn't the same as what I felt for Patrick.

"Hello, new me," I whisper to my reflection with a smile. "This is where you live. Reality. Don't forget that."

"Ready for my help?" Veronica asks from outside the dressing room door, and I open it to let her in. "Ooh la la!" she exclaims theatrically. "You look gorgeous!"

I smile at her in the mirror as she starts to lace up the back of the gown, then I shift my gaze to my own reflection again. I can imagine walking down the aisle in this dress. I can envision Dan standing there beaming at me. Surely that's a good sign. And as Veronica cinches the bodice, I can feel myself relaxing a little.

When she's done, she has me turn to look at the back of the dress with a hand mirror, and she tells me I look beautiful. Then she leads me out to the showroom, where Gina beams at me, and Susan claps her hands together. "Kate, you're a vision!" she exclaims.

"You look beautiful," Gina breathes, her eyes wide.

I turn to look in the three-way mirror, and as I twirl around, I see what they're seeing; the dress flatters my shape perfectly. In the mirror, I can see the reflection of the street outside, with a steady stream of people passing by, a few of them glancing in. I wonder if they're looking at me. Do I look like a joyful, first-time bride? After all, there's nothing that marks me as a widow. The black ribbon I wear is around my heart.

"This might just be the dress," I say, turning to Veronica. "I don't think I need to try on any more."

"Nonsense," she says. "You'll look lovely in each one."

I look warily at the rack of dresses waiting for me. "You want me to try on all of these?"

Veronica smiles thinly. "That's what brides do, dear."

Susan gives me a warning look, and I shrug and head back into the dressing room. For the next forty-five minutes, she and Gina *ooh* and *ah* over each dress I put on. The buttons and laces get more intricate with each subsequent gown, and I'm beginning to feel like I'd need a degree in rocket science just to figure out how some of them work.

Then, Veronica pulls a beautiful gown from the rack and brings it over. "This is my favorite," she tells me. "I think you'll love it too."

I gaze at its clean, flowing lines, the scalloped sweetheart neckline, the empire waist, and the long, detailed train. My lungs constrict. "Venetian lace," I murmur, reaching out to touch it.

"That's right," Veronica says, looking surprised. "How did you know?"

I sigh. "It looks a lot like the dress I wore to my first wedding."

"Wonderful!" she exclaims, entirely missing the point. "Then you'll love this one too. I think it'll fit you perfectly."

"I don't want to—" I start to say, but Veronica hustles me into

the dressing room with the gown anyhow and tells me she'll be
back in two minutes to help me into it.

It takes me a full minute of staring at the dress before I tentatively reach for it, fingering the pearly buttons on the back. I
remember Patrick running his hands over the buttons on my
dress a dozen years ago at our reception and whispering in my
ear, "I'm going to love taking this dress off, Mrs. Waithman."

I shudder and move my hand to the lace at the top of the
neckline. I remember Patrick's touch, his warm fingers caressing
my skin, just below my collarbone. "I can't believe you'll be mine
forever," he'd whispered in my ear as we danced our first dance
together.

My sigh is interrupted by Veronica's shrill voice outside the
dressing room door. "Ready to be buttoned in?" she asks.

I sniff and wipe my eyes. "Almost. Give me one second."

I resolve once again to push thoughts of my first wedding
away as I shrug into the beautiful ivory dress. "Ready," I say
through the door, and Veronica bustles in.

Her fingers are deft and nimble on the buttons, and I don't
look in the mirror until she's led me out to the main room.

"Kate," Susan says softly as Gina gasps.

I look up at my reflection and realize that on me, the dress
looks even more similar to my original gown than it did on the
rack. I turn slowly around to look at the girls, who are gaping at
me.

"It looks like . . ." Gina begins.

"I know," I say softly.

The two of them stare at me while I smooth my hands over
the delicate lace. I feel like I'm standing in a memory.

"You look beautiful, Kate," Susan says after a moment.

"Thanks." My voice is hollow as I turn back around to my
reflection. As I stare at the dress—a dress I know I can't wear to

marry Dan—something outside on the street catches my eye in the mirror. The world around me seems to slow down as I lock eyes with a girl staring in the window of Elisabetta's Bridal. She's holding the hand of a man—her father, I'm guessing—and her expression is sad. I know her immediately. But what I'm seeing isn't possible.

"Hannah?" I whisper, my heart thudding wildly as I spin around. I could swear that the girl whose face I just saw is the girl from my dreams, but I must be wrong. She can't be real.

The girl is staring back at me, her expression perplexed, as the man continues to lead her up the street. But is her confusion because she thinks she knows me too? Or because I'm a crazy lady in a wedding dress staring at her like I've lost my mind?

"Kate?" Susan says, but her concerned voice sounds very far away. "Kate? What's happening?"

I ignore her and call out "Hannah!" again, as if the girl can somehow hear me through the glass. But she's already disappearing from view, and the others in the shop—including my best friend and my sister—are staring at me like I'm a lunatic. Maybe I am. But all of a sudden, I don't care.

I stumble off the pedestal toward the door, but Veronica grabs me, her grip viselike. "Not so fast!" Her voice is an angry staccato. "You cannot leave in one of our dresses unless it's paid for!"

"Of course, of course." I begin to try to peel the dress off, right there in the middle of the store, and behind me, I can hear Susan screaming at me to stop, and Gina asking what's going on, but their voices are a blur. I can't get the dress off; the buttons are too tightly done, and I can't reach them. "Help me!" I cry out. Susan just stands there, but Gina rushes forward and begins unfastening my dress as quickly as she can.

But by the time she's done and I've discarded the gown and kicked off my heels, I already know it's too late. I rush to the door in my bra and slip anyhow, ignoring the whistles and laughter as I spill onto the sidewalk. "Hannah!" I cry. "Hannah?" I look desperately up and down the street, but the little girl and her father are nowhere to be seen. I turn around and come back inside, where Veronica is staring at me with disgust and Susan and Gina look worried.

"Kate?" Gina asks after a moment. "What just happened?"

"I thought I saw someone I knew," I answer, my voice shaking.

"Okay, let's get you dressed and out of here," Susan says in her take-charge voice, putting her arm around me and leading me back to the dressing room.

"If the dress was damaged at all, you'll have to pay for it!" Veronica calls after us.

Susan whirls on her. "It wasn't damaged," she snaps. "Now if you'll kindly hang it up, we'll be on our way." She shuts the dressing room door behind us and gestures to my pile of clothes in the corner.

"I'm sorry," I say, "I-I don't even know how to explain what just happened."

I expect Susan to say something biting about how she went out of her way to book this appointment for me, but when I look up after slipping my shirt over my head and buttoning my jeans, she's staring at me worriedly. "Are you okay?" she asks.

"I don't know," I mumble. I'm well aware that what I've just done is the behavior of a mentally unstable person, but I'd do it again in an instant. And that scares me as much as it should.

Fourteen

Outside the store, Susan and Gina hustle me up the street to Starbucks, and I can't help but scan the sidewalks in the vain hope that I'll see the girl who looked like Hannah again. My head is spinning and my mouth is dry. Was the girl in the window a figment of my imagination? Or have I been somehow dreaming of a real girl? Either way, it makes me feel like I'm going insane.

"Tea?" Susan asks once she's coaxed me into a seat in the corner of Starbucks. "I think a cup of tea will help."

I nod, wordless.

Susan glances at Gina. "Come with me to order, will you, Gina?" she asks. "Kate, you'll be okay for a second, right?"

"Sure," I say in a voice that sounds hollow to my own ears.

I watch as Gina and Susan converse in low tones near the Starbucks counter, shooting me a few furtive, concerned looks. Then I turn to look out the window, searching the faces, but it's just a sea of unfamiliar people immersed in a summer Saturday. Couples holding hands. Children skipping alongside their mothers. Women with huge shopping bags from Bloomingdale's and Henri Bendel. I feel painfully, starkly alone all of a sudden.

"Here you go, sweetie." Susan interrupts my train of thought. She puts a steaming cup of tea in front of me and takes the chair on my left. Gina settles into the chair on my right with an iced coffee. They exchange looks.

"Want to tell us what that was back there?" Gina asks gently.

I take a moment to gather my thoughts. "You know those dreams I've told you about?"

"About Patrick?" Susan ventures, glancing at Gina.

"Right." I return my gaze to my lap. "Well, there's a girl in the dreams too." I take a deep breath. "And when we were in the bridal shop, I could have sworn I saw her out the window."

My statement is greeted with silence, and when I look up again, they're both staring at me. "I know it sounds irrational," I say quickly. "And I know she doesn't really exist. She can't. You don't have to tell me that. But seeing that girl on the street—it was like the real world was colliding with the world I've been dreaming. Or maybe it's not a dream." I pause and draw a deep breath. "I'm crazy, aren't I?"

"When you say a girl, what do you mean?" Susan asks carefully, and I notice she hasn't refuted my suggestion of craziness. "Like someone our age? Or a child?"

"She's twelve," I tell them. "Well, she'll be thirteen next week, actually. It's her birthday." I smile faintly before it dawns on me how stupid I sound. "Sorry, I know you must think I'm nuts."

Susan and Gina exchange looks. "No. Not nuts," Gina says softly.

I glance out the window again before adding, "I dream her in so much detail. I mean, right down to the chipped purple polish on her nails, the crush she has on one of the guys from One Direction, and the fact that she's hard of hearing." I pause and without meeting their eyes add, "Also, in the dreams I've been having, she's my daughter."

When I turn back to them, I'm surprised to see Susan looking relieved. "Well, this makes complete sense now," she says. "You're just upset because you can't have children. This is a natural reaction to that, to dream up a little girl. As for her being hard of hearing, that's obviously because of that class you started taking."

"But I had the dream first," I say without looking at her. "Before I started taking the class."

"Kate, is that why you enrolled?" Gina asks carefully. "Because you were dreaming of a deaf daughter?"

I hang my head. "Maybe."

"Okay," Gina says after a moment of silence. "You know what? Let's get you home. It's been a stressful morning, and I don't think today's the best day for dress shopping. We can go again in a few weeks."

"Can we sit here for just a minute?" I ask in a small voice.

Gina scoots her chair closer to mine, and Susan does the same. "Honey," Gina says, rubbing my back, "we can stay here for as long as you want."

Susan eventually takes me home, and after I hug her good-bye and retreat to the bathroom to get some ibuprofen for my throbbing head, I can hear her talking to Dan in low tones in the living room.

"I told him you've been having some really vivid dreams about having a child," she whispers as I walk her to the door. "He needed to know." She pauses and adds, "But I didn't tell him the part about Patrick. I don't think you should either." She hugs me good-bye with a promise to call me tonight, and she's gone before I can reply.

I close the door behind her and walk slowly into the living room, where Dan is sitting on the couch, his elbows on his knees, his hands clasped. "Babe," he says, jumping up as I enter. "Are you okay?"

I nod as he pulls me against his chest. His hugs have always felt safe to me, and now, I close my eyes and relax into him, falling into the familiar rhythm of his steady breathing.

"So Susan says you've been having dreams about being a mother?" he asks once I've pulled back. "About a little girl who's ours?"

I blink at the word *ours,* but of course he'd assume that. "Something like that."

"And you thought you saw her today?" he asks cautiously.

I take a deep breath. "I saw someone who looked like the girl I was dreaming about," I tell him. "I think— Maybe I'm just overtired or something." But I realize as soon as I say the words that there's a little piece of me that believes that somehow, I really *did* see Hannah on the street. But that's impossible.

"Why didn't you tell me?" he asks. "These dreams, they were obviously powerful enough to make you sign up for those classes . . ."

I hang my head. "I knew how stupid it would sound."

"Kate, I wish you'd said something. I thought you'd lost your mind when you decided to learn sign language for no apparent reason. Now it makes sense."

"It does? You don't think it makes me sound crazy?"

He sighs. "I think it sounds like you're sad. And I'm sorry you're sad." He sits back down on the sofa and stares straight ahead for a moment. When the silence makes me uneasy, I sink down next to him. "About kids," he says hesitantly after a moment. "I . . . I'm afraid this is going to drive a wedge between us. I think we need to make sure we're on the same page." He pauses, and when I don't say anything, he goes on. "I just assumed you were thinking like I was: that we were too old to become parents. But I should have discussed it with you. It's just that everything with you has felt so easy. I figured we'd be in agreement about this too."

"Yeah," I agree softly. *But maybe it shouldn't have felt easy,* I realize. *Maybe that's one of the problems.*

"Kids are a difficult topic for me," Dan continues without looking at me. He scratches the back of his head and sighs. "My marriage to Siobhan broke up over fertility issues. She wanted a baby. We couldn't have one. And we drifted apart because of it."

"I thought you split up because she cheated on you."

"We did. But it was the baby thing that drove a wedge between us in the first place. I just don't want that to happen with you."

I stare at him. "I wish you'd told me."

He shrugs. "Yeah, well, you don't spend a lot of time talking about Patrick, either. The past is the past, Kate."

"Except it's not," I hear myself say. Dan looks at me quizzically, and I shrug. "What I mean is, the past isn't gone. It's what brought us here. So what happened with Siobhan, what happened with Patrick, those are things that matter."

"But you shut down every time we start to talk about anything serious," Dan says softly. "You won't talk about the past. You won't talk about the future." He pauses. "I've been trying so damned hard, Kate, to just focus on the here and now. But now it seems like you're angry at me for that."

"I'm not angry at you," I say, but I know that's not true. There's been something dark simmering beneath the surface lately, and I have the uneasy feeling that it's because deep down, I'm irritated at Dan for not being Patrick. I wasn't supposed to grow old with this golden boy who does everything right. I was supposed to have a big, messy, brilliant life with a man whose flaws were as endearing as everything else about him. It's just not fair.

"Yeah, well, you're never angry, are you?" His tone, suddenly sharp, stings. "But you've been on edge with me ever since you found out about your infertility. Like it was my fault."

"It's not your fault." My answer is automatic. "Of course it's not."

"*I* know that," Dan says. "I'm just not so sure you do."

I bite my lip and look at my hands. "I'm just not ready to close the door on having kids."

"Kate—" Dan begins, but I cut him off.

"No. I need to say this. I don't think I knew how much I wanted to be a mother until I found out I couldn't have a child," I say in a small voice. "And I know we should have discussed this before now, and maybe it's my fault for not doing that. But now . . . Well, maybe that's why I'm dreaming of having a daughter. I know it doesn't sound logical. But I want to be a mom, Dan. I really, really do. I think that's what I was supposed to be all along."

He's silent for a minute. "So what are we talking about? Adoption?"

I nod, holding my breath.

"Baby, you're forty," Dan says without looking at me. "I'm forty-five. By the time we went through the whole process of getting a child . . . Well, I just don't want us to be old parents."

"So maybe we could adopt a child who's a little older."

"Or we could admit that maybe your infertility is a sign." His tone is gentle, but his words make me cringe. "Maybe it's fate telling us parenthood isn't in the cards for us."

"But—"

"It's just that I've seen too many of our friends' marriages ruined because of issues related to their kids," he interrupts. "And those are their biological kids."

The words make me bristle. "An adopted child wouldn't be any less ours."

"I don't mean it like that. I just mean they could come with extra complications."

"So could a child we give birth to, Dan," I shoot back. "Maybe life isn't supposed to be a cakewalk. Maybe the greatest things in life come from the greatest challenges. Kids complicate things. That's just the way it is. But the complications are all worth it in the end. Why are you refusing to see that?"

"I'm not refusing to see anything, Kate! I'm just expressing my point of view."

"But you say it like it's a final decision! Like I don't have the right to an opinion!"

"You have the right to an opinion, of course," he says with a dramatic shrug. "But that doesn't make you correct."

I stare at him. "So now I'm wrong because I feel differently than you?"

"No, you're wrong because you can't just change course midstream."

"I'm not changing course, Dan! I never made my mind up in the first place."

He looks at me for a minute. "You seriously think that we wouldn't be terrible parents, Kate? We love to eat out and travel and buy nice clothes and drink nice wine. Where's there room in that kind of lifestyle for a kid?"

"Those are your things, not mine," I reply softly. "And no, Dan, I don't think I'd be a terrible parent." I think about the way I love Hannah so much in the dreams, the way my insides flip-flop with joy every time I look at her, the way she's turned out to be such a sweet kid. "I think I'd be a good mother, actually."

"Too bad your ovaries don't agree."

My mouth falls open, and I stare at him, wide-eyed and wounded.

"Shit, I'm sorry," he says immediately. "I don't know why I said that."

But I don't reply. Instead, I turn to stare out the window, blinking back tears. The streets below are still full of people enjoying the warm summer afternoon. A couple walks by holding hands; a woman in shorts and a tank top pushes a stroller and tugs a wobbling toddler behind her; two teenage girls decked out in leather and lace slouch past. My eyes fix on a man carrying a smiling little boy on his shoulders; the boy has a baseball glove on his left hand and a Yankees cap on his head, and he's chattering excitedly about something while the man listens, his expression amused.

"What if I already had a child?" I ask, almost without meaning to.

"What?"

"When you met me, I mean," I say, turning back to Dan. "If Patrick and I had had a child together before he died. If I was a single mom, would you have still asked me out?"

Dan looks at me for a minute. "Honestly, I don't think so. But Kate, it's a moot point. So let's just be glad that wasn't the case, okay?"

Wordless, I nod.

It's not until we get into bed that night, Dan wrapping his arms around me and murmuring that he loves me, that I realize we haven't really decided anything at all. We talked circles around the subject and then retreated back to our own corners, just like we always do. Maybe that's what I've been doing for a long time now—walking a road to nowhere because it's easier than letting go of the past.

Finally, I drift off to sleep, the face of the Hannah lookalike from the wedding shop window imprinted on my mind.

Fifteen

The next morning, I know before I even open my eyes that I'm back in my life with Patrick once again. The light is brighter here, the scent of the sheets familiar in a different way, the sounds of the street outside distinct from the sounds of the Murray Hill apartment I share with Dan.

"Morning," I say, opening my eyes and rolling over to face my husband, whose face is illuminated by the sunlight streaming in. *He looks like an angel,* I think for a fleeting second before I realize just how on the nose I am.

This time, though, the dream—or whatever it is—is different. It still feels incredibly real, but there's a milky fog filling the room; it reminds me of being in an airplane slicing through a wispy cloud. For the first time, I wonder fleetingly if I'm in heaven. But I push the idea quickly away, because that would mean Hannah's dead too. And she can't be dead, because she doesn't exist. Patrick's eyelids twitch a bit, and he slowly opens them, blinking into the morning light for a second before focusing on me. "Katielee," he murmurs, leaning forward to kiss me sweetly on the lips. "Is your head feeling better?"

"My head?"

"The headache you had last night," he says, raising an eyebrow.

The problem with getting only glimpses into this world is that I miss so much of the in-between. But obviously, even though I can't recall most of it, I *am* somehow in this dream world on a regular basis. Life seems to keep happening here with me in it. This both confuses me and makes me feel deeply sad.

"Yes," I manage. "My head's fine."

Patrick smiles at me, then glances at the clock. "Well, up and at 'em. We've got Hannah's recital this morning." He kisses me again then gets out of bed. I watch as he slips on a pair of pajama pants over his boxer briefs and pulls a white T-shirt over his head. "You want to handle Hannah's good luck pancakes? Or should I?"

I'm silent for a second as the information rushes in. I know in an instant that Patrick's referring to a piano recital, that Hannah adores her teacher, who goes by Miss Kay, and that she's excited about the Beethoven piece she'll be performing. I'm so startled by the sudden influx of knowledge that I manage only a confused, "Um . . ."

"Okay, I'll do it. You just get dressed." Patrick disappears out the bedroom door before I can reply, and in a few seconds, I can hear clattering in the kitchen as he takes the frying pan out of the cabinet.

I climb out of bed and open the closet door. I'm strangely unsurprised to find that my clothes are a mix of items I have in my real life and items I've never seen before. It makes sense, doesn't it? If this is an alternate reality, I would have seen some of the same clothes in the stores and found them desirable, simply because I'm the same person with the same tastes.

But *am* I the same person? It occurs to me how much losing Patrick changed me. In this dream world, maybe I'm carefree, happy, a person who throws caution to the wind and who doesn't know yet that the smallest moment can twist your life into something unrecognizable. I hope I am. That's who I was before Patrick died and the world shifted on its axis.

I pull out a dress that catches my eye; it's tea length and flowy and made of a silky fabric of deep purple and forest green swirls. I love it, but in my real life, I never would have bought it, because Dan would have laughed and called it "hippy dippy." I swallow a sudden surge of annoyance, throw the dress on quickly, add some strappy sandals, and head to the bathroom to wash my face and put on some makeup.

When I head into the kitchen a few minutes later, Hannah's already at the table, dressed in a blue dress and black Mary Janes with low heels. She smiles when she sees me. "Morning," she says aloud, then asks in sign language, *Is your head better?*

Yes, I sign back by nodding my right hand while I nod my head. *Thank you*.

Patrick winks at me as he approaches with a pan full of pancakes. "Blueberry and peanut butter, you weirdos," he says, flipping several onto Hannah's plate and two onto mine.

We both make faces at him, and as Hannah digs in to her breakfast, I carefully sign, *You look beautiful.*

She grins and signs back *Thank you* while nodding and smiling. I mirror the sign, because I know from Andrew that although its meaning is closer to saying *thank you* in return, it's also a common way to indicate the phrase *You're welcome*. I glance over at Patrick, who's standing at the stove, watching us closely.

Love you, he mouths to me, and it hurts my heart so much that for a few seconds I can't breathe.

"So," I say, turning back to Hannah and forcing myself to act normal. "Are you ready for this recital or what?"

"Mom!" she says aloud, rolling her eyes at me. "You know I've been practicing every day for a month."

"Right. Of course." I know somehow that she's good. Really good. And she's serious about it. I also know suddenly that she's been playing since she was three, that I took her to her first lesson six months after she got her cochlear implants because I wanted her to be exposed to music, and that Patrick and I fought about it at first, because he thought we would be influencing her interests by pushing her into something she hadn't asked for on her own.

It reminds me suddenly that in real life, Patrick and I used to fight sometimes, big and messy. Sometimes we'd argue about the important things—where we'd live, who we were spending the holidays with—but other times, it would be about something small and stupid, like who left the lid off the mayonnaise jar. And I hadn't been scared to argue with him, because I'd never feared him walking away.

So why am I so scared to fight with Dan now? Or with anyone in my life, for that matter? I've spent the last decade thinking of myself as even-tempered and reasonable. But what if I've just been a chicken? What if I'm so terrified of losing the people I love that I've been slowly giving away pieces of myself just to avoid confrontation?

"Uh, hello? Earth to Mom."

I snap back to the conversation I'm having with Hannah and shoot her an embarrassed smile. "Sorry, honey."

She makes a face at me and signs, *You're being weird again.*

Patrick joins us at the table, and when I'm finished eating, he grabs my right hand with his left and holds it clasped in his lap while he eats. I squeeze back and hope he knows what I'm saying: that this moment, the three of us here together, is perfect. I never want it to end.

Get dressed, Dad! Hannah signs, jumping up from the table. *We're going to be late!*

"Do the dishes, kiddo," he replies. "I'll be changed in a minute." She nods and heads over to the sink, while Patrick beckons for me to follow him.

I sit on the edge of the bed while he strips off his T-shirt and pajama pants. Desire sparks in my belly again, and I have to remind myself that we're running short on time, that we have to leave soon. Still, I can't stop myself from longing for him.

I watch as he pulls on khakis then grabs a white linen shirt from the closet and buttons it over his chest. "You look amazing," I murmur.

He smiles. "I was going to say the same to you. You get more beautiful with every passing year, you know."

I snort. "No, I get older and heavier and more wrinkled."

He rolls his eyes. "First of all, that's not true. Secondly, getting older is beautiful, because that's life."

"Right," I murmur. "Life." I feel guilty and foolish for ruing the things that are merely evidence of a life being lived.

"I'm sorry, Patrick," I whisper into the silence after he leaves the room.

Outside, we pile into a cab and I try to memorize the address Patrick gives the driver—*321 Bleecker Street*—so that I can find it later in the real world. It turns out to be a second-floor studio with hardwood floors, big beamed ceilings, and three dozen mismatched folding chairs set up facing a single piano at the front of the room. When we walk through the door, Hannah hugs us both quickly, then she bounds off to where two other teenage girls are deep in conversation. One of them high-fives her, and the other greets her with a friendly smile.

"What is this place?" I whisper. Patrick gives me an odd look and the room fades a little, so I force an innocent smile as I wait for my mind to load all the details I'm somehow already familiar with. And just like that, I suddenly know that this is the studio of a woman named Dolores Kay and that Hannah loves it here. "What I meant is, it's a beautiful place," I amend, and the room comes back into focus.

Patrick nods. "Miss Kay has done a great job."

Just then, a tiny, elfin woman in her sixties with a salt-and-pepper pixie cut and a black shift dress interrupts our conversation by banging a few of the keys on the piano until the room quiets down.

"Welcome, welcome, friends and parents!" she chirps in a British accent. "For those of you who don't already know me, I'm Dolores Kay, and of course this is our annual summer recital! Now let's find some seats and we'll get started!"

She strides purposefully toward the cluster of girls that includes Hannah, and Patrick and I find seats in the second row. "Save that one for my mom," he says, nodding to the seat beside mine. He checks his watch. "She should be here any minute now."

"Your mom's coming?" I ask with a smile. I hadn't expected to encounter anyone real in this dream world, but seeing Joan will ground this fantasy in at least some degree of reality. I'm surprised by how elated this makes me feel.

"Of course," Patrick says, and as if on cue, the door in the back of the room swings open, and Joan enters. For a moment, as she walks toward us, all I can do is stare.

"What's wrong with her?" I whisper to myself just before Joan arrives beside us, leaving Patrick only enough time to look at me in confusion. But before the words are even out of my mouth, I already know. Breast cancer. Stage 2. Diagnosed two and a half months ago after I insisted she get a mammogram. I run my thumb over the healing cut on my fingertip and worry: If Joan is sick in this dream world, what if she has breast cancer in the real world too?

Her cheekbones jut out, and she looks gaunt and drawn. "Hi, you two!" she says, beaming at us. She pecks me on the cheek first before planting a kiss on Patrick's forehead. Then she surprises me by pulling her loosely wrapped red scarf down, revealing a fully bare head. "It's too darned hot for this thing!" she exclaims, fanning herself with an issue of the *New Yorker* she pulls from her purse. "I'll tell you what, the one good thing about cancer is that I get to feel the cool breeze on my head in the summer." She winks at me and adds, "Ever the optimist, right?"

I continue to gape until Patrick nudges me, which snaps me out of it. "Joan," I murmur, and then I can't continue, so I settle for pulling her into a tight hug. I can feel her bony frame through her baggy shirt. "Are you okay?"

"Oh, I'm feeling fine, Kate," she says with a sigh. "Today happens to be one of the good days. The chemo's just a little harder on my body than I thought it would be. But you know that. I must sound like a broken record to you, sweetheart."

I take a deep breath, trying not to cry. I want to say more, but Miss Kay claps her hands then and brings the recital to order by introducing the first student to perform, a girl named Hira who looks about Hannah's age. As Hira plays Bach's Prelude No. 1 in C Major, stumbling over a few notes here and there but staying in rhythm, my mind whirls. I have to call Joan as soon as I wake up. I have to make sure she's okay. I almost don't notice the corners of the room going fuzzy.

The audience claps when Hira is done, and her performance is followed by four others. Hannah is the last to go, and Miss Kay tells us she'll be playing the first movement of Beethoven's Piano

Sonata No. 32 in C Minor. I know it's an extremely complicated piece of music, and I'm concerned that Hannah's being set up for failure. It's more than a typical child, even a talented one, should be able to master.

"Patrick?" I murmur, but he just puts a gentle finger on my lips and smiles as Hannah removes her cochlear implant processors and sets them on the bench beside her. As she begins to play, the room goes still. I'm frozen as I watch her fingers move swiftly across the keys, coaxing a complex melody out of the piano. Her tempo is a little slower than I expected, but she stays in perfect rhythm, and I realize after a few moments that I actually *like* the speed at which she's playing. It's becoming clear that this is her interpretation of the piece, and that she's deliberately putting her own touch on it. I'm floored.

When she finishes, the room is so silent and motionless that it seems frozen. For a split second, I wonder if I'm the only one who heard how beautiful her playing was. But then the audience bursts into applause, a few parents even standing and whistling. Patrick squeezes my hand and tears of pride sting my eyes.

When the clapping subsides, Miss Kay steps to the center of the room and gestures to the piano, where Hannah is still sitting, looking self-conscious. "As I mentioned," Miss Kay says, "that was one of Beethoven's piano sonatas. In fact, it was the last one he wrote, about five years before his death. By the time he composed it, he was almost entirely deaf."

I hear a few people mumble words of surprise to each other, and I can feel myself leaning forward to hear what she'll say next.

"Perhaps then," Miss Kay continues, "it's appropriate to tell you now that Hannah, my star pupil, is deaf too. She has cochlear implants, which help her to process speech, but they have a different effect on music, so Hannah removes hers to play. Much like Beethoven himself, whom Hannah says is an inspiration to her, she played this entire sonata with only a very small fraction of the hearing most of you have."

The room seems to explode in a cacophony of astonished voices and exclamations, and I feel the warm heat of pride spreading across my face. But do I have the right to feel proud of a girl I have no real recollection of raising, a girl I've only just met?

Patrick interrupts my train of thought by squeezing my hand.

"I want to stay," I blurt out before I can think about it. The room goes instantly dark and blurry, and I regret the words right away.

"What?" Patrick asks from somewhere far away. "Kate, we promised we'd take Hannah and my mom to brunch, honey."

"Right!" I manage to say into the void. He thinks I'm saying I want to stay in this room—not this life. "Brunch!" The room comes back into focus, and I'm relieved to be here again but sad to know it's only temporary. There's no way to make this world mine.

After pierogis at Veselka, the Ukranian restaurant on Second Avenue where Patrick and I used to love having lazy Sunday breakfasts, we put Joan in a cab back to the train station, then Patrick, Hannah, and I decide to walk home because it's an unusually crisp summer day, at least fifteen degrees cooler than it was yesterday. It occurs to me as we make our way down Second that the real-world forecast hadn't called for a temperature drop, which is just a further reminder that this dream isn't real. I take a deep breath and reach for Hannah's hand on one side and Patrick's on the other. I'm determined to enjoy every second of this fantasy before it fades away.

On the way home, Hannah keeps up an almost endless stream of chatter, telling us about her friends, her obsession with One

Direction, and her burning desire—as she puts it—to have a new iPhone. I can see Patrick suppressing a smile as she extols the virtues of the phone, and when he and I exchange amused looks, I feel a deep sense of sadness and regret. The simple perfection of this moment is the kind of thing I would almost certainly have taken for granted if this was the life I was really living. Instead, because it's the life I missed out on, every passing second feels like a miracle.

I look away, pretending to study a billboard, so that neither Patrick nor Hannah can see how close I am to crying.

Back at our apartment later that night, I'm stunned to still be here; it's the longest I've spent in this reality. Might I be able to stay for the night, awaken here tomorrow morning? I think I already know the answer is no, but I want to believe in the possibility.

"Want to tuck Hannah in?" Patrick asks me with a gentle smile as she emerges from the bathroom in a cloud of steam and plods into her bedroom. "I'm going to finish the dishes."

"Of course." My heart flutters at the prospect of a few minutes alone to tell her I love her and that I hope she has the sweetest of dreams.

I head down the hall and knock on her door then peek in to make sure she's dressed. She is, in a long pink nightshirt. "Hannah?" I say loudly, and she turns.

"Hey, Mom," she says, smiling back. Then she signs, *I am going to brush my teeth,* before disappearing out the door.

I stand still in her room, breathing in and out, while I wait for her to return. Her walls, I notice, are plastered with One Direction posters, a poster from the first *Hunger Games* movie, and a few dozen snapshots of her and her friends, taped crookedly on the walls by her bed. I see a list on notebook paper, written in pink and purple marker, that says *Hannah's Best Qualities,* signed by Meggie. I lean closer and smile as I read items such as, *Hannah always makes time for her friends* and *Hannah snorts when she laughs really hard.* I smile sadly at the list, memorizing Meggie's list of Hannah's attributes. It feels desperately unfair that I haven't had a chance to make a list of my own.

But then again, I have, somehow. All the things written in Meggie's girlie hand, with hearts over the *i*'s, are the things I already somehow know and love about Hannah too. Still, I can't help but feel deprived of the opportunity to discover them myself instead of being implanted with memories that aren't really mine.

I push the sadness away and turn to study her walls, which are also covered with pencil sketches. I smile when I notice that they're each signed by Hannah—and they're good. The sketches are of all sorts of things: people's faces, animals, seascapes, street corners. I lean in closer to examine the sketch that hangs just to the right of her bed. It's clearly Patrick and me, each of us holding one of a younger Hannah's hands. In the picture, she looks about nine or ten, and she's beaming. A Mickey Mouse balloon floats aloft, tied to her wrist. Behind us, Cinderella Castle rises behind Disney World's Main Street U.S.A. I wait for the rush of memories to fill my brain—and suddenly I remember walking toward the castle; I remember eating chocolate-covered Mickey Mouse ice cream bars; I remember watching Hannah's eyes widen as she looked out over the deck of a pirate ship at the fictional London below us on the Peter Pan ride. I feel my eyes fill with tears; the memories seem so real, but I can't understand how.

Hannah bustles back into the room then, hair still damp and face freshly scrubbed. I slowly sign to her, *You are very good.* Then aloud, I add, "You're really talented, Hannah. Your drawings, they're amazing."

She rolls her eyes. *You are being weird again,* she signs. *You have seen them a million times.* But I can tell she's hiding a smile; the compliment means something to her.

This one? I sign, my face a question mark as I point to the sketch of our family of three at Disney World.

Hannah's face softens. *My favorite,* she signs back. "It was the best day," she says aloud. "The first time you and Dad took me to Disney World."

"Oh," I say, my heart aching. "Maybe we can go again some-day. I'd really like that."

Hannah climbs into bed and smiles at me. *Good night, Mom,* she signs, followed by a big yawn.

Good night, I sign back. *I love you.* I repeat the words aloud, if for no other reason than to hear them for myself.

"Love you too," Hannah says. She takes off her headpieces, sets them on her nightstand, and rolls over, pulling her covers up to her chin. I sit by her bedside and watch her until she drifts off to sleep.

I find Patrick waiting for me in the living room. "You got her to sleep?" he asks as I join him on the sofa.

I nod. "We took her to Disney World," I say, thinking of the picture, of the smiles on our faces, of the way Hannah so expertly captured a moment I would have loved to see.

Patrick looks at me oddly. "Of course we did."

And then I remember a conversation we'd had early on, just a few months after we began dating. Patrick has asked me what my happiest childhood memory was, and I'd told him it was the time my parents took Susan and me to Disney World, in the late '80s. *One day, when we have a child, we'll go to Disney World too,* Patrick had promised. "We did all the things we talked about doing, didn't we?" I whisper, at once profoundly sad.

His brow furrows as the room grows a little dimmer. "Of course, Kate."

As he looks at me with concern, I think about Joan. "Patrick, your mother . . . ?" I let my voice trail off. "Is there anything I can do?"

"You've already done so much, sweetheart. And she's doing better," he says. "I think I might take a few days off next week to take her to her doctor's appointments." He yawns and pulls me close. "You ready for bed, hon?"

I listen to the pounding of his heart for a moment with my eyes closed. "I don't want to go to sleep yet," I murmur.

He doesn't say anything for a moment, then he takes my hand in his and traces the lifeline on my palm. "Do you know what today is?" he whispers, and I'm aware that the edges of my vision are growing ragged, and the dreamy film is once again descending over the room. "Patrick?" I say, but I can't hear my own voice anymore.

"Today's the day I proposed to you, thirteen years ago," he says, but his voice is already wrapped in a rushing sound that reminds me of the ocean sucking the waves back out to sea. "And when you said yes," he continues, "it made me the happiest man in the world."

Something inside of me bursts open. "Can't I stay this time?" I ask God, looking up toward heaven. "Please?"

"What?" Patrick replies, his voice far away and confused.

And then he's gone, his voice merely an echo in the darkness. "I love you!" I cry out, but the sound vanishes into the abyss.

Sixteen

"What'd you say, babe?"

Dan's sleep-drenched voice cuts into the haze and pulls me to the surface. I gasp and blink into the darkness. I know I'm back in my reality. I hate that my stomach twists with disappointment when I roll over and see Dan beside me instead of Patrick.

"Nothing," I mumble, forcing myself to take a breath and focus. "Just a dream. Or something. I'm sorry. Didn't mean to wake you."

He smiles and pulls me toward him. "Well, I love you too, babe." I realize that my last words to Patrick must have come out of my mouth, and Dan thinks they were directed at him.

I force a smile but can't seem to make myself say the words back. Each time I get a glimpse of a life that could have been with Patrick, I wake up seeing Dan a little more clearly.

But is that really true? Is it clarity that's flooding in, or useless nostalgia for a past I can't bring back? Because whatever the visits with Patrick and Hannah are, they're not real. Patrick is gone. And Dan is right here. I feel completely disoriented, and it occurs to me that maybe I've been standing in place with my eyes closed for so long that I have no idea where I'm supposed to be anymore.

"Kate?" Dan's voice is a question, and as I refocus on his face, I see longing there. He reaches out to stroke my cheek, gently, and then his hand travels down the curve of my collarbone, tracing my clavicle to my breastbone, on to the swell of my breast. "Kate," he whispers, and this time, it's not a question, but an answer. I close my eyes and try to wipe my mind clean as his lips meet mine, as he gently shifts the weight of his body on top of me. "Kate," he says once more, but his voice is low and pleading now, and it's what finally unleashes me from reality.

I don't respond, because I fear I'll say Patrick's name, but I let my body take over, doing my best to turn off my whirling mind. *Dan,* I say to myself, trying to root myself to the moment. *Dan. Dan is here. He's a good man. He loves you. He wants you.*

And, as it turns out, I want him too. My body learned how to replace the memories long ago, and so I let it do just that. I get swept away in the physical tide, and I only slip up once, when my brain comes crashing in, and I hear myself murmur, "I can't," just as Dan slides inside me.

"You can't what?" he asks, pausing and looking at me with concern.

I'm so startled that I've said the words aloud that I don't answer for a moment. But when I do, all that comes out is, "Nothing."

He looks unconvinced, but after a moment, he begins moving again, and I concentrate on the motion and try to forget about everything else.

The day turns out to be much cooler than the Weather Channel had predicted, and as we turn the news on that morning, the local anchor is talking about the unexpected cold front. I grab a cardigan on the way out the door and try to shake off the questions in my head.

It's not until later that day, after Dan and I have gone to brunch with his friends Jon and Christine, and after we've seen a movie with Gina and Wayne, that I finally remember what happened to Joan in my dream.

I gasp aloud, startling Dan, Gina, and Wayne on the way out of the theater.

"What is it, baby?" Dan asks with concern.

"I was just—I was thinking about Joan and wondering how she is," I say feebly.

"What made you think of Joan, Kate?" Dan asks carefully, in the kind of voice you'd use with a young child who's just said something outrageous.

I glance at Gina, who's looking at me oddly, then back to Dan. "The mother in the movie reminded me of her," I lie.

Dan nods and seems to accept this, and soon, he's involved in a long conversation with Wayne about the Mets.

"You okay?" Gina whispers, squeezing my hand.

"Sure," I say, but she doesn't look convinced.

"Anyone up for dinner?" Dan asks, saving me from any additional questions. Wayne says he and Gina have to get home because their nanny has dinner plans of her own tonight, so we say good-bye and Dan hails a cab to take us to Little Italy, which has always been my favorite place in the city for comfort food.

We get a spot at one of Puglia's long tables, and after the waiter has taken our order and brought us a carafe of red wine, I excuse myself and head to the bathroom. It's empty, so I quickly pull out my phone and dial Joan's number. I feel a bubble of worry when her answering machine picks up. I hang up and dial her cell, but there's no answer there, either, so I leave a message asking her to call me back as soon as possible. Knowing I've probably crossed the bridge to annoying now, I call her home phone again and leave the same message, adding that I have something important I need to ask her.

After I shove my phone back into my purse, I quickly splash some water on my face to brace myself, then I touch up my lipstick. I take a deep breath, nod at myself in the mirror, and head back out to Dan.

An order of garlic bread has arrived by the time I get back, and when I sit down, Dan hands me the glass of wine he's already poured. "To us, and to the future," he says.

I raise my glass and murmur, "To us."

"So," Dan begins a moment later, after he's eaten a piece of bread, "are you looking forward to seeing your mom this week?"

I blink a few times, embarrassed that I'd almost forgotten about her visit. "Of course," I say. I attempt a smile and add, "Although we both know she's just escaping the hundred-degree heat in Florida." My father died seven years ago, and after that, my mother decided to reinvent herself, moving south to a retirement community about twenty-five miles from Disney World. She goes to yoga classes three times a week, runs 5Ks, and swears she's in the best shape of her life. She's also had a steady string of boyfriends, which I found sort of amusing until she sat me down three summers ago and told me that if she could get back on the horse, so to speak, so should I. That was the day I knew she had turned the corner from worrying about me to simply pitying me. "I'm going to take the morning off on Thursday to go get her from the airport," I add.

Dan smiles. "All those years of living here, and she's still not comfortable getting to and from JFK on her own."

I roll my eyes. "I think she just likes the attention."

"Well, you're a good daughter," Dan says, his voice softening. "And a good person, Kate. I'm one lucky guy."

"I'm lucky too," I murmur.

"About the fight we had last night," he says, "I just wanted to say sorry. I don't think I listened to you very well. I'm not saying my mind's closed about kids, okay? I just need some time to process this."

I feel a small surge of hope. "Okay."

"Are we all right? You and me?"

It takes me a minute to answer. "I don't know. But I want us to be."

Over the next hour and a half, we stuff ourselves with gnocchi Bolognese and linguini with white clam sauce, followed by tiramisu and cannoli. We finish our carafe of red, and Dan orders a pair of chocolate martinis to go with our dessert.

"Are we celebrating something this evening?" the waiter asks when he arrives with our drinks.

Dan shrugs, his smile loosened by the alcohol. "Just a beautiful night in a beautiful city with my beautiful girl," he says.

We're laughing and reminiscing about the trip we took last year to Italy by the time our check comes, and as we walk up Mulberry Street toward Canal to grab a cab after dinner, Dan carries our leftovers, holds my hand, and continues to tell me an elaborate, funny story about a coworker's European trip gone terribly wrong.

It's not until we're in a cab headed home and the laughter has died down that the shame moves in. There's nothing wrong with Dan. He's the same man he's always been. It's just that I can't keep living two versions of the same life forever. And the truth is, this isn't the version I'd choose.

On the night before my mother arrives, I head to St. Paula's for my third sign language class with Andrew. I'm looking forward to it more than I expected, and I'm oddly proud of the fact that

I've spent my spare time in the last few days looking up signs I wanted to know. I've learned to say, *Good job, Now try this, piano, keyboard, guitar, maracas, sing, notes,* and *music,* and I've grown eager to work with the kids again. I'm hoping to talk to Andrew after class about scheduling another visit with Molly and Riajah as well as a first visit with the other girl he mentioned.

I'm sitting in my folding chair in the church basement, waiting for Andrew to arrive, when Vivian bustles in and sits down next to me. I look up from the file I'm reviewing on a new client named Simon and smile at her.

"Do you have the time?" she asks, pointing to her wrist.

I check my watch and tell her it's two minutes to seven, and she whoops loudly.

"I can't believe I've actually made it before class started for once!" she crows, and for the first time, I realize her accent is British. "Andrew isn't here yet, is he?"

"Not yet."

"Double score!" she cries, pumping her fist in the air. "Usually, I'm that complete slacker student who bounds in late and interrupts the teacher at work. You know, like last time. And the time before. But huzzah! An on-time arrival! Surely the world is spinning crookedly on its axis as we speak."

I laugh. "Have you taken many classes like this?"

"Oh, my dear, I take them all the time!" she says as she unzips the raincoat she's inexplicably wearing and wriggles out of it. "The last class I took was on origami. Before that, it was computer programming. I'm sixty-eight years young, and you want to know my secret? If you're continuously learning, you never get old."

"Well, that's a good philosophy," I say as she folds her raincoat over the back of her chair. "What made you decide to take an ASL course?"

"I've already taken seventeen other language courses, including

British sign language, which is completely different," she says with a shrug. "I like to know a little bit of everything. ASL has been on my list for a while, but I just hadn't found a class that appealed to me. Then I heard about this one from a friend. So what about you?" she continues, barely pausing for breath. "What brings you here? Why are you taking this class? Who are you learning for?"

"My daughter," I say, then I clap my hand over my mouth. I can't believe I just admitted aloud to taking this class for the benefit of a child who doesn't exist.

"Oh, how lovely," Vivian says, but she looks confused. "Now, help me to understand this. Why now? Did your daughter just go deaf?"

I look at my lap. "No. I just found her recently," I mumble.

"Found her?"

I realize I'm sounding crazier by the second, so I quickly amend that to the most logical explanation I can think of. "Adopted her, I mean. I just adopted her recently."

"Oh my!" Vivian says, her hands flying to her cheeks as she beams at me. "Kate, that's just lovely!"

"Oh. Yeah, thanks," I mumble. I've now dug myself even deeper into the crazy hole.

"You know, I truly believe adoption is one of the greatest unheralded blessings in the world," she continues, her expression turning earnest. "Think how beautiful it is to give a child a home and to become a family because you choose to! Maybe that's the best way to make a family, don't you think?"

"Sure," I say weakly.

"So," she says, clapping her hands. "Tell me about this daughter of yours. What's her name?"

"Um," I begin, but fortunately, I'm saved from answering when Andrew hurries through the door to the basement, his arms full of books and paperwork.

"Sorry I'm a little late, guys!" he says, dumping everything on the table at the front of the makeshift classroom.

There's a mumbled chorus of forgiveness, then Andrew asks if any of us have been practicing signing on our own.

"Raise your hand if you've been working on ASL signs independently, outside of class," he says. Amy's hand shoots up as Vivian and I exchange amused glances and raise our hands too.

"Terrific," Andrew says. "Amy, I saw your hand first. Did you learn something new that you'd like to share with the rest of us?" When she nods, Andrew says, "Do you want to show us?"

I'm sitting behind Amy today, so I can't see exactly what she's doing with her hands, but I'm close enough that I notice her ears turning red. I lean forward to see what she's signing, and I can feel my eyebrows rising when I catch the words *meal*—all five fingers pinched together, moving twice toward the mouth—and *with me*.

Andrew looks confused for a minute, but then his face brightens. "Amy, that's wonderful. You've learned how to say, *Do you want to have a meal with me?*"

Amy's face flames. "Right."

Andrew either completely misses the point or chooses to ignore the question, which is almost certainly directed his way, because he just grins and says, "You know, that's a wonderful and extremely useful phrase to have learned. You put me to shame that I didn't think to teach it to the class myself. You guys, let's go ahead and learn the phrase together. Amy, can you show it to us again? Here, stand up and face everyone."

Amy looks crestfallen as she stands up and repeats the signs again. Andrew puts his right hand on hers to show her—and us—how to more accurately sign *want,* which is two upward-facing palms, fingers spread, mimicking pulling something toward one's body, almost like opening a drawer. Amy jerks away like she's been burned when he touches her, which seems to startle him—and that's the moment that he understands that she wasn't just learning a phrase; she was asking him out.

His face turns a little red, and he glances at me before clearing his throat. "Wonderful job, Amy, just wonderful," he says quickly. "The rest of you, that's a phrase worth practicing at home."

He moves quickly away from Amy and gestures for her to sit down. When he's back at the front of the small room, he says, "Vivian, Kate? You also learned phrases?"

Vivian tells him that she's learned, *I take my tea with the Queen,* which makes us all laugh, and after she proudly demonstrates, he turns to me.

"Kate? What do you have for us this evening?" he asks.

"I learned how to say, *I'm very glad to be here with you,*" I tell him, picking a relatively innocuous phrase, although I've learned it so that I can say it to Hannah when I see her again. *If* I see her again.

"Great." Andrew smiles warmly at me. "Let's see it."

I point to myself, then I try to sign the rest of the sentence fluidly. *Very* is two peace signs touching and then moving apart from each other; *glad* is two open-palmed upward flicks to the center of the chest; *here* is a couple of upward motions with open, upturned palms; *with you* is touching the fingers of two closed fists together and then pointing.

"Wonderful," Andrew murmurs when I finish, then he puts his two palms up facing out and pats the air. "That's the sign for *wonderful,*" he adds. "Kate, you could even say, *It's wonderful to be here with you.*"

I nod, repeat his motion, and finish with *to be here with you.* He nods enthusiastically and says, "That's exactly it! Now, class, let's try both phrases and thanks, Kate, for bringing them up."

As the class mimics Andrew's more skillful repetition of my phrases, Amy turns and mouths, *Teacher's pet*. She's smiling, but the mirth doesn't reach her eyes.

An hour later, after we've learned two dozen new sentences, thirty common words, and a bit of history about ASL, Andrew looks at his watch again and says, "Well, folks, looks like we're out of time. Thanks again for being here, practice your signs this week, and I'll see you next Wednesday." We begin to gather our things, and Andrew adds, "Kate, could you stay after class for a few minutes? There's something I want to ask you."

This earns me a full-out glare from Amy, but I nod and wait for the other people to filter out of the room before approaching Andrew's desk, which he's currently shuffling papers on.

"Great work today. And I owe you an apology for not touching base sooner about the kids. Think you'd be up for another visit with Molly and Riajah soon?" he asks. "What does your schedule look like next week?"

"Actually, tomorrow works for me if it works for you."

He looks surprised. "Wow, your schedule must be a lot more flexible than mine."

"No, it's just that my mom's coming to town, so I took the day off to get her from the airport. Seeing the kids tomorrow would be perfect."

"You don't want to hang out with your mom then?" he asks.

"She's having dinner with my sister and her kids tomorrow night. She likes to see us separately, which is weird." I roll my eyes and add, "I think she tries to get dirt on us from each other. So believe me when I say I'd rather see Molly and Riajah than sit at home and wonder what my mom and sister are gossiping about."

"Only if you're sure," he says with a smile. "I was thinking maybe we could do two more short at-home sessions with the girls like last time. I should be able to clear their schedule with Sheila."

"And the other girl you mentioned? Do you want me to see her too?"

"You know what? Yeah." He frowns in concentration for a moment. "If it's okay with you, I'm going to see if we can set something up with her for Friday. Maybe I could bring her by your office. Would that work? So you don't have to make two trips out to Queens this week?"

"Sure," I say. "My assistant can schedule something. I'll talk to her tomorrow."

"Ah, you have an assistant," he says. "You're very fancy-pants, I see."

"The fanciest," I say, which makes him laugh. "Although I have to admit, I share her with the other three therapists in my office."

"So really only upscale-casual-pants, then," he says with a straight face, and I laugh.

We agree that we'll meet in his office at four o'clock tomorrow for the short walk over to Molly's and Riajah's foster home.

"Hey, I also wanted to apologize," he adds as I turn to go.

"Apologize? For what?"

"For unloading on you about my brother. I haven't done that in years." He pauses. "I know I should probably be past it by now."

"First of all, you should never apologize for talking about something like that. I'm glad you told me."

"Really?"

I nod. "And losing someone, well, it leaves you with a hole in your life. I get it. I don't think you ever get past that kind of loss. But I do think you get through it."

"Yeah, I think you're right." He smiles as I head for the door. "Oh, and Kate?" he calls after me.

I turn around. "Yeah?"

Andrew meets my gaze, smiles, and slowly signs something to me, ending with his right thumb and index finger pulling his left index finger up toward his chin. "See you tomorrow," he adds.

It takes me until I'm in the church above us, heading for the door, to realize that what he'd signed to me was, *You are very special.*

Seventeen

"You're putting on weight" is the first thing my mother says to me when I meet her by baggage claim at JFK after a long ride out to the airport on the E train.

"It's nice to see you too," I say with a sigh, giving her a hug. "I see you've been sticking with yoga." Her hair, dyed light brown with honey highlights, looks freshly blown out, and her figure is slender and toned. Admittedly, I'm a little jealous; she's twenty-five years my senior and looks better than I do.

"We'll have to get you to a studio, darling," she chirps. "Susan's been going to a place on the Upper East, and she just loves it. It'll be just the thing to get you into shape before you get married!"

We wait for her suitcases, two overstuffed Atlantic rollers, to come out on the conveyor belt, and when we're finally in a cab, she asks me, "So how are you, really?"

"I'm fine, Mom," I say without looking at her.

She's silent for a moment. "Susan told me about what happened at the bridal store."

I shake my head and look out the window so she can't read my face. "It was nothing. I just thought I saw someone I knew."

"A girl you were dreaming about? Honey, that doesn't sound normal."

I stare out the window for a moment at the outskirts of the city rolling by. Right now, I wish I could be walking somewhere among all those soaring buildings, on a street where no one knows my name.

"Do you think it's just nerves?" my mother ventures after the silence gets uncomfortable. "Prewedding butterflies?"

"Sure," I tell her. "Probably."

"I thought so," she says, leaning back in her seat and nodding knowingly. "Susan was very worried about you, but I said, 'Susan, she's fine. She's just getting used to the idea of being married.' Susan didn't understand how that feels, being that she's been married to Robert for such a long time, but you and me, we single girls get it, right?"

I glance at her. "I'm widowed, Mom. Not single. So are you."

"Well, of course," she says quickly. "But it's all in the perspective. I'm choosing not to dwell on your father's death. You know, you could choose not to dwell on Patrick's."

As my mother turns to look out the window, I study her profile and feel a pang of sadness. Within a year of my dad's death, my mom had moved to Florida and gotten herself a boyfriend. "It's just her way of dealing with it," Susan said when I expressed concern at the time. But I think she moved on so quickly because my parents had outgrown their relationship long before he died. I can't imagine ever having outgrown Patrick. I'm afraid that what my parents had was perhaps the norm and that what I had with Patrick was the exception, which makes me doubt even more that I'm supposed to find that kind of love again.

"So in these dreams," my mother begins. I blink a few times and refocus on her as she continues, "Do you see Patrick? Or just this imaginary deaf child you apparently had with Patrick?"

"Both," I say softly.

"Well," she says, brightening after a minute, "maybe it's just your mind's way of telling you you're ready for children. I mean, I would think you'd be dreaming of Dan, but who can know how the brain works, right?" She nudges me and adds, "Maybe this is just a sign that it's time to give me a grandbaby before I get too old."

I stare at her for a minute. "Susan didn't tell you?"

"Tell me what?"

"Mom, I can't have kids," I say flatly.

My mother stares at me for what feels like a full minute. Then, her face crumples, and she says softly, "Oh, Katie, I didn't know. What happened?"

"Nothing happened." I try to keep the edge out of my voice. "It's just—it's just the way it is, I guess." I quickly recap the doctor's visit, leaving out the technical terms because my mother won't understand them any better than I do.

"So Dan, he's okay with this?" she asks tentatively.

I nod. "Turns out having kids isn't that important to him."

"Oh." She pauses. "Well, I guess that's good. Life goes on as usual, right?" She nudges me again and gives me a sunny smile, but I know my mom well enough to see my own sadness reflected in her eyes. "I mean, I'm disappointed, of course," she adds. "But you enjoy being unattached, don't you? Think of all the things you'll be able to do in life without children."

The words are meant to be a comfort, but they feel like a slap in the face. "Right, Mom," I say. I intend to leave it at that, but then I hear myself add, "We could adopt, though, you know."

"Adopt?"

I nod.

My mother blinks a few times. "Of course. Why yes, you *could*. That's just an awfully big decision, honey. You don't want to rush into something you can't take back."

"But a second ago, you were ready to rush me into having a baby," I point out.

She purses her lips. "That's different."

"Is it?"

"Semantics, my dear," she says, and although I don't know what she means and am fairly sure she doesn't either, I let it go.

I get my mother checked into the Ritz-Carlton, where she has insisted upon staying despite the fact that both Susan and I have offered her our guest rooms. As we wait for Susan in the hotel's Auden Bistro, my mother orders flutes of champagne for both of us, and when they arrive, she raises hers and says, "To forgetting all about these dreams and getting on with your real life—and your lovely wedding, dear."

I force a smile and clink glasses with her, but I don't say anything aloud for fear of somehow jinxing the return of the dreams.

"I'm so happy for you, Kate," my mother says after she's taken her first sip. "Your father and I were both so worried that you'd never find anyone to be happy with after Patrick."

"I was worried about that too," I admit.

"But Dan, he fits the bill, doesn't he?" she continues. "He's such a nice man. I'm so glad you've found someone so perfect for you."

"Yeah, he's certainly good on paper, isn't he?" I ask before I can stop myself. I'm surprised by how bitter I sound, and I can tell by the look on my mother's face that she hears it too.

"Well, of course," she says, looking away. "But that's not important. What's important is that you're so compatible."

"Why?"

She looks at me blankly. "Pardon?"

"What is it that makes you think we're so compatible, Mom? You've been telling me since I first started dating Dan how perfect he is for me. But why?" I'm not sure whether I'm asking for proof so that I can justify staying, or whether I'm trying to blame her for pushing me in his direction. Either way, she doesn't take the bait.

"Well, you are, aren't you?" she asks. "I mean, you tell me, sweetheart. He's your fiancé. What makes him so perfect?"

"No one's perfect," I say instead of answering.

She takes another sip of champagne and sighs, then she completely changes the subject. "When you mentioned adoption earlier, Kate, I didn't mean to be dismissive."

I look up in surprise.

"Dan's on board?" she continues. "With the idea of adopting?"

I bite my lip. "We haven't really talked about it much."

"But if you think you *might* want to have a child someday, you need to make sure Dan agrees."

I take a deep breath. "And if he doesn't?"

My mother doesn't answer for a moment. "I love Dan," she says finally. "I know Susan does too. But the issue of a child can be a huge one that can take over a marriage. You have to be absolutely sure. Otherwise, regret will grow in spaces you don't even know are there."

I open my mouth to reply to the strangely spot-on pearl of wisdom, but Susan whisks up to the table then, dressed all in black, her hair freshly highlighted, her neck adorned with a Chanel choker. "Mom!" she exclaims, hugging our mother tightly and then giving me a peck on both cheeks when I stand to greet her. "So sorry I kept you two waiting. Let me order myself a glass of bubbly, and we'll catch up!"

The conversation about children and Dan gets washed away by the tide of Susan's arrival, and although my mother glances uncertainly at me a few times, she eventually gets drawn entirely into a conversation with my sister about the merits of opera versus theater.

As they talk, I try to focus on what they're saying, but my mother's words keep ringing in my ears. *You have to be absolutely sure.* And it occurs to me that there's almost nothing in my life that I'm sure about right now.

We catch up over a long lunch—crab capellini in tomato cream sauce for my mom, a quinoa salad for Susan, and a grilled chicken sandwich for me—then I check my watch and realize it's nearly three. I'd intended to stop by my apartment to grab my guitar before meeting Andrew in Queens, and if I don't leave now, I won't make it.

"This was great," I say abruptly, interrupting the stream of their conversation as I pull a couple of twenties from my purse and lay them on the table, "but I have to get back to work."

"I thought you took the day off," Susan says with a frown.

I shake my head. "I have an appointment late this afternoon. Sorry."

My mother firmly pushes my money back toward me and insists that lunch is her treat. "Come on, honey," she adds. "I'll walk you out."

I hug Susan good-bye, and as she digs back into her salad, my mom stands and follows me out into the lobby.

"Listen, honey, I have dinner with Susan and the kids tonight, then a spa treatment tomorrow morning and lunch with a few old friends at one. But how about dinner with you and Dan tomorrow? Will that work?"

"Sure, Mom."

My mom puts her hands on my shoulders and pulls back to look me in the eye. "Kate," she says softly, "whatever decision you make will be the right one, as long as you follow your heart."

"Thanks," I murmur.

"The thing is," she adds, "you have to listen hard to what your heart's saying before you know what you're supposed to do."

I spend the ride out to Queens thinking about what my mother said, but I ultimately realize I can't hear my heart, because it's wrapped in a thousand layers of defenses. I've been so busy trying to do the things I should do, to get back on the "right path," as my mother and sister would say, that I've forgotten how to read my internal compass.

It's a few minutes past four by the time I hurry up the front walkway of St. Anne's. "Sorry I'm late," I say.

Like last time, Andrew is in front of the building, sitting on the steps. Today, he's in a faded heather gray T-shirt with an equally faded outline of a smiley face on it, paired with jeans.

"Three minutes doesn't count as late," he tells me, "and by the way, you look great today."

"I do?" I look down at myself doubtfully. I'm in a faded button-down chambray shirt and skinny black jeans, which I quickly threw on when I stopped by the apartment after our late lunch.

"Much better than when you wear a suit," he says. "Purely from a clinical standpoint, of course."

I can feel myself smiling. "So we're off to see Molly and Riajah?"

"Actually, I have a little surprise for you." He scratches his head and looks suddenly worried. "Wait, I'm just now realizing that I should have called you. I can't just spring an appointment on you without telling you, can I?"

"An appointment with whom?"

"Well, I didn't want to interfere with your schedule tomorrow, especially with your mom in town," he says. "You're already being so nice by volunteering with us. So I made some calls this afternoon, moved some things around, and arranged for Molly and Riajah to be brought here. That way, you can meet with them now, then we'll head over to see the other girl I told you about. If that's okay."

"Sure. That sounds great."

"Okay, good." He looks relieved. "In the future, I'll give you more notice, I promise. I just don't want you to have to waste too much of your time on us."

"Andrew, it's not a waste at all." I'm surprised by how deeply I mean the words.

Andrew beckons for me to follow him. Inside, the building is homier looking than I thought it would be; framed children's drawings and splotchy finger paintings line the wall of the long front hallway, and as we pass by open doorways, I glance inside and see dozens of offices filled with photographs and bright colors. Many of the rooms look pleasantly cluttered, which surprises me; I had somehow expected something more sterile and bureaucratic.

"This looks like a nice place to work," I say as we turn a corner and Andrew opens a door for me.

"Well, the hours are long, and I won't be buying a yacht anytime soon," he says with a smile, "but I can't imagine a job where I'd feel more rewarded."

Andrew leads me into a conference room littered with toys. Molly and Riajah are at opposite corners of a large table, ignoring each other. Molly is playing with a couple of Barbie dolls, and Riajah is hunched over a notepad, sketching something with colored pencils. For a second, my heart lurches as I think about Hannah and her drawings, but I blink and push the thought away. These kids need me now; I can't be lost in a world of my own making.

"Kate!" Sheila stands from her seat at the middle of the table to cross the room and give me a warm hug. "It's so nice to see you again. I know the girls are looking forward to meeting with you."

I glance at them. Molly is still ignoring me entirely, and Riajah is studying me with a pensive look on her face. After a few seconds, she returns her gaze to the notepad in front of her and goes back to drawing.

"I'm looking forward to meeting with them too," I tell Sheila. "Thanks so much for bringing them by the office."

"Oh, it's no problem at all," she says, waving her hand dismissively. "It's nice to get out of the house, you know?"

"Let's see how this works out today," Andrew says, "and if the girls seem comfortable, maybe we can make this a regular appointment."

"I think they got a lot out of the session last week," Sheila says. "I'm happy to keep bringing them back."

Andrew touches my arm. "How about we start with Riajah, if that works for you. I've got a spare office set up down the hall for us. Shall we?"

I hesitate. "You know, I think it might be better if it's just me and Riajah this time," I tell him. "Besides, I learned some new ASL phrases on my own this week."

He looks surprised. "But understanding her will still be tough if she decides to speak to you only in sign language."

I shake my head. "That's kind of the point. I want her to *have* to communicate through spoken words or through music. Besides, if this is going to work, I'm going to have to get her to trust me, which means some one-on-one time."

Andrew looks skeptical, but after a moment, he nods. "Okay. That makes sense." He pauses. "You said you learned some new phrases? On your own?" He turns to Sheila and adds, "Kate's my star pupil."

I can feel myself blushing, which I know is silly. "I learned to say this." I take a deep breath and slowly sign, *I know you want to act like I'm stupid because I'm not good at ASL. And that's okay. But today, we aren't going to use words. Today, we're only going to use music. You have to speak my language.*

Andrew looks at me in surprise. "You learned all that just to work with Riajah?"

"Yeah. Did I say it okay?"

"Kate, that was perfect. When have you been finding the time to practice?"

"In my sleep," I say with a faint smile, and he laughs, clearly believing I'm joking.

"Okay, then," he says. "Let's get started." He crosses over to Riajah and kneels down in front of her, then he signs something so rapid I can't keep up. I watch his hands, and then hers, as they have a fluidly signed conversation back and forth. My hand signs are still choppy and uncertain, whereas Andrew's and Riajah's look like visual music. They're smooth, delicate, deliberate, and completely beautiful.

Riajah seems to be arguing, but eventually, she rolls her eyes and stands up. Andrew winks and beckons for me to follow as Riajah strides out of the room.

As promised, Andrew has set up a spare, unfurnished office for us to use. It's devoid of any furniture except for two chairs, and the room looks stark and sparse when Andrew flips the light on. I tap the wooden floor lightly with the toe of my right foot, and I smile when it vibrates a little in response. It'll be perfect for us.

A closet? Riajah signs with a smirk, and I recognize the word from reading over the ASL dictionary last night.

"No, a music theater," I say before Andrew has the chance to reply, and his eyebrows shoot up in surprise. Riajah simply snorts, sits down in one of the chairs, and turns away.

"Well," Andrew says to me, glancing at Riajah uncertainly. "I guess I'll leave the two of you alone, if you're sure you're okay."

"I'm sure." I say. "Oh, and one more thing: it may get loud in here for a few minutes. Is that okay?"

"Sure. I'll let my coworkers know." He looks from me to Riajah and back. But he makes no movement toward the door. "You're positive you don't need my help?"

"Andrew," I say with a smile, "let me do what I do."

My words must project more confidence than I feel, because he finally nods and heads for the hallway. "Have fun, you two," he says before shutting the door behind him.

When he's gone, I turn to look at Riajah, who is still studiously ignoring me. I say her name a few times, but she's clearly set on pretending I'm not there. I walk around her, until I'm standing in front of her, and she glances at me then turns away, her movement deliberate.

It's what I'd expected, based on our last interaction, but this time I've come prepared. From my big bag, I pull my iPhone and two small but powerful Bluetooth speakers.

"Riajah, Andrew tells me you like to listen to music," I say.

No reply.

"But have you ever *felt* music?"

Again, no answer.

I scan my phone for the short playlist I put together this afternoon, then I plug the speakers in, turn the volume to high, set everything on the floor, and say, "Because music isn't just something you hear with your ears. It's something you experience with all your senses." I don't wait for a reply; instead, I push Play.

The room explodes with the Philadelphia Orchestra's recording of Tchaikovsky's "1812 Overture." I know I'm playing the song loudly enough that Andrew and his colleagues can hear it down the hall, but that doesn't matter. What matters is that the sound is strong enough to vibrate the floor Riajah's chair is sitting on. I need her to feel the rhythm, to discover that hearing isn't the only way to appreciate a song. I continue to stand behind her and smile as I see her body respond, involuntarily, to the rise and fall of the music. She twitches each time the piece reaches a crescendo, and by the end, I can see her chest rising and falling with the rhythm.

I wait for a moment—I've programmed silence between the songs—and as I'd hoped she'd do, Riajah turns to look at me. *The music,* she signs. *Where?*

I don't reply. I simply smile at her and wait for my iPhone to provide her with an answer. A second later, it does; Outkast's "The Way You Move" begins to play, the bass line vibrating the floor. Riajah looks at me once more, her expression startled, and then she notices I'm mouthing the lyrics to the chorus. She blinks a few times then slowly rotates her chair until she's watching me closely.

When the Outkast song ends, the playlist transitions into the Who's "My Generation," but Riajah holds up her hand and stands up. I push Pause, then she signs something rapid to me, and I recognize the words *what* and *singing.*

"I like the way you move," I reply.

She signs the words back to me, and I nod. Then I say repeat very deliberately, "I like the way you move."

She stares at me and signs the words again.

I nod and say them aloud again, but this time, I say them in rhythm, stomping the floor hard enough for her to feel it.

She signs the words back to me, and in reply, I say them again, still stomping. When I'm done, I keep tapping my foot hard on the ground, waiting for her to jump in. She stares uncertainly at me, and then I have an idea. I bend down to my iPhone, go back to the beginning of the Outkast track, and stomp hard along with the cadence I know she can feel. When the song gets to the chorus, I sing, "I like the way you move," with the vocals in the song. It takes us until the third repetition of the chorus before Riajah finally joins in.

Her voice is raspy and sweet and although very off-key, she's completely in rhythm. She watches my lips and my tapping foot for a while, then I'm surprised to see her close her eyes as she waits for the next chorus. This time, she doesn't look at me; she plunks herself down on the floor, touches it with both hands, and sings in perfect time with the lyrics.

When the song ends, I push Stop on my iPhone and wait for her to open her eyes.

"You sang," I say.

She looks at me for a moment before smiling. "I sang," she says clearly.

Not wanting to lose the momentum of the moment, I ask, "Do you have a favorite song?"

She nods and surprises me by naming "You're Beautiful," a guitar-driven James Blunt song from a decade or so ago. I scroll through my iPhone, and when I find it, I look up.

"Do you know all the lyrics?" I ask.

"Yes," she says aloud. "I like it."

"What do you like about it?"

She considers this. "It says someone can be thinking about you even if you can't see them. Maybe they even love you and you don't know."

I nod, trying not to show her how elated I am by the interaction. "Do you think there's someone out there thinking of you, even if you can't see them right now?"

She shrugs.

"Like who?" I prod.

"Maybe someone who's supposed to be my mom or something."

I feel a lump in my throat. "Want to feel the rhythm of the song?"

She nods.

"But you have to sing with me or I turn it off," I tell her. I push Play, and we stare at each other as the first few guitar chords fill the room with sound. Then, Blunt's beautifully reedy voice pipes from the speakers, and I hide a smile of pride as Riajah loudly sings, "My life is brilliant," along with him. Again, her rhythm is perfect, even if her pitch is off.

For the next three minutes, with James Blunt's voice echoing off the walls, we sing together. I don't know every word like Riajah does, but I know enough to keep up, and when the final note fades, she turns to look at me. "The end is kind of sad," she says.

"But that's just the end to his story," I remind her. "Not yours."

She shrugs, but she doesn't add anything.

"So you like music," I say a moment later.

"Some," she says. She pushes her hair back over her ear, revealing the headpiece of her right cochlear implant. "Gift from St. Anne's," she says. "They let me understand the words to songs, which is cool."

"Do you like them?" I ask.

She's silent for a moment. "I like the quiet sometimes," she says finally. "But music, I like that too."

Her gaze turns guarded and she signs something to me that I don't recognize, so I sign back, *Repeat please? I don't understand.*

A cloud passes over her face, and just as quickly as she opened up, she begins to close down. "You know what?" she says out loud, her words melted and fuzzy on the edges. "You don't know anything."

She shakes her head, stands up, and walks out of the room before I can say another word.

* * *

I work with Molly for a half hour too, playing "If You're Happy and You Know It," and a One Direction song I downloaded while thinking about Hannah. Molly is less sullen than Riajah, but there's still a gulf of distrust between us, a feeling that I have to jump through hoops to climb over the wall she's on the other side of. I know all about taking baby steps with clients, and I know we're moving forward. Still, I'm frustrated, and I'm feeling the first tinglings of doubt that I may be out of my league, especially with Molly, who doesn't have implants and has very little residual hearing. But, I remind myself, she can feel the vibrations. And being moved by the rhythm of a song is a huge part of being touched by it.

After her session, I sign *good-bye* to the girls and decide to look at it as a small victory when Molly signs back *thank you,* then I shake hands with Sheila and tell her I'll see them all next week. Andrew and I walk them to the door of the building, and when they're gone into the balmy night, he beckons for me to follow him down the front steps.

"You got Riajah to sing," he says flatly, "and Molly to interact again."

"I wish I could have done more . . ."

"Kate," he says, shaking his head, "you've got to give yourself a little credit here. This was always going to be an uphill climb. Fortunately, you seem to have brought your climbing gear." He winks at me and checks his watch. "We're right on time for our other appointment. You ready to head out?"

I sling my bag over my shoulder and nod.

"You're going to really like this girl, Kate," Andrew says. "The two of you are sort of kindred spirits. She's an enormously gifted musician; we all call her Beethoven around here. She's just having a tough time right now, and none of us seem to be able to get through to her. I thought you might be able to."

"What instrument does she play?"

"Piano," Andrew says, and my heart leaps to my throat. *A twelve-year-old prodigy who likes Beethoven?* "But we only have a crummy old keyboard to lend her, poor kid," he continues. "And no budget for piano lessons."

"What's—what's her name?" I croak. I know it's impossible, but what if he says *Hannah*? What if the dreams were leading here all along? What if she's real?

"Allie," Andrew replies.

"Oh," I say, surprised by how disappointed I feel. *Stop being so dumb,* I chide myself. *Hannah doesn't exist any more than Patrick does.*

"Shall we head over?" Andrew asks, apparently oblivious to the pangs of disappointment shooting through me.

"Lead the way," I manage.

Eighteen

As we walk up Thirty-Fifth Street and turn left on Thirty-First Avenue, Andrew fills me in on Allie's history. She's in seventh grade and has been in the system on and off for the last two years. Her dad's not in the picture, and her mom has been arrested a handful of times on minor drug charges. The mother got out of a drug rehab program recently and is visiting Allie twice a week in compliance with ACS reunification guidelines.

"So Allie will go back to her mom soon?" I ask.

"That's the general plan if everything goes right, although it may take a while." Andrew sighs and shoves his hands in his pockets. "I think that a lot of the time, it *is* better for the kid to go back to the parents, you know? If the parent is decent, the sense of stability is usually helpful for the child. But I don't know Allie's mom yet, and I don't have a good sense of the situation. I worry about Allie."

"You worry about all of them," I say softly.

He cocks his head to the side and looks at me. "It's probably not too good for me, because there's only so much I can fix. But yeah. I worry. A lot. And Allie's one of the ones I worry about the most right now."

"You say she's been difficult lately? Behavioral problems?"
Andrew nods.

"Do you think it's because she's worried about going back to her mom?"

"Maybe," Andrew says. "Although that's hard to unravel. Is she worried because there's some sort of problem in the home we need to be aware of? Or is she worried her mom will lose custody of her again? Does she want to go back, or doesn't she? It's hard to get these kids to open up sometimes, but Allie's grades have been slipping; she's gotten into three fights in the last two months; and she refuses to talk with any of us about any of it. I'm hoping she'll respond differently to you."

"Why?"

Andrew smiles. "Because you're the one who speaks her language."

We arrive a few minutes later at a modest-looking apartment building on Forty-Second Street. Allie's foster family lives in a third-floor walk-up, and as we scale the stairs, Andrew pats me on the back and says, "Good luck." The words hang as ominously as a storm cloud as Andrew raises a fist and knocks on the door to unit 304.

A man with red hair, a thick mustache, and a goatee answers the door and smiles when he sees Andrew. "Man, you're right on time," he says. "Come on in."

Andrew introduces him as Rodney Greghor, Allie's temporary foster father. We shake hands, and Rodney explains that he and his wife, Salma, take many of the St. Anne's kids who are likely to be reunited with their biological parents.

"Our goal is usually to place kids in foster situations that have the possibility of becoming permanent," Andrew says. "But Rodney and Salma only do temporary situations, which has become a godsend for us. They love these kids, but everyone goes into the situation knowing it'll be temporary, so we don't run into the kind of problem where there's an expectation of adoption."

"We just want these kids to have a good home for how-ever long they're with us," Rodney adds as he leads us into the kitchen. "Salma's out right now, but you can meet her next time. You ready to meet Allie, Kate? I can take you back."

"I'm ready," I say.

Rodney hesitates, and I get the sense he's evaluating me. He nods to himself after a moment and gestures for us to follow him down a narrow hall. "Come on," he says over his shoulder.

The door to the room at the far end of the hall is open, but Rodney knocks lightly anyhow and motions for me to follow him. I feel the breath knocked out of me as I gaze around at a darkened room that reminds me a lot of Hannah's; the walls are covered in posters, including the same One Direction one I saw in Hannah's room. And where Hannah's walls were covered in taped-up sketches, Allie's are blanketed in handwritten notes. I lean closer to read the one closest to the door.

In here, the world is dark,
hope is stark,
but yet
I embark.
Make your mark,
they say.
Make your mark.

"She writes poetry," Rodney says, following my gaze. "I don't know much, but I think some of it's good."

"This one's sad," I murmur.

"I can hear you, you know," comes a voice from the shad-owy back right corner, and I jump, startled. With all the shades drawn and the lights out, I hadn't noticed there was someone sitting there, but as my eyes adjust and she turns, I can just make out the shape of a girl.

"Kate," Andrew says, "this is Allie. Allie, this is Kate Waithman, the music therapist I told you about."

"Hi, Allie," I say as the girl stands and steps forward into the pale slice of light from the hallway.

We study each other for a moment. Allie's a beautiful girl, with wide brown eyes, straight brown hair that falls just past her shoulders, and small, delicate features that remind me of a bird.

"Music therapist?" she asks, and her words have the same kind of rough edge to them that Hannah's did in my dream, but her cadence and the rise and fall of her speech pattern are off. I wonder how new her cochlear implants are. "You?"

"Yes," I tell her. "I've been looking forward to meeting you."

Her eyes immediately narrow, then she cackles, a surprisingly harsh sound. "Liar," she says simply, then she turns away and retreats back to her dark corner. My eyes have adjusted to the dim light enough now that I can see her, her arms crossed over her chest, her back ramrod straight as she stares at the wall. I glance at Andrew, who just shakes his head.

"Allie—" Andrew begins, and she whirls around angrily, her eyes blazing. She signs something rapid to him that I don't understand. He signs back, and she makes a huffing sound and rolls her eyes.

"What did she say?" I ask, which earns me another snort of derision.

"She said she doesn't need a psychiatrist," he says. "I explained that that's not what you are. You're here to work on speech with her. She doesn't seem to believe me."

I turn my attention back to the girl. "Allie," I say, "I'm just here to play music with you."

"I'm not talking about my feelings," she says, glaring at me.

I shrug. "I never said I wanted you to."

Andrew looks like he's about to say something else, but I don't wait to see what it is or what Allie's response will be. Instead, I walk over to her keyboard, which is set up on a rickety stand in the back left corner of the room. I turn it on, sit down in the small chair set up in front of it, and begin to play.

I don't think about what tune I'll pick out, but almost of their own accord, my fingers move across the keys to the Fray's "How to Save a Life." I'm less than a verse in by the time I've elicited a reaction.

"Hey!" Allie says loudly, stepping in front of the keyboard and glaring at me. "That's mine!"

I glance at her, but I keep on playing without missing a beat.

That's mine, she signs, her expression angry now. *Mine!* Then she switches back to spoken words and says again, "Mine!"

"Okay, then play it," I say without stopping. I dive into the chorus as she watches me, her jaw hanging slightly slack.

"What?" she finally asks.

I stop playing and look at her. "If it's yours," I say, "play it. Because if you won't, I will. That's what instruments are for."

"But I said it's mine," she says, her protest growing weaker as her expression grows confused.

I shrug. "You can't claim it as yours unless you play it. Musicians' rules."

Allie glares at me, and for a moment, we're locked in a silent staring contest. I'm starting to worry my bluff won't work when Allie finally rolls her eyes, snaps, "Move," and slides onto the seat I quickly vacate in front of the keyboard.

She pauses, as if to collect herself, and a second later, the room explodes with sound: angry keystrokes, sullen chords, all laced with a beautifully smooth melody that somehow manages to tie together the choppiness. When she closes her eyes and slips into the music, Andrew and I exchange glances, and I look over to see Rodney staring at Allie in awe.

A few minutes later, the song comes to an abrupt end and Allie turns to smirk at me. "See?" she says.

I keep a straight face. "What was that song?"

Her left eye twitches. "It's called 'Make Your Mark.'"

I think of the poem on her wall, the one in her slanty, girly handwriting. "You wrote it," I say.

She stares at me for a long moment. "So?"

"So," I say, "you're talented. And I look forward to working with you."

With that, without waiting for a reply, I turn and walk out of the room and back into the kitchen. After a moment, Andrew and Rodney join me. Rodney is scratching his head.

"That was it?" he asks. "That's the end of your session?"

I nod and glance uncertainly at Andrew. I'm relieved to see him smiling. He looks at Rodney. "Kate got Allie to engage with her," he says, and something changes in Rodney's face as he looks at me with grudging respect.

"You were right," I tell Andrew. My whole body is buzzing with energy. "I just had to speak her language."

"Any chance you'd want to grab something to eat before I head home?" I hear myself ask Andrew as we head back toward St. Anne's.

He glances at me. "Your fiancé won't mind?"

"He's out at a bar with his friend Stephen tonight. He'll be home late." Then, because I realize I sound a bit like I'm hitting on Andrew, I add quickly, "I just thought it might be nice to talk about the kids' progress. That is, if you're free."

The truth is, I know I can't talk to Dan about Allie, Riajah and Molly, because he won't understand how much the sessions with them meant to me. Andrew will. I'm not ready to leave my bubble of happiness yet.

Andrew grins. "As long as you promise to let me order for you again." I give him a look and he holds up his hands defensively. "Not because I'm some sort of chauvinist. It's because I loved seeing the look on your face when you took your first bite of that burger a couple weeks ago. I want to do it again and I have just the place in mind."

"Another burger joint?" I ask, but I can't help smiling, because that sounds delicious.

"Give me some credit here, Kate," he says. "I have a wide repertoire of culinary tricks up my sleeve. How do you feel about Caribbean food?"

We wind up at a narrow, hole-in-the-wall Jamaican place ten blocks from Allie's house. There are only a dozen tables in the restaurant, and the walls are painted black, green, and yellow.

"It doesn't look like much," Andrew says, reading my mind, "but I promise, the food here is incredible. Trust me?"

"I trust you." I smile, because the words are surprisingly nice to say.

"Good," he says, nudging me, "because I know my food, woman."

Andrew orders ackee and saltfish—which he tells me is Jamaica's national dish—as well as breadfruit and fried plantains.

"Breadfruit?" I ask when our waitress walks away to get us a couple of Red Stripes.

"It's a fruit," he says with a smile, "that feels and tastes like bread. In Jamaica, they traditionally roast the whole fruit and then slice it up. It's a pretty common accompaniment to ackee and saltfish."

"I'm almost afraid to ask what ackee is."

He grins. "Ackee is this wacky fruit that looks kind of like yellow stone-crab claws when it grows. But when you boil it, it winds up looking just like scrambled eggs. The Jamaican tradition is to serve it with salt-packed cod and a bunch of vegetables and spices. It's different, but it's definitely an experience."

"Fruit that tastes like bread," I repeat slowly, "and fruit that looks like eggs. Sure, that all sounds normal."

He laughs. "I thought you said you trust me."

Our waitress returns with our Red Stripes, and by the time the food comes, we're talking and laughing like old friends. There's something about being with Andrew that reminds me of being with Patrick, but the two men aren't the same at all. In fact, they don't have a lot in common. It's just that I have the weird sense that I can be myself entirely with Andrew. If I say something stupid, I have the feeling he'd say something equally ridiculous in return, just to put me at ease.

Our food arrives, and just like Andrew promised, the main dish looks just like scrambled eggs with tomatoes, peppers, and onions mixed in. I take a bite and scrunch my nose up as the flavors assault my taste buds. It's salty and very fishy.

"You hate it," Andrew says, his face falling.

"No." I take another bite. "Actually, it tastes nothing like what I was expecting, but it's pretty good."

He looks relieved. "And the breadfruit?"

I try it and nod as I chew. "Definitely tastes like bread. But really good bread."

"So I have your seal of approval?"

"You're two for two, Henson."

He pumps his fists in the air. "Victory!" he says dramatically, which makes me laugh. "So," he says, after taking a bite of his meal, "would that fiancé of yours like this too?"

I laugh. "He'd hate it. He won't eat anything with high sodium content, as I'm guessing this has."

"He has high blood pressure?" he guesses.

"Nope. Just an obsession with eating healthy."

Andrew looks confused. "But you said he would have loved that burger we had a few weeks ago. Which, by the way, is probably on the top ten list of the unhealthiest foods in the New York metro area."

I look down at my plate, my appetite gone. "No. I said my husband would have liked it."

"Your husband?" Andrew still looks perplexed, but there's something in his eyes that tells me he knows exactly what I'm going to say. He's lost someone too, and sometimes, you can just tell.

"His name was Patrick," I say.

"Oh," Andrew says softly.

"He died twelve years ago," I go on numbly. "Or it'll be twelve years on September eighteenth. And Patrick would have loved this place. And that burger."

Andrew looks at me for a minute, and I wait for his pat words of sympathy, a variation on the same theme I get each time I tell someone I'm a widow. But instead, he reaches out and squeezes my hand. "So when you told me you understand how it feels to lose someone, you meant it."

"Yes," I say.

He's silent for another minute. "He's the one who gave you the advice? About following your dreams?"

I smile. "He's the one."

Andrew nods. "So he has great taste in food. And he gives awesome advice. What else? Tell me about this guy."

"Really?" I'm surprised. People just want to say they're sorry for my loss and move on before the conversation gets awkward. But Andrew seems to genuinely want to know.

"Like was he a Mets fan or a Yankees fan?" Andrew asks, nudging me.

"Yankees," I say softly.

"Well, that's a relief. What else?"

I take a deep breath and begin to talk. I tell Andrew about how much Patrick liked to cook, how he loved woodworking, and how he was so good at his job because he really cared about helping his clients build better futures. I tell him about how Patrick's stomach rumbled loudly sometimes in the middle of the night, how he secretly loved Rollerblading but was afraid it was girly, and how he sometimes left little notes under my pillow telling me he loved me. I even tell him about the silver dollars.

In return, he tells me about his brother, and by the time we pay our bill and leave, we've spent over an hour trading stories, and I feel like a weight's been lifted. I haven't laughed about Patrick in a long time. Every conversation I have about him is cloaked in sadness and loss. It was nice to simply tell a new friend about a man who used to be such a big part of my life.

"Do you ever dream about your brother?" I ask Andrew as we walk toward the subway together.

I feel foolish for asking the question until he replies, "No, but I wish I did. He died when we were both so young, and he's been gone from my life for a while now. Sometimes I worry that my memory of him is fading." He pauses and asks, "Do you dream about Patrick?"

"Yeah," I say. "Recently, anyway. Really realistic dreams."

He nods. "Do you think your subconscious is trying to tell you something?"

"Like what?"

"I don't know. I feel like the only time I dream vividly is when I'm trying to figure something out." He looks at me. "Is there something you need to figure out?"

"Maybe," I say in a small voice.

We walk in silence for a moment. "You know, I like to think that part of honoring my brother is acknowledging that losing him made me who I am today," Andrew says.

"What do you mean?"

"I mean, a tragedy changes you, doesn't it? Like, I can't imagine I would be here tonight, walking with you, working with hard-of-hearing kids, if it wasn't for Kevin. When he was killed, there was a void in my life, and I think anytime there's a void, it gets filled by something that makes you different than you were before. It changes the course of your life."

I nod in agreement. "Loss colors everything."

"But I'm a better man because of what I lost and what I learned, you know?" He pauses. "Do you think losing Patrick changed you?"

"Yeah, I guess it did." I look up at the sky and add, "I'm just not sure I'm done changing yet."

It's not until we've hugged good-bye and I'm on a subway bound for Manhattan that I realize neither of us said a word about the kids of St. Anne's.

Nineteen

"So tell me about these dreams." My mother leans forward eagerly the next evening and reaches for my hand. "Quick, before Dan gets back."

We're eating oysters and drinking champagne at Noemi & Jean, a French bistro my mother read about in *New York* magazine. It's the Fourth of July, but Dan hates fireworks and my mother hates crowds, so we've retreated to someplace quiet and decidedly unpatriotic. We're the only ones here. Dan has just excused himself to the bathroom, and my mother's eyes are bright with curiosity.

"There's not much to tell," I say weakly, the words a lie. The truth is, I feel fiercely protective of the world in which Patrick and Hannah live, because I'm afraid that telling someone skeptical the personal details will invite derision and destroy the illusion for me.

"Oh, but there must be, sweetheart," she insists. She pauses to swish an oyster with a dollop of horseradish down her throat. "Susan told me how much they've been bothering you." She takes a sip of champagne and leans back in her seat.

I glance toward the bathroom. Dan will be returning at any

moment. "It's silly," I say quickly. "I'm just kind of seeing the life I would have had if Patrick hadn't died."

"Are you happy? In this dream?"

"Very happy." I consider my next words carefully before saying them. "It feels like the life I was supposed to have, if everything hadn't gotten all screwed up. What if Patrick had grabbed a different cab that morning, or what if his client had canceled the meeting? What if he'd stayed home sick that day? What if I'd asked him to fix the stupid leaky faucet before he left for work, so that he was running five minutes later? There are so many little ways it all could have been so different, and only one way it turned out like this. How can that be right?"

"Because it's simply the way it is," she says softly. "What's done is done. You have Dan. You have a nice life together. You're happy enough, right?"

I nod, struck by her choice of words. "Happy *enough*?"

"Isn't that what most people have?"

"What if I want more?" I ask. But the words get lost as Dan returns to the table and we abruptly stop talking.

"I hope I'm not interrupting, ladies," Dan says, smiling as he sits down.

"Not at all," my mother replies, batting her eyes at him. She's had a soft spot for him since the day I took him to Florida to meet her for the first time, and when my mom likes someone, she turns into a flirt. Of course it's harmless, but with my own confusion clouding things, her simpering smile and fluttering lashes just annoy me.

We polish off the last of the oysters and champagne and order our entrées and more wine. As the conversation turns to wedding plans, color schemes, and invitation fonts, I feel myself drifting. I turn to look out the window again. I can just catch the glow in the sky from the fireworks dozens of blocks away, and it makes me sad to feel like I'm on the outside of something, looking in without really seeing it at all.

I close my eyes for a minute, just to clear my head, while Dan launches into a long story I've already heard a half-dozen times about how he picked out my engagement ring. His voice and the clatter of the restaurant fade away as I breathe deeply in and out, trying not to think about how different this perfect dinner feels from the wonderfully imperfect one I had last night at a Jamaican dive.

And then, just as I've succeeded in tuning everything out, an image flashes across my mind, clear as a photograph. It's a frozen moment: Patrick, Hannah, and me smiling up at fireworks with the city sparkling behind us.

I gasp, and as my eyes fly open, I automatically reach for the table to brace myself, and I instead wind up knocking a glass of water over on Dan's lap. He jumps up to grab napkins, and I turn to look guiltily at my mother.

"What just happened?" she whispers.

"Nothing," I say, but my heart is still thudding, because I've never had a fragment from the dream appear while I was going about my real life. And with the Fourth of July celebrations in the background, it's clear that the image I was seeing is supposed to be taking place right now, almost as if there's an alternate version of my life playing out across town without me.

"Did it have something to do with the dreams?" she asks suspiciously.

I only have time to nod miserably before Dan returns, blotting the water from his pants as he sits down. "Geez, babe, you scared me," he says, rubbing my arm.

"Sorry about the water," I say.

"No problem. As long as you're okay," he replies before resuming his conversation with my mom, who's now giving me worried glances each time Dan looks away.

Neither seems to hear when I mumble, "Actually, I'm not sure I'm okay at all."

I pick my mom up in a cab the next morning at the Ritz-Carlton to take her back to the airport. She's quiet on the way there, and although she comments a few times about the weather, how nice it was to see my sister and me, and how she's looking forward to coming back to visit us again soon, she waits until we're almost at JFK for the heavy words.

"What was that last night, Kate?" she asks. "At the restaurant? Has that been happening to you?"

"No. That was a first. I closed my eyes and saw Patrick and Hannah. It just startled me."

"Hannah's the daughter?"

I nod and look away.

"Honey," she says gently, "you've always had the tendency to obsess about things. Remember that crush you had on Jon Bon Jovi in the seventh grade? When you were so sure you were going to marry him?"

"I was twelve, Mom!"

She shrugs. "I'm just wondering if that's what you're doing now—obsessing about these dreams because you need something to hold on to."

"Mom, I'm not obsessing. And these dreams have nothing to do with my childhood crush."

"Well, I think you need to figure out what it is you want," she says as we pull into her terminal. "I think these dreams are confusing you, Kate. If you don't figure out how you really feel, I'm afraid you're going to lose what you've built for yourself."

"Dan, you mean?" I ask, trying not to sound bitter. "You're afraid I'll lose Dan?"

"No, honey. I'm afraid you'll lose *you.* I'm afraid you'll lose everything."

She hugs me good-bye, and as I climb slowly back into the cab and ask the driver to take me back to Manhattan, I find myself wondering whether you can really suffer a loss if you have nothing left to lose.

But maybe I *do* have something to lose. What if the dreams are trying to give me some sort of a message, and I'm ignoring it? What if I'm meant to be following the clues the dreams are laying out for me? I know it sounds nuts, but there's nothing about this that's normal.

"Bleecker and Grove," I hear myself tell the cabdriver as we plunge into the darkness of the Queens-Midtown Tunnel. "Please," I say a little more strongly, "take me to Bleecker and Grove."

It's the spot where I saw Hannah's piano recital in my dreams. I have to find out if Dolores Kay is real, if she really holds piano recitals on the second floor of 321 Bleecker. If she's out there somewhere, then maybe the dreams aren't just a cruelly beautiful trick of my imagination. If she exists, maybe there's hope that Hannah does too.

Thirty minutes later, the driver lets me out on the northeast corner of Grove and Bleecker, and I stand there for a moment, looking around, my heart thudding.

I'm fairly sure I've never been here before in real life—certainly not enough to know exactly what it looks like—but the street scene is the just the same as it was in my dream. Blue construction scaffolding on the far corner. An alterations shop and dry cleaner across the street. I even dreamed of the white benches outside the café on the corner. And there, just where I knew it would be, is number 321, a narrow building with a high, arched awning. I hurry over and scan the businesses listed on the door. There's a tax attorney, a hair salon, an importer/exporter, and an ad agency listed, but no Dolores Kay and nothing related to a piano recital space.

That's okay, I tell myself. *Just because she's not listed on the door doesn't mean she's not here.*

My heart hammering, I push open the front door, which isn't locked, and take the stairs two at a time to the second floor. I turn left out of the stairwell, just like I did with Patrick and Hannah, then I barrel through the first door on the right, which is just where I knew it would be.

But when I tumble inside, it's not a rehearsal space or a music studio at all. It's an airy hair salon with hardwood floors, lemony overhead lights hanging from exposed beams, and a gum-popping receptionist who looks at me like I'm a lunatic as I stand there panting in the doorway.

"Ma'am," she says slowly, looking me up and down, "are you okay?"

"There's no piano," I say stupidly.

"Ma'am?" the receptionist asks again. I can see the stylists, and the two customers sitting in chairs, all staring at me. "Are you here for a haircut?"

"No," I manage after a moment. I blink and try to regain my composure. *Dolores Kay isn't real. There's nothing here. Hannah isn't real. You're a fool.* "Th-thanks," I mutter over the voice in my head. I back out the door before anyone can say anything else.

I rush back down the stairs, and outside, I hungrily gulp in the air. I feel like I'm about to pass out, and for a moment, the sidewalk wobbles below me. But then I feel a hand on my elbow, and I turn to find a teenaged girl looking at me with concern.

"Miss?" she asks. "Are you okay?"

"Y-yes," I manage, but she doesn't look like she believes me. I turn away, embarrassed, and head south on Bleecker, toward Seventh Avenue, my head spinning.

It takes me a few minutes to regain my composure, and when I do, I sit down on a bus stop bench to finish collecting myself. I can't understand why there are pieces of the dream that are real—my perfect awareness of exactly how the other storefronts on Bleecker would look, for example—but the most important components seem to be pure fiction. Why would I dream the poplar tree outside our old apartment window, for example, when the unit is now occupied by another family? Why would I be able to perfectly visualize the layout of Dolores Kay's studio, only to discover that it's occupied by a hair salon instead?

Is there really a girl named Hannah out there somewhere? How else can I explain what I saw from the bridal shop window without chalking this all up to insanity?

But then it occurs to me that Dolores Kay might be real after all, even if she doesn't occupy the studio I dreamed of. And if she exists, there's a chance Hannah does too. I pull out my iPhone, heart thudding, and enter *Dolores Kay* into a Google box. The search engine returns a slew of results, but my hope fades as I scroll through them. There are obituaries for women named Dolores Kay listed from Iowa, Pennsylvania, and Wisconsin, but none of the photos match the woman from my dreams. There are a few Facebook matches too, but again, none of the Dolores Kays looks familiar.

I add *New York* to the search string, but the results are even more hopeless. Census data from the 1940s. More obituaries. Nothing that connects to the piano teacher I saw so clearly.

Finally, feeling disappointed, I add *piano teacher* to the search string and hit Enter. Immediately, my heart is in my throat, for the picture that materializes on the top of my search screen is instantly familiar. It's the Dolores Kay I saw in my dream. She's real.

Except she's dead. My mouth goes dry as I click on the picture and it takes me to an obituary. Dolores Kay, I read, was a beloved piano teacher who died on March 6, 2004, in a convenience store robbery in Brooklyn. Like Patrick, she was in the wrong place at the wrong time. She was sixty-one, the obituary says, and she is survived only by a sister, Petula, who lives in London. *She will be missed most by her generations of piano students,* the obituary concludes. *In recent years, she had begun to develop a specialty in working with children with special needs.*

I can feel myself shaking as I stare down at the stark black and white of the obituary. There has to be a logical explanation for this. Perhaps, for instance, I skimmed Dolores Kay's obituary in the *New York Times* back in 2004, and it somehow stuck in my memory. How else would I have known who she was, or that she taught piano to special needs children?

But the explanation fails to make me feel much better. If I'm dreaming only of dead people, does that mean Hannah existed at some point and has died too? Maybe she's also wedged in my memory from an obituary I read years ago.

I put my head in my hands, ignoring the concerned whispers of the two women who have arrived at the bus stop and are staring at me from the far end of the bench. I hear the word *crazy,* and I wonder if perhaps they're not that far off from the truth.

But then I remember something else. Joan is in the dreams, and certainly she's real. She's alive. But she still hasn't called me back. If she truly does have breast cancer in real life, is it a sign that the dreams are something more than just a figment of my imagination? But if she doesn't, maybe I need to seek professional help. The idea scares me, but I feel like I'm spinning out of control.

I close the Google search results and dial Joan's number, but there's no answer, so I leave a message apologizing for being a nag but telling her I'm worried about her and am coming out to check on her. Then I jog to the corner, where I hail a cab to Penn Station.

Ninety minutes later, as I walk the twelve blocks from the Glen Cove station to Joan's house, I almost convince myself to turn around and go home. After all, Joan hasn't returned my call. Maybe she just doesn't want to see me.

Still, despite the last-minute trepidation, I find myself standing on her front porch. I ring the doorbell, but there's only silence inside. I ring once more, just in case, but it's clear she's not home. I feel even sillier for coming out here uninvited but I settle onto one of her comfortable Adirondack chairs to wait for her anyhow. *She's family,* I tell myself. *There's nothing wrong with this.* But if I really don't think I'm doing anything wrong, why haven't I returned Dan's calls? He's left me two messages since I got on the train, one asking if I'd be home for dinner and another telling me he was going to head out to Brooklyn to see Stephen for the afternoon.

"I'll be home by seven," his voice mail said. "Unless you tell me otherwise, I'll plan on making salmon tonight. Love you, babe."

I text Dan, *Salmon sounds great,* then I settle back to wait for Joan as I will the guilt to roll away.

She finally pulls into her driveway a few minutes before three and looks surprised to see me on her front porch as she gets out of her Volvo.

"Kate?" she asks, blinking at me. "Is everything okay?"

"Everything's fine," I assure her, as I head down the front steps to help her with the groceries I see piled in her backseat.

"Well, then, what are you doing here, dear? Not that I'm not happy to see you."

We embrace, and I can't help but notice that she feels thinner, less substantial than I remember. Or is that just my imagination?

Am I projecting cancer onto her because I don't want to believe the dreams are pure fiction?

"I just hadn't heard from you," I tell her as I grab a few bags and an eight-pack of paper towels from the backseat. "I wasn't doing anything else today, so I thought I'd just drop by and make sure you were all right."

She blinks at me a few times as she grabs the remaining bags and pushes the car door shut with her hip. "Sweetheart, I'm fine. I just hadn't gotten around to calling you back yet. I'm sorry."

I follow her inside, where her place looks just like it always does. I realize I'm looking around for evidence of illness: medication bottles, hot water bags, dishes piled in the sink because she's too worn out to clean up. But there's none of that. After I help her put away her groceries, I excuse myself to the bathroom, where I check the medicine cabinet for evidence. But there's only a bottle of Advil, a container of Pepto-Bismol, and a box of DayQuil tablets. In other words, she's fine. I feel like a fool.

I head back into the kitchen, where Joan is unloading the dishwasher. "Can I get you a drink? An iced tea, maybe?"

"That sounds great."

I watch her as she takes two glasses down from the cabinet, fills them with ice, and pours cold tea from a jug in the refrigerator. "Want to have a seat in the living room?" she asks, handing me a glass. "I'll be in as soon as I finish up in here."

"Need any help?" I offer.

"Oh, sweetheart, I get by just fine on my own, thanks. You go relax."

As I head into the living room and sit down, I'm hit with an old memory. This is the couch where Patrick and I sat, side by side, thirteen years ago, the evening we told his parents we'd gotten engaged. His mother had grinned from ear to ear; his father had asked if they could help pay for the wedding. Patrick had kissed me on the cheek and held up my hand for them to see. I remember how my diamond ring sparkled and caught the light.

I look down now at my hand, where Dan's ring has taken the place of Patrick's on my left ring finger. My hand looks older too; the veins are more prominent than they were when I was twenty-seven, and there are lines and folds that weren't there before. Time marches ever forward whether we want it to or not.

"Kate?" Joan's voice cuts into my thoughts, and I look up to see her gazing down at me. "Are you okay, dear?"

I nod, and she smiles, but there's concern in her eyes.

"You just looked lost in your own world."

"Just remembering the day Patrick and I came here together to tell you we were getting married," I admit.

Joan sighs as she sits down across from me. "Kate, I've been meaning to talk to you about something."

My heart pounds and I lean forward. *This is it. I know it. She's going to tell me she's fighting cancer.* "It's okay, Joan," I say. "I was hoping to talk to you too."

She nods and takes a deep breath. "Kate," she says slowly, "I wonder if I'm doing you a disservice by continuing to be so close to you."

I blink. "What?"

She looks at her hands. "It's why I haven't returned your calls. Ever since you told me about those dreams, I've been worrying about the role I'm playing in your life. I think that in order for you to move on, you need to let Patrick go, and I'm concerned that by making you feel responsible for me, I've made it impossible for you to do that."

"Joan," I manage, my voice shaky, "I don't feel responsible for you. I love you. You're my mother-in-law."

"But I'm not really, am I?" she asks, not unkindly. "Not any-more. I mean, of course I'll always love you like a daughter. And

I'll always be so grateful for the happiness you gave Patrick. But I'm not sure it's healthy for you to keep an old lady like me around."

I feel a bit like she's breaking up with me. "You're not an old lady, Joan. And I'm not here because I feel like I have to be. I'm here because I care about you. Deeply."

"I feel the same about you," she says. "But I imagine Dan isn't a big fan of our relationship."

"He doesn't mind," I say, although I know the words aren't one hundred percent true.

She shakes her head sadly. "I just don't want to be a burden on you, Kate. Patrick wouldn't have wanted to be a weight on your mind either. You know, that right?"

"I do," I say. "But you're not a burden. And Patrick isn't a weight."

Joan is quiet for a moment, then she nods. "What did you want to talk about, Kate? You said there was something you wanted to discuss?"

My concerns feel foolish now, but I say the words anyhow. "I was wondering when you last had a mammogram."

Joan looks startled. "A mammogram? Well, I guess it's been a while, but I feel just fine. What makes you ask?"

I can't tell her it's the dreams. Not after what she just said. So what I blurt out instead is, "Someone I really care about was just diagnosed with breast cancer. It just . . . It made me worry about you."

Her forehead creases. "I'm so sorry to hear about your friend."

I shake my head. "Just promise me you'll get checked out, okay?"

"Kate, I honestly feel just fine."

"Please. I need you to tell me you'll do this. For me."

She stares at me. "Okay. I will."

"Promise?"

"Yes. I promise."

"Soon?"

"Okay." She looks worried.

"And you're sure you're feeling all right?" I persist.

"Are you sure *you're* feeling all right?"

I nod quickly. "I'm fine," I tell her. "Just fine."

She studies my face. "You look like you're not getting enough sleep, sweetheart. Try to get some rest, okay? Take it easy. And don't worry about me. You're getting married soon, and this should be a very special and happy time in your life."

"It is," I say. *Just not as happy as the time I spend dreaming about your son.*

The first part of the work week passes quickly and uneventfully with appointments with Max, Leo, and several other clients. On Tuesday, I pray I'll wake up in the dream, for it's Hannah's birthday, but instead, I find myself in real life, so I think of her all day and hope that somewhere, in my strange alternate reality, she's happy. On Wednesday, sign language class goes well; I'm picking up words quickly, and I'm embarrassed to admit I'm enjoying my role as teacher's pet, even if it does earn me death stares from Amy. After class, I arrange to meet Andrew the following night at St. Anne's for a repeat of last week: appointments with Riajah and Molly at the office, then an in-home visit with Allie.

"How's your week going?" Andrew asks when I duck my head into his office on Thursday, just past four. He's in jeans and a vintage Beatles tee today, and his hair is rumpled, like he just got out of bed.

"I saw you less than twenty-four hours ago," I remind him with a smile.

"At which point I didn't have a chance to ask you properly how you're doing," he answers, returning my grin, "because to do so would have been to incur Amy's wrath."

"Ah, so you've noticed too."

"Noticed? She shoots daggers at you with her eyes every time you talk to me. Then she stares at me like I'm a Christmas present she'd like to unwrap."

I laugh. "Very humble of you."

His eyebrows shoot up. "I didn't say I deserve it. I'm just reporting the facts."

"Hey, in her defense, it's hard to be a single girl in New York," I say, although I don't know why I'm standing up for Amy. "Who can blame her for setting her sights on a cute, smart single guy?"

Andrew turns a little red, and I can feel my cheeks heating up too, because I realize the words sound flirtatious, although I didn't mean them to. Then we both start speaking at once. "I'm not exactly—" Andrew begins.

"I didn't mean—" I sat at the same time.

We both laugh uneasily, and he says, "You first."

"I was just going to say I didn't mean to sound like I'm hitting on you."

"Oh, no, of course not." His blush is gone, replaced by an amused expression. "Heaven forbid. I probably have cooties."

I roll my eyes. "I suspected as much. So what were you going to say?"

"Oh. Nothing." He checks his watch. "Let's go see if the girls are here, shall we?"

Twenty

The visits with Molly and Riajah seem to fly by quickly. Molly chooses a banjo from among eight instruments I scatter on the floor before she comes in, and when she's picked out a few notes on it, I show her a few simple chords, and we sing together, an exercise that's designed to help improve the natural cadence of her speech, her ability to watch and repeat, and her comfort communicating with others. Riajah is a bit more difficult; I try the same exercise with her, but she refuses to choose an instrument, so eventually, I wind up playing my guitar alone while she stares at me from the corner. But by the end of the session, she's tapping her feet and mouthing the words to the chorus, and although she refuses to acknowledge me on the way out, I count it as progress.

On the way to Allie's foster home, I tell Andrew about the sessions and what I'm thinking of for next week, but then an uneasy silence settles over us for the remainder of the walk, a strange contrast to the ease we usually enjoy. I'm relieved when we finally reach Allie's house, but the feeling is cut short when Rodney ushers us into Allie's room, and I see that she's torn down all her poems.

She's hunched over her computer, typing furiously, when we

enter, and she either doesn't hear us or is deliberately ignoring us. "Allie?" I ask loudly, but she doesn't turn.

"She's been like this all day," Rodney says softly.

"Any idea what's wrong?" Andrew asks.

Rodney shakes his head. "She won't talk to us. We've tried, but she just shuts herself in here."

"Let me try," I suggest. I take a deep breath and smile at the men. "I'll see you in a little while."

Rodney hesitates, clearly reluctant to leave, but he finally does, followed by an equally uncertain-looking Andrew. I watch Allie from the doorway for a moment. Her keystrokes are an angry staccato.

I walk over to her computer, and as my shadow falls over her, she jumps. "Allie?" I say loudly, trying to keep my voice gentle. "Everything okay?"

Her face turns red, and she slams her laptop closed then glances up at me with a deer-in-the-headlights look on her face. She doesn't say anything; she just looks at me stonily, so after a moment, I ask, "What were you writing?"

Her stare darkens into a glare as she signs the letters *NYB* to me. It takes me a moment to grasp that what she's saying is *None of your business*.

Instead of reacting the way she likely expects me to, I shrug and turn away. I bite my lip for a moment, my brain spinning over all the possibilities of what could be the matter. She's removed her poems from the wall, so maybe a boy she's had a crush on has rejected her. But then I realize none of the poems I'd glanced at last week had seemed romantic in nature. Maybe a teacher criticized her writing, but would that have put her in this sort of dark mood?

I spread out the same instruments on her rug that I used with Molly and Riajah earlier, then I pull out my guitar and wait for her to look up at me. When she finally does, still glowering, I nod to the items on the floor. "Want to choose one?" I ask.

She shakes her head firmly and rolls her eyes.

"You don't have to play," I tell her. "But I'm going to. I thought you might want to join me."

She snort-laughs and rolls her eyes at me again. I act like I don't care, and I begin strumming my guitar slowly, searching for a song that might elicit something from her.

I begin with Daughtry's "Over You," in case Allie's problem has to do with a boy, but she just ignores me. Then I transition into "Puff the Magic Dragon," and her expression grows bored. It's only when I begin playing the Beatles' "Hey Jude"—one of Leo's favorites—that I finally see a spark of interest on her face. When I finish the song, I let silence hang between us until she finally says something.

Who's Jude? she signs, her eyes still suspicious.

It's exactly the question I was hoping for. "Jude is John Lennon's son Julian," I tell her. "John Lennon is one of the Beatles."

"Duh," she says aloud. "Only idiots don't know the Beatles." Then she pauses and adds, "If his name is Julian, why do they call him Jude, anyways?"

I smile. "Paul McCartney—he's another Beatle, but I guess you know that—wrote the song for Julian when Julian's parents, John and Cynthia, were getting a divorce. Julian was sad, and Paul knew that sometimes, music helps people. He was originally singing, 'Hey Jules,' his nickname for Julian, but he changed it to 'Hey Jude,' because he liked the sound of it better."

She looks at me for a moment. "So why was Julian sad, anyways?"

I shrug. "I think divorce can be tough on a person," I tell her. "I think maybe Julian felt a little bit like his parents didn't care about him, or that he was being abandoned by his mom and dad." Something in her face changes. I've hit a nerve. "I think Paul McCartney was trying to tell Julian that it wasn't his fault, that he didn't have to carry the world on his shoulders, and that it was all going to get better."

She thinks about this for a minute. "Did it? Get better?"

"For Julian?" I nod. "Yes. He's all grown up now, and he's a musician too, just like his dad."

"Because his dad loved him, after all," Allie says.

"His mom and dad both did."

Allie turns quickly away and wipes furtively at her face. I wait for her to turn back around before setting my guitar down and signing, *What's wrong?*

"Nothing," she snaps. "And you don't have to sign. I can talk, you know. I'm not stupid."

I wait a moment before asking gently, "Did something happen with your mom?"

She snorts, but the pain that flickers across her face tells me everything I need to know. "No, nothing happened" is what she finally says. I assume she's stonewalling me again until she adds a moment later, "That's the problem. Doesn't she care about me? At all? She comes twice a week because she has to, and I have overnight visits with her in her new apartment sometimes, but the rest of the time, she doesn't even care if I'm alive."

"What makes you think that, Allie?" I ask, and her eyes narrow.

"Because why wouldn't she get her crap together quicker so she could take me home? Why would she be moving so slow and just leaving me here in some stranger's house in the meantime?"

"There could be lots of reasons that have nothing to do with you. Can you think of any?" It's my job to get her to cycle through the options herself and to explore what she's feeling about her mother, but it's hard to resist the urge to comfort her and tell her I know her mother must love her.

"Yeah," Allie says after a pause. "But I think it's because she hates me." She looks down, and I hear her sniffle a few times.

I wait for her to go on, but when she doesn't, I say, "It may not feel to you like your mother loves you, but she has a lot of problems in her life right now, Allie. Sometimes those kinds of problems make it hard for a parent to act loving."

She snorts. "You don't know anything about it."

"You're right. I don't. That's why I'm asking you to guess some reasons."

She's silent for a minute. "Fine. Maybe she's got some stuff to deal with, you know? Maybe she's just not ready to be a mom again yet. Okay?"

I smile at her. "That sounds much more likely, Allie. Don't you think?"

Allie makes a face and looks away. After a moment, she looks back at me. "I checked with my social worker, you know. My mom could get me back by September if she just grows up and stops doing all the wrong things. But I bet she doesn't even care."

"What were you doing on your computer there?" I ask, nodding to her laptop. "E-mailing her?"

"I don't even know her new e-mail address," she grumbles. "But I was going to give her a letter next time she comes for a supervised visit."

"What would the letter say?"

"It would say stop being a shitty mom."

"Well, that sounds fair," I say. Allie looks at me closely, and I know she's trying to determine whether I'm being sarcastic. I'm not. "But what if what you said a moment ago is true? What if she's just trying to deal with her stuff?"

Allie's face contorts into a look of disgust. "You know what?

You're just like everyone else. You say the right thing, but it doesn't mean anything."

I consider this and realize she's completely right. I'm just giving her platitudes. So I think for a minute and say, "Okay. What she's doing, it sucks. It sucks big time."

A tiny smile tugs at the corner of Allie's lips. "For real?"

I nod. "But what if you give her the benefit of the doubt? What if she really is trying to make a better life for you? Do you think that's possible?"

Allie doesn't answer. But after a moment, she gets up and crosses over to her keyboard. She doesn't do anything at first, but then she reaches for the keys and slowly, tentatively, pecks out the first few notes of "Hey Jude." Then she looks up, raises an eyebrow at me, and says, "Well?"

I smile, pick up my guitar again, and begin to play. And for the next twenty minutes, with me on guitar and Allie on keys, we play Paul McCartney's beautiful melody from nearly five decades ago again and again and again. I can hear Allie humming after a while, so I take her cue and begin to sing along with the music. After a few times through the song, I begin improvising the lyrics so that they connect more directly to Allie's situation. Soon, to the tune of "Hey Jude," we're both singing, "Hey, Mom. Where you been? I've been waiting . . . for you to come get me."

When we finally finish, our fingers tired, she gives me a high five.

I look up just in time to see Andrew watching us from the doorway with a smile on his face.

For the next several days, the session with Allie bothers me. I begin to have trouble sleeping, and the dreams—or whatever they are—don't return. I lie silently beside a lightly snoring Dan, willing myself to forget about Allie, to fall asleep, to see Patrick and Hannah again. But the tiles of my ceiling only grow blurrier, and the moments tick by until the room begins to gray around the edges as the first rays of dawn saturate the room-darkening blinds.

It begins to occur to me that maybe I won't get another glimpse into the life with Patrick and Hannah. Maybe being exposed to Hannah was a strange means to an end, a roundabout way to put me in Andrew's path so that he would lead me to Allie. I feel an almost gravitational pull to the girl. In fact, I can't stop thinking about her and how I might be able to help her, even when Dan surprises me with a weekend in the Hamptons. I lie beside him on the sand and pretend to read *People* magazine while my mind spins over the songs I'd like to try with her. At night, as we sit by a bonfire Dan has built on the beach, I pretend to listen as he regales me with stories about his coworkers, but really, my mind is on Allie.

On Tuesday, I have a session in my office with Max, and after we've played the xylophone together and talked about a new boy at school named Toby who isn't being very nice to him, he asks me a question that makes my heart ache.

"Miss Kate?" he says as he fidgets with the hem of his shirt. "How come some parents don't want their kids?"

"Max, why do you say that?"

"I don't know. Sometimes they just don't."

"Who are you talking about?" I ask gently. When he doesn't say anything, I ask, "Your mom?"

"No, silly!" Max says, rolling his eyes dramatically. "She loves me." Then his face falls. "But what about my dad? He didn't want me."

"What makes you say that, Max?"

"Toby at school told me that's why my dad went away."

I bite my lip as I search for the right words. Joya has been raising Max alone since he was ten months old, after his father left one day for work and never came back. Three months later, he had divorce papers delivered to Joya, and she'd signed them without fighting for more child support, because they'd also contained a provision that gave her full custody. She told me once that she didn't want Max having any exposure to a man who didn't want to be his father.

"First of all, Max, do you think Toby really knows anything about your life?"

He thinks about this for a minute. "Maybe not."

"So what do you think really happened with your dad?" I hold my breath, hoping I'm not inadvertently leading him down a hurtful path.

"I don't know. Mom never says anything." He pauses. "Maybe my dad didn't want to be my dad."

I think about how to respond. "Is it possible he just wasn't ready to be a dad yet at all? And that it had nothing to do with you personally?"

He looks confused. "But how come he'd be a dad if he wasn't ready to be a dad? That's crazy."

"Well, it's a bit like taking a test at school," I tell him. "Have you ever taken a test?"

He nods. "I'm good at spelling tests."

"Well, you study for the tests beforehand, right?"

He nods again. "Mom makes me."

"And studying is hard work, right?"

"Really hard!"

"But when you go in to take the test, you're prepared, and that's what makes you do well, right?"

"Mmm hmm," he agrees.

"Well, parenting is a bit like that. It's a lot of hard work. You have to always be learning and always be practicing and trying your hardest."

"Or you get an F!"

"Exactly," I say. "Sometimes, people just aren't ready to work hard. So they're not really good at being parents."

He thinks about this for so long that I start to believe my explanation has been a big flop. But then he smiles slightly and says, "So maybe my dad just didn't want to work hard and practice."

"Right," I say slowly, hoping I haven't instilled false hope.

When our session ends, I pull Joya aside and recap our conversation.

"I think it's just human nature to wish that the people who are gone from our lives are going to come back," she replies with a sigh. "Maybe this is something Max just has to puzzle through."

After she's gone, her words echo in my head. Maybe, like Max, I'm just going to have to wrap my head around the idea that Patrick is gone for good, and no amount of hoping for his return will bring him back.

"Well, you're tan," Andrew says as I walk into sign language class the next night. He's standing in front of the classroom, leafing through some papers, when I arrive, and I feel immediately awkward when I realize I've interrupted a conversation between him and Amy, the only other student who's already here.

"It's that obvious?" I ask, hoping that I'm dark enough he won't notice my blush. "I guess that must mean I was really pale before."

"Not at all," he says with a smile. "I'm jealous that you obviously spent your weekend at a beach or something, while I spent mine doing paperwork." He pauses. "No, wait! Maybe you didn't go away at all! Maybe you're one of those tanning bed girls. Is this a spray tan?"

He's teasing me, and it makes my cheeks even warmer. "Nope, sorry to disappoint. This is from a weekend in the Hamptons."

Andrew groans. "I knew it! Now I'm officially jealous."

"Did you go with your fiancé?" Amy asks loudly, injecting herself into the conversation. "I bet you spend a lot of time with him, right? With your fiancé?"

I blink at her. "Yes. Right. His cousin has a share in Montauk."

She whistles. "Fancy."

I shrug and glance at Andrew. "We thought so too. Until we arrived and found out we'd be splitting a three-bedroom house with four other couples."

Andrew chuckles, and Amy makes a face.

"Well, still, your fiancé must make some serious money, right?" she asks. "To be in the kind of social circles where Montauk is even an option?"

She's beginning to get on my nerves. "He does okay," I say vaguely. I'm heartened to see Andrew rolling his eyes behind Amy's back.

"Well, you should hang on to him," she says. "I know I would appreciate it if someone treated me to weekends away." She bats her eyes at Andrew, who looks embarrassed and goes back to shuffling his papers.

I sit down, and as the others filter in one by one, Amy picks up her things and relocates to the seat next to mine. "So you and Andrew seem pretty close," she whispers once Andrew is involved in a conversation with Greg on the other side of the room.

I don't meet her eye as I say, "Yeah, we do some work together. With foster kids. That's all."

She studies me for a minute. "So there's nothing going on between you two?" she asks.

"Nothing." I hold up my left hand. "Remember? I'm engaged."

"So you wouldn't mind if I asked Andrew out?"

I hesitate just a millisecond too long before saying, "Of course not."

She smirks a little, and it's obvious she's interpreted my pause as evidence that I'm secretly in love with Andrew. In reality, I'm trying to think of a way to tell her Andrew's not interested without being rude.

Andrew looks at me suspiciously as he calls the class to order, and I try to put Amy, Andrew, and their potential date out of my mind as I work on committing thirty new verbs and thirty new nouns to memory. At the end of class, Andrew lectures us for a few minutes about ASL sentence construction, then pairs us up with partners to practice twenty phrases he has provided for us on worksheets. I'm relieved when he assigns me to work with Vivian, but I feel uneasy when I realize that means he's working with Amy, since there are an odd number of us in class.

After class, I wave good-bye to him from across the room and hurry out with my head down. I'm halfway to the corner of Madison and Sixty-Ninth when I hear footsteps on the pavement and turn to find Andrew jogging after me.

"Wait up!" he says, his armful of papers and books precariously waving back and forth. "You rushed out," he says when he catches up to me.

"Didn't want to stand in Amy's way." I can't resist.

"There's no—" he begins, but then he shakes his head. "Don't worry. I won't be dating Amy."

"I wasn't worried," I say too quickly.

"Right," he says. He falls into step beside me. "Anyway, I wanted to tell you that Molly's gone back to her mother. It was a court order we weren't expecting, or I would have told you sooner. Her caseworker was in support of it, but none of us really thought the judge would sign off. It just happened this afternoon."

"Is she okay?"

"Seemed like she was really excited about it," Andrew says. "I've never seen a kid pack so quickly in my life."

"Well, that's good." I'm surprised to feel a lump in my throat. It's unsettling to realize one of these kids could vanish from my life so quickly. "I wish I'd gotten to say good-bye."

"I wish you had too. I'm sorry. But I think it's for the best. The parental reunion, I mean. I think the mom's not a bad person, and maybe this was the wake-up call she needed. I think Molly's going to be fine."

"That's good." I pause. "But what if you're wrong?"

He just looks at me.

"I mean, how do you deal with the not knowing?" I ask. "You'll never know whether Molly's okay or not unless she winds up back at St. Anne's, right?"

"Right," Andrew agrees after a pause. "Of course there are follow-up visits. But you're right; it's hard to tell how everything's going when you're only with a family for an hour. I think you just have to hope—and believe in the fundamental goodness of most people."

Twenty-One

I wake up the next day back in the too-bright, bizarrely familiar world for the first time in two and a half weeks, but this time is different from the rest. I'm not waking up at home, beside Patrick. Instead, I'm slumped forward uncomfortably on a mahogany desk, a piece of paper stuck to my cheek. As I struggle upright in my chair and blink in confusion, the only way I know I'm dreaming is that the colors in the room are too rich and vibrant for real life. Everything here always seem to be strangely oversaturated, as if someone exposed a photo reel for far too long, making the images bleed into one another too brightly.

I look around, puzzled. *Where am I?* But the second the question crosses my mind, the now-familiar information download happens. Instantly, I know that this is my office. I know I'm in a brownstone on the Upper East Side and that I work only three days a week so that I can be home with Hannah. I know I can afford to, because my music therapy practice has become very successful. The phrase *Music therapy services for adults: discretion, professionalism, and healing,* flashes across my mind like an advertising slogan. A second later I realize it *is* an advertising slogan. *My* advertising slogan. But does this mean I don't work with kids?

I frown and look at the file folders spread out on my desk. I open the one on top and read the case notes, written in my own handwriting, on a twenty-six-year-old patient named Travis Worthington III. Apparently, he has schizophrenia and I've been working on a treatment plan in conjunction with his psychiatrist. My notes tell me he's been having trouble expressing himself in words, but that he's been slowly opening up through music. According to what I've jotted down, his psychiatrist has recently recommended another six months with me.

The next file folder is for Samantha Lynn Berkley-Fournier, forty-two, a mother of two suffering from depression. My notes tell me she's been coming to me for a month now and that we've been working on finding music that makes her feel some happiness and using that as a jumping-off point to discuss how she's feeling. My eyes practically bug out of my head when I flip to her billing statement and see how much I'm charging her per session. It's nearly four times what I make in my real life!

But as I gaze around my office, I wonder suddenly if I'm happy here. In real life, my office is filled with pictures kids have drawn for me, artsy photographs of musical instruments I've collected over the years, and random knickknacks people have given me as gifts—everything from candles to marmalade jars to framed baseball cards. I love the managed chaos, and it gives the kids I work with something to look at too. I think of all the objects as possible entry points into conversations with each client I serve.

But here, my office is stark and professional, lined with books and medical journals. The walls hold my framed degrees and a handful of awards I've apparently won. The only traces of my personality are the photos of Patrick, Hannah, and my niece and nephew displayed on my desk.

I lean in and look at the photo of Patrick, a picture I suddenly know I took of him during a beach vacation to the Outer Banks of North Carolina a few years ago. He's standing knee-deep in the water and laughing as he looks right at the camera. Now, his eyes seem to sear into me from the photograph.

"What happened to my life?" I ask aloud, staring at his image. I don't have the sense that I'm unfulfilled here, necessarily, but it occurs to me for the first time that choosing to work with kids was a decision I made *after* Patrick died in my real life. I never considered it a choice influenced by his death, but what if it was? What if it was a subconscious need to work with clients I considered the most helpless, because Patrick had been helpless at the moment he died too? Or what if I'd simply found comfort in working with kids when I thought my own chance to have children had vanished? Should that have been a sign to me all along that I had a deep-seated desire to be a mom?

My heart thudding, I reach for my office phone to dial Patrick, but I realize that to my surprise, I don't know his number. I shake my head and grab my cell phone instead. It takes me a minute to discover that my security code is our wedding date, and when I unlock it, I'm relieved to find Patrick first on my favorites list. I call him, but it rings and goes straight to voice mail. "Hey, honey," I say, shaken by hearing his beautifully familiar voice on his outgoing message. "Can you give me a call when you get this? I have a question for you."

I hang up and look at the appointment calendar on my desk. My next session isn't until two thirty, and it's only noon. Suddenly, I know exactly how I'll fill the time. I need to go out to Queens to sign up for a volunteer position at St. Anne's, so that the next time I'm here, I'll feel a bit more comfortable with the work I'm doing. And I need to go home to see Hannah, if she's there, because I can't imagine spending time in this world without her.

I stride out of the office, telling my assistant—whom I don't recognize, but who I instantly know is named Judith—that I'll be back in time for my next appointment. As soon as I'm in the hall, I call Hannah's cell—the second number on my favorites list—but it goes to voice mail. I leave her a message, then I text her: *Thinking of coming home for lunch. Where are you?*

The second I hit Send, the world fades a little, and I realize too late that of course I should I already know where my daughter is. She's barely thirteen. That's too young to leave home alone, isn't it? I'm embarrassed to discover I don't actually know the answer to that.

At Aunt Gina's, just like every M, W and Thu in summer, Hannah texts back.

Can you tell Gina I'll drop by around 1:30? I text back.

Ok.

Love you, honey. So much, I add.

U 2, Mom.

I take a deep breath, tremendously grateful that I'll be seeing not only Hannah shortly, but Gina too. It appears that in this world, she and I got even closer to each other—close enough that my daughter refers to her as an aunt and stays with her when I'm working. I wonder if her first husband is still alive. If Patrick and Dolores Kay—both of whom died tragically in real life—are here, maybe Bill is too. Oddly, I'm not sure how this makes me feel, because if Bill didn't die, Gina never married Wayne, and they never had Madison. And I can't imagine a world in which Gina isn't Madison's mom. I close my eyes and take a deep breath. The more time I get to spend in this world, the more complicated the questions get.

I hail a cab outside my office and give the driver the address of St. Anne's. When we pull up in front of the familiar building twenty-five minutes later, I breathe a sigh of relief; it's still here. The fact that it's a constant between both worlds makes me relax a little. At once, I'm excited—giddy almost—to see Andrew. He may not know me yet, but like Joan, he'll be an anchor to my real life. And maybe he'll be able to help me understand what's going on.

But when I approach the receptionist, the one I never see in real life because Andrew usually meets me outside, she looks confused when I ask for Andrew Henson.

"There's no one here by that name," she says blankly.

I blink at her a few times. "He runs the deaf services program."

"Ma'am, we don't *have* a deaf service program," the receptionist says.

I feel a sense of panic beginning to rise within me. "But what about Riajah Daniels? And Allie Valcher? And Molly Parise?"

The woman looks at me with concern. "Ma'am, none of those people work here."

"No, they're children," I say softly, already backing away. "They're children, and now I don't know if they're okay."

I'm trembling by the time I reach the front steps of St. Anne's. I can see an image in my mind of Andrew standing here, his hands in his pockets, a superhero shirt making him look charmingly boyish, his smile lighting up his face. "Where is he?" I murmur.

I sit down on the bottom step and pull out my iPhone again. I search for his name, and before I even have a chance to scroll down to the text results, I see his picture pop up as the sixth Google Images option.

I click on it quickly, and when it enlarges, I click on the attached link. It takes me to a profile in the *Atlanta Journal-*

Constitution of a pair of brothers who own a restaurant called Griddle in the Atlanta suburb of Roswell. My eyes widen as I scan the story and find a second picture—of Andrew and a second man, who the caption tells me is his brother, Kevin.

Kevin's alive in this world. The thought startles me, and I realize instantly that without Kevin's death, Andrew wasn't compelled to work with deaf children in his brother's honor. His life took a completely different path, and that means that children like Riajah and Allie don't have a place like St. Anne's to look after them. I assume they're okay and that they're being cared for by another social services agency. But I can't imagine it would be the same as being looked after by friendly, hardworking, caress-o-much-it-hurts Andrew.

My stomach twists as I read the article. Griddle, which specializes in inventive grilled specialties, apparently opened nine months ago with Andrew as the head chef and Kevin as the manager. It's their second project together, after a restaurant called Mojo that closed in 2012.

"We're hoping that our old friends from Mojo give Griddle a shot and that we can become a strong part of the Roswell community," Andrew is quoted as saying. "Kevin and I grew up not far from here, and I think you'll find that the menu consists of unique twists on local favorites that should feel familiar to anyone who remembers a childhood in Georgia."

I enlarge the photo of Andrew and stare at it for a moment. Is it my imagination that he doesn't look as happy as he does in real life? He's ten pounds heavier—surely a result of working long hours in a restaurant kitchen—and his face is more lined, his eyes tired. There's something in his expression that looks sad, but it could just be me projecting. After all, *I'm* sad to see that he lives miles away and hasn't had a chance to help turn children's lives around. It feels like a waste.

I close the article and shove my phone back into my purse, then I take a deep breath and stand up. I walk up to the corner and hail a cab, and all the way back to Manhattan, I think about Andrew and how he's not where he's supposed to be. *Anytime there's a void, it gets filled by something that makes you different than you were before,* he said that day at the Jamaican restaurant. *It changes the course of your life.*

His words reverberate through me as New York rolls by outside my window. Life is wonderful here, in a way, because Patrick and Hannah exist—and Andrew's brother didn't die—but it's also different, because neither Andrew nor I had the chance to grow from our losses. Nothing knocked us off course and made us reevaluate everything.

The cab pulls up outside Gina's place, and after I hand the driver a couple twenties, I get out and stare up at the sky, which is too blue, too brilliant. It's beautiful, but I miss the sky where I live. The more time I spend in this world, the more I realize it can't possibly be reality. The overly bright colors should have been a dead giveaway all along. This may not be a dream in the traditional sense, but it's not real life either. My eyes filling with tears, I walk up the front steps to Gina's place and buzz her apartment.

"Hello?" an unfamiliar woman's voice answers.

"Hi. I'm looking for Gina."

"There's no one here by that name," the woman says. Startled, I look at the name beside her buzzer and see that, in fact, it says Trouba, a name I don't know.

"Oh," I say. "I'm sorry." As I walk back down the steps, confused, it occurs to me that I have absolutely no idea where Gina could be. It's the only apartment I've ever known her in; she even lived here with Bill before he died.

I consider texting Hannah back to ask her for Gina's address, but I suspect that will make the dream fade away, because there's no reason I shouldn't know. I can't ask Patrick, either. So for a moment, I just stand in place on the sidewalk like a rock in the middle of a stream as people flow by.

My phone rings a moment later, startling me. I'm relieved to see Patrick's name on the caller ID.

"Hey, honey," Patrick's warm, deep voice calms me instantly. I close my eyes. "Hi."

"What's wrong? You don't sound like yourself."

I sigh. "It's just been a long, confusing day."

"Honey, what's the matter?"

I have no idea how to even begin to answer that. So instead, I ask him the question I had this morning, even though I suspect it will probably pull me right out of this world, the way that questioning things always does. But I have to know.

"Am I happy, Patrick?" I ask him. "Really and truly happy?"

"What do you mean, Kate? Of course you're happy." He sounds concerned.

"I don't mean with you and Hannah. I know the two of you make me happier than anything in the world." I pause. "But with the rest of my life. Am I happy at work?" The world grows a little dimmer, and I know I'm skating on thin ice.

He's silent for a moment. "I think so," he says. "I mean, you're happy enough."

It's the same phrase my mother used in reference to Dan, the one that made me balk. "But happy enough isn't the same thing, is it?" I ask sadly. "How did I get here?"

The world is almost gone now, and I have to strain to hear Patrick's voice over the phone. It sounds tinny and distant, and I can no longer understand what he's saying. As I struggle to hold on, the faces around me melt and the buildings turn into blurs.

"Patrick?" I cry, but I know no one can hear me, for the rushing sound has begun. Just before the world disappears entirely, I realized I've made a choice. I didn't hang on long enough to see Patrick and Hannah this time.

But then again, maybe what I chose was life.

Twenty-Two

"How's Riajah doing now that Molly's gone?" Andrew asks Thursday afternoon as we leave my session at Sheila's place and walk toward the Greghors' row house. I want to hug him, to tell him how glad I am that he's chosen this life for himself, but I can't reference the restaurant in Georgia without sounding like a crazy person. So I settle for a warm smile.

"She'll be okay," I tell him. "She misses Molly. But to be honest, I think it's also that she feels like Molly's parents cared enough to come back for her. I'm trying to discourage her from drawing a parallel with her own situation."

He sighs. "Poor kid."

"You know, you don't have to walk me to Allie's," I tell him. "I'm sure you have plenty of stuff to do."

"What if I like walking with you?" he asks.

"Then by all means, carry on," I say formally. As soon as the words are out of my mouth, I feel like an idiot, but Andrew just laughs.

At the Greghors' place, he introduces me to Rodney's wife, Salma, a slender, thirtysomething, olive-skinned woman with a lopsided smile, a slightly crooked nose, and big brown eyes. She takes my hands and tells me she's so pleased I've been working with Allie. Then she and Andrew head for the kitchen while I make my way down the hall to Allie's room.

I find her sitting cross-legged on her bed, sketching something on a notepad. She looks up when I walk in, and I'm heartened to see that instead of glaring at me, she half smiles before returning to what she's doing.

"What are you drawing?" I ask.

She blinks a few times then reluctantly hands over the picture she's been working on. "I only just started," she tells me. "I'm not very good."

I look down at the sketch, which is incomplete. It looks like Allie was trying to draw a girl about her age, with dark, wavy hair. I have to blink a few times to get a hold of myself; the hair, even inexpertly drawn, reminds me of Hannah. Or maybe it's just the idea that Allie, who's about Hannah's age, has drawn it. I push images of the daughter from my dreams—and her bedroom wall covered in beautiful sketches—out of my head.

"This is good, Allie," I say.

"Whatever," she mumbles. "My friend Bella is a good artist. I suck."

"That's not true," I say. "This drawing looks really nice."

She makes a face at me. "Don't lie. I don't even know why I tried. Bella drew a picture of me, so I wanted to draw one of her too. But I can't do it. Not as well as her, anyways."

"Isn't it the thought that counts, though?" I ask.

"That's what people with no talent say," she says.

When I don't respond, she looks up and mumbles, "Sorry. No offense."

I shrug and begin unpacking my bag of instruments. I'm hoping I'll be able to get Allie to sit back down at the piano today, because she seems to loosen up and become a different, lighter version of herself when her fingers are on the keys.

"So who's Bella?" I ask as I lay a xylophone on the floor and fumble in my bag for the matching mallet.

"She's my friend," she says. "My best friend. And I'm not going to play your stupid xylophone. I'm not a baby."

"I didn't say you were. What do you want to play, then?"

"Who says I want to play anything?"

"Oh, you don't? Fine." I act nonchalant. "I'll play your keyboard while you draw."

I know this will elicit a response, so I'm not surprised when she snaps "No!" and jumps off her bed. She pushes past me and sits down at her keyboard. She pauses for a moment, and I can see her thinking. Then, suddenly, she pounds out the dramatic opening chords of Beethoven's Fifth. The sound is so sharp and sudden that I jump, startled, which makes her grin.

She plays for the next few minutes, and I listen, awed. "Beethoven was misunderstood too, you know," she says, stopping right in the middle of the song. "Like me."

"Was he?" I ask innocently. I like where she's going.

"Lots of people thought he was mean and had a bad temper," she says confidently. "But really, he was just a genius. He was thinking about music. And he didn't have time for people who made fun of him."

"Do people make fun of you?" I ask gently.

She ignores the question. "He was from Vienna. Did you know that? It's a city in Austria. And when he went deaf, all these people who pretended to be his friends were talking about him behind his back. They thought he didn't know because he couldn't hear anymore. But he knew. He always knew."

"Do people talk about you because they think you can't hear them?"

She frowns. "It doesn't matter anyways, because now Bella goes to my school. And she's deaf too. So when people make fun of our cochlear implants and call us robots, we can just ignore them together."

My heart lurches a bit, both in pain for Allie and gratitude for this friend who's in the same boat. "Bella sounds nice," I say. "She has cochlear implants too?"

"Yeah." Allie reaches for the keyboard with her left hand only and plays a short, haunting melody that sounds familiar but that I can't quite place. "She plays piano too, only she's better than me. We're kind of like twins."

I smile. "It's nice to have a friend like that."

She plays another verse of the strangely familiar song then says, "Today, at school, Tony Beluti, who's such a jerk, called me a bastard child because my mom is all messed up and I don't know who my dad is. Bella waited until the teacher's back was turned, then she spitballed Tony right in the eye."

"That's some friend."

Allie smiles. "The best."

"Speaking of your mom," I begin carefully, "how are things going with her?"

"I don't want to talk about it," Allie says, crossing her arms.

"Okay," I say. "How about we just play some more music?"

She looks relieved. "Cool."

"Can you teach me that song you were playing?" I ask. "It's really pretty."

She nods. "Bella wrote it."

For the next thirty minutes, we don't say a word, but we speak volumes with our instruments. Allie plays keyboard, and I imitate the melody on my guitar until we've gotten the hang of it, and we're playing in perfect harmony. Finally, our hour together is up, and I stand to leave.

"Today was great," I tell Allie. "See you next week, okay?"

She nods, and I turn to go. But she calls out, "Kate?"

I turn, and she looks at me for a moment before signing, *Thank you,* her hand moving away from her mouth like a blown kiss. *You're kind.*

"You are too," I say aloud. I pause at the doorway to add, "'Never shall I forget the days I spent with you. Continue to be my friend, as you will always find me yours.'"

"Huh?"

"It's a quote from Beethoven," I tell her with a smile. I walk out before she can respond.

That evening, dinner conversation with Dan is stilted. I can feel the awkwardness radiating from him in waves, but he keeps our small talk polite. The silences between the chatter seem to stretch on indefinitely.

I consider bringing up my session with Allie, just to make conversation, but I know he won't understand, so I keep quiet. I feel oddly buoyant after today's interaction with her; I'm really beginning to believe I can make a difference in these kids' lives, but the thought of telling Dan feels like giving a piece of it away. Like giving a piece of *myself* away. And I've already given away far too many of my pieces.

I twist my engagement ring on my finger as I wait for Dan to finish his food, and I'm hit with a new wave of shame. I never should have said yes to him, never should have taken the ring. Misgivings were already rumbling in the pit of my belly, but I had grown accustomed to ignoring them, since I thought there was no real pressure to make up my mind.

In fact, I realize as Dan chews, maybe I never should have gotten serious with him in the first place. The first time I met

Patrick, there was an instant spark between us, a glimmer of something that seemed to grow brighter and brighter the longer we talked. I felt butterflies and tingles and all the things you read about in bad romance novels. But with Dan, there weren't butterflies. There were nerves, of course, which perhaps I mistook for something else. But most of all, there were whispers of logic. *He's great. He's perfect for you. It's time to move on.* And in retrospect, not all those whispers came from my own head. The people who were most concerned about me—my mom, Susan, Gina and other friends—thought Dan was the answer to a question I hadn't actually been asking.

I thought, at the beginning, that it was only natural that I wouldn't feel the things for him that I felt for Patrick. Patrick was one of a kind, after all, and so was the love we shared. But that shouldn't have meant giving up a chance to have butterflies in my stomach again, nor should it have made me talk myself into falling in love with someone simply because he was there.

"Penny for your thoughts," Dan says, smiling uneasily at me as he finishes the last of the frozen lasagna I threw in the oven when I got home.

I force a smile back, take his plate from him, and chicken out. "I'm not sure they're worth that," I say, heading for the kitchen without looking back. I know I've wimped out again, and the longer I hide my head in the sand, the harder it will be to blink it all away.

It's not until the glowing red numbers of my bedside clock have ticked past midnight that I wonder for the first time if Allie has triggered a latent maternal instinct in me, and that everything else leads back to that. Am I so attached to her because I know she needs a good mother and she reminds me so much of Hannah? And is that making the gulf between Dan and me even wider, because the more I realize I want to be a mother, the less likely it is that my future includes him?

I roll over on my side, away from Dan. It's foolish of me to be thinking like this anyhow. Allie already has a mother, and it's not me.

Just then, the text alert goes off on my phone, a bright *ding* that pierces the silence of our bedroom. Dan shifts in his sleep and mumbles something, and I glance at the clock. 12:37. Who could be texting me this late?

I pick up the phone, angling it away from Dan to avoid waking him with the bright light. The text that's shown up on the screen is from an unfamiliar 917 number, and it reads, *No one wants me.*

I frown. It must be a wrong number. But just as I'm setting the phone back down, it beeps again with another text: *So you don't care either?*

Who is this? I type back.

There's silence for a moment, then a single-word reply: *Beethoven.*

Dan stirs again. "Everything okay, babe?" he asks.

"Um, I'm not sure," I say, my mind racing.

He mumbles something else then rolls over to go back to sleep. I hunch over my phone and type, *Allie??*

Yeah, she replies.

How did you get my number? I write, then I cringe a split second after hitting Send. If something's wrong, I don't want to push her away by making her feel like I'm accusing her of something. My phone is silent for long enough that a pit of dread starts to form in my stomach. When it dings again, I'm relieved.

Andrew wrote it down for my foster mom. I saw it on the paperwork. U mad?

No, I reply. I hit Send, then I type, *Are you ok? Where are you?*

Silence for a moment. Then her response comes: *What do u care anyways?*

Of course I care! I respond immediately. The dread is back. Something's not right. *Are you at home?* When there's no reply, I try again. *Allie? Where are you?*

But there's no response. I watch the clock as one minute ticks by, then two. *Please answer,* I type after three minutes have passed. *I'm worried.*

But she's gone silent. I try calling her, but it goes straight to voice mail. I sit there for another minute, staring my phone, before gently shaking Dan awake. "I have to ask you something," I say.

He rolls over, and when I turn on my bedside lamp, he blinks into the sudden light. "What's wrong?"

I tell him quickly about Allie and the cryptic texts I just received from her. "What do you think I should do?"

"It's not really your problem, is it, babe?" he asks, punctuating the question with a yawn.

"Of course it is," I insist. "She reached out to me. What if something's wrong?"

"She's probably just messing with you," Dan says. "You said she was sort of a brat."

"I never said that!" I exclaim, wounded on Allie's behalf.

Dan shrugs. "Well, I don't know. Call that Andrew guy. He'll take care of it. But this isn't your job, Kate."

I don't reply, and after a moment, he rolls over and mumbles, "Turn out the light when you're done, okay?"

I wait another few minutes to see if Allie will text back, and then I quietly get up from bed, go into the kitchen, and scroll through my phone until I find Andrew's cell number.

"Kate?" he says as he answers, his voice cloaked in sleep. "What's wrong?"

In the background, I can hear a muffled woman's voice asking who it is. "Um," I begin awkwardly, immediately flustered.

"Kate? You there?"

"Sorry to bother you," I blurt out, "but I just got a few weird texts from Allie. I have a feeling that something's wrong. Do you think you could call Rodney and Salma and have them check on her?"

"Yeah, of course." He sounds concerned and instantly awake. "Can I call you right back?"

"Of course."

I hang up and stare at the phone. The seconds tick by, stretching into a minute. Finally, my phone rings again. I answer right away. "Andrew? Is she okay?"

"I don't know." His voice is grim. "Kate, she's gone."

Twenty-Three

Andrew and I agree to meet at Allie's foster home in a half hour. In the meantime, I'll continue trying to text and call her on the way there.

"Should we call the police?" I ask before I hang up.

"From what you've said, it sounds like she ran away," Andrew says after a brief hesitation. "It's against the agency's rules, but let's give it an hour. I don't want to do anything that will affect her mom's custody proceedings."

"Her custody proceedings?"

"Yeah. I'm sure you know she's been visiting with Allie a couple times a week and working toward getting her back. I'm on the fence about whether she deserves another chance, but if it turns out to be for the best, and if it's on Allie's record that she ran away, it could complicate things. So let's cross that bridge in an hour, okay? We'll see if we can track her down first."

I try calling Allie's phone four times from the back of a cab on the way to Queens, and I text her another dozen times, but there's no reply. I'm beginning to think Andrew's making a mistake; Allie's twelve years old and is out there all alone. Anything could happen to her.

Andrew is already outside Allie's foster home when my cab pulls up. "Rodney and Salma are out looking," Andrew tells me, holding the car door open as I pay the driver and get out. "They went left. I told them we'd go right. There's a strip of bars and restaurants in that direction that are open late."

"Okay." We begin walking quickly up the street. After a few seconds, I add, "Andrew, I'm worried."

"She'll be okay. She's a smart kid. She'll be fine." The words come out in a rush, followed by a moment of silence. "Yeah, I'm worried too," he concedes.

We decide to split up at the corner, keeping in touch by cell phone. I head right on Thirty-First Avenue, and by the time I reach a long string of restaurants and bars, I'm almost running. I walk into the first place I come upon, a restaurant called Pace Caldwell's, but it's closing for the night, and there's no one there.

"Have you seen a twelve-year-old girl, brown eyes, straight brown hair?" I ask a busboy hurrying by with a stack of plates.

"No, ma'am."

I thank him and head back out into the night. My luck is similar at an Italian restaurant called Prosecco and a twenty-four-hour coffee shop called Up Latte. I'm passing three darkened storefronts when I hear it: piano music wafting out of a restaurant up ahead. It takes me a few seconds to recognize the tune, but when I do, I break into a run. It's the song Allie played the first day I met her, the song she wrote herself.

The place is called Simond's, and when I duck inside, the lighting is dim, the place looks seedy, and there are three middle-aged men sitting at the bar, each in various states of drunkenness. A couple's making out in the corner, and a trio of men who look like they just stepped out of *Duck Dynasty* are hunched around a table, a dozen empty beers between them. No one seems to be paying any attention to the girl in the corner, who's now playing "Hey Jude" on a piano that looks like it's seen better days.

I sigh in relief then pull out my phone. *Found her,* I text Andrew. *Place called Simond's on the main strip of 31st.* Then I put my phone back in my pocket and cross the room. Allie doesn't look up as I slide onto the piano bench beside her, but she finally stops playing when I put my right hand over hers on the keys.

"Allie," I say gently, "what are you doing?"

She doesn't make eye contact as she signs, *Who cares?*

Me, I sign back.

"Whatever," Allie says aloud. "You didn't even text back."

I stare at her. "Allie, I texted you like a hundred times!" When her eyes narrow, I add, "Check your phone if you don't believe me."

Muttering to herself, she pulls her phone from her bag and pushes the Home button. Nothing happens. She looks up at me sheepishly. "My battery must have died."

"Boy, you really thought this running-away thing through," I say.

She glowers at me. "I wasn't running away. I just needed to be alone."

I look around pointedly at the other restaurant patrons. "You're not exactly alone."

"Whatever," she grumbles. She reaches for the piano keys and plays a few notes with her right hand. "So I saw my mom," she says nonchalantly.

"On one of her visitations with you?"

She shakes her head without looking at me.

"Well? What happened?" I press. When she doesn't answer, I say, "She came to see you at your foster home?"

Allie laughs, a bitter sound. "Yeah, right. No. I went to go see her at her stupid apartment after school. But the guy who answered the door said she was busy. Said my mom had to be by herself for a little while and I should go home."

"So then what happened?"

She shrugs. "I went around to the side window and looked in. And there she was. Not alone at all. She was talking to this other lady, and then she was laughing like the lady said something real funny."

"Oh, Allie." I sigh. "So she didn't see you?"

"She totally did. I know she saw me, because she stared like she'd seen a celebrity or something. Then she turned her back on me. Like I wasn't important to her at all. Like she'd rather be laughing with some stranger."

"Allie, maybe you're wrong. Maybe she just saw her own reflection in the window or something."

"She saw me!" Allie snaps loudly enough that the couple playing pool in the corner glance over at us. "She saw me," she repeats more quietly. "She just didn't give a crap."

I look surreptitiously at my watch, wishing Andrew were here. He'd know what to say. I'm at a loss, so I settle for speaking from the heart. "Maybe it's true that she saw you," I concede. "But it's important that you know that adults just do the wrong thing sometimes."

"Yeah, no kidding."

"What I mean is, it's hard to realize a parent has flaws. But everyone has issues. So her seeing you and turning away, if that's true, doesn't necessarily mean she doesn't care. You said she had some problems with addiction; maybe she's just trying really hard to get clean, and she's acting kind of weird. Lots of adults are a little messed up, and they do the wrong thing because of it."

"*You're* not messed up," Allie says.

I think for a second. "Maybe I am."

"Whatever." She looks at my hands then shakes her head. "I don't believe you."

"Allie, no one's life is perfect."

She snorts. "Oh yeah? Give me one example of how supposedly messed up your perfect life is." She smirks at me, clearly certain that I won't be able to provide any evidence.

"This isn't about me, Allie. It's about you."

Her eyes get watery, and she blinks quickly a few times. "See? You're full of crap. You don't have any problems. You probably have a perfect husband and a couple of perfect kids and some perfect brownstone somewhere. People like you always have perfect lives and try to tell people like me what to do."

I'm not supposed to get personal, but it's the middle of the night, and not only is my patience wearing thin, but I suspect it will help a little if I can blow Allie's stereotype of me out of the water. So I take a deep breath and say, "I don't live in a brownstone, and I don't have kids, Allie, because I can't get pregnant."

She stares at me then drops her gaze and mutters, "Yeah, well, I bet your husband is some perfect Prince Charming who has, like, a yacht or a limousine or something.."

"My husband's dead, Allie," I hear myself say. I feel instantly guilty for the overshare, but her expression tells me it was the right thing to do. The triumphant look on her face is sliding away.

"For real?" she whispers.

My eyes feel damp now, and my heart is suddenly thudding too quickly. "For real."

"Well, when did he die, anyways?" Allie asks.

"A long time ago."

When she doesn't say anything, I elaborate. "It'll be twelve years on September eighteenth."

"What happened to him?"

"Car crash."

"Oh." She pauses and looks up, a guilty expression on her face. "I'm sorry. About your husband, I mean."

"Thanks." We're silent for a moment, then I add, "No one's life is ever perfect, Allie. And most of the time, there's more going on beneath the surface than you know. What if your mom is so focused on getting clean that she can't process the big stuff—like you—right now?"

Allie looks like she's about to say something, but then there's a commotion at the front door, and Andrew bursts into the restaurant, his face full of worry. It takes a moment for his eyes to adjust to the light, and then he scans the bar and spots us. He looks relieved for a split second, but then his expression turns stern as he strides over to us, his fists clenched.

"Allie!" he says, his voice sharper than I've ever heard it. "What on earth were you thinking?"

She glances at me, and for a moment, I can see guilt in her eyes. Then it's gone, replaced by something cold and defensive. She juts her chin out. "Like you care."

"Of course he cares, Allie," I cut in before a fuming Andrew can reply. "Do you think he's happy that he's up in the middle of the night chasing after you?"

She glances at him and then back at me, but she doesn't reply.

"You're lucky I didn't call the police!" he continues. "Do you know what would have happened? They would have taken you away from the Greghors. And you'd be back in a group home until your mom got custody. *If* she got custody. Your little stunt here could have messed that up."

"Geez, sorry," she mumbles.

"I hate to say it, Allie, but all the apologies in the world aren't going to change things if you get yourself into real trouble," Andrew says firmly. "I know you've got some stuff going on. But this has to stop. The fights at school, the acting out against Rodney and Salma, and now this? I'm really disappointed in you."

Allie looks like she's about to cry. "Well, why didn't you call the police anyways?" she mumbles.

Andrew glances at me, his expression softening. He looks back at Allie and says, "Maybe because everyone deserves a second chance."

Back at the Greghors' house, Allie gets ready for bed, while Andrew and I explain to Rodney and Salma where we found her and that she was upset about her mom.

"So it wasn't something we did wrong?" Salma asks.

"No, not at all," Andrew reassures her. "Allie's just struggling with some things. I don't think this will happen again."

Salma clasps her hands together and looks up at Rodney. After a moment, he says, "We were assured this placement would only be for a few months. We can't keep her any longer than that. That's why we do temporaries."

"It's not that we don't want her," Salma rushes to add as my heart sinks for Allie. "It's just, well, we've recently found out I'm pregnant. And if this is going to be a continuing pattern of behavior . . ."

"I don't think it will be," Andrew interrupts firmly. "And she should be going back to her mother within the next month or two. You know that."

"Congratulations on the pregnancy," I murmur, and Salma smiles at me slightly before turning her attention back to Andrew.

"I'm sure everything will be fine," she says, and I know she's trying to convince herself.

Andrew nods and thanks them stiffly for their help tonight.

Then he asks me to go check on Allie, to make sure she's all set for bed.

As I walk down the hallway toward her room, I feel like my heart is splitting open, and I wonder if part of the reason Allie fled was because she could sense the fact that the Greghors are ready to move on. I wonder if she knows they're having a baby, if she feels pushed aside already by a little person who hasn't even arrived yet.

I find Allie in bed, in a pink T-shirt and pink pajama pants with hearts stamped on them. With her face freshly scrubbed, she looks younger than her twelve years.

"You okay?" I ask, sitting down on the edge of her bed.

She shrugs.

"Allie, what happened tonight, I get why you did it," I begin carefully. "But you have to trust us. We all care about you. No one's going to let anything bad happen to you. If you feel hurt or mad or sad about something again, you just need to call me or Andrew, or talk to Rodney and Salma, okay?"

She nods again and slides down in her bed so that she's under the covers. I start to get up, but Allie grabs my arm.

You're wrong about my mom, she signs.

"What do you mean?" I ask aloud.

"You said she was probably trying to stay clean," Allie says. "And that's why she pretended not to see me."

"You have to give her the benefit of the doubt, I think."

"Well, then why was she smoking meth?"

I blink at Allie a few times. "What?"

"She was smoking something in a pipe," Allie goes on, her voice flat. "Had to be meth. That was always her favorite. *That's* why she looked away when she saw me, Kate. Not because I'm so important. But because I'm *not* important enough to quit drugs for."

Before I can reply, she rolls away from me, takes her head-pieces off, and pulls the sheets over her head.

"Allie?" I say, and when I realize she can no longer hear me, I touch her shoulder lightly. "Allie?"

"Go away!" she says, her voice muffled. "Leave me alone!"

I stay for another minute, just in case she changes her mind, but there's only silence, so I say, "We're going to make this right, Allie." I know she can't hear me, but I needed to make the promise. I give her shoulder a comforting squeeze and turn away.

In the hallway, I find Andrew waiting for me. "She okay?" he asks as we walk out into the warm night and head back toward a main street so that I can flag down a cab.

I shake my head. "Andrew, she said that when she saw her mom today, her mom was smoking something."

His face falls. "I'm going to assume from your expression that you're not talking about a cigarette."

"She said she thinks it was meth."

"Damn it!" Andrew rakes a hand through his hair. "I was hoping she could stay clean. I'm going to have to report this."

I nod. "How much longer can Allie stay here?"

Andrew sighs. "A few months, at most. The Greghors are right; they're only signed on to provide temporary care. And now with a baby coming . . ." He shakes his head and sighs again. "I just wanted Allie to have some stability."

I could take her. The thought is so immediate and so clear that it startles me. I blink a few times and tell myself it's a silly thought. I can't even get my own life in order. But then again, what if I could? What if I could become the stable person Allie needs? My heartbeat quickens a little as I consider the possibility that the dreams were leading me here, to Allie.

"—about your husband?" Andrew is saying something, but I'm so lost in thought that I only hear the end of it.

"What?" I can feel my cheeks turning red.

"Allie said you told her about your husband?" Andrew repeats, looking concerned.

Instantly, I feel terrible. "I'm so sorry. I know I shouldn't have said something so personal to her. I was just trying to show her that no one is perfect, and that even if a life looks perfect on the outside, sometimes it isn't perfect in reality. But I'm really sorry. It was totally unprofessional of me, and it won't happen again."

"Kate." His voice is soft, and I realize I like the way he says my name. "I wasn't criticizing you. I was going to remind you that you always have someone to talk to if that's ever something you want."

"You?" I ask, and it's not until he flinches that it occurs to me how rude that must have sounded. "Sorry," I mumble. "I didn't mean it like that."

He shrugs. "No pressure, but sometimes it's better to talk to a stranger than to someone who's been there from day one. Not that I'm a stranger, exactly. I'd like to think we're becoming friends." He looks down. "Besides, I owe you after unloading on you about my brother."

"You didn't unload on me," I murmur. I consider, for a moment, whether I should tell him about Dan and the problems we're having, but it feels oddly disloyal to share my relationship worries with another man. Still, I realize I'm longing for someone to tell me that this will pass.

"What is it?" Andrew asks softly, reading my mind.

"Nothing," I say quickly. Then I pause and reconsider. "Okay, well, you know how I told you I was having some really vivid dreams?"

"Of Patrick," he says with a nod, and for some reason, I'm startled that he remembers my husband's name.

"Right." I glance at him uncertainly. "Well, they've reminded me what it felt like being with him. And being with my fiancé—Dan—isn't anything like that." My words border on too personal, too much, and I wonder if my good judgment has evaporated. "Not that I don't love my fiancé," I hurry to add. "I do. It's just different."

Andrew nods. "But it's supposed to feel different, I think," he says after a pause. "The question is whether you're happy and whether it feels right. That's what you have to think about."

"I know," I mumble, already feeling silly for saying anything.

"Look, what happened with your husband changed you forever, just like what happened with my brother changed me," he says, and this time, I really listen, because it feels different from the advice I've gotten before. "So you can't compare the present with the past, not really, because you're a different person than you were when Patrick was alive. You have to look forward, at the things you want, not back at the things you once had."

I can feel tears prickling my eyes. "How'd you get so wise?"

He laughs. "Trial and error. Emphasis on the error."

We've reached Thirty-First, and we're silent as Andrew raises a hand to hail a passing cab. As it pulls over, he gives me a hug and I climb into the backseat. "Hey, Andrew?" I say just before he shuts the cab door.

"Yeah?"

"I'd like to think we're becoming friends too."

Twenty-Four

On Monday morning, I awaken again in the life I share with Patrick, and I'm so grateful that for a minute, I can hardly breathe. I'd feared, after my last dip into this reality, that I'd ruined my chance to come back.

But Patrick is there beside me in our bed, real and solid and warm. I feel tears in my eyes as I reach for him. He stirs and wakes up slowly as I nestle into the nook under his right arm.

"Morning, honey," he says, his voice still thick with sleep. He pulls me closer and kisses the top of my head.

"Tell me you love me," I say urgently, clinging to him like he's a life raft.

Patrick laughs and ruffles my hair. "I love you, weirdo," he says. Then he softens, the corners of his eyes crinkling into crow's-feet that weren't there twelve years ago. "I knew before I met you—" he adds, looking into my eyes.

"—that I was meant to be yours," I whisper. I listen to his heartbeat for a moment before asking, "How's your mom doing?"

He sighs. "I talked to her yesterday, and she doesn't sound great. This chemo's really taking a toll on her. I don't know what I'd do if we lost her."

"We won't lose her," I tell him firmly. "She's going to be fine." I feel another twinge of guilt over the real-life Joan, whom I haven't called since the day I showed up on her porch. I've gotten so absorbed with my own life and problems that I let it go. I make a mental note to follow up with her as soon as possible.

In the kitchen a few minutes later, Patrick pours me a cup of coffee and I struggle with the words I want to say. "Can I ask you something, Patrick?" I finally ask. "Am I . . . Am I a good mother?"

He turns around to look at me.

"I mean, do you look at me and see problems and shortcomings?" I go on, thinking of what Dan said to me about our ability to parent. "Or have I been mostly good for Hannah? Have I been there for her and made the right choices and made her feel loved?"

"Of course you have, honey," he says. "Where is this coming from?"

I shrug. "I don't know. I guess I'm doubting myself."

He frowns. "Kate, I don't know if I've ever told you this, but the first time I saw you hold Hannah in your arms, I just knew."

"You knew what?"

"I knew that this was exactly what was meant to be. You always had those maternal instincts, I think—it's one of the million things I've always loved about you—but from the very first moment I saw you holding her, it was like everything fell into place, like the universe was suddenly in total alignment. You were meant to be a mother the way that rain was meant to be wet and grass was meant to be green and ice was meant to be cold."

I smile. "You're sure?"

"You're a *great* mom," he replies.

Our conversation is interrupted by Hannah coming into the

kitchen, her pajamas rumpled, her hair sticking up at weird angles.

"I had a bad dream," she says, rubbing her eyes. "I dreamed that—"

But before she can finish her sentence, I've pulled her into a tight hug. I'm so glad to see her, so relieved that for a few moments, at least, I get to be here with her, that nothing else seems to matter.

"Geez, Mom, are you trying to suffocate me?" Hannah asks, but when I finally let her go, she's smiling.

"I'm just so glad I'm your mom," I tell her.

"Ooooookay," she says, making the sign for *cuckoo* around her ear and rolling her eyes at Patrick, who playfully rolls his eyes back but shoots me a quick look of concern when Hannah looks away.

"Okay, you two, enough mocking me," I say, and when they both laugh, it sounds like music.

"Come on, slowpoke," Patrick says to Hannah. "Get yourself some cereal and get moving."

"Wait, where's she going?" I ask, suddenly panicked at the thought that my already-limited time with Hannah could be cut any shorter.

"You're so weird, Mom," Hannah says before Patrick can reply. "You and Dad took the day off, remember? We're going to Coney Island. Duh."

"All of us?"

"Duh," Hannah says again. "You promised after I saw *Uptown Girls.*"

"That Brittany Murphy movie?" I have a sudden memory of seeing the movie in 2003, just before the first anniversary of Patrick's death. My sister thought it would cheer me up to go out to a theater and see a silly romantic comedy. Instead, the love story made me cry, and we left before the movie ended.

"It's, like, the best movie," Hannah says. "I mean, it's old-fashioned, obviously. But Jesse Spencer is so hot. For an old guy. And I love the part where they ride the teacups ride."

"Fun," I manage. But what I'm really thinking is that if some-one had told me in 2003, as I sat inside a darkened theater with Susan trying not to cry, that I'd one day be riding the teacups with my dead husband and our imaginary daughter, I would have thought they were crazy. But here we are. On second thought, maybe that just makes *me* crazy.

As Hannah pours herself a bowl of Corn Pops, I move closer to Patrick and touch his elbow. "I love you," I murmur.

"I love you too, Katielee."

An hour later, we're all on the N train heading for Coney Island. Hannah is sitting across from us, her nose buried in a young adult novel with a stiletto heel on the cover, and Patrick has his arm slung around my shoulders. We watch our daugh-ter together in silence, and I don't break it with conversation, because there aren't enough words in the world to describe how this moment feels. Patrick's warmth beside me. A daughter we love deeply, here with us. A whole life, stretching out before us. None of it real.

It occurs to me how mundane this moment would be if this was really the life I was living. Would I be taking the time to marvel at how beautiful Hannah's hair looks when it catches the light, or how happy it makes me feel to see her eyes crinkle slightly at the corners each time she reads something amusing? Would I be pausing to appreciate the scent of Irish Spring lin-gering on Patrick's neck, or the warmth that floods me when I notice the few errant hairs he missed on his jaw when shaving this morning? Would I stop to think how safe I feel tucked under his arm, like nothing could possibly hurt me as long as he's here?

No, because before I lost him, I thought we had a lifetime of endless moments like this stretching before us. I loved him deeply, but I never really knew that every second we had together was a gift until he was gone.

"What are you thinking about?" Patrick whispers as we roll through the Eighty-Sixth Street stop, the last one before we get to Coney Island.

"Just how lucky I am to be here," I tell him.

He smiles and squeezes my hand, but he doesn't reply until we're pulling into the Coney Island station. "We both are."

He stands up and nods at Hannah, who snaps her book closed and smiles at us. "We always said we have to make the life we want," he adds. "And I think we're doing a pretty good job, don't you?" I start to reply, but we're already getting off the train and heading for the station exit. I let myself be pulled along, swept by the tide, until I begin to wonder if perhaps that's been my mistake. Maybe I've been riding the tide all along instead of using the current to propel me in the direction I choose.

After eight hours at Coney Island, during which all three of us scream our heads off on the Sling Shot, giggle through the Cyclone, get dizzy on the teacups, and eat so many Nathan's hot dogs our stomachs hurt, we head home, dazed smiles plastered across our faces.

"It's no Disney World," Hannah concludes. "But Coney Island rocks. Can we go back next weekend?"

Patrick just arches an eyebrow at her, and after a minute, she giggles and says, "Okay. I'll let the hot dogs settle first. Then we'll talk."

Patrick reaches for my hand as Hannah digs her book out of her bag and begins to read again. "This has been a pretty perfect day, hasn't it?" he asks.

"The best," I agree, putting my head on his shoulder.

At home, we tuck Hannah in together, and I can feel myself growing wearier by the second. I know the dream is already beginning to fade, and I can't stop it. "Love you guys," Hannah says with a yawn as Patrick ruffles her hair and I bend down to give her a kiss on her warm, smooth cheek.

"We love you too, honey," Patrick tells her.

I don't know what makes me say it, but I hear my words for Patrick come out of my mouth. "I knew before I met you—" I say to Hannah, my heart aching.

She smiles, yawns, and takes off her headpiece. For a moment, I'm sure she's not going to reply. Then, she signs, *That I was meant to be yours,* and I find myself blinking back sudden tears. So she's part of our secret language too. But how can I love this girl so powerfully when she doesn't really exist?

Patrick flips Hannah's light off and closes her door behind us as we walk out into the hallway. "Let's go sit in the living room for a little while," he says.

We settle on our sofa, and he pulls me toward him. I rest my head on his shoulder.

"What would you want for Hannah if you weren't here?" I ask after a while. The room fades a little, but I mentally hang on. After all, I'm not asking anything outlandish.

"You trying to get rid of me?" Patrick teases, but when I don't laugh, he adds seriously, "I'd want to know she was taken care of and loved. I'd want to know that *you* were taken care of and loved too. I would want you to be happy, no matter what. I'd want the two of you to stick together and love each other for the rest of your lives, because you're the two best people I know."

I begin to cry, and once I do, I can't stop. "*You're* the best person I know," I manage through sniffles.

"Are we going to have to fight about this?" he asks with a smile.

I laugh, despite myself, and he kisses me on the cheek.

"Kate, you're really good with Hannah," he continues, his tone serious again. "She's lucky to have a mom like you. You know that, don't you?"

I hesitate. I love her, and even though I don't remember most of it, it seems I've done my best to give her a good life and to help her grow into a good person. It makes me believe that I have those skills somewhere at the core of me, just waiting to be used. "Yes," I say softly.

"Promise?"

"I promise," I say.

"Good." He's quiet for a moment, and I feel myself growing wearier, the room growing hazier, as he strokes my hair. "I knew before I met you—" he finally whispers, his voice already far away.

"—that I was meant to be yours," I murmur. It's the last thing I remember before drifting off to sleep.

Twenty-Five

When I wake up, I finally know with a calm certainty that I have to break up with Dan, and I have to do it today. I can't put it off any longer, not if I want to have a chance at a good life, a real life. I've spent months now—maybe years—overriding my gut, letting other people's opinions become my own. But it's time to take control of my own destiny.

I can't have Patrick—not in the real world—but that doesn't mean I can't go after the future I want. Maybe it's time to stop getting in my own way.

I want to be a mother. I used to know that for sure so many years ago, back when Patrick was alive. But after he died, it's like I forgot who I was and where my life was headed. If I couldn't have children with him, what was the point?

But the dreams have shown me that parenthood is still something I might be good at. They've made me reevaluate my life, forced me to see everything in a new light. I'm good with Max and Leo and all the other kids who come through my door because I'm not afraid to speak their language or care about the things they care about. I'm not afraid to open my heart to them. And I can only imagine that if I had my own child, that openness and readiness to love would increase tenfold, maybe even a hundredfold.

Andrew has taught me that too. By exposing me to kids who don't just need a music therapist but who also desperately need an adult on their side, he's helped me to realize that I'm someone of value, and that I have the maternal instincts I always worried I would lack. I know how to love. I've just been doing it the wrong way for the last twelve years, because I made a decision—albeit an unconscious one—to shut my heart off when Patrick died. Now it's time to let the light in.

"We need to talk," I say bluntly when Dan gets home from work that evening.

"You look awfully serious," he says with a faint smile as he hangs up his keys. "How was your day?"

"I didn't go in to work," I tell him. "There were some things I needed to think about."

From the way he averts his eyes, I have the feeling he already knows what I'm going to say. "Like what?" he asks, his tone flat.

For a moment, I have trouble speaking, because of course it's not anything Dan's done wrong. It's that all along, I've been in love with the idea of moving on. I just haven't been completely in love with the man I've moved on to. None of this is fair to him, but I can't stay in a relationship simply because it's easier not to rock the boat.

"I'm sorry," I whisper. "But I can't do this."

He looks taken aback but somehow not totally shocked. "Do what?" he asks.

"Marry you," I say. "I'm so, so sorry. It sounds like a cliché, but it's really not you. It's me. It's about the life I know I want, Dan."

I slide the engagement ring off my finger and hold it out to him, but he doesn't take it. I'm surprised to see so much pain on his face. "This is about kids? You're throwing me away over something you didn't even know you wanted a few months ago?"

"No," I reply, still holding the ring awkwardly. "It's not just that. It's everything. It's about the fact that you can't make a square peg fit into a round hole, and that's what we've been trying to do, Dan. I just didn't see it until I opened my eyes. I'm so sorry."

His gaze hardens. "You know this isn't fair, right? In all the time we've been together, you've never once mentioned wanting a child. And now, out of nowhere, it's the thing that has to define our relationship?"

"Dan—" I begin, but he goes on as if I haven't spoken.

"You can't just change your mind like that!" he says. "It's like the last two years have been a lie!"

"I was never lying," I say. "Not on purpose. I just wasn't being honest with myself."

"Or with me," he adds coldly.

"I'm sorry," I say. "I never meant to hurt you."

He stares at me for a moment then laughs in disbelief. "Jesus, this is about Pat, isn't it? Everything's about Pat! And now you're finally punishing me for not being him."

"No," I say firmly, resisting the urge to correct the nickname. "This is about you and me."

"That's a load of crap." Dan crosses his arms and glares at me. "You're obsessed with your dead husband. You know that's crazy, right? You know what you're doing is insane?"

"This isn't about him; it's about knowing now that things aren't right between me and you. I want it all, Dan, the heartaches and the pain, the ups and the downs, that feeling of being equal partners facing the world together. And I don't think I can have that with you."

"Bullshit," he mutters.

"Dan—" I begin.

"Bullshit," he repeats more loudly, looking up and meeting my eye. "This has *nothing* to do with me. This has to do with you finding out you're infertile and getting scared. That's all this is. You'll come to your senses."

He says it so smugly and with such certainty that my skin crawls.

"You really think of me as a child, don't you?" I ask. "Like someone who isn't as bright or sensible as you are."

He shrugs, but I can see the corner of his mouth twitching into a small smirk. "I don't want to fight, Kate."

"But you never do!" I shoot back, my voice rising. "We never fight! Don't you see that that's a problem? I'm just as guilty, Dan. We never really talked about anything important. We never dug any deeper than the surface. And that's not a real relationship! That's not healthy! You're supposed to fight for the things that mean something to you! And neither of us cared enough to do that, because it was easier not to!"

He stares at me, and I feel terrible, because he looks like I've slapped him across the face.

"I'm sorry," I say after a minute. "I shouldn't have yelled."

Silence falls between us for a minute. There's a piece of me that wants to take it all back, to tell him I'm wrong, to say we can fix things. But none of that's true.

"You know, Kate, you're going to have to let him go sometime," Dan says, after a moment, his eyes on mine. "If you don't, you'll never find happiness with anyone. And you know something? I feel sorry for you. What you're doing, it's pathetic."

The words hit me hard. I open my mouth to apologize again for hurting him, but he's already walking away. The door slams behind him, leaving only silence in his wake. I slowly slide the engagement ring onto the dining room table and let out the breath I didn't know I was holding.

Dan returns sometime after midnight, sleeps on the couch, and is gone—along with the ring—by the time I wake up the next morning. He's left a note saying he'll send movers for his things later today. I feel sad at the closing of another chapter in my life. But I'm also filled with a sense of resolve that grows as the day goes on.

I manage to push Dan to the back of my mind all morning while I work with Leo, a longtime patient named Sierra, and a new girl named Katia who has just moved here with her parents from Eastern Europe. They're concerned she's not picking up English quickly enough, and they've asked if I can work with her to help expand her vocabulary through music. It's an interesting challenge and one that provides the perfect distraction from my personal life.

Thanks to a last-minute cancellation, I have a two-hour break between the end of Katia's session and my first afternoon appointment, so I decide to take a walk to clear my head. Somehow, my feet carry me down Park Avenue, through bustling Union Square, and all the way to our old apartment on Chambers Street, the one I visited to no avail when I first started having the dreams.

It's almost one o'clock by the time I get there, and I hesitate outside the front door for a moment before pressing the buzzer next to our old apartment number.

This time, someone answers. "Yes?" a woman's voice crackles from the speakers.

"Um," I begin. I have no idea how to explain why I'm here.

"Hello?" the woman asks.

"My name's Kate," I say quickly. "I used to live here. Twelve years ago."

There's silence for a moment, then the woman says, "Yes?"

"I . . ." I pause. I don't know what to say. Finally, I settle on the truth. "My husband died while we were living here. It's why I moved. I was just wondering if I could come up for a minute. I-I'm trying to put some old ghosts to rest."

The woman is silent for a minute, then her voice crackles through the speaker. "You're alone?"

"Yes. I'm alone." I refrain from adding that this is true in more ways than one.

"All right." The buzzer sounds and I pull the front door open before I can second-guess myself. I trudge up the stairs to my old front door. The hallway has been painted a somber maroon; new lights have been installed; and the broken seventh stair that Patrick and I always used to skip has been replaced. But the air feels the same—damp and musty—and the familiar smell of the stairwell—pine mixed with laundry detergent wafting from the basement—makes me feel short of breath.

The door to 5F is open when I reach the fifth landing, and a woman about my age is standing there, her hands folded over her belly, her expression somber. "You're the one who buzzed up," she says, extending her hand. "I'm Eva Schubert."

"Kate Waithman," I tell her, shaking her hand.

"Ah yes, Waithman," she says. "I remember the name. We're the ones who moved in after you left."

"You've been here for a while, then," I say.

She nods. "You said you lost your husband? He must have been very young."

"Twenty-nine."

She bites her lip. "I'm very sorry. That must have been terrible for you." She gestures into the apartment. "Would you like to come in?"

I follow her inside, my heart pounding, but my bubble of expectation bursts the moment we're over the threshold. The apartment doesn't look familiar at all, except for its basic structure. I realize I'd hoped that it would look the same as it had in my dreams, and that this would somehow legitimize them. Instead, every trace of Patrick and me is gone.

In the living room, where our slate gray loveseat and sofa were the perfect pairing for white walls covered in black-and-white photographs of the city, the Schuberts have placed a maroon sofa and two brown leather chairs. The walls are now a pale yellow, and the floor, which was once beautiful old hardwood, is now tiled. Colorful family pictures are propped on every available surface. The kitchen looks completely different too; the breakfast bar has been scrapped to make the nook into more of a dining room, and even our trusty old white appliances are gone, replaced by stainless steel.

"It's not ours anymore," I whisper, more to myself than to Eva. I already feel like a stranger in this place. But what did I expect? That it would look just like it used to? That it would look like it does in my dreams? That Patrick would actually be here, waiting for me?

"Is there something you need, Kate?" Eva asks a moment later. "Something I can do to help?"

"No," I say, collecting myself and forcing a smile. "I'm sorry, but I have to get back to work. I shouldn't have come. I shouldn't have bothered you."

Eva pats my shoulder. "It's no bother," she says. "I'm very sorry for what you've lost. I can't even imagine. I hope you find what you're looking for."

After we've said our good-byes and she's closed the door behind me, I linger in the hallway for a moment. I close my eyes and try to remember exactly what it used to feel like to stand here, to know I shared this home with the love of my life, to know he was just over the threshold, waiting for me.

But he's gone. And it's about time I close the door to the past.

For the next couple of days, I feel hollow, and there's a small part of me that's already doubting my decision. After all, even if Dan wasn't right for me, he wasn't a bad guy. And without him, the loneliness is palpable. I hoped I'd get to spend more time in the world with Patrick and Hannah once I was free of Dan, but I've had trouble falling asleep since Monday, and when I finally drift off, my dreams are empty and dark.

"You okay?" Andrew asks, looking up from his paperwork as I round the corner into his office just before four on Thursday.

"Just fine," I say, forcing a smile.

"It's just that you look kind of . . . sad."

I'm surprised that he can tell, but I just shake my head and mumble something about being overtired. I haven't told anyone about the breakup yet; I'm not ready for it to be picked apart and analyzed and discussed. So I merely tell him, "I'm having trouble sleeping."

"Bad dreams?" he asks.

"Not exactly." I clear my throat. "So is Riajah here?"

He puts his pen down and leans back in his chair. "She's actually come down with a bad cold, so Sheila's keeping her home. I didn't call because I figured you'd be coming out for Allie anyhow. And I thought maybe she could use a little extra time with you today, if you're up for it. Is that okay?"

"Of course."

He smiles. "I'll walk you over."

As we make our way down Thirty-Fifth Street, we make small talk, and I have the feeling Andrew knows something is wrong but is kind enough not to be pressing me about what it is. He tells me about his day, and I find myself laughing as he explains how frightened he is of the ever-growing pile of paperwork in his office.

"How did you get here, anyhow?" I ask him, thinking of how in the dream world, he had ended up miles away, in a different life. When he looks startled by the abrupt change in topic, I smile and add, "To this job, I mean. You told me about your brother and why you know ASL. But how did you wind up at St. Anne's?"

"I came to New York for college and never left," he says. "I wanted to open a restaurant, so I studied business and management, but after working in the restaurant industry for a few years, I just wasn't that happy. I liked cooking, but I didn't *love* it. I didn't feel fulfilled. So I went back to school for social work."

"That's a big deal to switch tracks like that," I say, my heart thudding. I couldn't have possibly known that his first career path was in the restaurant business, could I?

He shrugs. "Maybe. It was a leap of faith, but looking back at it, I can't imagine my life going any other way. Sometimes, you have to take the risks in order to wind up in the right place. In my case, it was about choosing happiness. You know what I mean?"

I feel a lump in my throat. "I do," I say. I pause. "So you're from Georgia?"

He looks startled. "Geez, I thought I'd lost the accent. You can still tell?"

I shake my head in disbelief. The dreams just keep proving to be something more than that.

"How about you?" he asks a minute later. "How did the music therapy thing come about?"

I glance at him. "I guess you could say I chose happiness too. I always loved music, and I always saw myself working with kids someday, but my parents were pretty set on the fact that I was supposed to go into business or finance or law, something where I could make a lot of money. But then I met Patrick and he was so firm about the idea that I should do what I loved that I finally got the courage to quit my job and apply to graduate school for music therapy. He always used to remind me that it was okay to choose happiness. That's what life is supposed to be about. I've only realized recently that I kind of forgot his advice over the years."

"About being happy?"

I nod. "Yeah."

"Are you happy now?"

I consider this. "I'm getting there," I say finally.

Andrew gives me a friendly hug good-bye at Allie's front door, saying that he has a few more hours of paperwork to do before he's able to go home.

"Stop by after your session with her if you need to talk or anything," he says. "I'll still be at the office." He looks concerned.

I smile. "I'll be fine. But thanks."

Rodney greets me with a handshake, then walks me down to Allie's room. She's sitting cross-legged on her bed, and she looks up when I get there. *Hello, Allie,* I sign.

"You know, you sign like a three-year-old," she says, but she's smiling.

I know this is the part where I'm supposed to joke back with her, to tease her in return, but I can't quite muster the humor, so I just shrug and say, "Yeah, well, I'm learning."

"I'll leave you two alone," Rodney says before disappearing down the hall.

When I look back at Allie, she's frowning at me. "What's wrong with you?" she asks.

I shake my head. "Nothing."

Her eyes narrow. "Fine. Lie to me like everyone else. That's cool." She crosses her arms and turns away.

I'm startled to realize she thinks I'm upset at her. "This has nothing to do with you," I say, and she snorts in reply. I wait for her to look at me before adding, "Just some problems in my personal life. I'm just a little sad, that's all."

She stares at me. "What, did you get dumped by some guy you like or something?"

I blink at her a few times, startled.

"Wait, seriously?" she asks when I don't answer. "I'm right? You got dumped by some dude?"

"Allie, this isn't really appropriate for us to be discussing. These sessions are about you, not me."

"How long were you dating him, anyways? How did he dump you?" She pauses. "Wait, or did you dump *him*?"

"Allie—" I begin, trying to sound stern.

"Whatever." She's back to glaring at me. "That doesn't exactly seem fair, you know? I'm supposed to pour out my heart and you don't say anything about yourself?"

"I'd love to tell you about my life. But it's not what we're supposed to be doing in here. We're supposed to be talking about the things bothering you."

She stares at me for a minute. "Like the fact that my mom is probably going to dump me someday the way this mystery dude dumped you?"

"Allie, no one dumped me," I reply. "Yes, I had a guy. And yes, we broke up. But it was just because we weren't right for each other. I promise you, it has nothing to do with what's going on with you and your mom."

"Why, because my life couldn't possibly be as interesting as yours?" she snaps. "Anyways, if I'm so important to my mom, she'd work harder."

"Maybe she's working as hard as she can," I say. "Maybe she's made a lot of mistakes and is trying to climb her way back out of the hole she dug for herself. Chances are, some of the things that are wrong with your mom are actually an illness."

Allie snorts. "Yeah. And the medicine she's taking is meth. Or crack. Or whatever she's into right now."

"We don't know for sure that she was smoking anything, Allie. But from what you've said, she's an addict," I say. "It's not always that easy to stop."

"I would stop if I had a kid."

"I would too," I say. "But we're not your mom. And your mom's not us. She's a different person with her own demons to fight. Is she doing the wrong thing? Yeah, absolutely. But it's really important that you know it has nothing to do with you."

Allie picks at a stray thread in her bedspread. "Yeah, well, I've never been able to rely on anyone, okay?" Her voice trembles a little.

"Allie," I say. I wait until she looks up and meets my gaze. "You can rely on me."

She stares at me for a long moment before looking down again. "I know," she says. Then she looks me right in the eye and repeats, "I know."

"Now, should we play some music?" I ask, smiling at her as I change the subject. I've already gotten way too personal with her, treated her like a child I love instead of a client. I need to pull myself together.

She shrugs. "Whatever." But she gets up from the bed and crosses over to her keyboard. "What do you want to play, anyways?"

"It's up to you. Why don't you choose something with lyrics that talk about how you're feeling about your mom?"

"That's dumb," she mutters. But after a minute she says, "Fine. What about 'Because of You'?"

"Kelly Clarkson?"

She nods. "Not all the words are how I'm feeling, but some are. And I don't know the whole thing."

"Want to listen to the song first?"

She nods, and I download it from iTunes then play it for us. As we listen to Kelly Clarkson belt out the lyrics about someone who let her down, my eyes fill with tears for Allie. I quickly blink them away as the song ends.

"In the song, she says it's hard for her to trust people," I say. "Do you feel like that?"

Allie looks down. "Can we just play the song?"

I nod. "On one condition. Whenever you don't know the words, you have to make up your own. And they have to be about how you're feeling."

She looks at me for a minute. "Yeah. Okay."

We launch into the song, with me playing harmony and helping her with her articulation and listening closely as she makes up her own lyrics about being let down. I stay for an hour and a half, because really, I have nowhere else to be. As I pack my guitar up and get ready to leave, Allie stands up from her seat behind the keyboard and surprises me with a hug. "You're not going to walk out of my life someday, are you?" she asks. "Like everyone else?"

"Never," I promise. "And I'm pretty sure Andrew's not going anywhere, either."

On the walk back to the subway, I take a deep breath and dial my sister's number. It's time to start facing the music. I need to tell her what's happened with Dan.

"Hey," I say when she answers. "Do you have a minute?"

"Sure," she says, and I can hear Calvin screaming in the background, followed by Susan's muffled voice telling him to quiet down or he'll have to go to time-out. "What's wrong?" she asks, returning to the phone. "You okay?"

"I am," I tell her. As I say it, I know the words are true. "But I need to tell you something." I take a deep breath. "Dan and I broke up on Monday. The wedding's off."

There's silence for a moment, and I imagine her standing in her kitchen, lips pursed, judging me. After all, she's always been the perfect one; I'm the one whose life is a complicated mess. "Well," she says finally, "it's a good thing we didn't buy a wedding dress."

"Yeah," I say tentatively, wondering if she's about to launch into a criticism about my irresponsibility.

"Do you think you made the right decision?"

"I do. I really do."

"Then I'm proud of you, Kate," she says, and I'm so surprised I almost drop my phone.

"I thought you'd tell me I was being immature and short-sighted," I admit.

"Well, are you?" she asks.

"No," I say, bristling a little. "I think I'm finally taking responsibility for being happy."

"Then you're doing the right thing," Susan says. "Are you okay?"

"Yeah. I think I am."

"Good. Then come over this weekend and tell me all about it in person."

As we hang up, I smile and shake my head. Her reaction wasn't the one I expected, but it was the one I needed, and I'm grateful for it. A feeling of peace settles over me as I walk through the falling night.

Twenty-Six

I call Dan a few times over the weekend to attempt to apologize, to explain myself, but he doesn't answer, nor does he return my calls. I'm afraid he hates me, and I can't blame him. At times, I hate myself a little too. By Sunday night, I have to admit that I'm calling him for my own good, not his. I'm looking for absolution, forgiveness. And maybe that's not something I deserve.

At lunchtime on Monday, after a restless, unsettled weekend during which the dreams don't return, I text Gina and ask if she's free tonight after work. *I need to talk,* I tell her. She texts back and asks if I want to meet her at Hammersmith's.

"I broke up with Dan," I tell her as I slide into the booth across from her.

"I know," Gina says, looking at the table.

"Susan called?" I ask, both annoyed at my sister and grateful that I won't have to break the news to anyone else. I have no doubt Susan's already told our mother too.

"She made me promise I wouldn't say anything to you until you reached out to me," Gina says. "I'm sorry. I didn't know whether I should call anyway. She thought you needed your space for a few days."

"I guess I did."

"So?" Gina leans across the table and takes my hands. "Are you okay? I mean, really okay?"

"You know what? I am."

"Susan said the breakup was your idea?" Gina asks, and when I nod, she looks worried. "Do you think you did the right thing?"

"Yes," I say immediately. "What do you think?"

She hesitates. "I think it depends why you did it. Did it have to do with . . . the dreams?"

I shrug. "The dreams—or whatever they were—opened my eyes. I think I was so grateful to finally fall in love again that I never stopped to think about the fact that it's possible to feel something for someone without him being the *one,* you know? I think that being with Patrick again, even if it wasn't real, made me remember how I felt when we were together. Safe. Accepted. Totally free to be myself. I didn't feel that way with Dan. At all."

"Oh, Kate," Gina says sadly, but I see recognition in her eyes.

Oliver comes over and takes our drink order, returning a moment later with a gin and tonic for Gina and a Guinness for me. Gina takes a sip of her drink before saying softly, "I'm so sorry I never said anything."

"What do you mean?"

She sighs. "I always liked Dan. But I used to look at the two of you together and think, 'That's not what love's supposed to look like.' Wayne always said I should stay out of it, because it was impossible to know what was going on inside your relationship. Now I wish I hadn't."

Her words make me feel even more certain that I did the right thing. "You know what? I think this was a realization I had to come to on my own." I take a long sip of my Guinness and use my thumbs to absently wipe the condensation from the outside of the glass. "Do you think I'll ever feel the way I felt for Patrick again?" I finally ask. "Or was that a once-in-a-lifetime kind of thing?"

When Gina doesn't say anything for a moment, I add, "I think maybe that's why I settled. I thought I'd had my chance at love." My stomach twists.

Gina takes another sip of her drink. "Do you remember Donnie?"

It takes me a few seconds to realize why the name rings a bell. "The guy you dated right before Wayne? The one in the band? What were they called? Heavy Metal or something?"

She laughs. "Heavy Leather, I believe. Stupid name. But do you remember how into Donnie I was?"

"I can't believe I forgot about him! You were so sure he was your dream guy." Donnie had a tenth-grade education, greasy dyed black hair that hung to his shoulders, muscles the size of bowling balls, and only a mild proficiency on guitar, although he always used to brag that there were scores of record producers interested in him. "I thought you'd lost your mind," I add with a laugh.

She makes a face at me. "In retrospect, he was about as far away from Bill as I could get," she says. "It was entirely stupid— although in my defense, he was a really good kisser—but I think maybe I just had to get it out of my system. All I wanted to do was run away from all those thoughts of what could have been, because I knew that the life I'd planned died right along with Bill. I look back now and think that maybe Donnie was a necessary part of moving on. But it wasn't the right time, and he wasn't the right guy."

"Understatement of the year," I mutter.

She laughs. "Okay, tease me all you want. But here's the thing: When I was desperate to move on, because I thought it was what I was *supposed* to be doing, I chose wrong. Then, when I wasn't looking for it, Wayne came along. Now I'm happy—really happy. And in a way, I don't think that would have happened if I hadn't kind of burned through all the bad stuff with Donnie."

The words hit home. "The bumps in the road have a funny way of turning into stepping-stones, don't they?" I ask.

She smiles. "In the best cases."

"Do you think it'll happen for me someday? Finding someone who's as right for me as Patrick was?"

"I think it *could,* but only if you let it," she says carefully. "Only if you're not in a rush."

It's good advice, and it makes me feel hopeful. "Well, cheers to Donnie," I say, raising my glass. She makes a face, so I hurry to add, "For being a good kisser and a building block for a better future. Also for being a perfect example of why people should shampoo their hair at least every few days."

Gina laughs, but when she raises her glass to mine, her expression is serious. "To a better future, Kate."

Two days later, I skip sign language class, because I'm not ready to discuss my breakup with Andrew yet. Of course I'm probably deluding myself that it matters to him, but he seemed to sense that something was wrong last week at Allie's. I'm afraid he'll ask again, and aside from my sister and my closest friend, I'm not ready to discuss it with anyone yet.

So instead of going to class, I call Susan and Gina and ask if they feel like grabbing dinner, just the three of us. Both of them are way too eager to say yes, and as I meet them at the entrance to Swifty's in Susan's Upper East Side neighborhood, I can see in their faces that they're worried. I suspect they both believe I've been sitting at home feeling despondent, but the opposite is true; I've been spending my free time researching how to become a foster parent in New York State, and it's making me feel hopeful. Now that Dan isn't a factor anymore, I'm feeling more and more convinced that I'm ready for a child, and right now, fostering with a possibility of adoption seems like the best route. After all, I'm already involved with the foster system through my work at St. Anne's. Beyond that, I'm harboring a hope in the back of my mind that if Allie's mother doesn't come through for her, I might have the chance to step up to the plate.

Gina and Susan seem determined to fill any potential silences with chatter, probably because they're afraid of how I'll react if they bring Dan up. I smile and nod along as Susan tells me about a drawing Calvin did in preschool that looked just like a juvenile version of the *Mona Lisa,* and I laugh in all the right places when Gina tells a story about Madison getting into a bag of chocolate chips in the pantry last night when her back was turned, but my mind is wandering by the time I'm on my second Guinness and Susan has launched into an explanation of why she's fairly sure Sammie is a math prodigy.

I scan the restaurant while half paying attention to an anecdote about how Sammie helped Robert figure out the tip when they went out to brunch on Sunday. Susan has just dramatically concluded that Sammie is on the cusp of understanding long division when I see someone familiar across the room, on the other side of the bar. It's Andrew. We lock eyes and he grins and begins to head over.

"Hey, Kate!" he says, interrupting Susan's story as he arrives at our table. She and Gina look up, startled, then they both look at me. "Playing hooky, I see," he adds.

He's still smiling, and I can't help but smile back as I reply, "Sorry I skipped class. I'll be there for Riajah and Allie tomorrow night. I promise. I just needed some girl time. I should have called."

"No, not at all," he says. "I was just worried. But it looks like everything's fine."

Andrew smiles at the girls, and I realize I haven't introduced them. "Sorry," I say, "This is my sister, Susan, and my best friend, Gina."

"Pleased to meet you, ladies," he says, shaking their hands.

"And you are . . . ?" Susan asks, arching an eyebrow and looking pointedly from him to me.

I can feel myself blushing as I rush to say, "This is Andrew Henson. He teaches my sign language class. And he works with the kids at the foster agency I told you about."

"Ohhhhhhh," Susan and Gina say in unison, exchanging looks.

"So how was class tonight?" I ask, trying to make small talk.

"Oh, the usual. Amy flirting. Vivian trying to learn phrases about peace, love, and rock 'n' roll. We missed you." Then, before I can respond to that, he continues brightly, "So am I intruding on a girls' night out? Are you talking wedding dresses and wedding vows and wedding . . . I don't know, what is it you girls talk about when it comes to weddings?"

He grins, clearly joking around. Susan and Gina squirm uncomfortably and look at me.

I clear my throat. "Um, not exactly. The wedding's off. Dan and I broke up."

Andrew looks surprised, then embarrassed, and I realize in an instant that even after the talk we had, he didn't believe I'd make the choice to end the relationship. I'm startled that this hurts my feelings. "Oh, Kate, I didn't know," he says right away. "I'm so sorry."

"No worries. It's been a week now. I'm okay."

"But why didn't you tell me?" he asks after a long pause, earning him an eyebrow raise from Susan. "I saw you Thursday."

"I don't know," I mumble, feeling like an idiot.

An awkward silence descends.

"Well," he says a moment later, "now that I've completely stuck my foot in my mouth, I'm going to go wash it down with a drink. And what do you know, my date just walked in. Only"— he checks his watch—"twenty-five minutes late."

I look toward the door and see a tall, modelesque girl with honey-blond hair, a deep tan, and a form-fitting beige dress scanning the restaurant impatiently. I force a tight smile at Andrew. "Well, you don't want to keep her waiting," I say.

But he doesn't make a move to go. "Kate, I'm really so sorry."

"Thanks," I say.

He nods, tells Susan and Gina that it was nice to meet them, and heads toward his date, who's found herself a place at the bar. I watch him go for a minute, confused. Am I *jealous* of the girl at the bar? Is she his girlfriend? Is she the girl I heard in the background the night I called him about Allie?

Just before he reaches her, he turns and smiles at me, and our eyes lock for a beat. Then he turns back around, and the moment is over. I watch as he kisses the girl on the cheek, wraps his arm loosely around her waist, and disappears with her around the corner.

When I finally look back to Susan and Gina, they're both looking at me with amused expressions.

"So *that's* why you're so into sign language," Gina says knowingly.

"What? No!" I can feel my cheeks heating up.

"You know it's okay to have a crush on someone," Susan says. She glances in the direction Andrew disappeared and raises an eyebrow. "Especially someone that cute."

"He's not . . . I'm not . . ." I realize I'm stammering. "I swear that's not why I'm taking the class," I finally manage to say.

"But you admit he's cute," Susan prompts.

I hesitate before saying, "Well, I'm not *blind*."

Gina and Susan laugh, and I can tell they're relieved.

After dinner, Gina grabs a cab outside the restaurant, and Susan says she'll walk me to the subway before hailing a cab to take her back uptown. She loops her arm through mine as we walk. "I just want to see you happy, sis," she says.

I think about that for a minute, then I lean my head on her shoulder and smile.

"I'm getting there," I tell her. And I really am.

Andrew calls me the next morning and leaves a voice mail while I'm working with a client. I call him back on my lunch break.

"You okay?" is the first thing he asks when he picks up.

"Yeah. Why wouldn't I be?" I hear how defensive I sound, how standoffish. I don't know if I'm annoyed at him for being concerned about me in general, or whether I'm annoyed that he found the time to be concerned while spending the evening with a supermodel. Either way, I know I'm being ridiculous.

"We just didn't have much of a chance to talk last night," he says.

"Did you have a good time on your date?" I can't resist asking.

"What? Oh. Yes, it was fine." He sounds flustered. "Look, I just wanted to make sure you're doing okay. It must have been hard to break up with someone you were planning to marry."

"Honestly, I probably should have made the decision to leave Dan a long time ago."

"But it's always easier to see that in retrospect, isn't it?" he asks. "I mean, when you're in it, sometimes it's just easier to keep moving forward."

"Even if it turns out you've been standing still," I murmur.

"Exactly." He clears his throat. "Well, anyway, I was actually calling to let you know that you don't have to come in this afternoon. Riajah has a dentist appointment that Sheila forgot to tell me about until this morning, and Allie has after-school detention."

"Detention? For what?"

"Apparently she and her best friend skipped school yesterday and got caught."

"What?" I demand.

"Yeah, it was pretty dumb," Andrew says, echoing my thoughts. "They didn't do anything terrible—they just went to the cemetery where her friend's grandma is buried—but since they were caught, there were penalties."

"Wow," I say softly. "I can't believe she'd do this after what she pulled a couple weeks ago."

"Yeah, well, I think the incidents are connected, to be honest. She had a tough visit with her mom a couple days ago, and I think it screwed with Allie's head a little."

My heart sinks. "How did her mom have a visitation? I thought Allie saw her smoking meth."

"Her mom tested clean. Allie must have been wrong about what she thought she saw."

"Do you think she was smoking?"

He's quiet for a minute. "I don't think Allie would lie about it. But it was dark and Allie is prone to jumping to conclusions." He pauses. "The bigger problem facing Allie right now is that Salma and Rodney have officially given their notice."

"What?"

"Allie doesn't know yet. But this skipping school thing was the final straw, apparently. To be honest with you, I think they've been wanting to get out of this since they found out Salma was pregnant. I'm surprised they didn't dump her after her little incident last week."

"Oh, Andrew." I don't know what to say. Just when Allie is learning that not everyone in her life will let her down, two of the people who are supposed to be the most stable are about to do exactly that. It breaks my heart for her. "How much time does she have left in their home?"

"Eight weeks tops. That's what Salma said when she called earlier. She kept saying she was terribly sorry, but they just couldn't justify keeping her once Salma's through her second trimester." Andrew sounds pissed.

"Are you going to tell Allie?" I ask.

"Not yet." In the deep breath he takes, I can hear the pain he's feeling for her. "I want to see what her options are first. Eight weeks from now is about the time her mother should regain custody if she keeps all her visitation appointments and the social worker assigned to the case signs off on a reunification, assuming her drug tests are all clean. But if that doesn't happen, I'm going to have to find another home for her, and I may not be able to right away. She might have to go into a group facility for a while."

"Poor Allie," I murmur, feeling helpless. "You sure I can't come today? Maybe a music therapy session would help her if she's feeling confused."

"No. She's in detention until five, then Salma and Rodney are grounding her. Besides, she doesn't know yet about having to move, and I've asked them not to say anything for now. So she should be fine tonight. But I'll let you know before I tell her, okay?"

"Thanks."

"And hey, about your breakup." He lets the fragment hang there for a minute, and I have the weirdest feeling he's nervous.

"Yeah?"

"For what it's worth, I think you did the right thing."

Twenty-Seven

For the rest of the day, I struggle to keep my mind on work, but by four thirty, the time I should be leaving to head out to Queens, all I can think about is Allie.

Well, Allie and Hannah, actually. I keep seeing snippets from my world with Patrick and Hannah, images of tucking Hannah in, of watching her across the breakfast table, of hearing her laughter as she spins around in Coney Island's teacups. And the more I think about it, the more I'm convinced that the purpose of seeing those things has been to lead me to Allie all along.

I've stopped trying to explain away the glimpses into the alternate world; there are just too many connections to real life. But since I have to admit that the existence of Hannah is impossible—despite the girl I saw through the bridal shop window—I have to wonder what the dreams were trying to tell me. Perhaps they were supposed to show me that I deserved to be happier than I ever would be with Dan, and if that's the case, they worked. But I still have the feeling there's something I'm not getting, something unfinished, and I'm beginning to think it's all about motherhood.

I let myself wonder, just for a second, if Patrick is up there somehow, pulling the strings, showing me the way. But the world

I experienced a mere handful of times seemed to be reality for him; it's not like he was aware I was dreaming and was actively trying to tell me something. In fact, he'd looked confused and alarmed each time I acted like I didn't belong.

I take a deep breath, push my client notes aside and log on to my computer. I spend a few minutes googling how to be a foster parent in New York until I land on a page at nyc.gov that tells me the basics of the process. I fill out the application and then print every form I can find from New York's Office of Children and Family Services site too. I walk out the door without looking back.

It's six thirty by the time I walk through the front entrance of St. Anne's Services, and although the place is relatively empty, I'm not surprised to find Andrew in his office, a lone lamp illuminating the stack of papers on his desk.

"Hey," I say from the doorway.

He looks up in surprise. "Kate! What are you doing here? I told you you didn't need to come today."

I take a deep breath and prepare to say the words that could change my life. "Andrew, I want to apply to be a foster parent. I don't want Allie to go into a group home or to land in a house with strangers if her mom doesn't get her back. If she needs a home, I want to be the one to give it to her."

Andrew just looks at me. "Kate—" he says, raking his hand through his hair. He doesn't say anything else, but he looks upset.

"What?" I ask when the silence grows uncomfortable. "I thought you'd be happy about this! It's the perfect solution for Allie."

He pauses before replying. "I'm just not sure the timing is right."

I stare at him in disbelief. I'd expected him to jump up and hug me, or at the very least to thank me for helping provide a safety net for one of the kids he cares about. But instead, he's looking at me with what resembles pity. "The *timing?*" I ask, trying unsuccessfully to keep the edge out of my voice.

He sighs. "You just broke up with your fiancé, right? I think it's wonderful that you're interested in becoming a foster parent, but this is a huge life decision, and not one you can make lightly."

"This has nothing to do with my breakup!" I exclaim. "This has to do with *me*—and Allie."

"But, Kate, there's no guarantee you'd even get Allie," he says gently. "I mean, if we decide this is a good idea, I can expedite your paperwork, get you a home visit right away, and get you enrolled in the parenting skills class you have to take before you're certified. But even if we rush everything through—and even though you've already cleared the background checks, which will save us some time—it may not be soon enough. The process takes time, and Allie might need a home before you've been approved."

"But—"

"Besides," he says, cutting me off. "You need to remember that her mother is still very much in play. She's not perfect, but she's been trying. Allie might be returned to her, Kate. We don't know what's going to happen. And I don't want you to get your hopes up and then wind up getting hurt."

"I know it's possible I won't get her," I say, although what I'm thinking is, *I'm absolutely positive the dreams led me here.* "But I have to take the chance. And if it's not Allie, then I'll be there for another child who needs a home."

"I just don't know if you're ready," he says after a minute. "I'm sure that you feel like there's a hole in your life with your fiancé gone. That's normal. I'm sure you're feeling a little lonely. But, Kate, you can't fill that hole with a child."

I can feel my cheeks burning. "How could you think that's what I'm doing?" I demand.

"I'm just saying it's a possibility," he says. "It's possible you don't even know you're doing it."

"I can't believe you're saying these things!" I cry, although deep down, part of me understands his trepidation. "I've been thinking about a child for months now, Andrew, and working with you—working with these kids—has made me sure. I know the timing isn't ideal, and maybe on paper it looks like I'm not ready, but if there's even a chance I could provide a home for Allie, I need to do this now, or I let her down. And isn't that what being a parent is? Taking chances in your own life because you know it will make your child's life better? I want this, Andrew, and it has nothing to do with having a hole in my life or feeling lonely or anything else. It has to do with me being ready to be a mother—and Allie being ready for a home."

He stares at me before nodding slowly. "Let me think about it."

I stand there for another minute. I don't know whether to feel angry, hurt, or hopeful. I don't know if he's really planning to consider what I'm saying or whether he's just trying to get me out of his office. So finally I settle for a mumbled "Thank you," and I leave without another word, feeling like I've just lost something I never had.

I spend all day Friday thinking about what Andrew said and waffling back and forth between doubting myself and feeling as if I've just made the best decision of my life. I even consider going around Andrew and contacting the Office of Children and Family Services myself, but what holds me back is the knowledge that if Andrew won't give me his stamp of approval, I probably don't deserve it. After all, he wants what's best for Allie and the other kids he works with. And I know him well enough now to be able to say that his instincts are generally good. Perhaps that's why it's so hurtful that his first reaction was to doubt me.

Still, I'm holding out hope that he'll see I'm right, that I *am* in a good place now. So I wake up early on Saturday morning and begin clearing out the guest room, which I've been using primarily as storage. I'm already imagining Allie here while I pack up bags to take to Goodwill and put aside things I want to keep. As I pull box after box from the closet, I can almost see the walls decorated with her posters and her poems. I can visualize her keyboard set up in the corner.

"Thank you, Patrick," I whisper as I think about how all the dreams have led me here, to this. "Now if you can just help Andrew see my point . . ." My eyes blur with tears, and as I cross the room again to put away a lamp I've never liked, I trip over one of the boxes from the closet, spilling its contents. I curse, my toe throbbing in pain, and as I bend to pick up the pieces of paper I've scattered across the floor, I freeze.

Inside the cardboard box, which has been tipped on its side, I see the hand-carved wooden chest Patrick gave to me when he proposed, filled with a hundred slips of paper, each of them inscribed with the reasons he loved me. I haven't seen it in years. I sink slowly to the floor and pick up one of the slips.

I love how you go out of your way to help people, it says. I pick up another and read in his narrow, slanted handwriting, *I love the tiny dimple in your right cheek when you smile really wide.*

I read the rest one by one as I put them slowly back in the chest. There are big ones, such as, *I love the way you always look for the good in people,* and silly little ones, such as, *I love the way that when you laugh really hard, you double over.*

There are also specific ones: *I love the fact that when your mom broke her arm, you moved home for two weeks to help out. I love that you refused to quit softball in eighth grade after you were hit by a pitch that broke your nose.*

The last one I put away touches me the most. *I love the idea of having children with you one day. You're going to be an amazing mother.*

Tears are streaming down my cheeks by the time the slips are all put away. I grab a stool, stand on my tiptoes, and push the box as far back on the top shelf of the closet as I can manage. It makes a dull clinking sound as it pushes something at the back of the shelf into the wall, and a second later, a silver dollar tumbles to the ground.

I stare at it for a moment before climbing down slowly and picking it up. With the exception of the one I wear around my neck, I had given all the remaining coins to Joan after Patrick had died, because after all, they were her father's tradition. So I can't imagine where this one came from. Regardless, the coins are meant to carry good luck, and having this one fall from the sky—almost literally—feels like a nudge in the right direction.

Any doubt that it's a sign is erased a moment later when my phone rings. I tuck the silver dollar into my pocket, climb off the stool, and hurry out to the kitchen, where my cell is illuminated on the counter. The caller ID tells me it's Andrew.

"I'm sorry," he says before I can even say hello. It sounds like he's rehearsed the words, and they pour out quickly. "I think you were right. I had a kneejerk reaction based on a typical situation, but you're not typical, are you? And I believe you when you say you're okay. I agree that you'd give Allie—or any child—a good home."

"Really?" I whisper, my heart fluttering. I reach into my pocket and touch the silver dollar.

"Really," Andrew says firmly. "I've already gotten your paperwork rolling. You need to officially fill out an application—

which I'll fax to you today, if you want—but I've signed you up for an accelerated parenting course and contacted a colleague of mine about getting you a home visit as soon as possible. It'll still take five or six weeks, though, at the very minimum. And that's only because I've pulled every string I can think of. Usually the approval process takes a few months, but I agree that we should make every effort to have you available to take Allie, just in case that becomes an option."

"I don't know what to say," I whisper.

He clears his throat. "I also put in a personal recommendation for you, but you'll need two other references. Maybe your sister and your friend Gina, the ones I met at dinner? It just has to be two people who will recommend you and vouch for your character. So let's get all that in order, and as long as you can commit to three-hour classes each Tuesday and Friday evening for the next five and a half weeks, we should be good to go."

"Andrew," I breathe, "I don't even know how to begin to thank you."

"You don't need to thank me," he says. "In fact, I owe you an apology. You're trying to do exactly what I'm trying to do—give these kids a better life—and I didn't listen to you like I should have. You're going to be an amazing foster mom. So if you can go into your office today, I'll fax the paperwork right over, okay?"

"I'll head there now."

"Great. I have a really good feeling about this, Kate."

I close my eyes and smile. "I do too."

An hour and a half later, on my way home from my office after faxing all the initial paperwork back to Andrew, I make a detour by the East River and throw the silver dollar from the closet in, returning my good luck to the universe, just like Patrick always did.

* * *

The next day, I drop by Susan's to tell her about Allie and my decision to become a foster parent, as well as to let her know I put her down as a personal reference on my application. As I talk, her eyebrows shoot up, and she gapes at me.

"What is it?" I finally ask, sighing.

"You're sure you're ready for this?" she asks. "Being a parent isn't as easy as it looks."

I bristle immediately. "I never said it was easy. You know I work with kids every day. I understand what a challenge it is."

"Do you, though?" she persists. "You see these kids for an hour. But you're not the one worrying about putting food on the table for them, or disciplining them, or making sure they do their homework or grow up right."

I can feel my blood boiling. "So you're saying I shouldn't be a mother? Because it's hard? And I'm somehow not equipped?"

"It's just that these foster kids have so many problems," Susan says.

"That doesn't mean I can't work through those issues," I shoot back. "They've just had fewer advantages and fewer people looking out for them. Not everyone's as lucky as Sammie and Calvin."

"It's not luck," Susan says stiffly. "Robert and I have worked hard to give them a safe, secure home and a good upbringing."

"I know," I say. "I'm just saying that they're fortunate to have gotten you two as a mom and dad. Not all kids get to have parents like that."

"Exactly my point. And what do you think happens when a child grows up without any of the good values we've instilled in our kids?"

"Just because these kids haven't had traditional upbringings doesn't mean they don't have good values," I argue. "You sound like an elitist."

"No. I sound like a realist. And you sound like you have your head in the clouds."

"Not everyone gets handed the perfect life on a silver platter," I snap. "I know you did, so maybe that's hard for you to understand. But you have everything, Susan. I *lost* everything. And I'm doing my best to build a life for myself now."

"Yeah, you had a tragedy, and it's terrible," Susan shoots back. "But you're forty. You've got to stop mooning over your dead husband and agonizing over what was or wasn't meant to be. Besides, how are you ever going to wind up in another relationship when you're all of a sudden a foster mom? Do you think you're going to have time to date? Or that any guy in his right mind is going to want to accept this lifestyle choice you're making?"

And suddenly, I understand. "So that's what this is about. You think I'll never find a boyfriend if I have a child."

"A foster child, anyhow." She shrugs. "Fine, so Dan wasn't right for you. But I'm sure there's someone out there who is. If you go ahead with this fostering thing, though, you're just shooting yourself in the foot. Besides, do you really think you can do this alone? Be a single mom?"

"Yeah, I can," I say softly. "I know it'll be hard. But I have a good job, I can easily afford a few hours of after-school care each day, and I have the space in my life for this. I've never been so sure of anything, Susan. Besides, I'm not talking about fostering an infant and raising that child for the rest of his or her life. I'm talking about shorter-term situations with older kids, and if one of those situations turns permanent, it's still only another five or six years until that child is off to college."

"*If* they get in to college," she mutters. "And it's not like your responsibilities as a parent end there."

I open my mouth to reply, but she cuts me off.

"Maybe I'm not being fair to you. And yes, if you're asking me to be a personal reference for you, of course I will. You're the best person I know, Kate. But do I think you're doing the right thing? No. I think you're making a mistake. I think you're giving away your chance to find your happily ever after."

"The thing is, not every happily ever after needs to end with a Prince Charming," I say after a pause. "I already had my prince, and if there's another one out there, great. But I'm not sitting around waiting to get rescued. It's time that I'm the one doing the saving."

Twenty-Eight

Over the next few weeks, I throw myself into preparing to be a foster parent. I talk to Gina—who's more supportive than Susan—and after attending an orientation, I jump right in to the twice-a-week Model Approach to Parenting Preparation courses, the required ones Andrew signed me up for. Much of what is taught is information I already know—some of it instinctually, some of it from my therapeutic background. But the class also teaches me things that are new to me, such as how to help a foster child integrate into a new home, and what my legal responsibilities as a foster parent will be. I find myself imagining Allie in every sample scenario the instructor mentions, and I have to keep reminding myself that she may very well not be mine. But the dreams don't return, and I'm beginning to feel more and more strongly that they were leading me here all along.

I have weekly meetings at my apartment with a social worker named Karen Davidson who has been assigned to my case. Typically, she tells me, a home study could take months, but I come highly recommended by Andrew, and he has stressed the emergency nature of the potential situation with Allie, so she's trying to move things along. "Plus, I understand you're learning sign language and that you have experience working with both hard-of-hearing and developmentally challenged children. That'll make you a real asset to us, and I'd love to get you into our program as quickly as possible. The fact that you're already a volunteer with St. Anne's helps."

She takes my income tax returns from the last several years, makes copies of my birth certificate and social security card, and requests medical records from my physician. She also asks me what feels like a thousand questions each week about everything from where a child would be housed (in the guest bedroom) to how I'd provide child care while I'm working (I've already found an after-school program) and whether I'm involved in any romantic relationships (the answer to which is a resounding no). And she examines every nook and cranny of my apartment with pursed lips, jotting notes on a clipboard.

At Andrew's request, I don't say anything to Allie about my foster parenting training. "We don't want her to get her hopes up, because this isn't a sure thing," he reminds me. "And we don't want to get in the way of her bonding with her mom." So instead, I keep visiting her each Thursday, as usual, and I'm relieved to find her opening up and sharing stories about school and her best friend, Bella, whom she always calls *BFF* in sign language—her middle and index fingers crossed while she mouths the letters. I'm happy to see her friendship flourishing and grateful that she's found in Bella someone who can identify with both her hearing difficulties and her foster situation. I laugh when she begins telling me the ways she and Bella are plotting to get the purple-haired Jay Cash to ask Allie out.

"I've never even kissed a boy," Allie confides one day. "Bella says it's kind of gross, all tongues and everything, but I don't think she's kissed anyone either, even though she won't admit it, so I don't really believe her."

My heart swells with affection and love for Allie with each new stride forward she makes, and I'm relieved when she doesn't bring up her mother again, although it's probably my responsibility to be poking at the subject to see if she wants to talk. But I'd rather envision a life where I'll make everything okay for Allie, where I'll take away the pain of all the times she's been hurt before.

So I keep my head down and go through the motions of my life. I go to the MAPP class for prospective foster parents every Tuesday and Friday, to Andrew's ASL class every Wednesday, and out to Queens every Thursday, where I work with Allie, Riajah, and a young boy named Tarek, who has 90 percent hearing loss and who just entered the foster system a few weeks ago. At work, I joke around with Max, help Leo with his situation at school, and make music with two dozen other kids with various challenges that need addressing.

Life is slowly getting back to normal, a new normal, without Dan. But the glimpses into the world I share with Patrick and Hannah are gone now, and I miss them terribly. Each night, I wait to wake up in a life where I still have Patrick, and where Hannah exists. Each morning, I awake crushed and missing them anew. I try Joan a few times, but we seem to be playing phone tag; I keep getting her voice mail, and when she calls back, she keeps getting mine.

Four weeks after the breakup, Dan finally agrees to meet me for lunch, and after he lets me go on for a full five minutes, apologizing for hurting him, he tells me that he's pretty sure he never loved me in the first place. The words sting more than I would have thought.

"You can't mean that," I say. "We were together for almost two years."

"Well, it was easy enough for you to walk away," he says, his eyes hard. "That doesn't say a whole lot about your love for me, does it?"

"Dan, I did love you," I say. "I still do. But that doesn't make us right for each other."

He rolls his eyes. "Spare me the psychobabble. You haven't dealt with your own shit. You brought a whole load of baggage into our relationship, and that's not my fault. It's yours. One hundred percent your fault. I deserved better."

"I know," I say softly.

"So you can't just sit here and say you love me and expect me to smile and say, 'Well, then, I forgive you for treating me like I'm disposable.'"

"But I didn't mean to hurt you," I protest. "You have to know that."

He looks away, but not before I notice the pain in his eyes, which wounds me just as much as anything else. "Kate, I really don't give a shit what you meant." He gets up to leave before the waiter even arrives to take our order.

A few weeks later, I finish the MAPP training, so all that's left to do is wait for official certification as a foster parent. I've been told this is the part that can take the longest, because of bureaucratic red tape. I try to hang in there and believe it will all work out.

August gives way to September, the air turns cooler, and the numbers on the calendar begin to tick down to the anniversary of Patrick's death. The day before the anniversary is a Wednesday, and Andrew corners me after sign language class to tell me—in sign language, which I'm beginning to truly understand after all these weeks—that I don't need to come by St. Anne's tomorrow.

Why? I sign back carefully.

Because it's September eighteenth, he signs.

I stare at him for a minute. "You remembered," I say aloud.

"That it's the anniversary of you losing your husband? Of course I did. I don't want you to worry about us tomorrow. Just take care of yourself."

"Thanks," I reply, but I'm a bit sad that I won't get to see Andrew, Riajah, Tarek, or Allie. It'll mean a day alone with my thoughts and my sadness.

"Are you okay, Kate?" Andrew asks aloud as I turn to go. "Is tomorrow going to be hard for you?" Before I can answer, he shakes his head and says, "What am I saying? Of course it'll be hard. That was like the dumbest question I could have asked you."

I smile. "It's really nice of you to be concerned. And yeah, it's always hard. But every year, it gets a little easier to bear, you know? I'll be okay."

"Look, come by St. Anne's if you want," he says. "I didn't mean you shouldn't come. I just didn't want to make you work. But if you're feeling down and you want to talk, I'll be there all day and most of the evening." He stops short and adds, "I mean, not that you don't have other people to talk to. That's not what I meant."

"I know."

"I just meant, you know, if you need another friend, I'm here. Or there, I mean. At St. Anne's."

"It's a really nice offer," I tell him. "And it's really nice to know you care."

"Of course I care," he says. "I don't say this enough, Kate, but I appreciate all the work you've been doing with us. Some-times, I feel like I kind of roped you into it. You just showed up to take a sign language class, and before you knew it, I had you committed to volunteering with us every week. I feel like kind of a jerk."

"Andrew, stop. I love it. It makes me really happy to work with the kids. I'm grateful that you asked me to help out."

"Well," Andrew says, "I owe you. So if you're ever looking for something to do at night, and you're not out with your sister and your friend, let me know. I'll take you out to another fabulous and educational dinner sometime. To say thanks for helping me with the kids."

I stare at him. Is he asking me out? I quickly dismiss the thought, because after all, I've seen his girlfriend, and she looks like she belongs on the cover of a magazine. He must be asking me as one professional to another, even if he looks almost like he's blushing. "Sure, that sounds good," I say, because regardless of his motivation, spending a little more time with him seems like a nice idea. I hadn't realized quite how lonely I would feel without Dan or the dreams around. Sometimes, the nights seem to stretch on forever.

"Cool," Andrew says. He gives me an awkward hug goodbye and reminds me to call him tomorrow if I need anything.

Thank you, I sign back. *See you next week*.

He grins. "Well, look at you, Miss Fluent-in-Sign-Language. I'll see you next week too."

I take the next day off, as I have each year on the anniversary of losing Patrick. Even though I'm trying hard to put the past behind me, there's just something about coasting through life normally on the day Patrick died that feels wrong to me.

I lie in bed that morning, wondering how twelve whole years could have possibly passed since the day it happened. In some ways, it feels like it was just a year or two ago. In another way, I feel sometimes like it's been decades since Patrick died.

I've just sunken into the first stages of feeling sorry for myself when my phone dings with a text. I'm surprised to see it's from Allie.

U ok? she writes.

Yes, thanks, I write back, not sure whether Allie's asking me a general question or whether she remembers about Patrick. I told her the date of his death the night she ran away.

I just thought u might be sad about ur husband, she texts back a minute later, and I feel overwhelmingly grateful.

I am, I text back. *Very sad. But it really helps to know you're worried about me.*

Well, I really like u, Allie texts back after a pause. *U R really nice to me.*

I really like you too, I text back. *You're a wonderful person, Allie.*

Allie doesn't reply at first, and I wonder for a moment if somehow I've said the wrong thing. But then she writes, *Come by my house if u r sad later. I can cheer u up.*

I smile. *Thanks, Allie,* I write back.

My mom's hearing is today, she writes after a minute, and my heart stops beating for a minute. Why didn't Andrew tell me? *My social worker says she doesn't know what's gonna happen,* she adds a moment later.

I swallow hard. Maybe Andrew didn't say anything because he didn't want me to get my hopes up. But then again, maybe it's because he doesn't want my heart broken yet again on the worst day of the year. *Good luck,* I settle for texting back.

Thx, Allie writes back. *Gotta go to class.*

After the conversation is over, I turn my phone off, lie back down, and stare at the ceiling, feeling very much alone. But today's about Patrick, not Allie and her mother, and I won't let myself get sidetracked by yet another thing I can't control.

A little after eight, I roll over and look at the digital clock on my nightstand. I watch the minutes tick by, and I think about how twelve years ago, at this very time, life for both Patrick and me was blissful, virtually worry-free. We had no idea that in just a matter of minutes, everything would change.

I'm still watching when the clock turns to 8:36, a minute before it happened. I know I'm torturing myself, but I'm somehow unable to stop.

The clock turns to 8:37, and my heart sinks, just like it does every year. This is the moment, twelve years ago, that Gennifer Barwin—her blood alcohol level more than twice the legal limit—changed the course of my life forever. *I was just trying to show my baby Times Square, that's all,* she'd told the police later as an ambulance took her away. She'd merely broken her arm, and her daughter, safely strapped in her car seat, literally didn't have a scratch on her.

I lie there until 8:52, the moment Patrick breathed his last breath in a cage of twisted metal, then I get out of bed, shuffle to the kitchen, and go through the motions of making myself a pot of coffee, although I don't actually want to drink it. At 11:00, I finally pick up my cell phone again and return missed calls from Susan, my mom, and Gina. Susan and my mom want to make sure I'm okay and let me know they're thinking of me. The conversation with Gina is, as it always is, cathartic. We cry together for a few minutes and then we remind each other of some of our favorite funny stories about Patrick and Bill.

"Remember the time we were all going to the movies, and Bill's jacket got caught in the revolving door?" Gina asks with a ragged laugh. "Patrick was the only one who noticed, and he and Bill were yelling at the people behind us and trying to get them to stop the door, and you and I thought they'd gone nuts."

"Or the time that little girl came up to the four of us at dinner and was convinced that for some reason that Patrick was actually—what's the name of that guy who played Mark Darcy?"

Gina laughs. "Right! Colin Firth, right? Because she'd just seen some movie with him in it, and she thought Patrick looked just like him?"

"He kept trying to tell her that he was just a normal guy. But that just made it worse, because the little girl kept saying, 'That's exactly what Colin Firth would say.'"

"God, Patrick held that over your head for months, didn't he?" Gina asks, then deepens her voice for an imitation of Patrick trying to talk with a British accent: "'I'm Colin Firth, so you have to do what I say. I'm very famous, you know.'"

I laugh at the memory, but after a moment, my laughter dies down, and so does hers.

"I really miss them," Gina says softly.

"Yeah. Me too."

We hang up after making plans to see each other for dinner one day next week, then I take a deep breath and dial Joan's number.

"How you doing, sweetheart?" she asks when she answers.

"About the same as every September eighteenth," I tell her.

"It never really gets easier, does it?" she asks. "Every year, we think we're a little further along the path to being okay again, and every year, it turns out we're wrong."

"Exactly," I say. I knew Joan would understand. "How are you?"

We talk for a few minutes about Patrick. Then, thinking about my dreams, I ask Joan, "Hey, did you ever go get that mammogram we talked about?"

"Oh yes, I've been meaning to tell you!" she exclaims. "I did go in. The mammogram person—what are they called, a radiologist?—said everything looked okay, but they were just worried about one little spot, so they did a small biopsy. Everyone was very upbeat, and I'm supposed to get the results back any day now. I'm sure everything's fine, but thanks for urging me to go in. I'll feel a lot better when I know for sure that things are okay."

"Good," I say, but her mention of a biopsy bothers me. I can't shake the image of her bald and weakened by chemotherapy. "Just let me know as soon as you get word from the doctor, okay?"

"Of course, sweetheart," she promises.

After we hang up, I sit down in my kitchen and stare at my now-cold cup of coffee. The pain of missing Patrick is visceral today, and no amount of reminiscing about him or crying about his absence can make it feel any better. "Patrick, if you can hear me," I say aloud, "I love you. I've never stopped loving you. I miss you every day." I pause for a minute before adding softly, "I knew before I met you—"

But the only response is silence.

Then my phone rings, startling me, and I see Unknown Caller on the caller ID. Usually, I'd let it go to voice mail, but today I'm lonely and sad, and so I pick the phone up and say hello.

"Is this Kate Waithman?" The female voice on the other end sounds vaguely familiar, but I can't place it.

"Yes . . ."

"Excellent. It's Karen Davidson."

My heart is immediately in my throat. "Karen, of course."

"Well, I'm calling today with some wonderful news, Kate. You've been approved to be a foster parent. Your certification is official."

I can hardly believe it, so I ask her to repeat the words, and she does.

"We think you'll be a wonderful foster mother, Kate," she adds. "Congratulations. We're very happy to have you on board."

My heart is thudding double time. "I get to be a foster mom?" I whisper in disbelief.

"You sure do," Karen says.

"Do you think there's a chance I'll get to foster the girl I've been working with?" I ask. "Allie Valcher?"

I can hear Karen's smile through the phone as she says, "I don't see why not, if she needs a home; you have the specialized skill set to be able to work with her."

I blink back tears and look skyward. This must be Patrick's doing somehow. I was right. The dreams were leading me here. On September eighteenth of all days. "Karen, I don't even know how to thank you."

"No need," she says warmly. "We're grateful to you for opening your heart and your home to a child. We'll get everything officially rolling later this week, if you have time to come by my office."

We agree to meet tomorrow at noon, and after she gives me her address, we say good-bye, and I hang up.

Elated, I walk into the guest room and close my eyes. This will be Allie's room if everything goes right. I'll go out today and buy a bed, a comforter a preteen would like, maybe even a nice electric piano and a Mac with recording software. My life is about to change, and the fact that it's all happening today is, at the very least, poetic and beautiful.

"Thank you, Patrick," I whisper, feeling my husband's presence. If I close my eyes and imagine hard enough, I can almost feel his strong arms wrapped around me, his warm breath on my neck, his body pressed against mine. "I know you did this. Thank you for Allie."

Twenty-Nine

I'm at the Macy's in Herald Square early that afternoon, trying to choose between a teak trundle bed and an oak full-sized bed with storage drawers underneath, when my phone rings. Andrew's name shows up on the caller ID.

"How are you doing?" he asks when I answer. "Since today's the, um, anniversary and all?"

I smile, grateful for his concern. "I'm actually doing okay."

"You sure?"

"Really."

"Okay. Good." He clears his throat. "Look, I'm sorry to ask you this today, of all days. But if you're at all able, could you meet me at St. Anne's now? There's something I need to talk to you about, and I'd rather do it in person. If you're sure absolutely you're okay."

My heart skips. Is it possible that Allie's mother was denied custody today and that Allie will need a home? *My* home? Surely Andrew knows by now that I've been approved. "Sure," I tell him, trying to keep my voice from shaking. "I'll leave now. I'll be there in about forty-five minutes."

Karen Davidson had sounded so optimistic on the phone, and

as I think about it on the subway ride out to Queens, I become convinced that this is what Andrew wants to tell me. Maybe he's called me in to inform me that Allie and I have been officially matched. Can it happen that quickly?

Maybe September eighteenth can stop being the anniversary of the day the world ended and begin being the anniversary of the day I officially became a foster mom to Allie. It would be a beautiful end to my story. And I have the feeling this is what Patrick would have wanted for me.

When I get to St. Anne's, Andrew isn't in his office, so I shoot him a text saying I'm here, then I head down the hall, looking into office windows to see if I spot him anywhere. I reach the conference room and when I peer in the door, I'm startled to see Allie, her back to me.

I rap lightly and walk in. Her face lights up as she turns. "Kate!" she exclaims. "Hey, thank you so much!" She crosses the room to hug me, and as I hug back, I'm suddenly positive that Andrew has already told her the news. Allie's coming home with me. This is all coming true.

"Thank you?" I ask, feigning ignorance. I'm unable to stop myself from grinning at her, though. "Thank you for what?"

"Thank you for telling me not to give up on my mom," she says warmly.

A bad feeling develops in the pit of my stomach as I blink at her in confusion. "What?"

"The judge said she can come get me today. Kate, I'm going home!"

That's when I notice that the corner of the conference room is filled with battered suitcases, as well as a folded-up keyboard stand, and a keyboard standing on its end. I look from the pile to Allie, and for a moment, all I can do is stare.

"Kate?" Allie asks after a moment. "What's wrong? Are you

sad about your husband still? Do you want to talk about it or something?"

I shake my head, still mute with shock, just as Andrew comes in behind me.

"Kate," he says, and I can hear in his flat tone that he's realized in an instant what's happened. "Kate, can you come with me for a minute?" He doesn't wait for an answer; he just puts a gentle hand on my back and leads me out of the room. I feel dazed as he moves a stack of paperwork from a chair in his office and sits me down.

"Kate," he begins as I lean back in the seat. "I don't even know what to say."

"I thought you'd called me down here to tell me I could foster Allie," I say numbly. "I got the call today from Karen Davidson. I've been approved as a foster parent."

He blinks a few times as the information registers, and I can tell he feels a hundred times worse. "Oh, Kate. I had no idea. I called you because the judge awarded custody to Allie's mom, which means she's going home today. I know it's not what we expected, but I thought you might want to be here, to say good-bye. I didn't tell you on the phone because I thought it was the kind of news that should be delivered in person. I assumed I'd catch you before you ran into Allie, though. God, I'm sorry."

"Today of all days," I say dully.

"Oh, Kate," Andrew says again. He squats down beside me and pulls me into an awkward hug. "Was I wrong to call?"

"No," I say into his shoulder. He feels warm, solid. Suddenly, I don't want to let go, but that's irrational. Everything I hold on to disappears, so I pull away before he has a chance to. "I'm glad I'm here to say good-bye to her. It's the right thing."

"It's not a forever good-bye. It's just for now. As long as it's okay with her mom, I don't see why you can't continue working with her once she's settled, if you want to."

"Yeah, okay," I say flatly. I know he's trying to cheer me up, but I feel dead inside. "So the meth thing? Allie was wrong about what she saw?"

He nods. "The judge ordered another random drug test, but it came back totally clean too. It was just tobacco."

"Or maybe her mom's just good at beating the system." I take a deep breath and hope that I'm wrong. "Do you think she'll be a good mom to Allie this time around?"

Andrew looks sad as he shrugs. "I don't know. I wish I could say yes. But I've seen so many of these kids come and go, and there's often no way of telling whether things will work out. Let's hope that Allie's case is one of the good outcomes."

I'm silent for a moment, then I say, "I thought I was going to get to be her mom. Her foster mom, at least. I really thought that's what was supposed to happen." *How could I have gotten everything so wrong?*

Andrew doesn't reply. He just pulls me into another awkward hug. When he finally stands up, his expression is somber. "Her mom should be here soon. Are you ready to go say goodbye?"

"I guess," I say, although I'm fairly sure I've already had my fair share of good-byes in this lifetime.

"It's going to be okay, Kate," Andrew says. He reaches out and squeezes my hand. "I know it sounds like a foolish thing to say now, but I really believe things happen the way they're meant to. There must be a reason for this."

"That's a dumb thing to say," I snap. "There's not a reason for any of it. There's no reason my husband had to die. There's no reason I can't have a child. There's no reason that everything that means anything to me gets taken away."

I glare at him for a minute before realizing that it's not his fault. He's just trying to help. "Sorry," I mumble.

"No, *I'm* sorry," Andrew whispers, and when I finally look up at him, I see tears in his eyes. His emotion touches me more than I expect.

"I didn't mean to throw a pity party for myself," I say, wiping my own eyes and forcing a smile. "Let's go see Allie, okay?" I stand up and hurry out of his office before he can say anything else.

Andrew walks me back down the hall and stands by my side as I hug Allie tightly and tell her she's going to be all right, and that I'm so happy for her.

"Are you going to come visit me, Kate?" she asks, looking worried.

"You couldn't keep me away, kiddo."

"What about my piano recital next month? Are you coming to that? Bella's playing a Beethoven piece too, and Jay's going to be there. He said he'd come. Isn't that awesome?"

I nod, and at once, my whole body feels numb, exhausted. I'm too tired to even share in her obvious excitement about her crush. "I forgot that Bella plays too," I manage to say.

Allie nods enthusiastically. "You won't believe how good she is. On a scale of one to ten, she's like a fifty!"

I force a smile. "That's great."

"So you'll come?" Allie persists. "To my recital?"

"Wouldn't miss it for the world."

That's when Allie's mother arrives, accompanied by a harried caseworker balancing a big pile of papers in his arms. I'm startled to see how young she looks—maybe late twenties or very early thirties—and it occurs to me that she must have had Allie when she was only a child herself. This makes me irrationally sad. By the time she's my age, forty, Allie will be grown and out on her own. Her mother will have had all those years of having a child, and she has already squandered so much of it. How is it fair, in any universe, that she would get to be a parent and I wouldn't?

I can feel my hands balling into fists of frustration, and as if sensing how I'm feeling, Andrew puts a hand on the small of my back and begins rubbing small circles there. It's an intimate gesture for someone I only know professionally, but he doesn't seem to notice, and I realize I don't mind. Already, his touch is soothing me.

I watch as Allie's face lights up and she throws herself into her mother's arms. The woman, who looks like a slightly older version of Allie, appears startled, but she also looks happier to be holding her daughter than I'd expected her to be. I had pictured her as a villain who had carelessly thrown her child away. But I'm forced to admit the reality might be different. She looks pleasant, and I can see tears sparkling in her eyes as Allie holds on.

Maybe Andrew's right. Maybe Allie's mother really is trying.

"I'm going to do better this time," she tells Andrew as she helps Allie gather her things together. She turns to me, and although I know she hasn't the faintest idea who I am, she adds, "I'll be the mom she deserves. I promise."

All I can do is nod, and I turn away and leave the room without another word before Andrew has a chance to introduce us. I know I'll meet her eventually. I'll see Allie again, and I may even continue working with her. But I can't do this today.

I can hear Allie calling to me, but I don't turn around. There are tears streaming down my face now, and I don't want her to see them. I don't want our good-bye to be like this.

I retreat to Andrew's office, which is where he finds me standing a few minutes later, staring blankly out his window.

"You okay?" he asks carefully.

"Just peachy." I know I sound sarcastic, but I can't help it. My heart's been shattered into a million pieces.

"How about I take you home in a cab? I can keep you company for a while."

I turn around and look at him for a moment. His expression is earnest, his eyes sad. "Andrew . . ." I begin.

"I just think maybe you shouldn't be by yourself tonight," he blurts out. Then he shakes his head and says, "I didn't mean that like a come-on. I'm just worried about you. I could stay with you for a few hours, make sure you're okay . . ."

"I'm fine."

"I just don't think you should be alone," he repeats, looking at me helplessly.

I smile faintly at him. "Andrew, I'm alone all the time. Why should tonight be any different?"

I walk out of his office without another word, hail a taxi, and ride the whole way home staring straight ahead in silence.

For the second time on this very same day, I feel like I've lost a piece of myself. Twelve years ago, the man who was my family was taken from me in an instant. Today, I watched as the family I'd hoped to have disappeared too.

I crawl into bed, and for the first time in months, I'm not hoping I wind up back in the world where Patrick and Hannah exist, because I don't trust it anymore. What could it have been telling me if it wasn't about Allie? I just want the dark comfort of a dreamless night.

Susan and Gina spend the next few days trying in vain to pull me out of the funk I've slipped into since realizing that I won't be Allie's foster mother. It dawns on me slowly, over the course of several days, that even if Allie's mom had continued to disappoint her, Allie never would have looked at me as a parent. She might have loved me and come to rely on me, but I saw the way she looked at her mother with such hope, despite everything. It's too late in her life, I think, for her to ever have that kind of love for another parent.

Allie and I text back and forth a handful of times, and I'm happy, despite my own intense feelings of loss, to hear that she seems to be doing well. Her mother really seems to be trying, which makes me feel both relieved and jealous. There's a part of me, a very selfish part, that wishes it hadn't worked out, and that I could have been the one to swoop in and save Allie. But this outcome, the one in which she's returned to a seemingly loving home, is obviously for the best.

I go through the motions of work and dodge two calls from Karen Davidson, who leaves me messages about a hard-of-hearing teenager who has just come into the system recently.

"She's a really sweet kid," Karen says in the first message. "Her custodial grandmother died recently, and there are no other relatives willing to take her, so this is her first experience with foster care. She's been in temporary care for about three months now, but she obviously needs something more permanent. I think the two of you would be a really good match."

I finally call her back late Tuesday night, relieved when I get her answering machine. "I know this is going to make me sound like a flake," I say, "but I was really hoping to foster Allie, the girl I told you about. I definitely want to take a child in, and I want to be able to help the girl you're mentioning. But I need some time. I'm sorry. I'm really sorry. I hope this doesn't screw things up, and I promise I'll call you as soon as I'm ready." As soon as I hang up, I wonder if I've made a huge mistake, but everything feels jumbled right now. In truth, I probably shouldn't have been thinking about taking Allie in either; I need to get myself straightened out first.

I skip sign language class on Wednesday and leave Andrew a voice mail telling him I won't be able to make it in to meet with Riajah and Tarek the next night. He calls back, but I don't pick up, and when I listen to his message, in which he tells me he entirely understands and that I should take all the time I need, it makes me feel even worse. On Friday, I meet Susan for happy hour at Hammersmith's, and she starts on me right away.

"You need to let this go," she tells me before Oliver has even had a chance to deliver our drinks. "All of this. The dreams. The obsessing over a child who will never be yours. This whole depression thing. Mom and I are concerned about you."

"I'm fine," I mumble. I'm irritated that she thinks it's just that easy, that I should be able to simply flick a switch and turn off all my problems.

"No, you're *not* fine," Susan says firmly. "Obviously. Look, I get that you want to be a parent. But there are plenty of ways to go about that. You've been approved as a foster mother, Kate. Let them know you're ready for a child. Or begin the process of applying to adopt through an agency, if that's what you want. But you've got to stop harping on these dreams and what you think they're telling you. They're just dreams."

"You still don't understand how real they were," I say. "I was so sure that they were telling me Allie needed me. And now, she's gone, the dreams are gone, and Patrick's gone. It all feels like lies."

Susan sighs. "Kate, Patrick has *been* gone. For twelve years. It's a tragedy, and we all miss him. But he hasn't been visiting you in your dreams. You have to admit how ridiculous that sounds. You were just nervous about your wedding, because you knew deep down it was the wrong thing, and that triggered stress dreams. Any psychologist could tell you that. But the dreams are gone now, and that's obviously your brain telling you it's time to let all this go and get back to real life."

"Easier said than done," I mutter.

When I get back to my apartment building that evening, I'm feeling hurt and unsettled by Susan's words. Does everyone think I'm pathetic? Maybe I am. I'm so deep in thought that I don't notice Andrew sitting on the front stoop outside until he says my name.

"What are you doing here?" I blurt out, then I feel instantly bad, because the words sound rude, and I hadn't meant them that way. "Wait, did something happen to Allie?" I ask.

"No," he says. "She's fine, as far as I know." He's dressed a little more formally than he normally is, with a button-down sky blue shirt and gray slacks. He even appears to have combed his hair.

"You're all dressed up," I say.

He looks down at himself, as if he's surprised to see what he's wearing. "Oh. Yeah. I'm supposed to be at a dinner thing."

I imagine the tan, willowy blond girl waiting for him some-where, probably pissed off that he's not there yet. "Why aren't you at dinner then?"

"I called and said I'd be late." We look at each other for a minute, and then he says, "Kate, you skipped class, and you left me a message on my office phone in the middle of the night on Wednesday saying you couldn't work with Riajah and Tarek this week. Today, I got a call from Karen Davidson saying that she got a voice mail from you and that you sounded really upset and aren't ready to foster yet. I got your address out of your file, because I wanted to make sure you're okay."

I stare at him for a minute before hanging my head. "That's really nice of you." I don't wait for a response before I move past him toward the front door of my apartment building. "Do you want to come in?"

He follows me without a word. Inside my apartment, he gazes around curiously as I lead him into the living room, and we take seats opposite each other, me on the love seat, him on the couch. "Nice place," he says.

"Thanks." I feel nervous, awkward.

"Kate," he begins slowly, "you're upset. And I want to talk to you about it. Is this about Allie?"

I study his face for a moment, sure that I'll see judgment there, or maybe pity. But he only looks worried. Finally, I look away. "Yes and no. I mean, I thought I would get to help her."

"You *have* helped her."

"I mean, I thought that I was going to be the one to take her in for a while. To be the parent she needed, you know? But it turns out she didn't need that at all. It makes me feel . . ."

I trail off, and Andrew nods in understanding, waiting for me to go on.

"I just feel lost," I conclude in a small voice, feeling foolish as I say it.

"You're not lost," he says after a pause. "In fact, from everything I've seen in the last couple of months, Kate, it seems like you've been found. Or at least you've found where you're supposed to be."

"Where's that?" I ask, unable to keep the bitterness out of my voice. "Old and alone?"

"You just have to have some faith that life will work out the way it's supposed to," Andrew says, apparently choosing to ignore my self-pity. "Maybe Allie wasn't supposed to be yours. Maybe she was just supposed to show you something about yourself. Maybe, in turn, you were supposed to help her heal. Maybe this is *exactly* the way life was supposed to go."

"*None* of this is how life was supposed to go!" I exclaim. "My husband wasn't supposed to die! I wasn't supposed to find out

I couldn't have kids of my own! I wasn't supposed to be all by myself at forty!"

"How do you know?" Andrew asks. "How do you know what life intended?"

"What are you saying?" I shoot back. "That it's a good thing Patrick's dead? That I'm somehow fortunate that it took me twelve years to get my shit together? That now the road ahead of me is full of rainbows and sparkles? I'm sorry, but I just don't believe any of that."

If I were having this conversation with Dan, he would shrug and walk away with an annoyed expression on his face. But Andrew stays right where he is and says, "You're angry. I get that. And you have every right to be. Life has let you down. But what if the dreams you talked about were real?"

I stop fuming and look at him. "What?"

"I mean, who are we to say they're not? Maybe they're not just dreams. Maybe we all have this whole other world out there that we could be living in. But you have to choose, Kate. Do you want this life, the one you're living in, where you get to make a difference? Or do you want a life that might have been, where you're not really *you*?"

I think about the Andrew I read about in the dream, the one who didn't seem to have the passion that the man in front of me has in spades. And I think about the disservice I'm doing to Patrick by not allowing his absence to transform me into something better. He deserves more, and I do too.

I look down at my lap for a long time. I know Andrew probably thinks I'm pitiful, and I feel humiliated. "So can I get you a drink or something?" I ask finally, changing the subject as I remember my manners.

"No thanks." Andrew stands up. "I have to get to that dinner. I just wanted to make sure you were okay."

I'm surprised by how disappointed I feel. But of course he's leaving. "I'm sorry I snapped at you," I say in a small voice.

"Kate, you're allowed to snap! You're allowed to be messy. *Life* is messy. You should say what's on your mind more often. Honesty is sexy on you."

"Oh," I say, my cheeks flaming. "Right. Well, um, thanks for coming by to check on me. That was nice."

"Kate," Andrew begins, letting the word hang here for a moment as he gazes at me. My chest constricts as I stare back. "Kate," he finally begins again, "the way you are with these kids, it's amazing. I want you to know that. You get them to open up in ways I've never seen before."

"It's just the music," I mumble.

"No. It's you."

The words mean a lot to me, not least of all because I can tell he really means them. "I'll come back to St. Anne's next week," I say. "I promise. I just needed some time."

"Go see Allie. I think it will help both of you."

"I will," I say.

I walk him to the door, and as I open it for him and turn back around to say good-bye, he's just inches away, and for a strange, frozen moment, I have the feeling he's about to kiss me. What's even crazier is that I want him to.

We stare at each other, motionless, for what feels like a full minute, and then Andrew blinks, takes a step back, and mumbles, "I have to go. Look after yourself, Kate."

"Yeah," I say as he disappears down the hall. "You too."

And then he's gone. I stare after him for a long time, wondering whether I imagined the friction in the air between us.

Thirty

The next morning, I take the train out to Glen Cove to see Joan. The whole way there, I find myself thinking about Andrew. The way he looked in that sky-blue shirt. The way he understood how I was feeling and didn't leave just because I took my frustration out on him. The way I felt when his eyes held mine at the door. The feeling of loneliness that crept in when he was gone. Even as I'm heading up Joan's front walk to the house I used to visit with Patrick, it's Andrew's face I'm seeing in my mind. Strangely, this doesn't make me feel guilty.

I haven't phoned ahead, so Joan looks startled to see me when she opens her door and finds me standing there. "Kate!" she exclaims. "What are you doing here?"

"I hope you don't mind," I say. "I just figured I hadn't seen you in a while. I wanted to check on you."

She studies me for a moment. "Well, come in, sweetheart."

She leads me into the living room, and I notice as we pass the kitchen that there are dishes piled in the sink and a few rags sitting on the counter. "Everything okay?" I ask as we sit down on her couch.

"How did you know?" she asks right away.

"Know what?"

"About the breast cancer," she says softly. "You told me I needed to get checked out, that you just had a feeling. And you were right, Kate. They called two days ago. It's stage three. I'm supposed to meet with an oncologist and a radiologist on Monday morning. They want me to begin treatments in the city as soon as possible. I may need to have surgery too, if they're able to shrink the tumor a bit."

"Oh, Joan," I breathe. A wave of guilt sweeps over me—I didn't look out for Joan the way I should have—but I push it quickly away. *The dreams aren't real, Kate,* I tell myself. *This is a coincidence.* Still, I feel terrible for not urging Joan to get a mammogram sooner, dreams or no dreams. When Patrick died, I made a promise to myself that I'd always look after his parents. I feel like I've failed.

As if reading my mind, Joan leans forward and says, "Honestly, Kate, I wouldn't have gone to get that mammogram if you hadn't been so insistent. I was feeling fine, and you know me: if it ain't broke, I don't see the need to fix it."

I nod. Joan is a stoic type who doesn't even go to the doctor for a flu. I should have assumed she wasn't getting checked regularly. "So you'll be okay, right? With treatment? The doctors are optimistic?"

Joan looks at her hands for a while before looking up with a forced smile. "They tell me stage three breast cancer comes with about a 40 percent chance of survival. But other risk factors, such as my age, make the prognosis a little worse."

I can feel my eyes filling with tears. "You're going to be fine, Joan. I know it."

"Maybe, sweetheart. But if things don't work out, it just means I get to see my husband again sooner. And Patrick."

"No!" I say instantly. I have days too when I wish I wasn't

here, when I wish I was dead already so that I could be with Patrick again. But I know how valuable life is. I'm not about to let Joan throw in the towel. "You have to fight this, Joan. You have to."

"I will, dear. Of course I will. But I'm not like you. I don't have as much to live for anymore."

"Yes, you do," I say fiercely. "You have me."

"Kate, you have your own life to live. You don't need to worry about your former mother-in-law. Really, maybe it's for the best."

"You're not my *former* anything." I take a deep breath. "You're my family, Joan, You always will be. And I think you should come live with me for a while."

Joan looks startled. "What?"

My mind is racing. The dreams, whatever they were, led me here, led me to encourage Joan to get a mammogram. The dreams made me see that Dan was never meant to be my family. The dreams even prompted me to clear out my guest bedroom in anticipation of Allie moving in. I know now that that wasn't meant to be, but maybe *this* is. Maybe this is the family I was supposed to be making space in my life for.

"Look," I say firmly, "I have plenty of room. Dan is gone now, and the place is too big for just me. If your chemo treatments are going to be in the city anyhow, it doesn't make sense for you to be commuting in and out all the time. You'll be exhausted. Stay with me, at least until you're done with your treatments. We'll fight it together."

"Kate, I couldn't possibly impose."

"How is it an imposition if I'm inviting you? In fact, I'm insisting. Come stay with me. Let me help you."

Joan hesitates. "It would only be for a little while."

"It would be for as long as you want to stay," I say firmly. After all, this is what Patrick would have wanted. It's what *I* want.

I think about what Andrew said last night about making a choice. I can't retreat to a world I don't belong in every time life gets hard, can I? And if there's a choice to be made, I have to stay in the place where I can help Joan, where I can be a friend to Allie, where I can keep working with Max, Leo, and Riajah, where Andrew is a social worker and where I'm *me*.

I choose the here and now. If I can't have Patrick, I need to begin building a life without him—a real life.

Maybe this is the way to start.

By Tuesday, Joan has closed up her house in Glen Cove and moved into my guest bedroom, bringing only four suitcases of clothes, books, and toiletries with her.

"You sure you don't need more than this?" I ask as I help her put her things away that morning before work. "We can take another trip out to the house on Friday after I get home from work, if you want."

"Kate, this is more than enough. I even brought a winter coat just in case."

I went with her yesterday to what she referred to as a "strategy session" with her oncologist and radiologist, and already, I feel better about things. The radiologist, Dr. Habab, is a woman around my age, and the oncologist, Dr. Golden, is a man in his fifties with a crinkly-eyed smile. They both seemed energetic and committed to getting Joan through this.

"Don't you worry, Mrs. Waithman," Dr. Habab said on the way out, patting Joan on the back. "We are going to work together to kick cancer's ass."

"Oh!" Joan exclaimed, startled.

"Sorry for the language," Dr. Habab said. "But I want your

cancer to know we're coming for it. And we're not backing down."

"I like her," Joan said, squeezing my hand as we left the office.

Her first chemo treatment is scheduled for Friday, and I've taken the day off to go with her. Today, I've scheduled a lunch with Gina to fill her in on everything. As I walk to our favorite Italian place on Second and Fifty-Second, I breathe in the early autumn air and feel a spring in my step that hasn't been there for a while.

"I know I dismissed them, but maybe the dreams *were* telling you something," Gina says once we're seated. "After all, you're happier than you were a few months ago, aren't you?"

"I am," I admit. "I think I never looked at myself long enough to realize I was living a half life."

"The dreams woke you up," Gina says with a smile.

"So they did." If nothing else, they stopped me from letting life simply pass me by. I know I'm in a better place now, but I can't help feeling very alone, especially now that the dreams have stopped. "I just feel like I'm missing something," I add. "Like I've finally got my life on the right course, but all the pieces haven't exactly fallen into place yet."

"Maybe that's because you still have your heart closed off," she says innocently as she picks up her menu, blocking my view of her face.

"What do you mean?" I ask. "Gina?"

When she lowers the menu, she looks amused. "That Andrew guy," she says simply.

"What about him?"

"You like him."

"What?" I ask. "I do not. He's just a colleague."

Gina arches an eyebrow, but she doesn't say anything. I have the feeling she's waiting for me to go on, so after a pause, I add,

"Okay, fine, so he's a really *attractive* colleague. Who's very kind. And great with kids."

"And?"

"Okay, yeah, so he's pretty great," I admit in a mumble.

Gina gives me a triumphant look. "So why not go after him?"

"I think he's dating someone."

"You're positive?"

I hesitate. "No."

"Then what's the worst that can happen? He tells you he already has a girlfriend? Then at least you'll have tried." She doesn't wait for an answer. "You've *got* to stop letting your life pass you by, Kate, or it'll be too late."

Her words silence me for a moment. "Okay," I say finally. I look down at my menu until I feel Gina's hand on mine.

"What is it?" she asks. "What else is bothering you?"

And so I finally say aloud the thought that's been weighing on my mind for years. "It just doesn't seem fair for me to live a whole life, a happy life, when Patrick never got to live his. None of this is fair."

The guilt I've locked away surges toward the surface and spills over. A single tear rolls down my right cheek, and I swat it away, embarrassed. When I finally look up at Gina again, her eyes are watery too.

"You've got to let that go." Her tone is firm. "That was the hardest part for me, stopping the feeling that I was letting Bill down by living my life. But that's what Bill would have wanted for me. I know it. And it's what Patrick would have wanted for you."

I think of the words dream-Patrick said to me. *I would want you to be happy, no matter what.* Why hadn't I listened? Instead, I'd picked and chosen the messages I took away from the dreams. But what if that was the most important one of all?

"I'm a mess, though, Gina," I say. "What if I repeat the same mistakes I've made before?"

"You think I don't make mistakes?" she asks. "Kate, I've made a thousand of them. A million, probably. So has everyone else. But you can't learn if you don't try. That's what life is. Maybe that's what the dreams were about, wherever they came from. Maybe Patrick was reminding you to keep living. Now, it's up to you to do the rest."

"What if I don't know how?" I ask.

Gina smiles. "Then I'd suggest you start with Andrew and go from there."

That evening, after my last session of the day, I'm sitting in my office, staring at the phone like a nervous teenager. I've already picked up the receiver and put it down a dozen times. I want to call Andrew, but I'm scared. Terrified, even. Prompted by Gina's words, though, I've already made a promise to myself: I can't go home tonight until I've summoned the courage to make the call.

I check my watch. It's nearly seven o'clock, so chances are Andrew's already on his way home from the office. I decide to take the wimpy way out, leaving a message for him on his work line. That way, the ball's in his court. If he calls me back, I'll summon the courage to ask him out—or something along those lines. If he doesn't, I'll know I'm being foolish thinking I even have a chance.

Before I can second-guess myself, I pick up the phone and dial, fully expecting his work voice mail. I'm so unprepared for him to answer that I don't know what to say when he picks up after the first ring and says hello.

"Uh" is all I manage to say into the receiver.

"Hello?" Andrew says again.

"Uh," I repeat. Then I take a deep breath and blurt out, "Hi-it's-Kate." But I say it so quickly, the words mash together into one.

"Kate?" He's surprised to hear from me. "Hey. How you doing?"

"Oh, I'm good, just hanging out in my office, so I thought I would call you, and you know, I thought maybe you'd be gone for the day, but then you picked up, and now I'm talking to you." Okay. So I'm babbling. I hit myself on the forehead with the receiver. *Get it together, Kate.*

"Thanks for the recap," Andrew says. I can hear the smile in his voice, and it makes me relax a little.

"So," I say.

"So," he repeats.

I close my eyes. "I just, uh, had a question for you."

"I'm all ears."

I don't say anything for a moment, because for the first time, I realize how different this is from Dan. I *never* felt this kind of jitters with him. Never. It reminds me that there are stakes here, real stakes. And that's scary. With Dan, I just coasted along on autopilot with my emotions closed off, but if I put myself out there now and Andrew rejects me, it will really hurt.

Then again, isn't that what life's about? Exposing yourself to the possibility of hurt, of disappointment? Patrick once told me, *I think a life where you don't put your heart on the line for the things that matter isn't really a life worth living.* The words play in my head now, like Patrick himself is whispering them in my ear. Strange that it would be his voice urging me toward Andrew. But then again, maybe Gina was right. Maybe he would have wanted this for me. Happiness. A life fully lived.

"Kate?" Andrew asks tentatively, cutting into my thoughts. "You still there?"

"So what I was wondering," I begin immediately, "or I mean, I guess what I was asking is if you don't have a girlfriend, maybe you'd want to—"

"Kate?" Andrew cuts me off before I spiral even further into stupidity. "I don't have a girlfriend."

"Oh." I pause. "Well, I mean, I just assumed the girl I saw you with at the bar . . ."

"A friend set us up. We went out twice, but there wasn't really any chemistry."

I frown. How could he not have chemistry with a girl who looked like a supermodel? "Okay, but what about the girl I heard in the background the night I called you on the phone about Allie?"

Andrew chuckles. "An on-again, off-again girlfriend who is, and always has been, a very bad idea. I told her the next morning that we needed to end it once and for all."

"You did?"

"I like someone else," he tells me. "I think I realized that night just how much."

"Oh," I say, temporarily flummoxed. "Okay. Well, then, uh, if you would ever be interested, then maybe we could, uh—"

"Oh, I'm interested," he says, cutting me off. Again, I can hear him smiling through the phone.

"Oh," I repeat. I take a deep breath, knowing that with these next few words, I'll be thrusting myself into a new phase of life, one where my decisions matter again, where my heart's involved, where I'm living—*really* living—for the first time in years. Win, lose, or draw, I'm back in the game. "So I wanted to ask you—"

"Kate?" Andrew stops me. "You're spectacularly bad at this. But I'm glad, because I wanted to be the one to ask *you*. I just wasn't sure if you were ready yet. So . . . if you're ready . . ."

He's the one who sounds nervous now, and the tremor in his voice makes me smile as he continues.

"How about dinner?" he asks. "A date. A real date. Me and you. I—I like you, Kate. And I'd like to see what could happen between us, if we give it a chance." He pauses and adds, "If you want."

"I want," I say softly. I close my eyes and smile. It's a beginning. I don't know what will happen with Andrew, but I know I'm ready to find out, to make Patrick a beautiful piece of my past, and to choose to live in the present and build for the future. "How's tomorrow night?"

"I assume you mean after your class with your exceedingly charming and handsome sign language instructor," he deadpans, "who you'll no doubt be lusting over for the entire hour preceding the date."

I laugh. "Obviously."

"Then the answer is yes. Tomorrow night sounds great. But don't think you're getting away with a casual thing just because it's after class. I'm making a reservation somewhere, and you're getting an actual fancy first date, young lady, whether you like it or not. Even if Amy spends the rest of the class plotting ways to knock you off."

"Deal." I can't stop smiling.

"See you tomorrow, then, Kate. I'm really glad you called."

"I am too." We hang up, and in my stomach, I feel the fluttering wings of a hundred butterflies I didn't know lived there anymore. I close my eyes and lean back in my chair. I'm ready for this. I know that now. "Thank you, Patrick," I say aloud.

And then the silence is broken by a voice from my doorway. "What's wrong with you?" My eyes snap open, and I see Allie standing there, looking windblown and worried.

I scramble to my feet. "Nothing, nothing. What are you doing here? Are you okay? Where's your mom? How did you know where my office is?"

Allie makes a face and steps through my doorway. "I'm capable of doing a Google search, you know. You're right there. Kate Waithman, Music Therapist. Gave me an address and everything. Doesn't take a genius."

"Okay. But why did you look me up? Did something happen?" I quickly assess Allie. Physically, she *looks* okay.

"I need your help."

My heart skips a beat. "Did your mom do something?" As soon as the words are out of my mouth, I realize I'm actually hoping the answer is no, which means I've turned an important corner.

"No, nothing like that. My mom's fine. It's my best friend."

"Bella?" I ask, startled.

"Yeah. So you know she's in foster care too, like I was, right?"

"Right."

"So what happened was her grandma was her guardian, but she died like four months ago, and Bella had nowhere else to go, so she went into the system. They're still trying to find a home for her."

"That's so sad," I murmur. "So what's wrong? Is Bella okay?"

Allie kicks at the floor with her sneaker. "Technically, yeah. Physically, I mean. But the thing is, she's on her way to confront her mom. Her biological mom. She wouldn't listen to me when I tried to stop her. All these years, she thought her mom was dead, but then she saw her sitting in the back at her grandma's funeral a few months ago. Bella has been really, really pissed since then. Her mom didn't even say anything to her!"

"That's terrible," I murmur.

"I know, right? So she wants to go ask her why she got rid of her when she was a baby. She wants to yell at her or something. She finally found her on Facebook or Twitter or something last night and figured out where she works, and now she's going to confront her."

"Oh, no."

Allie nods. "It's just, I'm afraid for her. I think she's going to get hurt. Not physically, I mean, but, like, her feelings."

"And you want to stop her?"

Allie nods. "Will you help me? I know it's not your job or anything, but I don't know what to say to her, and you're really good at making people feel better. I thought maybe you could, you know, figure out the right thing to say or something."

"Oh, Allie," I say. She's come here, of her own accord, to stop a friend's pain. I'm so proud, my heart hurts. I stand and grab my jacket. "Of course I'll help you. Let's go."

Thirty-One

On the way, Allie fills me in. Bella's birth mother apparently works at a bar on First Avenue, just four blocks from my office, and her shift starts at seven thirty, which is fifteen minutes from now. Allie's hoping we'll get there in time to intercept Bella and calm her down.

"Maybe it's good for her to confront her mother, though," I venture, playing devil's advocate as we jog down the street. "Why are you so sure this is going to be a bad thing?"

Allie shakes her head. "Uh-uh. No way. Her mom gave her up when Bella was fourteen months old because she was deaf. She is *not* a nice lady. She just threw her away because she wasn't perfect."

I stop in my tracks, and I wait for Allie to stop too. "What?" she asks, her voice shaking a little. "We have to get there."

"Allie," I say slowly, "you know that to me, you're perfect, right?"

She sniffles and looks away. "Well, that's stupid."

"No, it's not," I say firmly. "You're with your mom now, and that's wonderful. I'm glad for you. But I want you to know that I wanted to take you in. I would have taken you in a heartbeat. I would have done anything for you to be my foster daughter."

Allie blinks. "But . . . I wasn't even nice to you at first."

"I could see beneath all your tough layers, kiddo. You're a good person, and I hope you always know that, no matter what."

"Yeah, well, you're a good person too," she says, then she surprises me by hugging me tightly. "Now come on. We have to go find Bella."

I nod, and we break into a jog once again. I wish I'd worn better shoes for this; I'm in kitten heels, and the balls of my feet are beginning to ache. Allie, in Converse sneakers, is oblivious to my pain and focused on finding her friend, so I struggle to keep up.

Finally, we round the corner onto First, and Allie points. "There it is. The bar where Bella's birth mom works."

I look up as I catch my breath. A sign with NICKEL NELLIE'S in peeling paint hangs above the doorway of a place that reminds me a bit of the dingy restaurant Allie escaped to in Queens in July. There's something about the place that feels familiar, something that tickles the far recesses of my memory, but I'm sure I've never been here before. "Have you mentioned this place to me?" I ask Allie. "I feel like I know it already."

Allie shakes her head. "I never heard of it until today. Neither had Bella."

"Weird," I murmur.

"So should we just wait out here on the street to see if Bella comes by?" Allie asks. "Or should we go inside? What do you think?"

I open my mouth to reply, but the words get caught in my throat as a familiar-looking woman rounds the corner of First and Fifty-Seventh, headed toward us and the entrance of Nickel Nellie's. Her hands are shoved into her jacket pockets, her head is down, and her stringy hair frames her drawn face. It takes me a moment to place her, largely because she's aged far more quickly than I would have expected. But when I realize who it is, my heart nearly stops. I gasp aloud at the same time the woman reaches the door of the bar and looks up, noticing me. Recognition flashes across her face, followed quickly by a look of disgust.

"Kate," she says flatly, stopping dead in her tracks.

I nod, stunned, my mind flashing back almost thirteen years, to the last time I saw her.

"Candice?" I finally manage to say. "Candice Belazar?" It's Patrick's old girlfriend, the one he'd dated right before he met me, the one we fought about the night before he died. In a way, even though Patrick and I had made up, I'd never forgiven the woman for causing any pain or strife between us on our very last night together.

"I was wondering when you'd show up," she says, looking me up and down with a strange lack of surprise, like she's been expecting me. "It only took you twelve years," she continues. "But, gee, you must have been busy." Her voice drips with sarcasm.

"You're still angry with me?" I ask. Patrick had broken up with Candice two months before he met me, but still, she'd always acted like I'd stolen him right out of her hands.

She ignores my question. "So is that your kid?" she asks, jerking her chin toward Allie, who's following our exchange with wide eyes. "That figures."

I shake my head, completely baffled by her anger, which seems wildly misplaced.

Allie is tugging on my arm now, trying to tell me something, but I hardly notice; I'm too busy staring at Candice, trying to puzzle out what's happening here. "Candice, I really have no idea what you're talking about," I say.

She rolls her eyes dramatically. "Right, just like you had no idea that what I had with Patrick was more than just some fling. Not that you cared."

Anger sizzles inside of me, along with a rush of possessiveness. "I'm sorry you got hurt. But you and Patrick were over before I met him. You weren't with him that long, Candice. You've got to let it go."

She laughs. "Oh, do I? Thanks so much for your advice." She shakes her head, and for a split second, I see sadness there before a smirk takes its place. "Anyway, it's too late, you know. I have no idea where she is."

I'm completely lost now. "You have no idea where *who* is?"

She rolls her eyes dramatically, and finally, Allie tugs my arm so hard that I have no choice but to look at her. *She is Bella's mom,* she signs quickly. *Why do you know her?*

I stare at Allie, completely perplexed. *Bella's mom?* I sign back. I know from Allie that Bella is thirteen, which means she would have been born a whole year before Patrick died. I'm absolutely positive that if Candice had had a baby, Patrick would have mentioned it to me. We didn't keep anything from each other, and surely he knew I would have been mildly amused to know that his ex had gotten herself knocked up so soon after they'd broken up.

It's true, Allie signs back. *I saw her picture on Facebook. It's her.*

Candice interrupts us then with a derisive snort. "Really?" she asks bitterly. "You learn sign language now because *you* got stuck with a deaf kid, but you couldn't be bothered when my kid needed you?"

I ignore her insult, because I'm so confused by her words. "You have a child?"

"So you're going to play dumb now? After all this time?"

"How many times do I have to tell you that I don't have a clue what you mean?" I snap. But my stomach is tying itself into knots as I stare at her. I don't know what she's getting at, but whatever it is, I have the feeling it's going to change everything. "Allie says you're Bella's mother?"

"Bella?" Candice asks. "I have no idea who that is."

Allie and I exchange confused looks. "Well, then who are you talking about?" I ask.

"Hannah, obviously," Candice adds, and for a minute, I stop breathing.

"Hannah?" I whisper.

"Seriously?" Candice says, throwing up her hands. "Why are you acting like this is news to you?"

"*Hannah*?" I repeat. "You're telling me Hannah actually exists?"

"What, did you think I was making her up? I mean, I'm no angel for the way I handled it all, but I told Patrick she was his daughter, okay? You can't accuse me of keeping it a secret."

"Wait, what?" I whisper as I go completely numb. Allie is tugging on my hand, but I can barely feel it. All I can think is *Hannah. Hannah. Hannah.* The name echoes in my head over and over. This is real. Candice Belazar is standing in front of me, telling me Patrick had a daughter named Hannah. Still, I can't wrap my mind around it.

"Kate!" Allie finally snaps at me, tugging so hard I feel like my arm is about to pop out of its socket. I look down, and she signs to me quickly, *She's talking about my BFF,* she signs. *Hannah Belazar. She goes by Bella because of her last name.*

My jaw falls as I stare at Allie. Slowly, I turn my attention back to Candice. "You're telling me Patrick had a daughter named Hannah?" I ask. "He really had a daughter?"

For the first time, Candice looks uncertain. "Wait, he told you, didn't he? He said he was going to tell you."

My heart is racing, and for a moment, I feel a sharp stab of betrayal. If Patrick really had a child, how could he have not told me? It's not possible, is it? We told each other everything. The possibility that Hannah is real, and that Patrick kept her a secret, boggles my mind. "She's thirteen?" I finally say. *Just like the Hannah in my dreams.*

Candice glances at Allie and shrugs. "Yeah. So what?"

"And Patrick knew about her all along?" The words actually hurt to say aloud.

It takes Candice a moment to meet my eye, and when she finally does, I see shame in her face. "Not exactly."

"Not *exactly*?"

She shrugs. "I told him when she was fourteen months old, okay? I just couldn't do it anymore. Not when I found out she was deaf."

Allie just stiffens and glares at her. I'm so stunned, I don't even have the words to come to her defense.

"When?" I finally ask weakly. "*When* did you tell Patrick?"

Candice grimaces and looks down. "The day before. The day before he died. I—I asked him to take her."

And suddenly, I understand. The fight I had with Patrick that last night. The fact that he'd been too involved in the conversation with Candice to call. The way he'd looked at me when he said he had something important to tell me.

He never had a chance to tell me about Hannah. *But he was going to.*

"I asked if he wanted her," Candice continues, apparently oblivious to the visceral reaction I'm having to her news. "He was surprised, of course, but he said he totally wanted to take her if it was okay with you. He said he'd talk to you."

"He tried," I murmur.

She ignores me. "He was real happy, you know. Happy to have a kid, even though he was pissed that I hadn't told him."

I feel numb. If Patrick had lived, he would have asked me that night about taking Hannah in. I would have said yes. I would have become Hannah's mother, just like in the dreams. "Why did you wait so long?" I ask. "Why didn't you tell him when you found out you were pregnant?

Instantly, I'm furious with her. Maybe Patrick's death was inevitable. But Candice's decision to take away his child wasn't. Sure, it would have complicated things for me to have Candice in the picture, but Patrick could have spent the last fourteen months of his life getting to know his daughter. Candice took that from him. From *us*.

She shrugs and looks away. "Patrick had already dumped me by the time I found out, okay? I had to have *some* pride, you know? And my new boyfriend, Carl, said he was cool with raising her as his own, just as long as Patrick never knew about her. Carl, he was worried that Patrick would mess things up for us and I'd want to go back with him or something."

"So what changed?"

She looks at me like I'm crazy. "I don't have health insurance. And Carl, he said he wasn't going to spend money on a kid who wasn't his. So I didn't really have a choice, did I? I was just trying to do what was right for her."

"Yes, you're a real saint," I mutter.

She narrows her eyes at me. "You got no right to judge me."

I don't even have a response to that. I shake my head in disbelief. "So what happened to her? To Hannah?"

"Hell if I know. I gave her to my mom. Then my mom stopped speaking to me when I had Tammy and Sandy. Said I was gonna be a crappy mom to them too, and she didn't have room for three kids. I told her to go to hell, and that was that."

"Tammy and Sandy?"

"Yeah. My twins. Who are normal. No offense." She glances at Allie, and I do too. Allie looks like she's about to punch Candice in the face. I'm not sure I'd blame her. Maybe I'd even help. "Anyways," Candice continues, "my mom was pissed I kept them while I unloaded Hannah on her. But they were just easier, you know? Then my mom died, and I don't know what happened to Hannah after that."

"So you just let her go into the system?" I demand. "You didn't even try to find her?"

"Don't you dare get high and mighty on me, Kate. You didn't want her either."

"That's not true!" I say, clenching my firsts. "I never even *knew* about her! Patrick never had a chance to tell me. I would have taken her in an instant. How can you not know that?"

Candice looks genuinely stunned. "I just figured—"

I open my mouth to reply, but we're interrupted by Allie, who steps pointedly between us and says, "Stop. Right now. She's here. Bella's here."

I turn, and the moment unfolds like it's happening in slow motion. I see Hannah, *my* Hannah, exactly as she looks in my dreams, walking toward us from around the corner, clutching a map in her hands. I watch, breathless, as she looks up from the map and sees Candice first. Her lips tremble a bit, and I can tell she recognizes her birth mother, the woman she's come here to confront. I can see the pain in her face.

But then her gaze shifts to Allie, and I can see confusion sweeping across her perfect features. Finally, her eyes slide to me, and that's when she stops in her tracks.

For a frozen moment, Hannah and I just stare at each other. I can't seem to move or to muster words, but there are a thousand thoughts running through my mind. I can't believe she's real. She's been real all along. *Does she know me too?*

I want to say the right thing, to say *something,* to tell Hannah

I know who she is without scaring her away. But there's nothing that could have prepared me for this, so I just stand there, staring. The world around me feels like a blur; I can only see Hannah.

She begins walking toward us again, slowly, but she looks puzzled now. She looks at Candice again, then at me, then finally at Allie. *What's happening?* she signs to Allie.

Allie shrugs and looks at me. *I don't know,* she signs back to Hannah. *I think your birth mother knows my friend.*

Hannah's gaze slides to my face again, and she regards me suspiciously. I can see something flickering in her oh-so-familiar eyes. *Patrick's eyes.* It's distrust, trepidation. But there's something else there too, a spark of distant, foggy recognition. Or maybe I'm just imagining things, because I want so badly to believe that Hannah has seen me before too.

Do you know me? I sign to her. It takes all my focus to keep my hands from shaking.

"No," Hannah says out loud, and her voice sounds exactly like I knew it would. "Who are you? You're friends with *her?*" She gives Candice a dirty look.

Candice jumps in. "Wait, you're normal? You can talk?"

I finally find my voice again as I turn to Candice. "You know what, Candice?" I say. "You are a complete jackass. Hannah *is* a normal kid. So is Allie. Just because they're hard of hearing doesn't mean they're abnormal. That's an incredibly ignorant thing to say. But then you've always been an incredibly ignorant person, haven't you?"

I turn back to Hannah, whose eyes are wide and alarmed. "I'm sorry," I tell her, and I'm not even sure what I'm apologizing for, exactly. It's just that it feels a bit like the universe itself owes these two girls an apology of some sort, and Candice certainly isn't going to be the one to deliver it. "Hannah, I hope you know you're better off without someone like this in your life. She did you a favor when she gave you up."

"Who are you?" Hannah asks, staring at me.

I clear my throat as tears sting my eyes. I don't know what to say. I doubt Hannah's been having the dreams too, because if she was, I think her reaction would be different somehow. But there's a spark of *something* in her eyes, although it's not the instant recognition I would have hoped for.

I think about saying that I'm just a friend of Allie's, a friend who cares about what happens to her too, but that wouldn't be the whole truth. I consider telling her I'm the woman who was meant to be her mother all along, but that would just scare her away. So what comes out of my mouth unbidden instead is the best way I know how to say what's in my heart.

"I knew before I met you—" I murmur, knowing that I'm telling Hannah in a language of my own, in a language she won't understand, that I love her, that I've always loved her, even before I knew she existed.

Hannah just stares at me for a moment, and I'm convinced she believes I'm crazy. Maybe she even thinks I'm somehow in cahoots with Candice and that I'm here to hurt her too. But then, her expression changes from one of defiance to one of confusion, and she replies tentatively, "—that I was meant to be yours." She looks at Allie then back at me.

My heart feels like it has burst into a constellation. "How did you know to say that?" I whisper.

Hannah shakes her head slowly. "I have no idea." She studies my face, like she's trying to figure something out. "You knew my dad, didn't you?" she finally asks.

"How did you know that?"

"I don't know." She looks a little scared now, and I know I can't reach out and comfort her, even though I want to. It's too soon. "My grandma told me he was a nice man," she continues. "She said he would have loved me if he'd ever gotten the chance to know me. But then he died."

"Yes," I say through the lump in my throat. "He did. But, Hannah, he would have loved you with all his heart. I can promise you that."

"You really knew him?"

"I was his wife." I hate that those words will always be in the past tense. But they have to be. I know that now.

"So you were supposed to be my mom or something?"

"Yes. I was. I . . . I think maybe I *am*."

"Yeah, well . . ." Hannah glances at Candice, then she looks away, an expression of resolve on her face. "I don't have anyone anymore." I know that whatever Hannah came here to say to Candice today has already been said. There are plenty of languages that don't make a sound, and I'm confident that Hannah has just closed the book on the woman who gave birth to her.

"Yes, you do," I tell her. "You have me. And you have a grandma named Joan, who will be so very happy to meet you. And an aunt Susan, and cousins, and a grandma in Florida too."

"You're saying I have a family?" Her lower lip quivers.

"You always have." I stare into the eyes of the girl who reminds me so much of Patrick and of the life we were supposed to have together. I don't see Candice in her at all, and I'm glad. Instead, I see everything I lost and everything I've found. This is the life I was intended to have all along. It just took me a little longer to find my way here.

Epilogue

Eight Weeks Later

"Did you have a good time, sweetheart?" Joan asks as I slip into the apartment on a chilly November night, trying my best not to make any noise. My lips are still tingling from the kiss Andrew and I shared in the hallway.

"It was pretty much perfect," I tell her.

Joan has already made up the foldout bed in the living room, and she's smiling at me as she dog-ears a page in the novel she's reading. Her hair is gone from the chemo, just like in the dreams I used to have, but she's fighting the cancer. She has a new reason to live.

Hannah.

Hannah, who's fast asleep in the room that used to be my guest room but that now belongs to her. Hannah, whose blood tests prove she's Patrick's child, Joan's grandchild. Hannah, whose adoption paperwork Andrew has pulled strings to expedite. Hannah, who will officially become my adopted daughter within the next couple of months.

Joan yawns. "I like him, you know. Andrew's a good man. And he's so good with Hannah."

"He is," I agree. I can feel my cheeks getting a little warm as I add, "I like him too, Joan. A lot."

In Joan's smile, I see genuine acceptance and happiness, and I'm glad; she has welcomed him into our lives with open arms. I think she's happy to finally see me moving on—not the way I did with Dan, but the way I'm doing now, with an open heart. Finally realizing that I shouldn't feel guilty for being happy— that Patrick wouldn't want me to—has changed me.

I know how lucky I am to have found someone who understands everything. Andrew treats Joan like she's an old friend he adores, and for this, I'm eternally grateful. After all, Joan's a nonnegotiable for me. A lesser man might not have understood why I need to have my deceased husband's mother living with me. But Andrew hasn't missed a beat. *Regardless of how they're in your life, family's family,* he'd told me the night I first hesitantly explained the situation. *And family is the most important thing in the world, no matter what.* That had been it. And he's been nothing but supportive of my decision to adopt Hannah.

"What time is Allie getting here in the morning?" Joan asks.

I nod. "Her mom's dropping her off at ten." We've decided to have Thanksgiving a day early this year so that Allie can join us. She'll be spending Thursday with her mother, who has indeed stayed sober and clean since getting custody back. Although Allie doesn't trust her entirely yet, she's getting there. She has one session a week with me in my office, and she spends a lot of her extra time over at our apartment with Hannah, talking about boys. The purple-haired Jay Cash, apparently, has finally kissed her.

"It'll be amusing to see the girls figuring out how to get the turkey into the oven," Joan says with a chuckle. Allie and Hannah have volunteered to cook for us, although it will be their first time doing so. *That way you can have time to flirt with Andrew,* Allie had signed to me mischievously last week, which of course made my cheeks heat up.

"Can you believe Christmas is only a month away?" Joan adds as I shrug out of my jacket and unwind the scarf from my neck. "Our first Christmas with Hannah. Who would have believed any of this was possible?" She looks off into the distance for a moment before adding, "I wish Patrick could be here to see this."

"I think he is, in a way," I tell her.

"I do too." She yawns. "Well, I should be getting to sleep, or I won't have any energy at all tomorrow. Stupid cancer."

"Stupid cancer," I agree. I hug her good night, and after bringing her a glass of water, I kiss her on the cheek and turn out the light. I make my way down the hall and crack the door to Hannah's room to make sure she's sleeping soundly.

Indeed, her chest is rising and falling peacefully. The moonlight spilling through the window illuminates her delicate features, which are as familiar to me now as my own. I tiptoe across her room and pull the covers up around her shoulders, just in case she gets cold during the night. She stirs and smiles in her sleep, and I wonder what she's dreaming of.

She's never been able to explain how she knew the words Patrick and I always exchanged, the words I told her myself in my dreams. But as I watch her eyelids flutter and her smile grow broader, I wonder if, like me, she saw a preview of this life before she got here.

On her dresser are the two things that have convinced me beyond a shadow of a doubt that something beyond our comprehension brought us into each other's lives. The first is a framed sketch of hers, a picture of a little girl and her parents at Disney World. When I first saw it as she was unpacking her things a few weeks ago, I gasped.

"What is that?" I'd asked, staring at it as if I'd seen a ghost. In a way, I had.

She frowned as she turned to look at the sketch too. "I drew it when I was ten, after I had a dream about going to Disney World with people who were my mom and dad in the dream. It was probably the realest dream I ever had." She leaned in to look more closely at the picture, then she turned to stare at me, a perplexed expression on her face. "Wait, the mom kind of looks like you, doesn't she?"

"She sure does," I said through my tears.

The second item that sits on her dresser is a small jar of silver dollars. "I find them all the time," she said with a shrug when I asked her about them. "It's weird, actually. Like, I'll just be walking down the street, and I'll look down, and there's a silver dollar. Like they're falling from the sky or something."

I look skyward now, to where I imagine Patrick must be. Maybe Hannah's explanation of the silver dollars isn't that far off. Maybe they *have* been coming from the sky, wishes from a long-lost father who wanted to help her find her way home. Someday, I'll tell her the story of the silver dollars and how her family has a long-standing tradition of throwing them back. But for now, knowing that they're there is enough. She'll have plenty of time to return her wishes to the world.

I kiss Hannah gently on the cheek, then I shut her bedroom door quietly behind me and make my way back out toward the living room. The lights are out, and I can hear Joan snoring softly already, so I'm careful not to make noise as I put my coat back on, open the apartment door, and slip out into the hallway.

I walk up Third Avenue to Forty-Second Street and grab the 5 train heading uptown from Grand Central Station. I get out at the Fifty-Ninth Street stop and head three blocks west to Fifth Avenue, where I turn left and walk until I'm standing in the square in front of the Plaza Hotel with the Sherry-Netherland behind me to the right.

In the middle of the plaza sits the Pulitzer Fountain, the fountain Patrick and I were supposed to throw a silver dollar into on the night of September eighteenth, 2002. I know now that he'd given me the coin that morning because he'd just learned about Hannah. It was meant to be a celebration of the daughter he'd hoped we'd soon bring home.

The bronze sculpture on top of the fountain is of Pomona, the Roman goddess of abundance, and I wonder if that's why Patrick wanted to throw the coin here, because suddenly and unexpectedly our lives were about to become so abundantly full. Pomona has been sculpted holding a basket of fruit, which reminds me a bit of a Thanksgiving cornucopia, making it quite apropos that I'm here the night before our family Thanksgiving. Never could I have imagined that I'd one day have so much to be thankful for.

Then again, there were always things in life to be grateful for, even after I lost Patrick. I just let my grief obscure the moments of hope. Maybe there were silver dollars falling from the sky everywhere, like there were for Hannah, if I'd just opened my eyes and looked for them.

I reach now for the silver dollar around my neck, which has served as a comfort to me for a long time now. But the metal circle has also been an anchor. As I pull it over my head and examine it, I'm almost surprised to realize it's just a coin, no different from the ones in Hannah's jar. I've spent a dozen years thinking that it was Patrick's final gift to me, but now I know I'm wrong. He's given me Hannah, and that's a gift that will never end.

But more than that, he gave me a foundation for a good life, which is something I should have recognized long ago. He encouraged me to follow my dreams, and that's why today, I'm able to make a difference in other people's lives. He loved me deeply, which taught me—even if I forgot the lesson for a while—that everyone deserves to love and be loved that way. He taught me to look for the good in the world, and to be profoundly grateful when wonderful things happen. And by dying, he gave me one more gift: he reminded me just how valuable life itself is.

"I won't waste another second," I promise him aloud as I look down at the silver dollar in my hand. Slowly, I unclasp the chain and slide the coin off. It's cool and shiny, but it's not magic. It's not a piece of Patrick. Patrick is in my heart and in my daughter and in every moment of my life, and now that I know that, I know it's time to let go.

You have to pass the good luck on, Patrick always used to say. *That way, someone else gets to make a wish.* I can almost hear his deep, reassuring voice in my ear as I squeeze the coin in my palm. I look up at Pomona and at the five basins of water spilling into the large pool at the bottom. I read once that the sculptor, Karl Bitter, had been killed in a car accident before he could complete the fountain and that someone else had to finish it for him. It makes me think of Patrick, because in a way, I know that for the rest of my life, I'll be finishing the beautiful things that he started, the things he never had the chance to see through. It's a privilege, I realize, to sculpt a life in his honor. But now I have to put my touch on it too.

I look at the coin one last time, kiss it for good luck, and close my eyes. I take a deep breath and throw it toward the fountain, smiling as I hear the tiny pinging sound it makes as it splashes into the water. I turn away without looking, because I don't want to know where the coin has landed. It belongs to someone else now, another person who needs its luck.

As I walk home, I'm eight grams lighter without the silver dollar. But there's been a weight lifted from my shoulders too, and for the first time in a dozen years, I'm not looking back to the past. I'm looking forward to the future. And I know it's going to be beautiful.

Back at home, as I slip under the covers, I find myself thinking about Hannah. Although she's just like she was in my dreams, and although so much of my early knowledge of her came from that, I'm savoring every new detail too. The musical sound of her laughter. The fact that she likes to paint her thumbnails different colors than the rest of her fingers. The crush she's recently developed on a boy named Eddie Colton at her school. The fact that she hates mushrooms but loves peas. The way she has a dimple in her right cheek when she smiles wide, just like I do. She even loves blueberry–peanut butter pancakes with honey. "My favorite!" she exclaimed the first time I made them. "How on earth did you know?"

The things I love about her are infinite, just like Patrick always used to tell me. And I've only just begun to know her. I drift off to sleep with a smile on my face.

When I awaken, I know right away that I'm back in the lemony morning light of the dream. Patrick is beside me, sleeping soundly, and for a moment, I just watch him.

The dream is hazier this time, and I have the feeling it's because my ability to see this world, whatever it is, is almost gone. Maybe it was only visible to me when I needed it. Maybe Patrick had something to do with showing me the way to Hannah, or maybe it was God himself. Either way, I know I don't need this life anymore. What I had with Patrick can never be duplicated, and there will always be a hole in my life where he used to be, but I have Hannah now, and Andrew too. And I know I have to keep moving forward and becoming a better version of me. I owe that to my husband, who never made it out of his twenties.

I wrap my arms around him, breathing in his familiar scent for what likely will be the last time. I begin to cry, and he stirs and rolls over, his body pressed against me, his eyes just inches from mine.

"Katielee?" he asks with concern. "Are you okay?"

"Yes," I tell him, because finally, I am. "Are you really here?" I ask a moment later, reaching out to touch his face, knowing that the question will begin to take me out of the dream. As the room grows a little dimmer, I can feel the stubble of his jaw, the warmth of his body. I ache to stay here forever with him, but the ache isn't as strong as it usually is, and that brings me comfort.

"I'm always here, Kate," he says, and I wonder if that's true. Maybe once someone is in your heart, they never really leave. "Where else would I be?"

"In heaven, maybe," I say softly as the room's edges grow fuzzy. "Or maybe living happily in a world that might have been, somewhere on the other side of the sky."

"What are you talking about?" He pulls me closer and dries my tears, but he's already beginning to fade, and I can barely feel his touch on my skin.

"I just want you to know that no matter what, I'll always love you," I tell him. "And I'll love Hannah with every fiber of my being. I'll take care of her always."

"Of course you will," he says, stroking my cheek. "You're her mom."

This makes me start crying again. "Yeah. I am."

"I'll always love you too, Katielee," he says after a moment. "I knew before I met you—"

Tears stream down my face. "—that I was meant to be yours," I reply.

He pulls me to him, and I close my eyes, feeling his warmth around me, hearing the steady beating of his heart, knowing that this is what could have been.

But it wasn't. It never will be. I know that now.

"Thank you, Patrick," I whisper. I hold on tightly one last time. After tonight, it will be time to let Patrick go, to move forward into the future, to begin living the rest of my life.

It's not the life I planned, but somehow, it's the life I was intended to have. And now, finally, I'm ready to embrace it.

Author's Note

When I first set out to write *The Life Intended*, I knew very little about the topics that would become integral to the book. I'd had little exposure to the foster system (except for an inspiring magazine article I worked on with *Orlando Sentinel* columnist George Diaz and his wife a few years ago), I didn't know much about music therapy (although it had always fascinated me), and I only knew a handful of people who were hard of hearing. It would be an understatement to say that researching this book was a huge educational experience for me.

At its heart, *The Life Intended* is the story of Kate Waithman finding her way back to the life she was supposed to have all along. But because the book includes many details about foster care, cochlear implants, deafness and music therapy, I want to mention a few things:

First of all, music therapy is a very, very broad field. I was fortunate enough to speak with Kristen O'Grady, MA, LCAT, MT-BC, a music therapist in New York State who, like Kate in the book, was educated at NYU. She made the excellent point that the definition of music therapy is widely contested, even among those in the music therapy community.

In the book, Kate explains this to Andrew, and I tried my best to make Kate's interactions with her clients as authentic as possible, but it's important to remember that not all music therapy is the same. And of course Kate herself isn't perfect. For instance, she overshares details of her own life with Allie as she lets her professional objectivity slip at times. This book is in no way suggesting that music therapy is meant to be practiced that way.

As for the scenes related to foster care, I was lucky to have the guidance of Arlene Goldsmith, LCSW, PhD, who has been the director of New York–based New Alternatives for Children (NAC) since its inception in 1982. Like the fictional St. Anne's Services where Kate volunteers in the book, NAC is an organization that works with the state system to provide high quality services in support of birth, foster, and adoptive families caring primarily for medically fragile children, including those with physical, emotional, and behavioral challenges as well as developmental disabilities. St. Anne's isn't directly based on NAC, but it was inspired by it, and I'm grateful to Arlene for the information she provided.

Finally, I'd like to address the issue of deafness. As Andrew mentions briefly in the book, there's a difference between deaf with a lowercase *d* and Deaf with an uppercase *D*. The first term is broader and refers to the actual condition of not being able to hear. The second term refers to the Deaf community, a group of people with a shared culture and language. Some people in the Deaf community feel that cochlear implants are unnecessary and that in fact the suggestion that they're needed can be insulting. Some resent what they see as the implication that hearing loss is something that needs to be fixed. Some don't feel they need—or want—sound.

In *The Life Intended*, Andrew is a big advocate for getting cochlear implants for hard-of-hearing children in the care of

St. Anne's. This is in no way meant to criticize the beliefs about cochlear implants among some in the Deaf community. This is simply Andrew's opinion; he feels that children in the foster care system have more advantages if they can hear and speak more easily, since many foster children who are hard of hearing or deaf don't have the advantage of being part of the cultural Deaf community. If the children in his care were being placed in homes where the parents were culturally Deaf, he might feel differently.

I hope that through reading *The Life Intended* you've learned a few things about music therapy, deafness, and foster care. As I mentioned in the Acknowledgments, any errors in the book are mine and are not related to the experts mentioned here who took the time to give me insight into the work they do.

If you'd like to learn more about music therapy, the American Music Therapy Association is a great resource. Find them online at musictherapy.org. If you're interested in finding out more about NAC or foster care in New York, visit nackidscan.org. And if you're interested in the fascinating topic of using music to work with the deaf and hard of hearing, visit Dr. Paul Whittaker's charity: Music and the Deaf at matd.org.uk.

Thanks for reading!

Acknowledgments

A thousand thanks, as usual, to my amazing literary agent, Holly Root, and my extraordinary editor, Abby Zidle, who comprise the best creative team I could possibly imagine. I also owe a huge debt of gratitude to both Farley Chase and Heather Baror-Shapiro, two amazing agents who go above and beyond, and to publicist Kristin "Kristin-with-an-i" Dwyer, Marla Daniels, Louise Burke, Jennifer Bergstrom, Michele Martin, Liz Psaltis, Melanie Mitzman, Mamie VanLangen, Laurie McGee, Diana Velasquez, Taylor Haggerty, Julianna Wojcik, and the rest of my wonderful team at Gallery Books and the Waxman-Leavell Literary Agency. I'm also very grateful to all of my foreign editors, especially Eva Schubert in Germany and Elisabetta Migliavada in Italy, both of whom have become dear friends of mine. What a gift to get to work with such wonderful people!

I am very fortunate to have received help and input on this novel from some wonderful people, including music therapist Kristen O'Grady, sign language expert Koli Cutler, "Music and the Deaf" founder Paul Whittaker, hearing instrument specialist Collin Andersen, Kari Andersen, Adam Kancher, Pam Kancher, Pamela Tonello, Jack Tonello, and New Alternatives for Children executive director Arlene Goldsmith. I'm inspired by the work that all of you do, and I'm so grateful that you took the time to help me. Any mistakes in this novel are entirely mine.

One of the main themes of *The Life Intended* is the importance of family, so it's also important to me to thank my own family, especially my mom Carol, my dad Rick, my sister Karen, my brother Dave, my brother-in-law Barry, my nephew James, my niece Chloe, my godson Colton, and his brother Eddie, my stepmother Janine, Aunt Donna, Uncle Steve, Aunt Janet, Courtney Harmel, Anne Walls, Fred Walls, and the rest of my cousins, my parents-in-law Wanda, Mark, Bob and JoAnn, my brother- and sister-in-law Jarryd and Brittany, and the whole Trouba family, who have taken me in as one of their own (although I'm about a foot too short to belong!). Thanks also to my wonderful friends, who have become like family over the years, especially Kristen Bost, Marcie Golgoski, Melixa Carbonell, Lisa Wilkes, Scott Pace, Walter Caldwell, Jon Payne, Christine Payne, Brendan Boyle, Kelly Galea, Amy Ballot, Amy Tan, Courtney Dewey, Amber Draus, Megan Combs, Scott Moore, Megan McDermott Lewis, Trish Stefonek, Robin Gage, Wendy Jo Moyer, Chad Kunerth, Gillian Zucker, Kat Green, Karen Barber, Nancy Jeffrey, Joe Grote, Kathleen Henson, Andrea Jackson, Ben Bledsoe, Jay Cash, Pat Cash Isaacson, Jason Cochran, and Broadway producer/film manager extraordinaire Andy Cohen. And thanks to my wonderful writer friends, especially the amazing Wendy Toliver and the other Swan Valley writers: Jay Asher, Linda Gerber, Aprilynne Pike, Allison van Diepen, and Emily Wing Smith.

Thanks also to my dear friend Chubby Checker, who has reminded me how very important music can be in life.

And of course thanks to my kind, intelligent, thoughtful, creative, and oh-so-handsome husband, Jason. I'm a lucky woman indeed.

The Life Intended

KRISTIN HARMEL

Kate Waithman thought she would only have one great love—her perfect husband, Patrick. But when Patrick is tragically killed in a car accident, Kate prepares for a life that is forever incomplete. Twelve years later, Kate has built an impressive career as a music therapist and is finally ready to move on with her fiancé, Dan. Soon after their engagement, however, Kate starts to have startlingly vivid dreams about the life she would have had if Patrick survived. Even more troubling, some of the details in these dreams begin to translate to real life. There is only one piece of the puzzle that doesn't fit: a daughter, Hannah, a prodigious piano player who is hard of hearing.

As Kate struggles to decipher her dreams, she finds herself wondering if her dream life is better than her reality. When she enrolls in a sign language class, she finds herself drifting farther away from Dan and closer to her charming instructor, Andrew. Finally, Kate realizes that she needs to make an impossible choice: cling to a lost past, or embrace a new future. *The Life Intended* is a captivating novel about the struggle to let go when our memories refuse to be forgotten.

Topics and Questions for Discussion

1. Before his death, Kate and Patrick share a special phrase, "I knew before I met you . . . that I was meant to be yours." How do you think this theme continues to echo throughout the novel as Kate struggles to understand her destiny?

2. Discuss how karma figures into Kate's story. Patrick superstitiously collects silver coins and then returns them to the universe when experiencing a stroke of good fortune. How do Kate's feelings about this habit change? What does it mean when she finally relinquishes Patrick's last coin?

3. When Dan proposes, Kate is besieged by memories of Patrick that are still fresh even twelve years after his death. Discuss how familiar relationship milestones can trigger the emotion of past loves. Do you sympathize with Kate in this moment? Or should she focus on moving on?

4. As Kate is swept into the past, she must also contend with a certainty about her future—her infertility. Discuss her

regret upon realizing that she can't ever get pregnant. How does she react to Dan's complete indifference to this news?

5. When Kate wakes up to a dream version of Patrick, she is confronted by a world that is strangely familiar yet full of differences from the life she knew with him. She meets Hannah, a hard of hearing girl who can't possibly be her biological daughter; finds that her sister, Susan, has a happy life in San Diego; and realizes that she no longer works with children. What kind of trade-offs have occurred in a world where Patrick is still alive?

6. Kate relies heavily on Gina, a friend who also lost her first husband, for emotional support. Are Kate and Gina alike in the way they handle grief? How are they different?

7. As both a music therapist and a volunteer for St. Anne's, Kate consistently witnesses the healing effects that music can have on struggling children. But not all of her students are easy to reach. Who do you think is the toughest shell to crack, and why? How does Kate earn their trust?

8. As Kate's dreams become more frequent, her experiences with Andrew are connecting her in new ways to the "real world." Why do you think she is so drawn to him? What about their pasts bring them together now?

9. On the day she goes wedding dress shopping, Kate is haunted by the lace gown she wore when she first walked down the aisle. She's also certain that she sees her dream daughter, Hannah, pass by on the street. Discuss the fine line between being stuck in the past and letting that past inform your future. What is Kate's gut trying to tell her here?

10. When Dan says his friend Stephen has accidentally gotten a girl pregnant, Kate feels very conflicted. Discuss this moment in the novel and how it relates to her confession to Joan about wanting to be a mother. How does this moment influence Kate's decision to call off her wedding to Dan?

11. Kate tells Dan that "sometimes the greatest things in life come from the greatest challenges." (pg. 134) What do you think Kate's greatest challenge was at the beginning of the novel? What do you think it is by the end?

12. During her dreams, Kate realizes that while some parts of her life are drastically different, her essential characteristics and tastes remain the same. How much do you think a person can change over their lifetime? And which aspects of an individual personality are more likely to stay constant?

13. Kate's mother reminds her that if she is not careful, "regret will grow in spaces you don't even know are there." (pg. 165) What do you think she means by this? Do you think Kate finds a way to take her advice?

14. Although Kate does not end up adopting Allie, she is cleared as a foster parent and finds her way to Patrick's lost daughter. She also realizes that Andrew might never have made such an impact at St. Anne's if he hadn't lost his brother at a young age. While the novel doesn't necessarily imply that life is fair, it does suggest that there is a balance and order to things. Do you agree with this outlook? Why or why not?

Enhance Your Book Club

1. In her dream world, Kate and Hannah like starting the day by making their favorite blueberry and peanut butter pancakes. Grab some fresh blueberries and start your book club by coming up with your own special recipe for this delicious dish.

2. During her music sessions at St. Anne's, Kate asks Allie to come up with her own lyrics to a favorite song. Share your favorite song with the book club and discuss how you would adjust the lyrics to describe your life. After she finished writing the novel, Kristin Harmel was inspired to write the lyrics to a song called "The Life Intended." Listen to it and find out more here: http://kristinharmel.com/the-song/. (Also available on iTunes.) How do you think the lyrics of the song relate to the novel?

3. In honor of Allie and Hannah, listen to Beethoven's The Piano Sonata No. 32 in C minor, Op. 111, which he wrote while deaf. Discuss what you hear and how it changes your definition of music.

4. Patrick's family has a tradition of "paying forward" good luck with silver dollars. How do you "pay it forward" in your own life? Discuss a family tradition you have, or start one of your own!